DOWSING FOR LOVE

Dick Croy

a Watershed Book
Marietta, Ohio

DOWSING FOR LOVE

By Dick Croy

Published by Watershed Books
1300 Glendale Road
Marietta, OH 45750

PRINTED WITH
SOY INK ™

Printed in the United States of America

10 9 8 7 6 5 4 3 2 1

Publisher's Cataloging-in-Publication
(*Prepared by Quality Books, Inc.*)

Croy, Dick.
   Dowsing for love / Dick Croy.
   p. cm.
   Preassigned LCCN: 94-62198
   ISBN 0-9645252-1-6

   1. Dowsing--Fiction.   I. Title.

PS3553.R55D69 1995   813
                           QB195-20049

This novel is dedicated to the late dowsers Wayne Cook and Don Wood...to my mother, who helped inspire it...to Vicki, Joy, and Phil, who helped give it shape...and to all true dowsers of this world.

FOREWORD

The human body appears to have two essentially parallel sets of nerve fibers extending from the sensory organs to the brain. Along one set, rapidly moving trains of signals of relatively large amplitude travel to the cerebral cortex for registration. This leads to conscious perception of the information content inherent in the sensory signals. Along the other set of nerve fibers, slowly moving trains of signals of subliminal amplitude travel to the brainstem (the old "reptilian" brain) and to the reticular network in the mid-brain location between the left and right hemispheres of the cerebral cortex.

This old brainstem is the seat of the primary thought processes of unconscious activity that controls involuntary muscle movement such as breathing, heartbeat, pupil size, genital erections, etc. Conscious processes are labeled secondary thought processes because they involve higher order processing in the cerebral cortex. During the sleep state, when the cerebral cortex has raised its neural firing threshold for consciousness so that the system will not be disturbed easily, it is the nerve signals from the reticular network that can automatically lower this firing threshold and produce wakefulness when the reptilian brain senses the need.

Ordinary neural signals play no role in dowsing. Rather, it is subliminal information, picked up by the body's sense organs and registered in the "old" brain, that leads to the dowsing response via a modulation of involuntary muscle activity.

Careful research on a water dowser, who is also very sensitive to various forms of electromagnetic energy, has shown that the adrenal glands (and perhaps the pituitary gland) are implicated as body sensors. Canadian research has shown that the upper arm muscles electrically fire an instant *before* the dowsing wand twitches downwards to indicate the presence of water. Further, conventional physics research on nonlinear systems shows that, for bi-stable systems (a dowsing wand is a bi-stable system) subject to both small amplitude periodic forcing and random noise forcing, an increase in input noise can result in an improvement in the output signal-to-noise ratio. This has been called stochastic resonance and is probably what happens in the body's neural system just prior to the dowsing response. It is the dowsing response itself that transforms the sensory information from the unconscious level to the conscious awareness level.

Although the dowsing response is most well known in the area of water detection, it can be utilized to enhance one's intuition in any area -- medicine, science, engineering, business, human relations, etc. To gain this enhanced intuition, it is necessary to practice just like for any other type of learning or muscle development. (But this is supervised neural learning.) However, it is first necessary to adjust one's mindset to allow (and even encourage) this subliminal signal transfer from one's unconscious level processing to the conscious awareness state.

My initial entry into this area of research activity was via some experiments with the dowser written about in this book. He was certainly a "character" but he had "something"! It took a great deal of patience and perseverance to carry out joint research with "Walter Barry" because he was a very nonlinear individual with many good qualities and many not so good qualities. However, he planted a couple of important seeds in me that have ripened well over the past two decades.

I now think that learning to develop and trust the dowsing response in oneself is extremely important at this point in human history. It opens our access to vast information and energy fields, present and available in the universe, that heretofore were blocked for most of us because they are detectable presently only at subliminal levels.

William A. Tiller 8/7/94
William A. Tiller, Professor Emeritus
Stanford University

ACKNOWLEDGMENTS

In addition to the dowsers from all walks of life to whom this book is dedicated, first among those I wish to thank for their generous and considerable contributions are Prof. William Tiller, for his foreword and permission to reprint the scientific paper which he co-authored with Wayne Cook (Appendix A); and author Christopher Bird. Those who wish to learn more about dowsing will find Mr. Bird's seminal work *The Divining Hand* an immense pleasure to read; it's as beautifully produced as it is informative.

The testimonial letters (Appendix B) from the initially skeptical, then grateful customers of dowsers Don Wood and Elaine Ralston were shared with me by Don's daughter Nancy; permission to include them in the book was granted by Nancy, Elaine, and the letter-writers themselves. Thanks to all of you!

The Jim Perkins Chapter (in northeastern Ohio) of the American Society of Dowsers welcomed my wife Joy and me into a number of their homes for monthly chapter meetings. Members and other dowsers who took the time to read the manuscript and comment on it are Carolyn Dumke, Roy and Sylvia Emerson, Cecil Lemmon, Harvey Lisle, Paul Sevigny and Jim Perkins. The ASD staff -- in particular Brenda Paquin, Susan Vanderpool and Alan Benjamin, manager of the organization's book store -- have been most helpful in my efforts to bring the book to the attention of ASD members.

The manuscript was also read by Claudette Wassil-Grimm and Barbara Temkin, whose meticulous and constructive criticism improved it greatly; by Dr. Anna Prince and Elizabeth DeYulia, who suggested some key last-minute revisions and encouraged me to seek a larger audience for the book than dowsers alone; my sister Rebecca Bennett, who is promoting the book for the publisher on the West Coast; and, in a number of different versions, by my wife, without whose moral, intellectual and financial support the ms. might never have become a book at all.

Parts of the ms. were read to members of the Ohio Valley Literary Group, whose interest in my writing has been creatively nurturing since my return to the Midwest. A number of characters in the story were inspired by real people who, along with many good friends and mentors of one kind or another from my stimulating sojourn in California, have immeasurably enriched and influenced my life.

Special thanks as well to Mark Harvey for illustrating the story's thematic elements so superbly on the book's cover; to Christine Blanke and all those at Thomson-Shore, Inc., who printed and produced the book; to my brother Douglas and cousin Jessica Mackinnon for helping an earlier stage play of the story reach readers at three theater companies; to Denise Gabriel and Madeline Scott for reading the play and introducing it to colleagues in the schools of dance and theater at Ohio University; and to Bill Miner and all the people at Miner Sales, Inc., who provided the supportive environment of worthwhile employment while the book was being prepared for publication.

Christine Price and the *Monterey (CA) Peninsula Herald* responded to requests for verification of incidents related by Wayne Cook in the long interview I conducted with him. Last I'd like to thank the staff of Watershed Books for their professional help in transforming *Dowsing for Love* from a much-edited manuscript to the book you have in your hands.

Lafayette, Ohio, gets its drinking water from seven municipal wells sunk into sedimentary sand and gravel of the Thothwillow River (that's Shawnee for "bright horn"), which flows into the Ohio River here. City Service Director Dean Channel has just been informed of a serious contamination problem in Well Six.

"We've never had any contamination in these wells before," declares Dean as if precedent alone will make the pollution disappear, "not the kind of contamination you're talking about. What the hell's the name of this stuff again? Tetrachlor..."

"Tetrachloroethylene," offers Russ ('Rusty' naturally) Fawcett, the city water director. "PCE. It's a solvent used in the cleaning industry."

"Like a dry cleaner you mean? There's never been a dry cleaner here by the Thothwillow that I know of."

"Well, it used to be used in diesel fuel and fire extinguishers too."

"There's a combination for you," says Dean, grimacing. "So how'd it get here?"

"Beats us, Dean. Could have been buried here years ago or dumped somewhere nearby fairly recently. There's a gas well on the Hindley property, the other side of the softball field, about 500 feet away -- the Department of

1

Natural Resources' Oil and Gas Division is taking some soil samples over there.

"And remember that tractor-trailer that spilled tar on Putnam Avenue last summer? We're tryin' to find out what was used to clean that up. We're also using metal detectors to see if we can locate some kind of underground storage tank."

"What about the river? Couldn't it be coming from the river?"

"That's what we thought at first. But, fortunately, Well Six is the only one contaminated so far -- and it's the farthest of all seven wells from the river."

"Well, I guess that rules out the river."

"Looks like it."

Lafayette is an historic community of tourism and agriculture, surrounded by industrial plants which rely on the Ohio River for its water and cheap transportation. Dean Channel is well-liked and respected by the city's employees. Without shirking his own workload, he allows managers to run their departments pretty much the way they see fit, as long as they get the job done and stay out of trouble. The latter is no small task with vigilant taxpayers on the lookout for misuse of their hard-earned money -- or, worse, their being unnecessarily inconvenienced in its application, as in the city's seemingly never-ending street repairs. Dean can see both sides of most disputes and is rightly considered indispensable by the city's popular female mayor. Borrowing from the technology that has situated all these plants up and down the Ohio, you might think of Dean as city government's primary cooling tower.

"You're sure none of the other wells are polluted?" he asks the water director.

"Not so far, and we're monitorin' 'em awful close."

"You keep saying 'so far'; what're the odds this could spread?"

"Can't say. Well Six tests out at 33 parts per billion --

that's not a dangerous level, even though this is a poison we're talking about. 'Fatal if inhaled, swallowed or absorbed through the skin,' according to Transportation's hazardous materials booklet."

"Jesus Christ."

"Course we shut the well down right away."

"You said test wells are necessary to locate the contamination source. What the hell's all this going to cost?"

"Depends on how many we have to drill -- fifteen- to twenty-thousand dollars to start. We need you to ask council for emergency legislation to drill four test wells around Number Six. That should tell us which direction the chemical's coming from. Once we know that, we oughta be able to expand out in that direction and eventually locate the source."

"That's not as much as I was afraid of -- if it works. Who would the drilling contract be with?"

"Capital Drilling, out of Columbus: they're supposed to be one of the best in the state."

"And if they're unsuccessful?"

The water director sighs, his expression a clear warning that he's putting his boss on notice. "Well, right now we can get along with one well down without too much problem. But give us a couple a dry months and we may have to add another shift -- pump from midnight to six. Or drill a new well, at a cost of $50,000 or so."

The two men walk toward the city vehicle they arrived in. "And if we don't find the source of contamination the first time out we'll have to drill more test wells," Dean says, thinking aloud.

"Which still isn't the worst that could happen," the director replies.

Dean stops and turns to him, to make his next question unequivocally direct. "The contamination could spread to the other wells, you mean."

"That and the fact that we may have to close the softball field for the rest of the summer. If the first wells don't tell us anything, we may have to dig the next ones out in rightfield."

It takes Dean a moment to realize that the completion of his report has resurrected the director's dry sense of humor. Dean plays along with him.

"Couldn't we call anything hit to rightfield an out?"

The director shakes his head in mock seriousness. *"That might work okay in slo-pitch, but we're talkin' about guys -- most of 'em right-handed hitters -- who could no more pull a pitch with some heat on it than they can see past their beerguts to the inside of home plate."*

"Worse than I thought," Dean chuckles. *"We do have a crisis on our hands."*

"After that oil slick came down the river last year," replies the director, serious again, *"I figured with our own wells drilled into an aquifer here we were safe. All those cities up and down the Ohio having to buy their water somewhere else for weeks, and all we had to worry about was keepin' our boats clean."*

"Nobody's invulnerable any more are they. Let's find this. Do whatever you have to to make sure it doesn't spread."

Dean pauses a moment to look over at Well Six's pale green steel superstructure: a twenty-foot piece of industrial sculpture enclosed in Cyclone fencing and surmounted by a steel-mesh catwalk. It looks the same as the other six along the riverbank. What if a few months from now they are all identical? Contaminated. Unfit for use. Just the thought of it makes him shudder.

1

CORK ROCKNER

Here I am, driving home from the office -- exhausted more from depression than a good hard day's work and not for the first time fantasizing an impulsive jerk of the wheel to send my Mazda hatchback swerving across the road into some ill-fated oncoming vehicle. At the same time recognizing my despair for its selfish transient nature and Lilliputian scale in the scheme of things -- though no less real for all that -- and knowing full well that the other drivers on this two-lane southeast Ohio highway are perfectly safe, from me and my morbid fantasy at least. Remembering again, too, my preoccupation with suicide as a possible solution to my adjustment problems in college. I didn't take such thoughts too seriously then either, though I eventually quit school not once but twice and never did graduate.

Living now with Carlotta, I remind myself for the hundredth time since moving in a little over a year ago, I have no real sanctuary anymore, no place to come home to where in seclusion I can lick the festering wound of spending the greater part of my day doing work I loathe, with people I have absolutely no desire to be with. Poor bastard. Self-pity's a mantra ray in the depths of the mind, poisonous tail lacerating its own thin skin. My bleak mood is not improved when I drive up to the usual chorus of Carlotta's furiously barking dogs.

"Pineal brains," I mutter to myself as Tom lifts his leg

beside my left-rear tire and aluminum-alloy wheel. Actually I like all eight of Carlotta's current menagerie individually; it's just *en masse* that they're hard to take, especially these clamorous and self-important greetings. It took me weeks to learn to plow through their midst with her confident aplomb. "Don't worry, they'll get out of your way," she kept assuring me, but I couldn't stop imagining the horrible feeling of one of their crushed bodies momentarily lifting one side or the other of whichever vehicle I was driving, nor help wondering how she'd react if in following her advice I happened to kill one of her animals.

She's been right so far; now I don't even slow down as dogs surge around the car like a wave breaking harmlessly against my ankles.

I stop to rub noses with Tina, Tom's pretty part-shepherd sister, giving her ears a perfunctory rub as well, and she sings to me happily. Spike, too, gets my attention and grunts his appreciation while the others square off with one another, jaws playfully interlocked or fastened affectionately around a foreleg, and the whole pack drifts off toward the shade of the back yard.

Carlotta's in the kitchen preparing this evening's macro meal -- that's short for "macrobiotic", the special diet emphasizing grains that has been her religion and way of life for several years now. We exchange a kiss and a few words of greeting -- as few as possible as far as I'm concerned; the last thing I want to do is talk about the miserable day I'm fleeing. Carlotta, on the other hand, is cheerful and energetic as usual and not really expecting me to elaborate. She's already started the rice -- brown of course -- in the pressure cooker and is blending the meat of a large zucchini from her garden with onions, eggs, garlic and Parmesan. Stuffed back into its skin, then sliced and baked with bread crumbs and a little olive oil, this delicacy of Carlotta's has become one of my favorite summer dishes.

I stand there listening to her chatter about what the

dogs and horses have been up to today -- how her ride went on Queen Anne, her bitchy, neurotic Arab mare, and how Sidney is progressing under her dressage training -- and am struck once again by Carlotta's strong presence. She has an aristocratic, almost regal bearing, tempered both with the grace of the dancer she still is in her late 40's and the robust, childlike enjoyment she extracts from life. Though I have occasionally found myself marveling at the homeliness of her features or expression in a particular light, this is largely because most of the time I'm enthralled by her unique raw beauty. I'm always photographing her.

Two images of Carlotta imbedded in my brain, from our first times together, must epitomize what I find most attractive in her nature and physical appearance. In one she is standing at the cash register in a fast food place where we have taken her fifteen-year-old daughter and a friend for a snack after a movie. Her well-worn boots and jeans and Levi's jacket, no less than the long natural blonde hair framing her angular face and the unconscious self-assurance in her cocky stance and dazzling smile, all tell you that this is a *woman*. A landmark. A force of nature.

Perhaps the other image reveals as much about me as it does about Carlotta. For some reason we drove separate cars to the restaurant where we had our first date. It was an enjoyable evening: laughter, good conversation, the stirring of desire. But my last picture of her that night is the one that lingers. As she drives past in her Bronco from the parking lot, what I can see of her in the front seat is mostly in silhouette. She's hunched over the steering wheel, elbows out, hair hanging softly around her face, looking over at me -- probably unaware I can see her, or not caring -- and everything about the way she's sitting there says so clearly, so eloquently: Who *is* this guy?

Carlotta holds nothing back. I guess that's both the best and the worst that she brings to our relationship.

While she finishes dinner, I go back to our bedroom to meditate. For me this is a quiet time of about equal parts prayer, contemplation and the same mental jabbering -- mantra of the mundane -- that goes on most of the time. Sometimes the interlude can be remarkably refreshing and invigorating. And when I'm really able to get in touch with the miracle of being alive...and, beyond that, healthy, with three beautiful healthy daughters, living a life free of personal tragedy in a society that for all its greed, stupidity, violence and other evils far surpasses the cultural environment in which most of the world's people must spend their whole lives, then I feel a sense of gratitude beyond measure. If only I could hang onto the wisdom of reverence!

Today, after several minutes of nonstop mental wallah (the sound-effects term for a roomful of voices) I remember why I'm sitting here -- often the way my meditations begin -- and become aware of birds singing outside the window, the faint rustling of leaves in a late afternoon breeze. I feel myself relax. A subtle lightness and warmth spreads through my chest and arms all the way to my fingertips.

I picture Carlotta in the kitchen, making a delicious healthful meal for us -- in my mind I can hear her singing or talking to whichever dogs have begged their way in to hang out with her. Then for a long, extended moment I seem to be aware of everything, good and bad, that has happened between us over the last three years. I become so filled with love and thankfulness that my heart feels as if it's expanding. My eyes even begin to tear -- this *is* a good meditation!

Then the emotion, the realization that prompted it, gradually subside, overwhelmed by dispassionate reflection, memory fragments, some of them painful; the annoying, compulsive mantric phrases with which I reassure myself, like a man fingering prayer beads or jangling pocket change. And finally the analytic faculty itself is roused from slumber and begins to prowl through my mind, finding fault here, there -- almost everywhere it looks.

Back to the real world, where in fact all is not well with mah baby and me. The tears of gratitude a moment ago may actually have sprung from the persistence of what's good about our relationship in the face of some serious problems between us. Such persistence is something I've never been very good at, made possible in this case by Carlotta's various strengths in addition to my own desire to transcend previous limitations, to break a pattern I've come to recognize in the way I make and break relationships with women. I had never anticipated meeting someone like Carlotta here in my hometown, where I naively hoped to remain only long enough to sell the family business before returning to California. Two years, I told my friends on the West Coast.

I'd been back for several months, grimly trying to become enough of a businessman to negotiate the sale of the company, when I was invited to a macro potluck by the owners of the town's only health food store and restaurant. I wasn't really enthusiastic, but swimming had been mentioned -- I assumed from a dock in the Ohio River -- and the summer had been long, hot and humid. Why not?

Fortunately the directions were good or I'd have been certain this was the wrong place as I turned off the highway at the entrance to a wooded area that had the look and feel of an estate about it. If anything, an effort had been made to conceal rather than announcing this. Around here many farms are surrounded by forest on a private, often gated road; but I felt the presence of more than a rustic farmhouse or "country contemporary" at the end of this gravel drive.

A hundred yards or so from the highway it divided and, perhaps to delay my arrival at a social gathering I was beginning to suspect I had greatly underestimated, I took the branch that descended to the river and a broad expanse of bottomland. Sure enough, here was a riding ring, a dock and an uncovered pavilion that could seat a hundred or more people, but no sign of a potluck for a few friendly and unpretentious health food folks. I turned around and took the high road this time.

It climbed away from the highway above a rock-strewn creekbed that was dry now in late August. Soon I spotted a small neat barn on the left and, beyond a hairpin turn, a wide green lawn laid out with orchard, shade trees and flower gardens around a massive stone house that would have been admired by tourists in the English countryside. Surely despite my directions and the signs of a party of *some* kind, this was the wrong place.

But I couldn't very well stop here and back all the way down this long private drive to the bottom of the hill; I had no choice but to continue on, braving the icy stares of the undoubtedly haughty country-club types preening for one another around this Gatsby-like mansion until I found a place to turn around.

Then I noticed as I came on up the hill that the cars I could see weren't all that fancy; one or two in fact were real sleds. This *must* be the right place -- as some part of my mind had been nervously aware all along. I found a place to park and, holding the big bowl of fruit salad I'd brought with me, surveyed the scene from a distance. There were maybe twenty or so people, a few of whom I recognized and all dressed as casually as I was, congregated beneath a canopy of beautiful big oak trees around a picnic table laden with food. I could see a large swimming pool in the background -- so much for mudding it out in the river, which was all right with me.

I took a deep breath and began to feel reallll good. There were several attractive women here who appeared to be alone -- women I never even knew existed in these parts all the time I'd been serving my family penance, not quite in celibacy but certainly not among a coterie of interesting, attractive female friends such as I'd known in L.A. either.

In fact, there were too *many* interesting people, of both sexes and all ages, around to confront all at once. I wandered over, smiling vaguely at faces both familiar and unknown to me, and deposited my contribution among an unappetizing assortment of lethally healthful-looking dishes, noticing with satisfaction that my fruit salad was the only one here.

I singled out Carlotta as the probable hostess right away: a tall slender blonde woman poised and sophisticated-looking, about my age, holding court amidst a small circle of admirers -- none of whom appeared to have taken note of my arrival. I asked a woman I recognized whether she thought it would be all right if I made a self-directed tour of the grounds.

"I'm sure Carlotta wouldn't mind," she replied, "as long as you stay outside."

Carlotta looked over at me with mild curiosity as I immediately left the gathering I'd just joined, to go exploring. I had decided before leaving home that a macrobiotic potluck with a bunch of health food enthusiasts was definitely an event that would benefit from a little herbal embellishment. And now the spectacular natural setting of Carlotta's estate was calling me from several directions at once.

The house and grounds occupied the top of a hill and ridgeline overlooking the Ohio. Directly across the river, bizarrely enough, was a factory complex which I'd get to know and detest -- although with nowhere near Carlotta's intensity -- later. At this time of year its unexpected intrusion was masked by the profusion of trees on her property. I strolled around to the north side of the house for the view upriver.

It was unreal: like a landscape by one of the great English or early American masters. Plowed fields and green meadows girdled with thick stands of hardwood forest. (I'm not exaggerating when I compare it to a painting; "girdled" was a word that came to me as I stood there gaping.) Here and there the sun shimmering off standing water and small creeks meandering toward the Ohio. And in the distance, a good three miles as the crow flies, the clock tower of the county courthouse. I stood there marveling that in all my years of growing up in this area I had never experienced a scene like this.

When I finally got around to socializing, I learned that Carlotta had been a dancer in New York for several years, then after a career-ending injury had come home to start her own modern dance company. The few of us still around at the end of the party got to see tapes of some of the disbanded company's performances. (Though receptive to ballet, West Virginia and Southeastern Ohio are not exactly bastions of modern dance.)

In her eagerness to show her work, tempered by years of disappointment at the lack of interest it had received here, I felt a kindred spirit. And in her direct gaze from eyes at once proud and humbled I thought I detected some recognition of this. By the time I left I knew I had met one of the people you can count on your fingers who will mean a great deal in your life.

...Three years have passed since then; we're in the middle of the summer again. I've experienced how in the winter the industrial plants across the river stand out in all their harsh alien squalor. How every two or three weeks year-round the wind changes to waft their putrid petrochemical odors over Carlotta's virgin acres. When her grandfather built this magnificent showplace it was surrounded by forest and farmland; the factories came later. Many are the times she has reminded me of this.

2

I don't know where Carlotta spends more time, in the kitchen or her barn, but she's more at home in either than anywhere else. If she's not embroiled in housecleaning, which she takes care of entirely on her own (she has full-time help for the grounds) or exercising in front of the mirror in her enormous cathedral-beamed living room, this is where you're most likely to find her -- baking zucchini bread or mucking out stalls, usually surrounded by her dogs.

When I come back downstairs five of them are sprawled out in their favorite spots on the gleaming red oak floor and the dilapidated couch in front of the fireplace which never fails to distress her elderly aunts on their infrequent holiday visits. Though the dogs have wrecked it, Carlotta leaves the couch in the kitchen to keep them from getting underfoot while she's working. The dogs live here, her aunts don't.

Stuffy, her favorite, a pudgy black part-cocker spaniel, follows me with a suspicious brown eye from the window seat, her exclusive territory. Stuffy's the only one -- of the dogs anyway, I'm still not too sure of Carlotta's daughter Emily -- who still hasn't completely accepted my moving in. Largely because Stuffy's neurotic jealousy has aroused the fiendish teasing side of my nature often enough that she wouldn't trust me any sooner than she'd allow another of the dogs to share her window seat. But even Stuffy and I get along. We have an understanding: I wouldn't dream of interfering with Carlotta's outrageous pampering of her, while Stuffy, on the other hand, has begrudgingly allowed me to take her place beside Carlotta at night. She sleeps now in a chair beside the bed.

Dinner's about ready and Carlotta has set the table for two; Emily eats with us only occasionally. Like most teenagers she prefers her own food, though she's no more repelled by Carlotta's macro diet extremes than is the average adolescent by the typical fare of more ordinary parents. Emily's been brought up on brown rice and azuki beans, after all, and rejects them now only on principle, in the same way her peers turn up their noses at meatloaf.

"Have a good meditation?" asks Carlotta.

"It *was* a good one," I reply, stretching. "I thought of us, among other things."

"Oh? That must have been interesting. What about 'us'?"

She's standing at the sink; I come up behind her and put my arms around her. "Just some of the things we've been through together...and how much I care for you," I say, kissing her on the ear. She stops what she's doing and leans back against me for a moment, allowing me to inhale the leather and hay and skin-lotion scent I associate with her. I take a slender wrist in each hand and kiss her lightly on the cheekbone, tasting the salty film of perspiration on her fine skin, and she twists around from the hips to offer me her lips. Her body is so limber she does this with ease, closing her eyes and smiling before returning to whatever it is she's doing in the sink. I slide my hands down to massage the backs of her thighs through her jeans.

It's ironic that while I stand here enjoying the warmth that has just surged into my heart, I'm also asking myself whether Carlotta is disappointed that a moment earlier I said "care for" instead of love. She noticed it, I'm sure; she notices every such omission -- often, it seems to me, to the exclusion of anything positive that may have accompanied it. But the warmth I'm feeling toward her overwhelms my self-questioning, my guilt if that's what it is. The feeling is what's important.

This is what I actually experience of love now: random, transient flowerings of emotion which come and go spontaneously. The rest is all just words -- words and concepts, word accretions.

When we started seeing each other and I was determined to win Carlotta's reluctant heart, it was easy to say, "I love you," because when she was in my arms I could *feel* what she was doing to me, what she was bringing into my life. I expressed the emotion and said the word with all the conviction in the world, not only because I knew I spoke the truth but because it felt so *good* to say it.

The fact that she looked askance at me when I dared to utter this frightening magic word so loaded with the detritus of the heart, to speak it with such brazen and insouciant assurance so early in our friendship, only spurred me on. Far from being intimidated by her inability, her honest refusal, to reciprocate -- to say what she herself wasn't feeling -- I declared my love with enough feeling for both of us.

If I recklessly bandied the "L" word about for the pure joy of sharing it with a woman again after so long, I don't think I can be accused of exploiting it to win Carlotta's heart. For our love-making, chaste as it still was at the time, was invariably followed or preceded by long sessions of...negotiation, I guess you'd have to call them, in which Carlotta articulated her demands. She'd been on her own for a long time now and wasn't at all sure she wanted to make a change, definitely not unless I was really serious about her, not just looking for what she dismissed as "romantic adventure". And I told her right at the beginning, at the risk of jeopardizing our relationship before it had even had a chance to begin: when you really love someone it's just between you and you. The only real commitment involved is the one you make, and keep, with yourself.

I shared this with her -- this hard kernel of wisdom I'd come across in my wanderings in the wilderness -- knowing full well that it's hardly the sort of thing a diffident lover expects to hear. I wanted her to see as many sides of me as possible. If I was willing to share this questionable revelation with her right up front, then my declaration of love must be genuine too, right? But more importantly, the talismanic phrase, "It's just between you and you," has done wonders in helping me reconcile all the heartache I've experienced; I thought, naively, that Carlotta, who'd been living a life of abstinence atop her hill for years, might see its salutary magic as well.

"That's the most selfish thing I ever heard," she said when I introduced her to the idea. "I'm glad you told me if that's how you really feel, because I don't want any part of that kind of relationship. That's the way I ended up living in New York -- in self-defense. I took what I wanted and made no bones about it. But I don't want to live like that anymore. I'm too content here with Emily and my animals to get sucked back into that kind of life."

We're on a blanket in front of the huge fireplace in her high-ceilinged living room, its open beams and most of its elegant faded furniture lost in shadow. Obviously designed by her grandfather for entertaining, the large room is used by Carlotta primarily for her strenuous daily workouts.

"Why is it so selfish?" I ask. "I don't think you understand what I'm saying. To me, this is the secret of success between two people; it's an acknowledgment that no one can hurt you but yourself."

"I'm not afraid of getting hurt," she says indignantly, her brown eyes flashing, "that's not the point. Why should I change my way of life for someone whose only commitment is to himself? I've already known enough people like that to last a lifetime. If that's all you have to offer, Cork, then no thanks, I'll continue to get along fine on my own."

"You're misinterpreting what I said, Carlotta," I patiently reply, well aware that I asked for this by bringing it up in the first place. "You asked me for a commitment and I've already given it to you. I told you, I'm more than willing to make our relationship monogamous if that's what you want. But as for the future, who can say what will happen between us? We hardly know each other yet, but neither of us has much of a track record where long-term relationships are concerned.

"I'm not talking about *my* commitment at the moment; I'm talking about *yours* -- to yourself. I'm suggesting that you go into this -- a relationship with me, I mean -- not on the basis of whether or not I'm going to love you, or love you enough, or love you in the right way or whatever...but on the basis of how *you* really feel. This relationship is for *you*, the same as the ones in New York you were talking about. If there's a difference this time it'll be because you want more out of this one. And how are you going to get it? by putting more into it. You see what I mean?"

Firelight and her volatile emotions play across Carlotta's expressive face. The defensive anger in her eyes becomes indignation, then a frank plea for honesty, clarity: help me understand you, it says.

"Don't you see, it all depends on you," I tell her, taking her slender work-toughened hands in mine. "Any weakness or thoughtlessness of mine can't hurt you, once you're really able to see that you're ultimately doing this for you -- and I'm doing it for me. If you find that I'm not up to the kind of love you want, you don't have to interpret that as some kind of betrayal. You can simply see it as it is -- a deficiency in character or whatever -- and walk away, withdraw your commitment....Do you see what I'm trying to say?

"I can't ask you -- and I'm *not* asking you, Carlotta -- to do anything but what's right for you, whatever that turns out to be. I trust you because that's all I'm expecting from you. If I choose to love you, that's my business; I have nothing to blame you for later if you decide you want something else."

I can see that Carlotta's *trying* to comprehend what

17

I'm getting at. At the same time, by now I don't know whether I'm making any sense or not. Do I *really* want a relationship to work this time, or since the last one I royally screwed up have I worked out some kind of elaborate rationalization with the dual purpose of *convincing* me I do while simultaneously covering my ass? It seems to me I've caught a whiff of bullshit in all this talk.

Carlotta seems to have read my mind. "Why are you so intent on protecting me -- on shielding me from you and your thoughtlessness and weakness, as you put it? Do you think I need protection? Are you really that bad -- or are *you* the one you're really protecting? All this sounds to me like nothing more than a fancy way to justify not making a commitment. But you can't expect me to look at life the way you do just to make things easier for you."

"...No, of course not," I sigh, feeling mentally exhausted, fuzzy-headed all at once. "I'm *trying* to communicate to you how I feel, but I know I'm not doing a very good job of it right now. Let's just shut up for a while."

"That's the best idea you've had all night."

This brings smiles to both of us. Meanwhile, the shutdown of my mind is allowing me to feel the energy Carlotta and I can generate between us. In no time the bright crackling flames in her enormous fireplace burn through the defenses we've been erecting all evening and we find ourselves wandering again in the mysterious, exciting new world we're discovering together.

3

THE MAKING OF A DOWSER
Walter Barry's Story

I came from lumber territory down in Florida, a town called Shannon. My father was in the lumber business and we lived in a real rough environment. A bunch of hard rough people worked in that mill -- at least fifteen hundred colored people and about 300 white people -- and the lumber camp was all that was there. Of course the town was gone years ago, the timber was all cut out.

In 1918 during the flu epidemic of World War I when my father and brother and two sisters and I were all down flat on our backs with the flu, my mother packed up and moved out on us -- just left us all there to die, as far as she was concerned. I guess this was the beginning of a heck of a lot of psychological stuff in my life. I was eight then; I was born in 1910 on the tenth of October: 10/10/10.

It's pretty hard for four children and a busy father to get along, so they started farming me out to boarding schools and relatives. I stayed with aunts and uncles and grandmothers, and I was always on the outer fringe of someone else's family, never a part of it, never feeling that I belonged to anyone in particular. My mother moved to Alabama and had to come back and steal my older brother out of school as a witness in her divorce case. It was sticky.

I was a hard worker and kind of a loner too. I always

19

took up with some old colored man like the iceman or the blacksmith. I looked up to the older ones and hung around them, and I guess I picked up a lot of knowledge, a lot of that old-time wisdom in that way.

At about the age of 14 I was sent to a boarding school in Montverde and by that time I had grown up physically. I was way above the normal size for that age and doing a lot of chasing around with some of the girls from school. I ended up getting caught in the girls' dormitory with a girl from Johnson City, Tennessee. Mother Parish caught us and I checked out before morning.

I was crazy about the ocean, the Gulf, so I hitchhiked over to Tarpon Springs on the west coast close to St. Petersburg. I hung around over there for two or three days until I spotted a little fishing vessel in the harbor and went down to the pier and got acquainted with the owner, a Greek fisherman. I talked him into a job by telling him I was an orphan who didn't have anywhere else to go.

We went out to the snapper banks, about 90 miles from Tarpon Springs, and picked up a load of red snapper, put them in the hold on ice and set sail for Santiago, Cuba. I thought it was rather odd that we were going all the way to Cuba with a load of fish. When they let the crew go ashore, this was the first exposure I'd had to being a big shot and going into a bar.

This was back during Prohibition and all I'd tasted before was a little wine, but I liked it so I went in with the crew and had my first real drink. It never occurred to me that it was strange they'd let the whole crew go ashore at one time. We sat around drinking all evening and I got drunker than a coot. The next day we got out of there and went back to the snapper banks, fished for no more than four hours, then came on into Tampa where we were dismissed.

Several years later I got to thinking about it -- about the waterline of the boat not rising very much when we came back in empty and about the fact that we only fished for a short while before loading these fish on ice in the hold -- and I realized I'd been aboard a rum-runner. They'd gone into Santiago, loaded up on Ron Rico and Bacardi and smuggled it into the country under a foot of red snapper. I guess they took me along to make it look like a family thing with a kid on board.

When I finally returned home I'd been gone about three months. Dad, of course, was very upset that I'd disappeared without letting anyone know where I was. In Cuba we'd gone from Santiago over to Havana that night, and I'd noticed the sailors down there with a girl on each arm and a bottle of booze and the whole works, and it really intrigued me. So I went down to the recruiting office and passed all the examinations at the age of 14 to get in the Navy. Passed all the physicals, all the mentals -- all I had to do was get a signature on the papers.

I went and confronted my father with this and he took a look at it and dropped it back down on the desk and said, "Are you crazy?"

"Well, maybe I am," I said, "but I sure want to go into the Navy."

"No way -- you're just a baby! You get in there with that bunch of men and they'll completely ruin you. You're bad enough as it is."

"Okay, if that's the way you feel about it." Of course to myself I said, I'll give you so damn much trouble you'll finally come around -- which I immediately did. I ran away from home three times in the next six or eight months. Every time he put me in school I would stay maybe a month or so and then I'd check out.

One day he called me in and told me, "Well, I've made a decision: I'm going to put you in the Florida State Reform School, or you go in the Navy."

"Okay," I said, "I'll go down and get all my papers together and get a new examination."

21

"There's one thing I want you to understand. If you come back with anything less than an honorable discharge, I'll break your neck." And I knew he meant it.

The Navy shipped me out of Daphne, Alabama, up to Birmingham; from Birmingham to Norfolk, Virginia; from Norfolk to Hampton Roads, their training station. I was only 15 years old, a rosy-cheeked country boy. I thought I knew everything in the world, had had a little sex and the experience to go with it to make me think I was a real man.

Back in those days the Navy was rough. They used to sentence people to four years in the Navy instead of sending them to jail. Some of the old salts said it wasn't far removed from the days of wooden ships and iron men. They gave me a little pamphlet that said, "You're in the Navy now. Keep your eyes and ears open and your mouth shut." I apparently read that backwards. I was in about two weeks when I got it the first time.

Some big old farm boy from South Carolina set me down so flat with his fist I sat there for ten minutes before I could get the nerve just to stand up, much less try to get back at him. I decided maybe this was a pretty good piece of advice after all. I went along with it for about three months before the same thing happened again. But then I made an about-face; I knew if I got booted out I couldn't go home again so maybe I'd better apply myself.

Although I didn't have enough education to feel confident of really succeeding, I put in my application for the Naval Electrical School. I began to see there was a heck of a lot to be learned not just about the electrical trades but about my own personal self and human relations too. I had to get along with people.

So I studied and got through the Naval Electrical School and went from there through the Gyrocompass School. From there they transferred me to the Navy Receiving Ship in New York at the Brooklyn Navy Yard. This was in 1927.

But the USS Henderson was on her way to China, and they put me on the Henderson. We went through the Panama Canal and up the West Coast to Seattle, where they transferred me to the USS Vega, a sort of supply ship for the naval base in Alaska. Ten days before the Vega was to sail to Alaska I got my transfer orders again -- right back to the Receiving Ship in New York. There they put me on the USS Dobin, a repair ship. The way I see it now, every one of these moves was to convince me that I was being guided into something.

I got into the Electrical Repair Department on the Dobin; and we were to keep up all repairs for the 36th Squadron of destroyers as well as four submarines. I don't know how many destroyers were in that division, but there were quite a few. I got into armature winding and electrical installations, did gyrocompass repairs, and all sorts of things. It gave me a background, as I see it, to understand the things we're into now: the human energy, bio-energetic forces involved in dowsing and healing.

Unfortunately, all this time I was also gaining momentum on my alcoholism. I'd go ashore and come back dog drunk; I kept getting into all sorts of scrapes with my booze. Our home port was New York City and we were in dry-dock the whole month of December. Saint Nick's Athletic Club up on 66th Street had a dance hall for the sailors, soldiers and Marines, and even though I kept getting beat up and thrown out, I got to thinking I was tough again. Once when we were anchored on the East River I was trying to get up to 96th Street on the subway, and I fell off the platform and had about six people down there on the tracks trying to get me out before the train came. It was just stupidity.

If I hadn't been a good man on ship who could do anything they told me to and very efficiently, I'm sure I'd have been in a lot of trouble. But they overlooked a lot because I was available to do anything they wanted me to at any hour of the day or night. They'd call me at three o'clock Sunday morning to get up and wind an armature in an emergency on one of the destroyers. The armature is the part in a motor that turns; rewinding it is an intricate operation where you've got to tear off all the old winding and put in new insulated copper wire. That's the sort of thing I did and I'd stay right with it until I finished.

I got through the Navy with what they call a minority cruise: three years and five months. I went in in May and was discharged in Charleston, South Carolina, on the 10th of October, 1929, on what was supposed to be my 21st birthday but was in reality only my 19th, about the time most young men go in.

I didn't expect the stock market crash to bother me any. When we were in Boston the last time, I'd gone to the office of an engineering firm there and told them about my abilities as an electrician, and they told me when I got discharged to report to the El Paso Electric Company and they'd have a job for me. (I asked for something in Texas because my father had tuberculosis and had gone to El Paso for his health -- or, as it turned out, to die.) So after my discharge I went to the ship's chandler in Charleston and signed on to the Gulf Pride, a tanker headed for Corpus Christi.

That was undoubtedly the most miserable trip I ever took at sea. We were empty, sitting on top of the water with no ballast, like a tin can. The ship was crummy -- this was before the time of maritime unions. The food was lousy, and there was brackish water in the fresh water tanks; the more you drank, the more you wanted. I think it took us about eight days to make that trip down through the Straits of Florida to Corpus. I got off the ship constipated, feeling just miserable, and caught a train to El Paso.

The El Paso Electric Company was building a big power plant that was the first with a combustion control system which would feed the boilers and maintain desired steam pressures automatically. I was very fortunate in working with the engineer in charge of installing this system, a man named Wheeler; when the plant went on line I stayed on as an electrician. And when I hit the Mexican border at the age of 19, with a job paying me about $150 a week when everyone else was working for $25, I really went wild.

I was too young for the older crowd in Juarez and too old for the younger ones so I had to pick up with the in-betweens, the misfits. I even took a shot at marijuana once. A bunch of high school kids asked me to go out in an alley with them and I smoked one joint -- that's the word they use now although I don't think they called it that then. It took me about twenty feet off the ground and I couldn't get back down, so I quit right there. It's probably a good thing I was also loaded with cheap Mexican whiskey because if I'd gone that route I'd really have been in for it.

In September 1932 my dad died of tuberculosis. The company doctors, who were there because they had TB themselves, called me in for a physical. I'd been getting maybe one good night's sleep a week, carousing and getting two or three hours the rest of the time, and these two boys gave me an examination and told me I had TB too. They said I had to go to the Veterans Sanitarium -- that the company would take care of it, my expenses and insurance and all -- and I told them to go to hell. I said just because my father died of tuberculosis doesn't mean I'm about to. So I acted exactly backwards again. New Yorkers were coming out to El Paso for their health, and I quit my job in El Paso right in the middle of the depression and went to New York.

4

Through connections I'd made in the service I got a job in public relations for a clothing concern in the garment district. This exposed me to all the booze in the world because I had to take out-of-towners to the Follies and all the shows and clubs and show them a good time, on an unlimited expense account. I'd always wanted to be an entertainer; I learned tap dancing from the colored kids down by the sawmill and had done a little singing in Mexico and around town. So we'd go into these clubs in New York and once in a while I'd get up and do something.

One night down at Jimmy Kelly's in the Village I did a number and Jimmy comes over and says, "I see you around here a lot -- how would you like to go to work for me as an entertainer? I need an emcee."

I said, "Well, I can't afford to quit my job."

"That's all right," he said, "keep your job. Come down here and do a show, then take your gang around, show them the sights, and come back and do another show."

So we started this and I was making two paychecks for several months until I got caught at it; they kept getting these expense accounts from Jimmy Kelly's, Jimmy Kelly's. I went to work for Jimmy, then three or four other clubs, did a little vaudeville, a little radio, and all the time the booze was the main thing. I couldn't go on, I couldn't work, I couldn't do anything without the booze. I was drinking at least a quart of whiskey a day.

I was living in the Park Central Hotel. My daily ritual was to get up around 3 o'clock in the afternoon and go down to the gym after drinking half a water glass of whiskey to get me started. I'd work out, get in the steam room, go swimming, have a massage, then come back up to my room and this time drink a full glass of whiskey while getting ready to go to whichever club I happened to be working at the time. One day -- I forget the date but it was in 1935 -- I got up and was sitting on the side of my bed, and it dawned on me that I had absolutely no talent whatsoever except what was coming out of the bottle. I called Newark Airport and asked how soon I could catch a plane to Jacksonville; they said there was one at 7:30. Between 3:30 that afternoon and 7:30 that night I packed all my belongings and made arrangements for a bellboy to ship them for me; quit my job, picked up my paycheck and bought everybody in the club a drink; then took a cab to the airport. I was running away from booze -- yet all I had in my bag were my toilet articles, a change of socks and underwear, and six quarts of Canadian Club.

In Jacksonville I ran into a man named L.L. Pray who was selling wheel alignment and balancing equipment for the Beeline Manufacturing Company out of Davenport, Iowa. Pray had a territory of four southern states -- Florida, Georgia, Alabama and Tennessee -- and he wanted someone to learn enough about this equipment to install it and stay there and instruct a man on it. He had a big Buick 90 pulling this huge trailer loaded with 5,000 pounds of equipment. We'd slide it off already assembled and put it into a garage or a dealership somewhere, and I would stay there to show them how much money it could make. Pray would come back and make the final deal, and I'd stick around till a new machine came. Then we'd load it so he always had a new one on his trailer. This worked pretty well for me for a while, but the booze still predominated.

I was back in Jacksonville sometime in 1936 to show a tall young country boy named Speedy how to use the equipment. He and I would get to drinking together early in the morning and we'd be pretty well oiled by the end of the day. One night I met a chick in a restaurant and made a date with her for a dance. The next evening after drinking all day with Speedy I got dressed and went down to Bay Street and picked up a pint of whiskey.

In Florida at that time you'd have a package store in the front and a place in the back where you could order a Coca Cola and sit down and have your drink. I went in back with my pint, took a big slug, then shoved the bottle in my back pocket and went to the restroom. I was standing there relieving myself when this young soldier from the local CMTC -- Citizens Military Training Camp -- came in a little drunk. He just kinda pushed me aside so he could go at the same time I was. I stepped to one side, then felt something warm and looked down, and he'd urinated on my beautiful imported Scotch linen suit, from the knee right down into my shoe. Without thinking, I came up with an uppercut that caught this kid right under the chin and lifted him clear off the floor. He went sprawling on his back into a bunch of beer cases. They tumbled over and broke, with beer running all over the floor, glass and everything.

It happened so fast I didn't realize I'd hit him that hard. I looked down at him, and his head was flopped over on his right shoulder with a knot about the size of your fist on his long neck. I just knew I'd broken it.

The man from the liquor store ran back with a couple of other people, and pretty soon people started coming in off the street. Then the police arrived and a druggist down the street was called. A policeman asked me if I'd hit him and I admitted I had. He said, "Well, don't you go anywhere, I think you just killed a man."

"Oh my God!" I said and sat down on a beer case. I'd forgotten about my suit by this time. Well, there was a lot of hullabaloo around there, when all of a sudden this fella sat up, raised his head -- and the knot disappeared.

I jumped up and knelt down in that filth, put my arm around him, and asked, "How do you feel?"

"All right," he said. "What happened?" When I told him he said, "I don't blame you for hittin' me." He was sober by that time and so was I.

I said, "My God, man, everybody in this room thought you were dead!"

When I asked him about the knot on his neck, he said, "Oh that," and twisted his head around. It was a goiter -- one of those south Georgia goiters from eating too much corn and not getting enough iodine in his diet. Boy, I never cried so hard in my life. Tears just started flowing -- I was so relieved to see that this guy was all right.

But you know what I did then? I went back down to the hotel, cleaned up and put on another suit, took a couple of big slugs from the pint I still had, then went out and bought another one and danced all night -- had a rip-roaring time. No way did I attribute any of my problems to the booze.

From Jacksonville we went to Orlando. I'm quite a fisherman, and the minute I rode into town and saw all those beautiful lakes again -- the boarding school I ran away from was just across Lake Apopka from Orlando -- I thought, boy, this is for me! I didn't want to go on traveling all over Georgia and Alabama and everywhere, especially with the booze the way it was.

We put in a wheel alignment machine there for Smith and Meadows Garage just off Orange Avenue, and I got to meeting people. Everyone was friendly and nice -- beautiful women -- there was a lot going on in this little town. As soon as we got the machine all set up I started campaigning to stay there and operate it. I quit the Beeline Manufacturing Company and stayed in Orlando.

And the same thing happened all over again: booze, booze, booze -- out all night every night, dancing and raising heck and chasing everything I could find. I even got to messing around with some married women, which is always conducive to problems.

In fact there was a beauty parlor right in front of our garage, whose owner had a cute little wife, and he was an alcoholic, out carousing all over, neglecting this little gal. I just couldn't stand to see this, no way did I want to see any cute little thing like that neglected. So I started taking care of his duties for him, and he found out.

One morning she called me at the house before I came down to work and said, "Charlie's got a gun and he's drunk and he's looking for you! You'd better not come down today."

I said, "Ah hell, he'll get over it all right."

I was under the wheel alignment machine, just starting my work, when I saw Charlie drive in. He parked his car, and I saw him go around and open the glove compartment. He stood there for what seemed like ten minutes at least, then closed the door and walked right up in front of the shop. "Walter?" he says.

"Yeah?" I answered.

"I want to see you a minute."

I got up and walked up to him, and he reached in his coat pocket, pulled out a .32 automatic and put it right in my belly button. He was shaking like a leaf, and the thing was fully cocked. He says, "You've been fooling with my wife."

I said, "Well, Charlie, you're doing all the talking; it seems you have a little advantage right now. Regardless of what I say, it's still going to be wrong. Besides," I said, "I've seen you out at all the night clubs with somebody else's wife for the past couple of years, and there is no way that you're not as guilty or more so than I am."

"That doesn't enter into it at all," he said -- "it's *my* wife I'm interested in. I'm going to blow your guts out."

Well, I thought, if he's going to shoot me, it might as well be in the back. "Okay, Charlie, it's your ballgame," I said and started walking away, expecting that hot bullet any second.

I went on in, got under the machine, and I could see him from underneath the car I was working on. He stood there for about five minutes until finally I heard that gun's safety click back on. He put it in his pocket, got in his car and drove off. He was gone for about two months, went on a real wild drinking spree. Then Smith and Meadows took in a new partner and bought a big elaborate place. When I moved over to the new garage I met my first wife.

I started fishing out at Lake Down, and this old man out there had a bunch of boats he'd rent, on about 18 acres of the most beautiful land you've ever seen. The first time I went out there I went with a kid by the name of Frank Jones. Frank told me, "Now you stay right in the car and wait till the old man comes out because if you get out of the car, he's got a dog that'll tear you to pieces. He'll come right at your throat." Well, I've never been afraid of a dog in my life. So I just got out and started walking up towards the house and, sure enough, here comes this beast -- half Airedale and half shepherd, with the hair on his neck standing up -- bounding out of the yard and running right toward me.

I just slapped my hands together, and he jumped up and put his feet on my chest and tried to lick my face. By this time the man had come out of the house and he walked up to me, stuck out his hand and said, "That's the first time my Princie has ever done that to anybody. I've got to be your friend." So he and I got to be close friends as of that minute.

Three or four months later a beautiful young girl came into the shop with the front end of her Dodge mashed in and the wheels all knocked out of alignment. After I put it up on the machine to see what the damage was and make out an estimate, we decided she should have somebody take her home. I did the honors and when I asked her for a date that night she said yes.

I picked her up and we went out and had a few

drinks, just riding around, until she said, "Let's go out to my grandfather's." I agreed and she directed me out toward Lake Down. When it was obvious that's where we were headed, I asked her who her grandfather was.

"He's an old Dutch out here on the lake."

"Gee," I said, "I've been fishing with that guy, fishing and drinking with him and everything else." The minute he knew I was interested in Jean, his granddaughter, he started arranging for our marriage. Actually, I think I married her on account of him.

5

Carlotta's about ready to put dinner on so I get the coleslaw she's made earlier from the refrigerator and take it and a dish of hummus, surrounded by triangles of pita bread, out to the picnic table on the patio and sit down. The sun is behind the trees now, and the lawn and orchard are their deepest, most vibrant green. Tina looks coyly out at me from the flowerbed, her favorite place to lie in the summer.

"Went to see my aunt today," says Carlotta with enthusiasm after joining me. Her face and voice are animated as usual, her deep-set dark eyes sparkling with silent laughter.

"The one at the nursing home?"

"Right, Aunt Elsa. She was really sweet today. Asked me to take her for a drive."

"Where'd you go?"

"Out Turkey Hen Road -- where Cindy and her husband bought that little farm last year."

"I know where you mean."

"I stopped by to see Cindy too, but she wasn't there. I hope she wasn't off somewhere with that contractor she keeps talking about."

"I thought she and her husband just got back together -- when they bought the farm."

"They did. I don't understand that woman. She can be so much fun -- we're both interested in a lot of the same things -- mostly horses of course -- but she doesn't use her head sometimes. If she starts runnin' around on Bill again she's liable to lose her kids this time."

"Think so?" I ask, mildly interested in the romantic peccadilloes of this young woman I've seen down at the barn a couple of times.

"I can't say that I'd blame him. And that little boy of hers -- Rooty, they call him -- is darling. He says I'm his girlfriend. When I'm over there he wants all my attention." She laughs at the thought of this.

"So tell me about your aunt," I say. "Where'd you end up taking her?"

"I was going to introduce her to Cindy, she's such a character. But since she wasn't there, we drove clear up the hollow just to give Elsa something besides other old people and crabby attendants to see for a change."

"She must've had a great time."

"Oh she did -- till we had to stop so she could go to the bathroom." Carlotta's eyes light up in amusement rather than revealing the least hint of disgust as she relates the incident.

"I said, 'Can't you wait, Elsa? I can have you back in fifteen minutes.' But she says, no, she can't wait and then she starts to get a little frantic because I guess she thought I wasn't going to stop. So we pull over, and I help her down out of the Bronco -- remember how she clung to me when she came to dinner with her sisters? She did the same thing this time. Said she couldn't walk, I'd have to carry her over where no one could see her. And I'm goin', 'You're doin' fine, Elsa; I'll help you, but I can't carry you, you're gonna have to walk there yourself.'

"Then she starts whimpering and getting panicky, says she can't wait -- so I just whipped her pants down right there and held her out away from me...." Now Carlotta wrinkles her nose for the first time although she's still grinning.

"Diarrhea. It went everywhere." Again she laughs her boisterous laugh -- almost a whoop at times, as it is now. "I tried to keep it off her as best I could. Then I found rags in the back of the Bronco to wipe off what did get on her. Of course she's terribly humiliated, and I'm reassuring her that everything's all right, these things can happen. What an

34

afternoon!"

Carlotta gives me that gleeful look that's so characteristic of her, and I smile back, admiring her immensely. How alive she is, and how giving! I don't know anyone else who lives life so flat-out, just from her own natural energy: no tea or coffee for Carlotta (though she does have quite a sweet tooth she struggles to control). And most of the time she's in excellent spirits, although her infrequent anger certainly isn't a force of nature you want to fool with.

For the first six months or so after we started seeing each other, I didn't think Carlotta had a dark side -- and it's no more than a dark grey in any case. She's opinionated as hell, congenitally unable to see how life looks to ninety-nine percent of the people on the planet. But her big heart ameliorates that shortcoming considerably.

Everything was great between the two of us until I began to feel -- or *not* feel, actually: gradually I stopped being able to feel the love between us which at first had been so electric, such a living presence that it was like...what? the opposite of a shadow, an entity of light beneath the skin? More like a special case of phantom limb pain maybe: the white hole in your chest you fall into when you've lost your heart to someone.

Was this emotional anesthesia a surprise to me? Not at all, just part of the pattern I mentioned earlier in how I handle relationships; I'd anticipated it from the beginning. The whole point of starting a new one with Carlotta was the turning point it was going to represent in my life. This time was going to be different. This time I wouldn't let the fadeout of my experience of love get to me; I was going to work through it. I had no idea what lay beyond this major barrier I'd always managed to erect between myself and my feelings in love, but I was sure as hell ready to find out.

This is part of what I'd been trying to tell Carlotta from the very beginning, that night in front of the fire. I didn't come right out and warn her that this was likely to happen, for two reasons. For one thing I'm not that stupid -- or honest, I guess. Carlotta would have been gone in a minute. But I also wasn't sure it would happen. I haven't been with enough women in my life for this pattern of behavior to have hardened into some kind of immutable law of nature.

Now the moment of truth had arrived in my love affair with Carlotta. It was time to tell her what I was going through and to reassure her that I was determined this time to cross the Cork Rockner frontier with her into new territory.

I remember clearly the day she and I first discussed this -- the first of *many* times to come -- but not how it happened that we were having lunch at her house in the middle of the week. Remember, this was some six months after we started seeing each other, a year and a half before I moved in with her. So although this obviously didn't mark the end of our relationship, I believe its gradual deterioration began with my disclosure, even as the intimacy between us continued to grow.

"What do you mean you're no longer 'in touch with your feelings'?" I recall her asking, a whole new tone of mistrust and incredulity in her voice. "How long has this been going on?"

"It just started a little while ago, Carlotta," I reply. "But I told you, it's nothing to worry about. I'll get through it; I just need your patience, that's all."

"You mean all this time together and you still don't know how you feel about me? I thought things were good between us. You said...all kinds of things that led me to believe you felt the same about me as I do about you. Now you tell me you're not sure? What am I to believe, Cork?"

"Trust your gut feelings. If they tell you I'm just leading you on and lying to you, then tell me to get the hell out of your life. I can say that because I'm *not* lying to you -- I haven't and I won't. I tried to prepare you for this right at the beginning, Carlotta, but I didn't *know* it would happen with you, I hoped it wouldn't. I did know if I told you then, it would be all over for the two of us, before it even began. And I didn't want that -- I wanted you in my life."

"But now you're not sure anymore?" she asks accusingly.

"No, I'm still sure, Carlotta -- as sure as I could be about anything! Just because my feelings have gone underground for a while doesn't mean I no longer know my own mind, or that I don't have any willpower to draw on."

"Oh, great, so now you need willpower to be with me? You sure know how to turn a phrase, Cork."

I smile more or less in spite of myself and reach out to her; at first she's having none of it, but then she relents and allows me to pull her against me.

"I *never* expected to find someone like you back here, Carlotta. I thought I was just coming back to try to sell the family business and then I'd be out of here. But now I feel you may be the real reason I came back -- I mean, if there's some kind of destiny guiding my life. If there isn't, fine, I know how important you are to me."

"Well I'm not sure it's enough for me, Cork. Not when your mind says one thing but your heart's not sure it agrees, or whatever the hell your problem is."

"My problem will go away, Carlotta, if you'll allow it to. If you'll just stay with me and trust your own instincts or intuition. I'm sure of it."

Carlotta's attempt to put that afternoon behind us has been a gift to both of us. But since then she has always been a little mistrustful in a way she'd ceased to be after finally making a commitment to the two of us. And she maintains that this mistrust is behind what I construe as her insecure and jealous behavior. She says that if she's at all insecure in our relationship, it's because I told her myself that I can't really *feel* how I feel about her. How can you argue with that?

6

I'm making it sound as if Carlotta and I have spent much of our time together bickering, but that isn't true at all. She has too great a love for nature and too much willpower to allow her spirits to languish for long. Out in the fresh air with her animals or in her garden, she is invigorated, replenished. Though she can be quick to take affront, character and her exuberant sense of humor play equal parts in restoring her positive outlook.

In the past year Carlotta has mourned the deaths not only of two of her favorite dogs but of Viceroy, the ancient palomino stallion she's had since childhood. The patient, swaybacked old horse had the run of the grounds between house and barn. He made his rounds in the shambling gait of an elderly boulevardier out for his daily constitutional. When she saw him Carlotta would sing out his name in three syllables, giving it a lilting melody in which you couldn't miss her love for him.

Apparently early one morning the poor animal stumbled over the side of the hill near her barn. By the time Carlotta discovered him he was already near death, wheezing softly, wedged into a gully that even a strong young horse would have found it difficult to escape. Distraught but in control, Carlotta got Hank, her groundskeeper, on the phone, and within minutes they were tenderly working ropes around Viceroy's twisted body, coaxing him, trying to winch him as gently as possible into a position from which he might struggle somehow to his feet. But we all knew this was futile.

By now Emily was there and mother and daughter were sobbing openly together as Viceroy's rasping breaths grew more and more feeble. Finally a great shudder shook his gaunt sides and they both wailed, while Hank and I looked on, not only helpless to intervene but humbled by the awesomeness of a life so powerful at last succumbing, the extraordinary dignity in the magnificent old horse's death.

Only two months earlier Carlotta had grieved over the death of Ronnie, her tough little hound who despite numerous wounds sustained over the years in the line of duty, continued his hyperactive love-life right to the bitter end. Mauled by a neighbor's rottweilers outraged by the brazenness of his poaching, Ronnie lingered for almost a week, thanks to Carlotta's round-the-clock nursing. After her vet had sewn him up, he supplied the medication and Carlotta provided the hospital bed and loving care but to no avail.

The only one of Ronnie's self-appointed tasks involving neither sex nor his obnoxious habit of goading the rest of the dogs into a barking frenzy at the least provocation had been his regular cleaning of the foulest-smelling pair of ears I ever hope to encounter. These belonged to Carlotta's 13-year-old German shepherd Good Ole Boy, or Bo, as he was more commonly called. Whether Ronnie considered this his duty or merely prized Bo's rancid secretions as a peculiarly canine delicacy, we were never sure, but his oral ministrations were probably all that kept Bo's encrusted ears from infection. And Ronnie's untimely demise was followed a few months later by Bo's. Though he'd already lost the use of his hindlegs a year or so earlier, Bo had learned to drag himself around the yard fairly well on a little cart Hank made for him. But his well-lived years finally caught up with him. Of all the dogs Bo had lived here longest, having been a Christmas puppy in a red ribbon for Emily, and his death after first Ronnie's and then Viceroy's was particularly hard on Carlotta.

It hasn't kept her from her routine of barn- and housecleaning, however, or her daily workout in the living room. She continues to ride every day, weather permitting, and I often accompany her on weekends, forgetting much of her instruction from session to session but retaining enough to perceive some progress and to imagine a time when I can handle horses skillfully enough to really share in Carlotta's joy with them, rather than tagging along on our trail rides perched atop the plodding overweight gelding she calls Beefheart or concentrating surreptitiously on protecting my balls during the lessons in her riding ring beside the river. For now, riding is still mostly drudgery, which I endure for the pleasure not only of Carlotta's company but of observing her in her element. All my shit-shoveling and -hauling, the hours spent brushing and currying her horses -- a tiny fraction of the time she spends in such endeavors -- are a price worth paying to see Carlotta fighting with her beautiful but crazy Arab mare, both of them headstrong and furious with each other; or astride her big thoroughbred Germanicus, with Carlotta reveling in their graceful union.

Though she'd prefer it the other way around, Carlotta's perfectly willing that we spend a lot more time walking than riding together: through the woods or on unpaved roads back into the hills away from the river. We've watched the seasons turn over our favorite isolated farmhouses and stark or lush forest settings, noting and discussing the people and landscapes and how they've interacted; thrashing out our own or the world's problems together; or remaining quiet for half an hour or more, just looking and thinking. Once last spring we happened upon a whole possum family, a mother and three or four babies, mashed utterly flat into the packed gravel roadbed, and silent tears ran down Carlotta's face. She brushed them away a little sheepishly, but I loved her for feeling what I could not.

We spend time on the river, as people do here, skiing or in less energetic pursuits. One night early this summer we amused a more conservative couple who are good friends of ours, Jimmy and Sarah Majors, by skinny-dipping off their boat. This time of year we virtually live in Carlotta's pool, entertaining our own and Emily's friends -- all of whom love her perpetually-teenage mother, who shares their humor, laughs uproariously at their jokes and translates for her dogs in cute little cartoon voices. On occasional hot sunny afternoons we even have the pool all to ourselves. Carlotta's at home in the water, a strong, graceful swimmer. Yet the first time we made love there, a look of wonder came over her face which reminded me of my eldest daughter's expression as I cradled her in my hands for her first bath.

Cathy lived with us for a few months recently, although she's gone back now to live with her mother in Chicago. Last fall Carlotta and I drove up with her horse trailer and brought Cathy and Shiloh, her four-year-old gelding, back with us. She went to school for a semester with Emily, who introduced her to her friends and made her feel right at home.

After hating my guts for the first year or more, Emily has finally come to tolerate me; I think you could even say that in our own ways we're close now. It's not surprising that she would deeply resent and fear my intrusion into the privileged life she'd shared exclusively with her mother. More impressive is that she should go out of her way to welcome and befriend Cathy.

I wonder what would become of Emily's and my friendship if her mother and I should break up? I've tried to avoid strong emotional attachments with the children of women I didn't expect to stay with, the time or two I've had such foresight. But Carlotta was supposed to last. Not too long after we started dating I told my mother I thought it possible that we'd eventually get married, the first time I'd said such a thing to her since my first marriage, more than twenty years ago. Right now that seems more than just overly ambitious, it seems naive -- if not downright deluded.

...This pretty well brings us up to speed in the story I'm telling. We're back now at the table under the pin oaks, on Carlotta's patio. After we've laughed at her tender, earthy

41

story about her aunt and shared a few minutes of after-dinner conversation, she informs me that she's having lunch tomorrow with Amy and Leslie, two women who are friends of ours -- though not so much of the two of us as a couple as the two of us as individuals.

Oops, I think to myself, who the hell set this up? Carlotta and Amy having lunch together isn't particularly noteworthy, but why would Leslie be included? Then I decide to relax and quit worrying about what may or may not come up as a topic of conversation. The chips are gonna fall where they're gonna fall anyway, right?

7

Come World War II, I went into the Key West Navy Yard as an electrician since I was familiar with all the old Navy ships and they'd put a lot of them back into commission. I stayed drunk in that place for 24 hours a day. There were Cuban gunboats coming in all the time, and every one of them was loaded with all sorts of rum -- at $.90 a fifth, so you know I was in heaven. But I was still functional, still doing armature winding and all; I hadn't forgotten any of it.

I was doing some real crazy things. We had a bond rally one day, and there was a commander standing up on the podium telling us we should all go without lunch and support the war effort by buying bonds and stamps. I had just come from a convoy that was headed for Russia; they had a whole railroad and just ship after ship, as far as you could see, loaded with this stuff for Russia.

And I got up and said, "I understand we're supporting Russia to the fullest extent in their war efforts." The guy said that's right, and I said, "Well where's Germany's material? I just came from the convoy center out there and I saw all this stuff going to Russia, and I think we ought to be sending Germany the same amount."

Everything came to a screeching halt.

"Just wait until one of them wins," I said, "then jump on him and clean him up and this thing will be over. Because Russia has told us in every book ever written exactly how we stand, and they're a bigger enemy than Germany ever thought of being."

Boy, they hustled me off to the administration building to find out what I was talking about and I stuck to

43

my guns. I said, "They show Joe Stalin as a benevolent pipe-smoking old man and he's in blood up to his elbows. The only plan they've got for us is to bleed us of everything we've got."

Not too long after this I was walking through the Navy yard one day without a shirt. They had a regulation against working without your shirt in the yard, but that good old sun was nice on my body. One of the guards came over and says, "You're supposed to be wearing a shirt."

"That's for the Navy people," I said, "not for civilians or civil service."

"No," he said, "it's for everybody in the Navy yard." He was kind of a belligerent character anyway -- had a gun on him. He says, "I'm gonna take you up to the administration building."

"You're not going to take me anywhere," I said. "I might go up there but you're not going to take me."

With that, he reached over and grabbed me by the arm and was going to put my arm up behind my back and push me down through the Navy yard. I just set him on his fanny, gun and all.

He reached for the gun, and I said, "If you take it out, you're either gonna have to kill me or eat it, cause I'm gonna swarm all over you, fella." He put it back, and I said, "All right, we'll go up to the administration building, but you walk ahead of me. You're not going to walk in back of me with a gun."

The reason this sort of thing didn't get me fired is that I could do things around there no one else could. For instance, a merchant ship came in that had the first RCA SOS system in the fleet. It was set up so that if an SOS came in, it would ring an alarm in the captain's cabin and in the radio shack and engine room so somebody could come pick up the message, without a radioman having to sit there 24 hours a day listening for distress signals.

Anyway, the alarm came on and they couldn't shut if off. So someone came over and took me as an electrician out to the convoy center where this big beautiful merchant ship was all loaded and ready to head out with the convoy for Europe. The African invasion was underway then.

I was taken to a man who had six big blueprints of the alarm system laid out and weighted down on this hatch cover. While he was studying them, I walked over to the equipment and opened up a panel about three by six feet, and you never saw such a maze of wires and resistors and tubes in the back of that thing. It looked like a real jumble. I asked the radioman, "What does this thing do?"

"Well, it comes on if you get a signal, and then you can't reset it, it just alarms all the time, with the bell ringing, and the captain says the only thing you can do is pull the main switch, which shuts the whole thing off."

So while this repairman was looking at the blueprints, trying to figure out which way to go or what to look for, I asked, "Where's the button that resets it?"

He says, "This little button here."

"Have you got a piece of paper?"

He tore off a little piece and I shoved it up into the contact behind the button. I pushed and pulled at the contact, which was loose, then asked for a pair of needlenose pliers. I fixed the contact so the button would seat properly with the paper in there, then pushed the button.

"Throw the switch," I said.

He threw the switch and the alarm was clear -- just that simple. Everybody's looking for something big. This was the type of thing I was doing, and I was doing most of it from a psychic standpoint.

Here's another example: We had an anchor winch that one of the helpers had gone down to do some repair work on. It had a huge, drum-type controller with about 50 or 60 wires coming into it, and this guy came in and took all these wires loose and just left them hanging out with no diagram of how to put them back together. It was on one of the older ships, and there were no blueprints on it, nothing. So I went down and sat there looking at that thing, and I just started picking up wires and putting them together, sticking them here and there, here and there, mostly by feel or intuition or something. When I got through with it, you could take that thing and just do anything with it.

Another time, the USS Nemesis, a Coast Guard cutter running off-coast convoys out of Boston, came into the Navy yard with a steering gear problem. It was an old ship. They had an electrical steering gear arrangement on that thing, and they would be floating along in the middle of a convoy and go two points starboard or two points port, and that thing would turn around right in the middle of the convoy -- they couldn't stop it.

It had been worked on by men from the Boston Navy Yard, the New York Navy Yard, the Brooklyn Navy Yard. The Sperry Company came down from their headquarters in Brooklyn with all their blueprints and worked on it. But the thing locked up again the next time the ship went out and made a full circle. Well, they repaired it again at the Charleston and Jacksonville Navy Yards without success, then finally brought it into Key West without telling us anything of their prior troubles.

A guy I worked pretty well with at the Navy yard there was one of the homeliest human beings, but one of the most lovable characters, I had ever seen. He was an old boy from Hamilton, Illinois, named Pig Dewiese. The day I met him we shook hands and he said, "Call me Pig, everybody else does." So he and I went to fix this steering gear. We didn't have blueprints, we just had our handtools.

We started out at the helm. This is the steering mechanism, which has a group of electrical contacts underneath so that as you turn the helm and the contacts are made, electrical impulses are sent down through a series of relays into the engine room and into the shaft alley where the steering gear is located. We disconnected each one of these contacts individually, tightened all the connections and sandpapered all of them; and we went from there step by step through each relay, all the way down to the steering gear itself. Then we took the brushes out of the motor and undercut the commutator and sanded it and tightened everything, each with a certain feel as we went along. It took us about two days altogether.

When we reported to the engineer that we were finished, he told us to go home and prepare for an overnight trip around the Dry Tortugas, islands at the westernmost tip of the Florida Keys. He said, "We're going to go out now and test it. We're not going on any more convoy duty until this thing handles right. If you guys haven't got it fixed, you're going to be with us when it locks up the next time to see if you can find the problem."

We went out to the Dry Tortugas and back, and that thing would answer to one point, two or ten just like clockwork. When we were ready to leave the ship we were standing up in the wings of the bridge with the captain and chief engineering officer, and the captain turned to us and started telling the whole story of how many different people and Navy yards had worked on this before us.

"I can't understand," he says, "how we can come into a second-rate Navy yard, and two country boys with no blueprints can come down here and fix something the people who manufactured it couldn't fix."

Old Pig spoke up and said, "Captain, we didn't have sense enough to know we couldn't fix it so we went ahead and fixed it."

I guess that's right. But as I see it from where I stand now, there has been a psychic ability in these things from the very beginning of my life, and there has been a healing ability. When I was about 12 or 13, down at the mill with my father, we had an alcoholic company doctor who would be laid up drunk somewhere, and when one of the workmen would get hurt I would go ahead and treat him. I cleaned their wounds and bandaged them and took care of them until they got back on the job again, and I've noticed all through my life that I have some healing ability, but I always kept it dampened down so it wouldn't exert itself.

Well, after my shirtless run-in with the guard I got to thinking that I'd better get out of there before I got myself into real trouble. Since we were at war anything that showed up might get me slapped in the can for a few years. I told them I had to leave and they let me go. I went back up to Fort Lauderdale and while I was there I got into an automobile accident drunk one night, riding with a friend of mine. I kept telling him that that old car he was driving wouldn't stand the pressure he was putting on it, until we went into a ditch. I ended up in the hospital with my left hand scarred up pretty bad and the right one nearly cut off.

8

When I left, the Navy reported to the draft board that I wasn't working as a civilian in the war effort. Right away they started calling me in for examinations and all, and I guess having a bad hand was the only thing that kept me from having to go back into the Army or Navy, which apparently was all part of the plan for me.

I'd always wanted to go to California. When I was out here soldiering at the Navy yard in San Pedro, I'd scouted around Hollywood and Los Angeles and gone up to San Francisco on one occasion. Then when I was out here in '34, '33 I guess it was, I was traveling in pretty good company in a chauffeur-driven limousine which belonged to my boss and staying at the Beverly Wilshire Hotel, and I really fell in love with California.

I'd done some wheel alignment work for a man in Orlando many years before the war who was from California, and every year when he came back to Florida he would come by and have me do his alignment again. He had told a Chrysler dealer in Beverly Hills about my work and I wrote to them about coming out to work for them. They said they'd be very glad to have me and sent me gasoline ration tickets and everything to get out here with. This was in 1945.

I got myself back on my feet again after the accident, sold everything I had -- which wasn't much at the time -- and bought a housetrailer. Then my wife Jean and my stepdaughter and I started out for California in a little '36 Oldsmobile six-cylinder coupe, pulling a much-too-heavy housetrailer fully loaded with everything we could put in it.

We had a very hazardous trip, with about eight blowouts on the trailer and that old car, with no spare available until we got into El Paso. I looked up an old friend in Juarez and asked what I could do for a set of tires. He sent me back across the border to a man in El Paso who was in the black market, and I bought a set of tires for the Oldsmobile and put the old tires from the Olds on the trailer and managed to make it out here.

I went to work for the Chrysler dealer and put the housetrailer in the first trailer park we looked at, in Santa Monica. We lived there for several months until I found a house over on Arizona Avenue. Right after the war I'd sent in an order to the Beeline Manufacturing Company in Davenport for a complete wheel alignment and frame-straightening machine, with a wheel straightener and balancer and the whole bit. I didn't have the slightest idea what I was going to be able to do with it at the time, but I knew full well that if I got my order in in time I would get first priority when steel was released after the war.

When I finally got my equipment the latter part of '46 or early in '47, I moved right around the corner from the Chrysler dealer, on Wilshire and Roxbury. I'd built quite a following that went with me into my own business, and I stayed there until '49 when the parking problem got too bad. Beverly Hills was beginning to develop pretty fast so I bought a garage business over in West Hollywood on the corner of Beverly and La Jolla. It was quite a large place, with not only wheel alignment and frame straightening but body painting and a service station. I got to feeling like a bigshot with all that business.

In the meantime, Jean and I had had a baby. Linda was a little thing of perfection, absolute perfection. We'd tried once before in Florida, but Jean got double pneumonia and then premature childbirth hit her. She had a stillbirth and was being operated on while Pearl Harbor was being bombed. I was down at the local bar telling everyone my problems. But since my automobile accident just before moving to California, I hadn't had a drink in almost five years.

I was out at the Elks Club one night, which I'd joined for business reasons, standing at the bar with the sheriff on one side of me and the mayor of Santa Monica on the other. I'd been toying with the idea of going back to beer, and when the sheriff asked me to have a drink with them, I ordered a Bud. The next day I was back to drinking a quart a day, just that fast.

Trying to get the business of some insurance adjusters, I bought a boat so I could take them out every Sunday and drink with them. I ended up with a bunch of freeloaders and a 32-foot boat down in Wilmington that I couldn't afford. We would go down late Friday or Saturday night and take a trip to Catalina -- go over to the isthmus and lay out over the weekend and pretend to fish for awhile, but mostly we'd just sit over there and drink.

My family relations were terrible. I was back into the old sick booze thing again, and it was so bad I was spending all my money and letting my bills stack up on me. I was about $4,000 behind on withholding tax on my crew and I had 12 men working for me, so an investigator came in to find out why I hadn't been paying it. I never will forget this guy; he was a real pleasant little man by the name of Shapiro. I invited him out on my yacht and of course he suggested I sell it. Then he went down and wrote a check on my bank account toward the tax bill that took every dime I had. Eventually I got it all cleared up and sold the boat.

By 1950 because of the booze my wife was beginning to talk about divorce and that worried me a little bit because I had a good thing there. I could run around anyplace and get home any hour of the night, knock lamps over and break up the furniture and everything, and not hear too much about it. We had brought the old man out from Florida to live with us because I thought so much of him and wanted him with me, and he was getting too old to stay by himself. I kept throwing my weight around, but they talked me into going down to an Alcoholics Anonymous meeting. I didn't know what kind of meeting I was at the first time until two or three people asked how long I'd been on the program and how long I'd been sober -- and I wasn't sober at the time.

I sat there at that meeting and every time they mentioned God I would go, "Hmmmm." No way was I going to go for any of that. I had had good religious training when I was a kid. But I went to AA, went to their dances, mainly to please my wife so she wouldn't leave, and I kept getting drunker and drunker.

By 1952 my morning ritual was to get up and pour a full water glass of Ron Rico rum and take it into the bathroom with me and set it down on the little glass shelf in front of the mirror. I'd take about four drinks of that and it would come up immediately along with green bile, until the fifth or sixth one I could get down. And the minute that stuff stayed down all my problems were gone. I could shave and I was steady. I could go ahead and drink the rest of it, pour myself another one and drink that too, and I was ten feet tall -- suave, debonair, intelligent, everything I wanted to be.

But I was still a slob. So one morning, on the 24th of March, 1952, I was standing there looking at my bloodshot eyes, and I said, "I'm not going to drink this morning. I'm going to skip it." And I lathered up and picked up my razor and I was shaking so bad I couldn't get my razor to my face without cutting my throat. So I looked right into my eyes there in the mirror and told myself, "You haven't got far to go -- you're of no value to anybody, your business and your family life are bankrupt.

"The problem with you," I said, "is that you think you're the greatest, there's no one in the world greater than you. You have no belief in anything but yourself and you've made a mess of everything you've ever touched. It's about time you looked to what they call the higher power in

Alcoholics Anonymous. You'd better take a good look at it. Because if you don't you're gonna die, and it will be a blessing when you do."

I shook my razor in my face and said, "You stupid so and so, from this minute on you are going to change." I said these very words: "Thy will be done, not mine from now on." Within 15 minutes, as if you had lifted a thousand pounds from my shoulders, the whole burden of alcoholism left me. I felt it when it went. I could breathe easier, my eyes started clearing up, my hands quit shaking. I shaved, picked up that water glass full of booze and poured it down the drain. Since then I have not had one drink of anything, not one-sixteenth of one ounce have I put into my system. And right away, everything started fitting together.

9

My problems at home were relieved to a certain extent, but I know now that by this time I had destroyed a good and beautiful woman. I had put her into such a psychological state that she could never come back, and my boozing had also had a lot of bearing on her physical health. But everything else started fitting into place.

I looked at that big business I had on Beverly Boulevard and decided it had to go, it was *too* big; if I sold off a large portion of it I'd be able to pay my bills. I started looking around in Santa Monica and found a small place at 21st and Pico that had a neat little service station with two pumps in front and a nice garage across the back. When I found out it was for sale, I went into escrow on it with $18 in the bank.

I also had the confidence of a lot of people who would just walk away from me when I'd been drinking. I called an old friend of mine I'd bought my house from and told her I needed about $5,000 to buy that piece of property and move my business, and she said, "Meet me at the bank at ten o'clock." The first phone call I made I got the money I needed. I started closing up the other business and selling off the equipment, and I got enough to pay practically everybody I owed, the ones that had kept carrying me on parts and everything. Those I couldn't pay I went around and told not to worry, I'd pay them off too.

I went out to Santa Monica with one body man and my nephew, who came with me when he got out of the Navy in 1947. I'd trained him as a wheel alignment man and first-class mechanic. We painted the place and did a little handbill advertising. Douglas Aircraft was just a few blocks from me, and they were going full-blast at the time. When we opened the place the business just flocked in. I cleaned up the rest of my old back bills with interest.

I had been dreaming about a little ranch up at Malibu for years, so after I got some money in the bank I found a two-and-a-half-acre rancho on Wildlife Road in Point Dume just south of Zuma Beach. We put down a down payment and I went up and started cleaning off a home site.

Next door to me there was the drunkest woman you ever saw in your life. She was drunk 24 hours a day. She had been a movie actress or bit player in her day -- doing bits with James Cagney and Walter Pigeon and all the real famous ones back in those days. She was a beautiful girl and when she started losing her looks she'd gone through the Hollywood mill. Her husband, a wino, was doing the running for her, back and forth to the booze store.

Several months after buying this property I put out feelers to get to know her. I got to talking to her and her husband about Alcoholics Anonymous and all they'd done for me and actually got her interested enough to go to a couple of meetings. I found out that her mother, who lived in Riverside and owned extensive property, had farmed her out to this place to get rid of her and away from everybody so she wouldn't kill somebody.

One time the old lady -- she was in her mid-70's then -- was up there to see about the property after her daughter had gotten herself into a fracas down on the highway and was in jail for 30 days. Her son-in-law told her I'd been trying to get her daughter interested in AA so she sent for me.

The daughter and son-in-law had a horse in the corral and I had a horse, so we agreed I'd put mine in the corral and feed and care for both of them until her daughter got out of the can. Her husband was generally too drunk to take any of the responsibility. The old lady and I got up quite a friendship. Every time she came up she would send for me.

She thought I was the only hope her daughter had for sobriety. "Don't ever desert us," she said; "keep working on her and see if you can get her rehabilitated."

Another time when her daughter was in the hospital for several months, the old lady called me in and said, "Walter, I've watched you work, and you're one of the hardest workers I've ever seen. Anybody that will work out here like you do and run a business in town has really got to be ambitious. I have a mine up in the desert that my husband discovered and operated for several years before he died. None of my family are interested or ambitious enough to work it. My nephew is the last one that tried; he went up there and as soon as the temperature got up to 115, he started to die and abandoned it. One of his uncles went up there and he couldn't stand the heat or the hard work either so he dropped it. I'd like to give it to you, out of appreciation for what you've done and are trying to do for my daughter."

I thought, well the old lady's getting senile, the way she talks about this being worth millions...I'll humor her. We talked about it but that was all. But every time I'd see her she'd bring it up again. So one Sunday my nephew and I and two Mexican fellows who were customers of mine all got together and made a picnic out of this thing. We got up early, picked up the old lady, and got to running up these winding roads way up in the desert, nothing anywhere. Looking through her thick glasses, she'd say, "There's a mesquite bush with a tire laying under it, turn to the right there," and we finally got up to this mine.

It was a placer or strip-mining operation, with quite a hole already dug into the side of the hill. Everything she had told me, which I had pooh-poohed, was just exactly like she'd said. So we stayed. We gathered up about 200 pounds of dirt in some bags and brought it back with us. Ran it through two different laboratories and both of them came back with some very wild mineral reports.

Her husband had been selling this to citrus and alfalfa

farmers as a soil supplement. So we started mixing different things with it, putting it on plants, and I had a good test with my own property, which I was landscaping. You could mix this material with adobe, put it back in the hole and water it, and it acted as a loosener for the soil so it wouldn't pack down again. We noticed a different texture of green in everything. So we got all excited about it and decided we'd go up there and start mining. There were five of us to start with, we were going to make a partnership out of it; but eventually I was all alone. I thought, well, I'm going to go ahead and do it anyway.

Trouble was, I didn't have any money to do this, over and above what I was supporting my family with and putting into my ranch. But the darnedest things started happening, a whole series of events.

I didn't have any building material and I didn't have a big truck. Then one day a brick mason came into the shop and said, "I've got two trucks in my garage, and one of them has a dump body and one has a flatbed body. If you'll take the dump body off and replace it with the flatbed, I'll give you the dump truck for the labor." There wasn't much to it, a day's work with a cutting torch and electric welder. He brought them in, I switched them around and he gave me this Dodge truck.

Then an accountant gave me all this plywood -- all I had to do was go over there and pick it up, it was already cleaned and the nails had been taken out. It was form lumber they had used for this big dormitory at UCLA; they'd already written it off on their taxes, and with a cost-plus-ten percent arrangement I think they wanted to make it cost as much as they could. While I was hauling it away, the accountant asked me what I'd give him for a three-year-old Dodge pickup with a burned-up motor.

"I'll give you $100 for it if you'll take it in trade."

He agreed and I took it back to the shop. When I pulled out a sparkplug to check the compression, water shot out of the cylinder. I pulled the head off and all that was wrong with the motor was that the head gasket was blown and the cylinders had filled up with water and locked the crankshaft in place. So for about $8 and my labor I had a $1,500 truck that's now part of the mining operation.

I started getting the mill ready and had to have a house up there too. Bill Bell, a friend of mine, was dying of lung cancer; they'd given him about two months to live. He had a lot of equipment up at his ranch, and he knew that as soon as people found out he was dead they would come in and just rip it apart. So he gave me a bulldozer, a skiploader, a 1,500-watt generator, many hand tools and a grain buster, a type of hammermill. That was the way I started out my mining operation: I'd take a tire off the truck and run a belt from the bare wheel right back to the hammermill.

Another friend in the construction business had bought ten cases of Japanese nails, and at that time they didn't have enough temper in them. They bent so bad you'd have to drive about ten nails to get maybe five in a board. So he gave me all ten cases. Then a sheet metal company wanted a motor overhauled, and the owner made me a 600-gallon tank to go on a trailer for hauling water, in trade. It looked like everything I needed was fitting into place. Looking back on it now, I can see a pattern here where everything kind of fits together to bring about a certain outcome; it may take years and years for it all to dovetail and come about.

My first summer at the mine I was doing all the work up there on weekends. I'd leave either early Saturday morning or Friday night. I was driving up there one Saturday with a load of plywood stacked high on my truck, about all it could carry, and as I started to turn off the Okala Mountain road going up to the Peg Leg Mine, I glanced to the left and for one fleeting second thought I saw the head of a man and two arms waving.

I went on up the road about a hundred yards after I'd made the turn, and it kept going through my mind: did I or didn't I see it -- because things like this happen in the desert; you get where you see things that aren't there. But I thought, if it *was* a man and I went off and left him when he needs me...I backed the truck down, pulled off the road and went over and looked around in the bushes. Sure enough, there was this old man lying face down, his nose stuck right in the sand, just barely breathing.

I turned him over, then hurried back to the truck and got my thermos jug and some ice out of my ice chest and a paper towel. When I started cleaning his face, he opened his eyes and groaned, "Oh God, I thought you'd gone. I heard the truck going on in the distance and I guess I passed out."

"What happened to you?" I asked. He tried to tell me but we had to get some water into him first. His lips were parched he was so dry. He said he'd been prospecting up back of Okala Mountain which was 12, maybe 15 miles from there, and that he had plenty of water when he went up. His pickup truck was in good condition and he had a full tank of gas and his bedroll. He slept in the back of the truck the night before, and he had bathed and just wasted water; when he was ready to come out he had just two or three swallows left. He drank that, got in the truck, started the motor and backed up to pull out into the road -- and the motor quit. He kept trying to start it but nothing happened; when he finally looked down at the gas gauge, it registered absolutely empty.

Well, he knew he'd had a full tank when he went up there, and he'd only gone half the distance from Barstow so he couldn't understand what had happened. He kept trying to start it, hoping the gauge was wrong, until he ran his battery down. Then he got frantic. When you're in the desert and you get frantic over anything you're in trouble because you'll get ten times as thirsty. He was 25 or 30 miles from the nearest town, with very few houses out there in that wilderness. So he just started walking.

He made it down to the fork in the road where I turned off, but that was as far as he could go. He was sitting on the ground in the shade of a greasewood when he heard me coming, and he must have used up all the rest of his strength to wave -- and then he fell. After I got him rational and back to the truck, we started up the road he'd taken driving in, and it was pretty hard climbing. We had to go all the way up to where his truck was in low gear. When we got there I raised the hood and found a small crack in the flexible gas line to the fuel pump.

Back when I first started going to the mine, the old lady told me, "Don't ever go into the desert without a full toolbox, tape, everything you can take along with you that you might need because it may save your life." This is what I'd always done. I had equipped a sidebox underneath the truck with all sorts of things, and I always carried plenty of water -- an extra five gallons and full thermos jug -- along with an ice chest with food and vegetables and cantaloupes in it.

I taped up the hole in his line, drained gas out of my truck and put it in his, and attached the jumper cables. While I was doing all this, he went out and searched around in the mesquite bushes until he found a forked branch. He cut that off and came back and said, "This is a witch stick and I can find water in the ground with it."

We'd been talking about the importance of water on our way up to his truck and how foolish it is to get caught out there without it, and he says, "This thing works for me and it worked for my father and my grandfather. All of them were water witchers."

I kind of laughed at him, probably with a real classic sneer of doubt, and he said, "No, it works -- I can show you how." He set my thermos jug on the ground and walked around, and every time he came over the top of that jug with the stick, that thing would darn near jerk him into the jug.

I looked for something he was doing that made it do that. I thought he was trying to kid me.

"No, it's a fact," he insisted, "I can show you how to do it. You may have this power yourself, a lot of people do." I asked what makes it work. "I don't have the slightest idea. Put your fingers around the stick like this, relax, then hold it out in front of you and start walking around. Bring it over the jug and see if anything happens."

So I did and when I got over the jug, I felt a pull on the end of that stick, and it was something I wasn't responsible for. I broke the connection on it and walked around out there, then closed my fingers around the forks of the stick...and the minute I got over the jug that thing started pulling again. It wasn't a strong pull but it was perceptible. I could tell something was happening that I didn't have anything to do with.

We got the old boy started, and I followed him down to the turnoff. We waved good-bye and he drove on into town while I went up to the mine. Who he was I don't have the slightest idea. I haven't seen him since, never heard anything about him, but the meeting with that one man, a prospector, changed the whole course of my life. There was no way I could put that stick down without trying to find out exactly what made it work.

10

CARLOTTA

"PAS DE DEUX"

SPACE
A man and a woman
on a bare stage
in separate pools
of light
He says she says
articulating
the obvious

TIME
How it's possible to be
together yet apart
Different timetables
The tulips next to the
chrysanthemums
in the bed
and neither dreaming
of the others'
existence

MOTION
Strangers on a train
Ships passing in the night
The gravitation of the
planets
in their orbits
All the Hollywood lovers
fleeing
1. the law
2. the bad guys
3. creatures from space
4. time's wing-ed chariot

SHAPE   Movement's design
Is it improvised or
choreographed
Unrestrained or
under control
Free
or not free

Dance
that paradox where
(when)
embracing
is letting go

Lafayette may be a small midwestern town but fortunately not too far removed from civilization to have a good health food store and restaurant. God knows we need all the help with our health we can get, living in the Mid-Ohio Valley. Brighter Earth's proprietors and hard-core clientele sponsored the macro potluck at my house where I first met Cork. And Brighter Earth is where Amy, Leslie and I have agreed to meet for lunch.

Amy is a pretty long-haired brunette who'd have prospered on the American frontier; she's that tough and self-reliant. Her brother Peter is one of Brighter Earth's co-owners. Amy works part-time for Peter as a clerk and waitress and part-time in a staff position at the local shelter for battered women.

Leslie, a slim redhead with an angular but attractive face, has run the shelter, quite successfully by all accounts, for the past year and a half. She and Amy are both strong independent women in their late-30's. The fact that Amy's a good ten years younger than I hasn't stood in the way of our getting together occasionally to talk and commiserate with each other about life in the hinterlands, including the general dearth of decent men around here.

Today, although the mood among us is fairly lighthearted as usual, there seems to be some kind of suppressed tension at the table. Maybe I'm only imagining it. Amy is giving us her front-line report in the war between the sexes as it's played out here in Southeastern Ohio.

"...I told him to be sure and call me when 'Lethal Weapon 17' is in town. I was going to say something about lethal boredom but I decided there wasn't any need to be nasty about it. I try never to insult a person's religion if I can help it."

"Good for you, Amy!" I congratulate her. "I hope he's smart enough to know you insulted *him*."

"You know, I'm not sure he is."

"Oh he'll figure it out eventually," Leslie assures her. "Think how much better it'll be when he realizes how long it took him."

Our laughter turns a few heads but we don't care.

"Why do men have to be so sneaking and secretive about it?" asks Amy, turning serious on us. "If they have to have two or three different women in their lives at the same time, why can't they be honest about it and hang out with women who can accept that?"

"Because no woman's going to admit she'll accept it, that's why!" says Leslie.

"Won't *admit* it maybe, but there are plenty who *will*," I tell her. "And who'll gladly be the 'other woman' who makes another woman miserable too."

"That's pretty cynical, Carlotta."

"I'm sorry but it's true. You know it is, Leslie."

"I'm afraid she's right," Amy agrees with me, "as much as we'd like to think otherwise. There are a lot of groveling women out there."

"Give me dogs and horses any day. You know where you stand with animals." For some reason Leslie seems to pick up on this.

"...That doesn't mean you and Cork aren't getting along these days does it?" she asks.

"Oh no, there's room for Cork up there on the hill too," I tell her, wondering where the question is coming from. "He and I and the animals all get along fine." A definite look passes between the two of them and there's an awkward pause.

"...Isn't this soup great?" Amy finally interjects, to break it. "Peter's got a new sous-chef -- a woman who commutes all the way from Athens every day. She's great with soups. Wait'll you taste her mushroom barley."

Leslie and I both answer at once. "It *is* good," I agree.

"Aren't we getting fancy," Leslie teases her: "'sous-chef' huh? What's next, fingerbowls and sorbet?"

"Hey, being macrobiotic doesn't mean you can't have a little class, does it? I doubt that Peter will ever put sorbet on the menu though."

"I don't know, Amy, I wouldn't exactly call this a macro menu any more," I have to tell her. "He even serves coffee for God's sake."

"Well this *is* a business after all, Carlotta; he's gotta make money. How long do you think he could stay open with a strictly macro menu?"

"I think we're lucky to have him," Leslie chimes in.

"*Damn* lucky. And there are plenty of macro items," exclaims Amy: "cucumber-wakame salad and soba noodle salad with tofu...brown rice and azuki beans with sautéed onions, carrots and squash...miso soup of course, hummus and pita...miso-tahini spread..."

By now she has Leslie and me both laughing. "All right, all right -- don't get so upset, Amy," I reassure her. "I'm glad Peter's here too. I just hope he doesn't forget what his original intentions were, that's all. How far is he willing to go to bring in customers?"

"I give up," she says, throwing up her hands good-naturedly. "You're hopeless, Carlotta."

"Well, she does have a point, you know. Really, where *do* you draw the line?"

"Thanks, Leslie!" I'm glad *someone* agrees with me.

"I trust Peter to know where to draw it," says Amy, continuing to stick up for her brother. "No sorbet, no fingerbowls, no beer and wine, no meat..."

"Can't we talk about something besides food, for God's sake?"

"Great idea, Leslie!" I'm eager to share my latest news from the barn. "I'm boarding a new horse -- Sidney, the cutest two-year-old," I tell them. "He plays just like one of the dogs. He fetches: I throw him a stick and he goes after it and brings it back to me."

"*Another* horse?" asks Amy, "I didn't know you had room for another one."

"I don't really. The others aren't too happy about him being there. Except for Queen Anne -- I think the old slut's got a crush on him now."

"You and your animals!" laughs Leslie.

"I know, they're a bunch of characters. The goats got out again the other day -- had to have one of my semi-annual roundups."

Pretty soon I have us all in stitches, describing the scene of the dogs and me spread out across the hillside trying to corral Capricorn, Lady Bug and the rest. The older dogs know to stay away from those sharp horns, but Tom and Tina almost got hooked once or twice before they finally wised up and backed off a little. All the time I'm thinking, "No more vet bills, *please!*"

"Are you still milking any of them?" Amy finally asks.

"Not any more. The people who said they wanted it didn't show up half the time. One woman called *pleading* with me to sell her goat's milk for her baby, couldn't drink anything else, she said. Said she'd come by twice a week without fail. I think she came twice, period."

"That's too bad," says Amy in genuine disappointment. "I'll miss your ice cream. What was it you called it?"

"Bah-moo," I reply with proprietary pride, "wasn't it great! Goat's milk and cow's cream."

"That's right," remembers Leslie, "you had some at your macro-potluck last summer. It was delicious."

"Ah-ah," Amy admonishes us, "we're talking about food again. Somebody change the subject."

Another pause as we finish eating. Again, it's Amy who breaks it.

"...You haven't said much about Cork, Carlotta. How's it working out with the two of you living together now?"

"It's working out okay, why? I saw you two exchange a look a minute ago. Is there something going on I don't know about?"

Another look pregnant with withheld information passes between the two of them, prompting the faint stirring of an unpleasant sensation I've gone without for so long now I'd almost forgotten how it feels. Amy decides to be the one to tell me.

"...Are you aware that Cork came to see Leslie the other night?"

How could I have forgotten *this*, I wonder, as the long-absent feeling lands in my stomach like some predatory bird, talons spread. "What? When?"

"Last Tuesday. A week ago Tuesday evening," Leslie answers.

"We thought maybe we ought to say something. I had a feeling you might not know about it."

"...What do you mean, 'came to see you'? Did something go on between you two, Leslie?"

"No, not really. I was just surprised he came to see me. He didn't call first, just dropped in. We just sat and talked, mostly."

"Mostly?" My lunch is beginning to curdle. It's not *what* they're saying but the way they're saying it, the way this is all taking place like some kind of dream that's either

67

occurring right now or that I'm beginning to remember faintly: a nauseous deja vu feeling.

"Well, nothing happened, but there was a feeling in the air if you know what I mean."

"Carlotta, we're not trying to make something out of this that isn't there -- at least I hope we're not -- but I just felt you should know about it."

"*Why*, if nothing happened?"

"*I'd* want to know," says Amy decisively.

"You mean just the two of you were there, Leslie?" I'm struggling to get a fix on this, to focus on what really took place. Could there be alternative versions? What are they implying -- or leaving out?

"No, the kids were there too."

"Well, I don't know what to say. You say nothing happened, but you're making it sound like something *did* happen. I know Cork was home when I came in Tuesday." *Wasn't* he? I'm trying to recall for certain.

"We're not saying that anything happened except what *did*," says Amy. "It may mean nothing at all -- I hope it doesn't."

"I probably wouldn't even have said anything about it. But Amy thought we should."

"I've told you before, Car. I think Cork has a wandering eye. If we're outa line in telling you this, fine -- so much the better. That's for you to decide. I don't wish any ill toward Cork and certainly none against you. But I wish someone had told me about Tim's nocturnal visits at the very beginning, it would've saved a lot of pain."

Amy reaches across the table to touch my wrist. "Maybe we shouldn't have said anything, but I feel we should look out for one another. Maybe this was a case where 'eternal vigilance' was overkill. Anyway, I really care for you, you know that."

"Well, I thought I knew that..." I'm beginning to feel some anger now -- not just emotionally but the *heat* of it, along with the searing pain in my guts.

"...It just seems to me, Leslie, that if you feel Cork was wrong enough in coming over there to tell me about it now, then you should have said something to him at the time. Did you?"

Leslie has no answer to this.

"I'm the one who thought we should tell you, Carlotta," says Amy.

"And I told Amy because I didn't feel quite right about it. But Cork never came onto me or anything like that, nothing blatant. There was just this...*feeling* in the air."

All of a sudden a coldness toward both of them comes over me. Is this why we're here? Did they really have to tell me like this? "Well," I hear myself saying, "I don't know whether to thank you or cuss you both out, but you've sure ruined my lunch."

I don't want to be with anyone right now. I manage to find my billfold and fumble through it for what's probably about the right amount for my share of the check, ignoring their entreaties to linger for any more of this. I leave quickly, trying not to make a scene but feeling my cheeks burn, seeing people at lunch, browsing in front of the stocked shelves, paying for groceries at the counter -- as if this were just any other ordinary day of the week -- all through a watery haze.

11

While Carlotta's ignominious lunch is taking place I'm in anything but blissful ignorance of the topic of conversation, at Rockner Hardwood Forest Products, the family business I've come back to lift from my father's sagging shoulders. What the hell *I'm* supposed to do with it is still very much in question.

My original naive intention, as I said earlier, was to unload it somehow as quickly as possible and get back to the West Coast, where I had been probably just as naively pursuing a career in the movie business -- as in dreams, in which the object of pursuit keeps receding maddeningly toward the horizon with every step you take. At least I've been able to continue to write here. That's one thing about writing that distinguishes it from making movies: if you're serious about it, you can do it alone, anywhere, for next to nothing.

As opposed, also, to running a business which has been in, and out of, bankruptcy. Coming back out again is something that only about ten percent of companies seeking shelter under Chapter 11 are able to accomplish. Largely, I now realize, because this is a dubious achievement most companies would just as soon leave to untrained and inexperienced pseudo-, quasi- or parabusiness-persons like myself. If going into bankruptcy can be a humiliating experience for small businessmen like my father, its debt-encrusted mirror image or reciprocal is most certainly a humbling one for the would-be entrepreneurial savior or white knight.

Forget about "alone and next to nothing" where the

business is concerned. I've been unable to make this company profitable with a payroll of thirty or so, a slew of understanding and forgiving supplier-creditors, and a whole cartel of lenders who, except for the bank that forced my father into bankruptcy in the first place, have been generally supportive. At the kind of interest rates they're charging, their stockholders have nothing to be concerned about where altruism is concerned, believe me.

At any rate, more in ornamentation than utility, in my uniform of chinos and tieless dress shirt, I'm sitting here digging impatiently through the incredible layer of debris on my desk when Irene appears in the open doorway of my cluttered, undistinguished-looking office. Nominally the office manager-bookkeeper, Irene's actually more like the company's general manager. Farm-reared and still very country, in her mid-30's, she has all the business instincts and a complete knowledge of the company's operations that I lack. Thank God.

"You don't wanta hear this," she says with an ironic little smile on her face.

I feel my stock Pained Expression appear reflexively on my own but say nothing.

"Thompson rejected that load of face-and-better red oak."

"...Why?"

"They said it has too much stress."

"Have you told Herman yet?"

"I buzzed him but he didn't answer."

"What do the kiln records show?"

"That load came out of Kiln Three, which had two days of conditioning. It *should* have been all right."

"It didn't get wet did it? Was it loaded in the rain?"

"No, I know it wasn't raining when we loaded the container, and Leonard said it couldn't have got wet during storage."

"What else did they say was wrong with it?"

"That was it. They said the color and surfacing looked okay, but they haven't graded it yet."

"Well they'll probably claim that it's off-grade too. If we conditioned it for two days it couldn't have any stress in it to speak of. They want me to bend over and hand 'em the Vaseline. If we're willing to make a three- or four-thousand dollar adjustment on the load, they'll be more than willing to take it off our hands."

Irene is uncomfortable with the remark but not surprised by it. "...That's probably about right," she agrees.

"What the hell are we gonna have to do to get a few loads out of here without a claim, Irene? It seems like every third or fourth load somebody's gotta call up here and bitch about it. If it's not the kiln-drying it's the surfacing, or the lumber's too wavy. If it's not that, then there's too much mineral or off-grade. If we can't get out a decent goddamn product we might as well shut down!"

Throughout most of this tirade I notice myself throwing things around on my desk, ostensibly trying to find whatever I was looking for when Irene entered, although by now I no longer remember what the hell it was.

"Do you agree?" I say, glaring at Irene in anger not at her personally but at her news of today's daily screw-up at Rockner, Inc. "Do you think I'm exaggerating? Have we managed to get five loads out of here in succession anytime this year without generating a claim?"

"Well, that may be a little bit of an exaggeration," she says, easily controlling what must be her own anger at my unloading on her for something that's not her fault. "But I know what you're saying. We're getting too many claims."

"Tell Leonard and Herman to get in here, will you please. I want to hear what the hell they have to say before I call Thompson."

She leaves and I grab a stack of papers and trade magazines spilling over a corner of the desk and slam it down into my overflowing wastebasket. Naturally the goddamned thing tips over.

"I don't *care* what you talked about, that isn't the point. If it was all so innocent why couldn't you have told me you were going over there?"

When I got home from work this afternoon, Carlotta wasn't around. Turns out she was off on a long ride on Queen Anne, her Arab mare, to cool off and think things over. Still wearing her riding boots, she's just returned to find me in the bedroom about to meditate. You can guess the rest.

"Because I didn't know it myself till I went over there," I reply, feeling less defensive than resigned to her interrogation. "It was just spontaneous. I feel sorry for her, Carlotta. She's lonely...she's got those two kids to take care of by herself, on not nearly enough money....I do feel something for her but it's compassion, nothing more."

"If it was so spontaneous why is it you just happened to go over there the night I work late with my dressage class at the arena?"

"*That's* why I decided to go. I knew you wouldn't be home anyway. And I made it a point to be back by the time you got here."

"But you never said a word to me about it then either -- which tells me you must have felt guilty about it. Why wouldn't you tell me unless you didn't want me to know? I had to hear about it from my friends. Do you have any idea how that made me feel, Cork?"

She plops down on a corner of the bed and homes in on me with her piercing eyes for confirmation of what she's just said. There's no heat in the look at the moment, just clear, focused hurt and indignation.

"You're right, Carlotta, I'm sorry, I should have told you. I *planned* to. It just never came up, the time was never right." I can smell the bullshit this answer reeks with as soon as it's left my lips. Get serious here, Rockner. Pay attention.

73

"What do you mean the time was never right?! What kind of bullshit is that?! You should have told me that evening. I'm sure I must have asked you how your day went or something. And you never said a word about going to see Leslie."

"Because I knew it would just make you uptight, Carlotta -- what was the point? She's tried to talk to us a couple of times when we were together, and you scared her off with your proprietary attitude." Might as well get to the bottom of this. But how deep is that going to take us?

"I *what*?"

"You know what I mean," I say, beginning to feel annoyed now myself. "You did everything but stand there between us. You're so damn possessive at times it's stifling. I knew if I was going to have a talk with Leslie I was going to have to do it alone."

"I don't know what you're talking about. When were the three of us talking when I 'scared' her off, as you so nicely put it?"

"Once in front of my parents' house when you drove up and we were standing there on the sidewalk talking to each other, and the other time at the arts and crafts festival."

"When I walked over and she got up and walked away -- I remember. *That* scared her off? Naturally I wondered what the hell you'd been talking about for her to react like that -- what do you expect? But I had no idea I was making you both so uncomfortable."

"You were standing there glaring at her as if you'd caught us at something. It did make me feel uncomfortable. I don't know how it made *her* feel."

"Not so bad that she couldn't come tell me about your little visit the other night."

Why the hell *did* Leslie tell Carlotta? Probably she said something to Amy, and Amy's the one who felt Carlotta should be told. While I'm standing here trying to carry on a coherent conversation with Carlotta, I look inside myself for

74

the real reasons, *all* the reasons, I went over to Leslie's the other night. Are these two women, both of whom I like and respect, over-reacting -- as I feel they are -- or trying to come between Carlotta and me for some reason? Or were they right in telling her?

"I don't know what the hell she could have told you to make you so upset, because absolutely nothing happened, Carlotta. You've just gotta ease up. You can't expect me to have no female friends just because you and I are going together. I don't know why you feel so insecure."

"Don't tell me what to do. If I'm insecure, it's because that's the way you make me feel, Cork. Doing things like this behind my back...Leslie slinking away when I walk up..."

"That's Leslie, not me -- and she probably did that after the way you reacted the first time. I can't believe she told you anything went on between us at her house. Believe me, I'm sorry I went over there -- and not just because your feelings got hurt."

"Now yours are too huh? Your little rendezvous isn't as secret as you thought it would be."

Actually, I'm not too sure how or what I feel right now -- other than weary of this conversation and the self-scrutiny accompanying it. I slump down on the bed beside Carlotta, a couple of feet away, and look over at her.

"...Will it make you feel better if I admit I was wrong? I already said I was sorry for not telling you. I *was* feeling a little guilty about it, I admit. I told you: I figured it would probably upset you and I wanted to wait for the right time. But then when you told me you were having lunch with Leslie today, and I started wondering whether or not she was going to say anything, then I realized this must be part bullshit too: not being able to just tell you I'd been over there.

"We've gotten ourselves into a vicious circle, Carlotta. I feel you're too possessive -- God knows I've told you that often enough -- and you feel I'm out trying to make it with

75

other women because I'm not satisfied enough with you or something. We're creating a self-fulfilling prophecy here."

Carlotta's listening to me: hurt and angry but open to what I'm saying. I'm speaking from the heart now, I can feel that. Maybe it's good this has all come up now, maybe we can gain something from it.

"It's true, part of the reason I wanted to see Leslie wasn't just because I felt sorry for her, although that was the main reason: to show her that somebody out there cares about her. But another part was just wanting to share some time with somebody else for a change. I feel suffocated by you sometimes. We end up talking about the same old things all the time -- which happens in a relationship. That's natural. We need to have some outside interests and connections to keep what we have alive. If you could just trust me more, you'd see there's no reason to be concerned about all these things you're so worried about. I'm *not* out looking for sexual conquests. I'm just trying to stay in touch with people. Maybe if you were less possessive I'd feel less *need* to get away from you occasionally, I don't know. I'd sure as hell feel less need to be so discreet about it when I did."

"Well that's just great, Cork. You start out saying you went over to Leslie's because you feel sorry for her, and now you tell me you did it to get away from me. If we keep talking long enough, what the hell else will you confess to? You may be deceiving *yourself* but you're sure not kidding me. You just need to know that other women find you attractive -- satisfy your ego with a little flirtation without any of the work a real relationship requires."

"...There probably is some truth in that, Carlotta. But a little harmless flirting shouldn't be lethal to a relationship, for God's sake."

"So you *admit* you were over there flirting with her! Tell me, Cork, did you or didn't you go over there to sleep with her?"

"C'mon, Carlotta. Don't get hysterical about it, for

76

Christ's sake. I told you, *nothing* happened."

Actually, this isn't quite true -- and it certainly isn't the *whole* truth. But it's sure as hell all I'm going to tell Carlotta. Why? Because she gives no weight at all to the changes I've already made in myself over the years, and am still making in my thinking and behavior, for her sake, for *our* sake. With respect to my selfish negative traits, all Carlotta's aware of or thinks about are the ones I still have, not those I've spent years weeding out of my character. So the ones still there are over-emphasized and give an unfair picture of me.

For example, there was a moment over at Leslie's when I'm pretty sure we could have ended up in bed together, although what preceded that moment *was* mostly just conversation. But when Leslie murmured something about my being "almost married", I didn't contradict her because I feel this is essentially true. After that things cooled down rather quickly. Which was fine with me, I'd accomplished what I'd gone over there for. I'd expressed the affection I feel for Leslie and let her know there's at least one man out there who finds her most attractive and sympathizes with the position she's in as a single parent with two children, a difficult and exhausting job, etc.

But can I tell Carlotta any of this? Can I tell her about passing up a possible roll in the hay, when just a few years ago I'd have done almost anything to score with Leslie under the same circumstances? Of course not; I can't tell her the good without revealing the rest. Maybe it's because of these silences between lovers that we give each other so little credit for the changes we *are* able to make in our lives. We don't consider the dynamic aspect of behavior; we lay down rules about how people should treat us, without regard to whether in breaking them they may actually be showing real improvement.

"You're telling me only a little bit at a time," interjects Carlotta, pulling the emergency brake on my train of thought. "And you keep changing it! First you say one thing, then you add something to it. Then a little bit more. How the hell do you expect me to believe you?"

"I expect you to believe me because I wouldn't lie to you," I say, reassuring myself that there is in fact more truth than lie in what I've just revealed about what is becoming, in retrospect, an increasingly unsavory incident. "If you *don't* believe me -- if you really think I was just over there to make it with Leslie, and you're not willing to listen to what I'm saying to you -- then I don't see any point in continuing our conversation. Do you?"

"No, I don't! And I don't want you living in my house while you're sneaking around seeing other women either. That's not right, Cork, no matter how you try to rationalize it."

12

I didn't move out that day or the next. Carlotta and I continued to discuss what was wrong between us, what dissatisfied each of us most about the other, what we wanted that we weren't getting -- oh, it was a fun time. Past arguments we'd thought safely buried emerged from the state of suspended animation we'd foolishly mistaken for extinction to haunt one heated discussion after another. These imperishable tales from the crypt stalked us through all the rooms and long hallways of Carlotta's big house, gradually wearing us down, until we came to realize that our love affair had been an accident waiting to happen for some time.

For a while I hoped the situation might produce the flashpoint a relationship needs occasionally to reignite passion, consume the deadwood of routine and accommodation. A lot of my own anger reeked of emotional putrefaction, it really was cleansing in some ways. Then one of us finally said the wrong thing once too often, and it turned out to be dishearteningly banal rather than liberatingly infuriating.

By the end of the week we've decided to try living apart again. When I move out with what I can get in the car we haven't patched things up at all. I'm still optimistic about some kind of real love and friendship between us, but now I see that down the road a ways, as we say around here.

I've decided to move in with my parents for a while until I can find a decent apartment or, preferably, a small house in the country to rent. I gave up a nice house and my two cats to move in with Carlotta. The cats are well taken care of, but I'll be lucky to find a house soon. The only ones really livable around here are those for sale that have been on the market so long their owners are willing to try renting them out. The catch is you'll probably have to agree to let the house continue to be shown while you're living there. Nice huh? Believe me, the alternative is even worse. Maybe it's time to admit that I'm not going to be returning to L.A. soon and think about buying some little place.

In the meantime, I'm sitting here at the kitchen table, talking to Mom, who's preparing dinner. Dad's lying back as usual in his recliner in the TV room. He's never quite recovered from the company's bankruptcy seven years ago, having descended gradually into clinical depression from which he intermittently struggles to recover, then succumbs to, in what looks as if it's going to be a terminal deterioration of spirit, mind and body.

"I was afraid you and Carlotta living together wouldn't work out," my mother says as I browse through this afternoon's edition of the *Lafayette News*.

"...I know, you warned me," I reply after a lengthy pause, since I've been only half listening to the one-sided conversation in which she's determined to engage me. I resolve to give her the small pleasure of my attention since that's why I'm sitting here. Our small local paper certainly doesn't offer much competition. "We had to try it eventually though."

"I hope we'll still see her."

"So do I. She's pretty bitter at the moment but I think she'll get over it."

"Do you think you and she can still be friends?"

"I hope so. I'm not even sure it's over between us. We just need a change -- at least I do. But I can see us getting back together again. Maybe just not living together."

"I know it's none of my business, but did something in particular come between the two of you?"

"Aw, I'd rather not talk about it, if you don't mind," I reply reluctantly, all of a sudden feeling a discomfort close to pain at having to contemplate life without Carlotta. "I mean it's no big deal but --"

"Oh no, that's all right," Mom interrupts. "I didn't mean to be nosy."

"I know you didn't -- you weren't. No harm in asking. I just don't feel like talking about it right now."

"I'm sure you don't. Of course it's certainly okay with your father and me if you want to stay here for a while while you look for a place of your own."

"Thanks -- I figured it would be. I appreciate it. I don't know how long it will take me to find something again though."

I continue to leaf listlessly through the paper while Mom busies herself at the sink, until I come across an article that captures my interest. They still haven't found the source of contamination in the city water well that I've been reading about for what must be several months now.

"Have you been following this whole business about one of the city's wells being contaminated?" I ask.

"Yes -- that's a heckuva note isn't it."

"Sure is. They don't know where it's coming from. If they don't find out before long, it's liable to spread. They're going to drill test holes around Well 6, that's the one that's contaminated."

She doesn't respond right away and I get to thinking. "...I wonder if a dowser would be able to find something like that?"

"A dowser...is that one of those people who can find water, like?"

"Right, we had a segment on a dowser in our TV series. Did I show you that one? He found water all over Southern California -- still does for all I know. We filmed him...what? must be almost ten years ago now. Walter Barry's his name."

"I don't remember seeing that one. I don't think you showed it to us."

"I may not have. He's also a healer -- Alex believes he saved her life. He's the guy I took her to when she'd been sick for weeks and couldn't get well. Remember? She really thought she was going to die."

"Well of course," Mom replies, invoking my ex-wife's name melodramatically, "naturally *Alexandra* would think she was going to die, or something equally dramatic. What *is* as dramatic as death anyway? Torture maybe. Having to listen to Dorothy tell me for the hundredth time at lunch about some tediously insignificant incident in her past."

"Well, she wasn't just being melodramatic this time, believe me. She *looked* like she was damn near ready to die."

"Alexandra will probably outlive all of us. What's all this have to do with a contaminated well though? Is he going to 'heal' it the way he supposedly healed her?"

"Right." Then I add seriously, "I'd think maybe a dowser might be able to use his dowsing rods the same way he does to find water. They use dowsers to find oil and minerals...missing children...lost items -- all kinds of things."

"*Who* does?"

"All kinds of people. A lot of those Walter has found water for are really wealthy, powerful people. They live on these beautiful ranches out in the middle of nowhere, with everything but water. That's how he makes his living."

"Well, finding water I can understand -- no, not really *understand*, but at least it's something I've heard about."

"Right, but dowsers do all kinds of things. The real ones, I mean -- the genuine ones. Map dowsing even."

"What in God's name is *map* dowsing."

"Just what it sounds like: instead of dowsing at the actual site, you do it over a *map* of the site, often with a pendulum rather than dowsing rods. It's usually just a preliminary step to focus in on the most likely area of finding whatever it is you're looking for -- not a substitute for dowsing at the location itself. That might be the way to get Walter involved in something like this."

"You're not really thinking of getting a 'dowser' involved in our problem here are you?"

"Why not?"

"Why *not*? Because you'd end up being the laughing-stock of the city, that's why."

"Why do you say that? If he found the source of the contamination he could end up saving the city thousands of dollars. It could be done discreetly enough."

"Oh come on, Cork, this isn't a Hollywood TV series on psychic phenomena we're talking about. It's the city's drinking supply."

"*Exactly*, that's my whole point! What could be more important?"

"I'd think you have enough to worry about with the business being the way it is. That's all we need right now: your name in the paper connected with some crazy water-dowsing scheme to go along with the company's financial problems. You've always wanted to be the knight in shining armor, ever since your football days -- maybe even before that, I don't know. I thought you were over that by now."

I wasn't expecting this. I feel my face heating up. "What the hell's wrong with wanting to help out?! I've been reading about this in the paper for months now, and they haven't been able to do a goddamn thing to solve their problem. I'm probably one of the few people in town who knows anything about dowsing and what it can do, or at least what it's done in other places. Should I just stand by and watch the city pour money it doesn't have down the toilet rather than risk making a fool of myself by coming forward with some controversial information that might help?"

"Yes, that's exactly what I'm saying. Concentrate on the business's problems and let the city worry about its water wells."

I get up angrily from the table, words just spewing from my mouth now. "That kind of attitude is exactly what's wrong with this country! Don't get involved if you can help it

-- and for Christ's sake don't try anything too new or different! And by all means: don't dare to give a damn. People might think you're trying to be a hero or something!"

I'm dimly aware that my mother is as stung by my outburst as I have been by her words, but I don't really care. We'll both get over it. No longer the least interested in dinner, I leave the house for a drive in the country to cool off and think things out. Maybe I'll go have a beer somewhere. God, living with my parents again is going to be fun!

13

I have a very inquisitive mind. The first time I went into town I cut myself a nice forked limb off a peach tree and whittled it down until it was roughly symmetrical, then took it back up to the desert with me. Every time I got my work done I'd pick up that stick, get myself a tub of water and go stand out there with that thing and let it work. I'd study it, thinking about all the things that could make it do what it was doing, but none of the things I thought of made sense.

I'd read Verne Cameron's book and the one on Henry Gross up in Connecticut -- both of them well-known dowsers -- and I'd written to the government for pamphlets, but they didn't have any. They'd thrown them all out because dowsing is witchcraft. I went to meetings, started listening and asking questions, and everything led straight back to "witchcraft", something that just didn't jibe with me.

I finally began making metal dowsing rods; I kept working with them and got to roaming around the desert with them out in front of me, and I found what I thought was an underground river that came down right through the mine property about a hundred yards south of the house. I traced this thing for about ten miles. I'd skip over it and run parallel with it, get off, then find it again, and the boundaries seemed to be pretty regular all the way across the desert. I marked it off on both sides with little piles of rocks. I just couldn't understand what was happening. I'd walk into the marked area and feel a pull, then when I'd get out of it I couldn't feel the pull anymore.

This kind of investigation went on for a year or so until I noticed that my dowsing energy, my ability to find

DICK CROY

water, was getting stronger; I could feel the pull more strongly, it was amplified. I couldn't understand this either. I kept reading, trying to find some reason for it.

Someone had introduced me to the crossrods bent at a 90-degree angle that plumbers use. After making a set of these I could walk across what I thought was this underground stream, and when I got to the edge of it the rods would cross. I'd walk across it and they'd stay crossed until I got to the other edge and then they'd uncross, so I had verification from two different instruments.

This went on for another year or two and my sensitivity kept gaining; another thing I noticed was that I had quit being ill. I used to pick up a cold in September/October and keep it till May or get another one right on top of it, and this no longer happened. Also, a lot of pain in my body from old injuries diminished and I started feeling good all the time. I attributed this to the fact that I was doing exceptionally hard work in the desert where the air was clean.

I went up to the mine one Saturday morning when it was raining. I had a nice warm house with a fireplace by this time, and I just held up there, reading everything I could find on dowsing and experimenting with a bucket of water. It rained all Saturday night and half a day Sunday: regular cloudbursts, one right after another. When the sun came out Sunday afternoon I picked up my witchstick or divining rod or dowsing rod, whichever you prefer to call it, and walked out on that wet desert just knowing that everything would read water.

But I got no reading at all -- until I got to where I'd marked out the edge of my river. It suddenly dawned on me that rain water has only the hydrogen and oxygen atoms in it; there are no minerals in it because it is purely distilled water. I set two unopened bottles of Sparkletts distilled water for my generator on the ground and checked them with the rod and didn't get any reading from them either.

I uncapped one of them and sprinkled just a pinch of the mineral from the mine in there and shook the bottle up. When I went over it with my divining rod it nearly jerked me in -- just as strong a reaction as with the water underground. This was the first indication of why this thing worked: it had to be the minerals. All the lights came on; everything started clarifying.

It also gave me a key to why my health pattern had improved, why I was no longer catching my colds every year. I had been mining a material containing silicon, aluminum, iron, sodium, magnesium, potassium, calcium, barium, boron, gallium, uranium, copper, titanium, zirconium, nickel, cobalt, strontium, chromium, manganese and sulfur. I had inadvertently absorbed into my body chemistry 20 additional minerals over and above my daily dietary intake, and in so doing I had apparently not only amplified the energy in my body but my sensitivity to certain types of energy as well.

That night I went in and threw all my books into the fireplace -- everything I had pertaining to dowsing. They made a nice fire. Next morning I went back to Santa Monica and opened my business as usual, then took off for the library and book stores, gathering anything I could find on simple atomic structures, the nucleus, solid state transistors, diodes, everything I could find on electronics. When I went back up to the mine the next weekend I started in on some serious research.

I guess the key for the whole thing came from a book stating that every mineral emanates from its nucleus a radioactive energy force on its own particular frequency; and this frequency is set by the proton-neutron balance in the nucleus of that particular mineral. I had already learned that your body chemistry requires 17 basic minerals to keep you functional in an intelligent healthy manner. Putting these two pieces of information together gave me the basis for understanding the energy required in your body to make the divining rod work. I started experimenting with everything I could find on how this energy is expressed in and around the body, and this research has taken many, many years. Every day, in every lecture, every seminar, everything I read, I'll pick up one or two key words that will reveal a little more insight into the principles behind dowsing and healing with the rods.

Although I had found a way to determine the boundaries of an underground stream, I didn't know any way to determine the direction of flow or the depth, and this was a real bugaboo with me. It looks as if the good Samaritan principle has to come into play every time you're looking for information; you have to be trying to help someone else, and he'll provide an answer.

Going up to the mine one Saturday morning, I spotted an old man about 85 years old on the side of the road beside an old Chevrolet with the hood up. When I pulled over and asked him what his problem was he said he had a dead battery. I asked if he had anything to drink and he said, "No, I've been here about three hours and nobody has gone by. I thought after a while some of the neighbors would go for their mail and find me."

So I gave him a drink of water, jockeyed my truck around in position for my jumper cables and got him started again. For some reason I proudly announced that I could find water underground with a divining rod. "So can I," he said, "done it all my life."

Surprised at this, I said, "Dad, maybe you can tell me something. How do you tell how deep it is?"

"Oh, that's simple," he says. "You get yourself a piece of wire -- in fact I think I've got one in the back." And he went around and opened the trunk of his Chevrolet and came back with a piece of wire about two, three feet long with a little weight tied on one end and a loop in the other end.

"You just take this thing in your right hand, hold it over the stream and it will tell you something," he said. "It'll start talking to you and if you really got the gift, it'll work for you."

"I may not have the gift," I said, "but I've sure got a lot of energy."

"That seems to be all it takes."

"Do you know how this thing works?" I asked.

"My pa could do it, and I can do it, but nobody knows what makes it work. There is no scientist in the world that knows what makes it work."

"Well that's what I'm working on," I said. "I sure hope that some day I can come up with an answer."

"Nope," he says, "there's no way you're going to do it. It's a gift from God. That's the reason they call it a divining rod. You either got it or you haven't -- one way or the other."

I tried to give the piece of wire back to him, but he said, "No, you keep it, you got my motor running and now I can get home, so you keep it."

So I took it up to the mine and I could hardly wait to get up there. I skidded the truck to a halt, grabbed that wire and ran out to the underground stream. I stood over it and the wire started doing crazy things. I'd back out of where I'd determined the boundaries to be, then come back in, and that wire would start doing more crazy things that I couldn't make heads or tails of.

I went along like this for two or three months and I still couldn't figure out what the devil this thing was doing. So one Saturday night I was sitting outside up at the mine listening to Ted Armstrong from Ambassador College. He was broadcasting from down in Mexico and it came out loud and clear out there in the desert. He says, "If you had a problem with your automobile, and you wanted a key to the answer to that problem, you would get the owner's manual out. There is one in the glove compartment that came with the car. And you would start reading that instruction booklet from the front to the rear until you found a key to the problem with your car.

"Now," he says, "if you happen to be a standard-size human being with fluid drive and hydraulic brakes and all, there is a book in existence that came with the baby -- it was here before the baby came -- and it's a book of instructions on care and feeding and all the problems that will come into the human sphere. If you have a problem of any kind, you get this book out -- and it's called the Holy Bible -- and dust it off 'cause I'm sure it will have a lot of dust on it," -- and he was right -- "...dust it off and sit down and start reading. Within the covers of that book you will find a key to the answer to your problem."

Well, I was up there by myself -- with my dog Nancy -- and Sunday morning I got up and made a pot of coffee, then went out on the patio and propped my feet up on the table. I dusted off my Bible and started reading. I read through Genesis and I got into Exodus. I read in Exodus about Moses and the rod. It said that God told Moses to take the rod and do wonders for the people and explained it to him.

Now, in my quest for information I had started going into home shows along about 1954. I'd get a booth and decorate it with the old Western stuff -- guns and boots and saddles hanging around -- and Nancy was with me then, and I'd get out there with a tub of water and my rods and I'd draw a crowd. I packed the front of that booth until the other guys around me would just close up and go home -- they couldn't even get anybody to look at their stuff. In a sense I had been doing wonders for the people too, and although I tried to explain them, I didn't know the answers anymore than Moses did.

So on this particular morning I read in Exodus that Moses said, "I am slow of speech and of a slow tongue," and God replied, "I will be with thy mouth..., and will teach you what ye shall do....And thou shalt take this rod in thine hand, wherewith thou shalt do signs."

Well now, I thought, this is the key I've been looking for. Maybe if I walk out into that stream and let the Master do the talking, maybe I can see a pattern in this. So I finished my coffee, then got up and put my Bible away -- one morning's reading -- and walked out into that underground stream with my rod.

I had improved on the rod by then; I held it out in front of me and I looked up and said, "Old Buddy, I'm pitch-hitting for Moses." I said, "I want some answers on this thing because I've got to know." And for the first time, this rod started in with a pattern. It oscillated up and down, at an angle, to a count of 81 -- 81 complete cycles -- and at 81 it switched to a *vertical* oscillation.

At that point I stopped. I laid the rod down, walked around it, came back and picked it up again -- then stepped back in between the piles of rocks marking the channel, and it did the same identical thing: went to 81 oscillating at an angle with the ground, then switched to an up-and-down movement. Every time it made that switch I'd quit because I didn't want to lock myself in. I kept doing this for about 15-20 minutes, counting, and then about the fourth or fifth time I decided, well, now I'm going to let it go on.

So this time I let the rod continue to vibrate after it switched to a vertical oscillation. It went to 81, 82...and I stayed with it, until it counted down to 110, I believe it was, and stopped. All of a sudden my hands started shaking: the vibration went all the way through my body, and I just stood there. Then, just as suddenly, the shaking cleared up, and the rod started wig-wagging back and forth, left and right.

It did this for a good minute and a half and stopped. Then here came the shaking again. It scared the devil out of me -- I couldn't understand this at all. Finally the shaking stopped, and the rod started counting down again. It counted down to 110, and when it got to 110 it went in a circle. Again I dropped it, and stayed away this time for about 20 minutes -- made some more coffee. When I came back out, I picked up the rod and went upstream about a hundred yards. Remember, I had this marked out for about ten miles. Whether I went downstream or upstream the rod would do the same thing.

Finally I went in and got a pencil and paper to draw up what I thought was happening underground. Then it dawned on me that if I had all the minerals in my body that were in the water, I might be tuning in on each of them on its own particular frequency. I also theorized that the angle the rod made with the ground when it was oscillating might be an indication of the stream's direction of flow. And perhaps the number of oscillations were units of measure. If so, then the first number, the point where the oscillation changed from diagonal to vertical might possibly indicate the distance to the *top* of the underground stream; and the second number, where the rod's reaction changed again, to a wig-wagging motion, could mark the bottom.

Of course, at this time all this was just guesswork on my part, just theory. Next I started looking for the energies within my body and how to measure them.

14

Up to this time I really hadn't had enough nerve to go out and do a water survey for anyone, but I decided I'd better try. At one of my home shows a guy came by and said, "I've got a little ranch over here close to Hemet. What would you charge me to come down and do a water survey for me? You seem to be an expert at this."

I said, "I am, I am -- the best in the business. I can come down there for $100."

So a couple of weeks later I went down and did my first water survey, and he paid me and got a well, a good well. I ran a small ad in the *California Farmer*, a little farm magazine that goes all over the world, it seems, because I got letters from Beirut and Calcutta as well as calls from all over California, wanting me to come and find water. But I didn't have to leave the country to stay busy.

Once in a while I'd get a curve thrown at me and get a dry hole, and I couldn't understand it. I'd get to thinking maybe my countdown was off or something and I'd go back and check it, and everything would check out fine. But on a couple of these dry holes, I found out that the well-driller had said something like, "Damn if there's water *here*; there may be water over there 50 feet because we've got a water table underground," and he'd drilled 50 feet from where I'd said the water was.

But although I ran into all sorts of things like this, the tempo began to pick up and I was getting calls now from Arizona, Oregon and Washington, and I started traveling all over. I've got some tremendous wells, but very few of these people will give you any kind of testimonial. You've got to run them down and try to pin them to the wall to get one out of them. And I found out why.

I got a well for a man named Herb Kellogg that was bringing in 2,200 gallons a minute. He was so pleased with that well he got up at an Alfalfa Association meeting in Lancaster, California, and said, "I had this guy come out with a divining rod and find a well for me and, man, did he get me a good one. It's the best well in this part of the country."

And somebody yelled from the back, "Hey, Herb, whattaya been drinkin'?" You see ridicule right away because this is in the realm of witchcraft. So Herb shut up.

While he was test-pumping this well, a guy named Leonard Griffith from Willow Springs came by and Herb told him about me. Leonard telephoned and I went to Willow Springs the following Saturday and found a cone up there in the mountain that was putting out a stream about 35 feet wide. It ran right down through his ranch, within eight feet of his reservoir, where he had all his pressure pumps and booster pumps connected. All he had to do was drill a hole eight feet from his reservoir and put in a pipe over to it.

I went up there after the drilling was finished and Leonard was test-pumping the well. He was standing there with his arm propped up on his fender, looking real sad. I said, "Boy, that's a good well. The driller tells me you're getting 1,400 gallons a minute out of this thing."

"Yeah," he says, "I'm awfully disappointed though."

My mouth dropped. I said, "Leonard, you're disappointed with 1,400 gallons a minute, and 400 is the best you've ever had on your ranch?"

"Yeah," he said, "I expected 3,000."

I just turned around and walked away. I couldn't even get him to write me a letter; I had to get Herb to write me a letter about Leonard's well. It's a funny thing. I got a report by the grapevine that there's a well of mine way back in the boondocks down in Mexico that is doing close to 3,000/4,000 gallons a minute -- they had to haul a heavy-duty diesel in there to handle this thing. But I haven't been able to get the owner to give me any information on it at all; he may have left Mexico for all I know.

Another guy down here at Lake Nacimiento called me about two years ago. He grows almonds all up through the hills in this perfectly dry area; what dampness they pick up is mostly atmospheric. I found him one of the best wells they've ever had in that part of the country. I asked him for a letter and never heard from him. Called him again -- "Yeah, yeah," -- still never heard from him. Why don't they put it on paper, as badly as we need documentation to shake loose some of these things?

A few years ago Cyril Chappellet, one of the principal investors in the restructuring of Lockheed Aircraft in 1932, called me to locate water on the Chappellet ranch in Big Sur: 500 acres atop a bluff about 1,250 feet above the Pacific Ocean on Highway 1. He contacted me on a Monday, and I told him I'd be there the following Thursday night. I left the mine Thursday morning, and along about San Luis Obispo it started pouring and it rained all the way into Big Sur.

I called his daughter and son-in-law, Bill Pittiney, from Ventana, an inn and restaurant in the area. They told me the gate combination but for some reason I couldn't get it to work, so I had to call back and have them come down and let me in. I figured this probably convinced them they had a nut on their hands. Here was an old codger coming up to find water, and water was running down the gutters, the ground was soaking wet, and I didn't even have sense enough to get a combination lock to work so I could open their gate.

They fixed dinner for me, and after dinner that evening we had a session where I explained how I worked. Not knowing that it's the mineral content in the water that gives me a reading, Bill and his wife were kind of nudging each other, wondering how I could find water underground with the surface completely saturated.

95

The next morning the sun was out. Mr. Chappellet came down to the Pittineys' from his house nearby, and his first statement was that he wanted to see what kind of phony he'd hired; then he laughed and I laughed with him. I said, "If we're going to look for water, let's find it in the most convenient place."

"Well, anywhere up around the house," he says. "Let's look up here first."

So, starting from the Pittineys' front porch, I held up the scanning rod -- that's the forked one, the equivalent of a witchstick -- and began scanning around in that area. About a hundred yards from the house, some 75 or 80 feet from the edge of the bluff the ranch sits on -- a cliff which drops straight down to the highway -- I got a reading as if a sailfish had struck on a deepsea fishing rod.

I put the rod up repeatedly and kept getting the same reading inland from the cliff, so I told Bill this was the first place we should look. I took the crossrods and walked into the area and got a reading immediately. I went down 20 feet from the first reading and I got it again. Then I climbed the fence and went down into this valley a little piece from the house and got the same reading. So I came back up to the edge of the cliff and started checking for the water's origin.

I could get a clear reading all along the edge. I began walking inland away from the cliff, toward the apparent source of my readings, from all angles; and it soon became clear that what I was dealing with was a complete circle, anywhere from 45 to 60 feet across, just like an underground lake.

I eventually surmised that the flow of water I had found was escaping from a volcanic cone through a crack some 15 feet long. Ancient volcanic activity had formed the cone, which must have cracked when the lava cooled and quit flowing -- just like Mama's cake if you cool it too fast. An underground stream was flowing inland toward the valley through this crack after rising vertically, parallel with the cliff, from many thousands of feet underground. There, molten lava was creating super-heated steam which was being pushed up through the cooler strata of the earth, then cooling and condensing into water, with constantly replenishing steam underneath it. This little tributary and others like it from other cones in the area were all feeding into a common underground river down in the valley.

I believe that every one of the valleys and canyons up here has an underground river which takes the water off and returns it to the ocean, in nature's own circulatory system. Just as we have a heart in our body which supplies the top of our head, the tips of our fingers, the bottoms of our feet with blood at the same pressure...so, it seems to me, is the planet's circulatory system powered by geothermal pressure. Great pressure on the ocean floor forces water into the deep open cones that made the suboceanic range of mountains. When this water is superheated by molten lava underground, steam is produced which of course is also under great pressure. It's pushed up toward the surface, condenses into water, and the cycle is endlessly repeated.

It's entirely possible that when this particular cone was originally formed, the ocean may have been 10 or 50 miles from here, and deterioration or decomposition of the cliffs over time brought the coastline into this close proximity to the cone.

I remember that it was 165 feet down to the top of this water. Now can you imagine telling a well driller that you want him to drill on top of a cliff 1,250 feet above the ocean, and that there's an underground river 40 or 50 feet deep flowing inland from the cliff? When Bill told his well driller this, the man took out a chew of tobacco and put it in his jaw and said, "There's nobody going to tell me there's water up here on this cliff. You're just going to waste your time."

Bill told him, "Well, I had two or three dry holes down in the valley that were located by geologists at about $1,500 to $2,000 apiece for their services, plus several thousand dollars for drilling the wells -- they even put in casings and pumps and didn't get a drop of water out of them. I've been through that, and this man seems to know what he's talking about. I want you to drill regardless of what you think."

So they drilled there and got 30 gallons a minute from that well; it's remained constant for four and a half years. On down the cliff about three-quarters of a mile south of the house, we found a similar cone though a bit larger, with a slightly wider stream coming from it. They put a well there too and again got 30 gallons a minute. Then they went down in the valley and put another well in there and got 40 gallons a minute from it.

Up to this time their total supply of water had been from a tiny spring at the foot of the cliff. They'd run a power line all the way down that cliff to a pump with a float like the one in your toilet. Every time that spring would put out 10 or 15 gallons of water, the float would close a switch and the water would be pumped up the cliff through a half-inch plastic line into a tank, and that's all the water they had on that ranch to take care of four houses and all their cattle. Of course there was no way they could have a swimming pool. Here was a multi-millionaire family that should have had everything they wanted, and they were limited to this tiny little trickle of water.

Now that they have the wells they can water their gardens and plants, and they've increased their cattle-raising. They have swimming pools and the luxury of flushing the toilet every time they use it.

15

A few days after moving in with my parents I'm having lunch at Brighter Earth with Jimmy Majors, an old high school buddy of mine who's been all over the country before returning like me to Lafayette to go into business with his twin brother Johnny. These two hell-raisers were my best friends in high school and the three of us have maintained our friendship over the years. Johnny never did leave town and has done quite well for himself in the wholesale grocery business. But I've visited Jimmy and his growing family in suburban homes in Phoenix, L.A., Baltimore and Minneapolis and still managed to set foot in only about half the places they've lived in.

I still remember vividly those late-afternoon and evening high-speed Mojave runs between L.A. and Phoenix, under sunsets that seemed to last for hours, gradually deepening the subtle desert palette of earth tones and drawing a whole spectrum of reds from the landscape into the huge desert sky. In the clarity of that air, distance and the barriers that normally separate us from the physical world become transparent. We've had some good times together, Jimmy, his lovely wife Sarah and I.

But things haven't worked out well at all for them here in Lafayette. Tired of traveling the world for Shell Oil and of listening to Sarah complain about it -- and against the advice of members of his own family -- Jimmy decided several years ago to come back and show his twin brother the corporate way to do business. Their partnership was a bad marriage almost from the beginning. Then, savvy but severely under-capitalized, Jimmy started not one but two companies of his own.

On paper the synergy between them looked great; in the marketplace it proved about as effective as that between him and Johnny. But rather than embittering him, the hard times Jimmy's been through the last couple of years, both personally and professionally, have scoured and clarified his soul like the desert he still loves and now longs to return to. His greying hair notwithstanding, he's getting his good looks back too, now that he's starting to work out again. I tell him so at lunch.

"Oh, man, getting that goddamn business off my shoulders was a lifesaver -- literally," he replies with the proverbial sigh of relief.

"Any leads on a new job yet?"

"Not yet, I just started sending out resumes last week."

"What're you looking for?"

"What I'm really good at: something in sales without too much administrative responsibility -- out of the Midwest. I've decided grey isn't a color I identify with. And I don't need any comments from you about my hair, Rockner."

"What makes you think I was going to say anything about your grey hair?" I ask innocently.

"Screw you, buddy. You're in no position to gloat."

"I'm not gloating, I'm sympathetic. You've gotta stand by your friends during their mid-life crises."

"You're real sympathetic all right. You're a goddamn bleeding heart."

This kind of banter has been going on between us for thirty years; there are few people I can relax with like Jimmy. I'd sure hate to see him go if I didn't agree that it makes the most sense for him now. Only one of his four children is still in high school and, like Jimmy at the moment, his marriage is not working. At least I can look forward to the possibility of visiting him in the desert again.

"If you leave, will Sarah and the kids go with you?" I

ask, having wondered about this for some time now.

"Who knows?" he sighs again. "Sarah's not about to share her plans with me. If she can find a way to keep the house, she'll probably stay."

"How would you feel about that?"

"I don't want to lose my family. I'd miss my kids. But bein' away from Sarah's sharp tongue would be a relief. She sure as hell hasn't been sympathetic through all of this, believe me."

"At least you've been able to watch them grow up in the same house with you," I reply, thinking of my own daughters.

"They've kept me goin'. That's a helluva lot more than I can say for Sarah. She's more selfish than they are. It's natural for kids to think only of themselves, but you expect a little understanding from your wife. The only thing she understands now is that we might lose the house. That and what to say that'll hurt the most -- she understands that *real* well."

"I know it's been tough. It's been hard for her too though, you know -- Sarah I mean." Unfortunately, although I love Sarah too, it's always been Jimmy's version of the story of their marriage I've been privy to. I know, though, that Jimmy is no more the model husband than I was in my brief tenure.

"She seems to thrive on an adversarial relationship. But what I need is some nurturing -- I really do. Aside from the kids, it's been so long since I had a little human warmth I forget what it feels like."

"I've told you before: you could take care of those needs if you were discreet enough."

"That isn't me though, Rockner. I couldn't lead that kind of life."

"Why not? It isn't as though you'd be being unfaithful to Sarah." (Which is why I feel no disloyalty to her in making the suggestion.)

"That's for sure," says Jimmy.

We fall silent for a minute or two, lost in our own thoughts, enjoying our meals.

"Sorry to hear about you and Carlotta," Jimmy says finally.

He seems to have read my mind, which isn't particularly unusual between us. Thinking of the breakup of his long marriage has naturally made me think of Carlotta and me.

"Yeah, I wish it hadn't happened -- the way it did anyway. But living apart may be the answer for us. We sure as hell can't live together. All those goddamn dogs goin' in and out, in and out all day long...and us staying up there on the hill most of the time without seeing anybody, partly because Carlotta's so judgmental there aren't too many people she really likes."

"I know what you mean. Sarah and I really like Carlotta, but she sure can be closed-minded sometimes," Jimmy agrees.

"But she won't accept that at all. She has no idea how privileged she is and how that affects her perceptions. She just doesn't wanta hear it. Not that it's all *her* fault that we can't get along. I'm willing to accept half the responsibility, at least. I guess I'm not demonstrative enough for her -- she feels I'm not loving enough. She thinks just because I want to have friendships with other women I must not care enough for her."

Jimmy chuckles. "You're not exactly the world's most compassionate person, Ace."

"Well I care a lot more for Carlotta than she seems to realize. It's hard to show it when you feel like you're under attack half the time."

"Tell me about it."

"My problem is, I guess sometimes when I need to be compassionate the most, that's when *I* get judgmental myself. When Carlotta starts whining about needing more love and

102

attention, it brings entirely the wrong reaction from me. I feel like she's too busy asking for more to feel what's already there, you know what I mean?"

"Sure I know what you mean."

"I know *I'm* not the easiest person to live with. No one else has ever been able to for very long. So maybe this change will be good for us, I don't know. I sure wouldn't want to lose Charlotte as a friend, no matter what happens."

Jimmy and I both notice the petite attractive brunette in her late 30's-early 40's, briskly putting things into a store-supplied shopping basket.

"Hi, Brook!" he sings out, "*shopping* on your lunch break?"

She comes over with a smile that seems almost as big as she is. "That's the life of a harried schoolteacher, Jimmy. How are you?"

"Couldn't be better. Do you know Cork Rocker?"

"Never had the pleasure -- but I've heard of you, Cork. Nice to meet you," she says, extending her hand.

I stand up, feeling her warmth reach out to me as if I were as good a friend as Jimmy obviously is and wondering why he's never mentioned her to me. "Nice to meet *you*, Brook. Where do you teach?"

"I'm a remedial reading teacher at Madison. Trying to squeeze in some shopping for a dinner party tonight."

"Who is it, some of those arts-and-crafts hippies you hang out with?" Jimmy rags her.

Brook gives him a burlesqued look of reproach, complete with pugnacious eyebrows that suddenly look almost muscular. "You'd fit right into that group, Jimmy. The main thing is, they know how to have fun -- same as you."

"I'm afraid all that's a little beyond me," he says.

"*What's* beyond you?"

Jimmy laughs. "Those naked sweat baths for one thing."

Brook laughs along with him but puts a finger to her

lips. "*Jim*-my! not so loud. You're liable to get me fired. I'd better hurry or I'll be late to class."

"Always on the run, Brook. You gotta take time to smell the flowers."

"If I'm late again all I'll smell is the poop when it hits the fan," she shoots back at him over her shoulder. "See you both."

Both of us are still chuckling when Jimmy says, "She's somethin' else. That's someone you oughta look into, Rockner, if you and Carlotta are history."

"She's cute," I agree, "but I hope we're *not* history. What's this about naked sweat baths?"

"I figured that'd get your attention, Ace. Sounds like your kind of activity doesn't it. That crowd's into all kinds of weird stuff. I kid Brook about it -- I call 'em retro-hippies, but they're good people. The ones I know anyway."

"I think *you're* the one who should spend some time with her. Looks like she could give you all the nurturing you could ask for."

"She could all right, I'm sure of that. But she and Sarah are good friends. Besides, I told you, that isn't my style. Sometimes I wish it were."

We finish eating in silence, then I ask, "What do you think of this fiasco about the city's contaminated water well?"

He shrugs. "It's no surprise to me. I think we're going to be hearing of a lot more of them before long, all over the state -- all over the country."

"Why's that?"

"Because of all the shit we've been dumping and burying for years, that's why. We have two Super Fund sites right here in Lafayette, you know."

This gives me the lead-in I need to launch a small trial balloon on the possibility -- remote, though it might be, I hasten to assure him right up front -- of hiring a dowser to find the source of contamination. He shoots it down so fast he almost spits out his coffee in the process.

"Now I've heard everything!" he says, laughing, spluttering and slamming his cup down on the table all at the same time. "I thought becoming a businessman was going to put some sense into your head, Rockner, but you must think you're still out there in La La Land."

I don't even attempt a come-back this time.

"You wanta learn something about industrial pollution around here, Ace -- including our water well? Talk to Andy Byers, he's a friend of mine works for Chemlab. You know who they are don't you?"

I tell him I'm familiar with Lafayette's only environmental testing company, a firm that has grown remarkably since its inception two or three years ago.

"Andy will tell you stories that'll have you drinkin' bottled-water along with the Perrier crowd," he promises me. "Tell him I said for you to call."

16

Andy sounds like a nice enough guy on the phone; more significantly, he seems really interested in my reason for inviting him to lunch, as if he has a story to tell. We meet the next day at the Boat Landing for an alfresco meal on Lafayette's historic Ohio River levee. Even on this sultry smoggy day there's a cool breeze off the river, and every outdoor table is taken. Though I'm five minutes early, Andy's already seated at the one I've reserved for us.

He's in his late-20's, clean-cut-looking, with an earnestness in appearance and tone of voice, tempered by a mild, dry cynicism that proves to be rather humorous at times. If he's a bit idealistic, as Jimmy claims, he's nevertheless learned to protect himself. After a few minutes of pleasantries and feeling each other out, with Andy no doubt looking for a possible hidden agenda on my part and me trying to detect any tripwires to avoid from his affable but guarded remarks, we get down to business.

To draw him out I've already decided to reveal my thoughts about bringing in a dowser, figuring that if I leave myself vulnerable enough I'm more likely to elicit frankness from him. I sketch in the story of filming Walter Barry for our TV series, emphasizing his professional credibility lest Andy think he was more a character in some sort of docudrama than a successful dowser in real life, and explain how I think he could possibly be helpful here. "Jimmy tells me you know a good bit about this well contamination yourself," I conclude, leaving the door open for what I hope will be Andy's turn to expose his secret musings.

"It's a sore subject at Chemlab," he says. "This well-testing project that Capital Drilling has literally been running into the ground for close to a year now was never put out to bid. It seems odd to us that the city would take this job out of the county when there are local companies that could do the job just as well."

"Who else besides Chemlab?"

"Geologic Survey, for one. We were working on a joint bid with them, with GS doing the drilling and us handling the chemical analysis -- and we weren't even allowed to make the bid. Why not? We've both done a lot of contract work for the city, they know we're *more* than competent for a job like this."

"...Why do you think they didn't let you bid?"

"Well, this is just speculation you understand -- but we think maybe they wanted to keep the lid on around here -- keep as much information as possible from getting into the wrong ears. That'd be a lot easier to do with an out-of-town company, right?"

"Maybe," I reply. "Is there anything else that makes you suspicious?"

We're interrupted here by our lunch, but after it's been set before us by the cute college-age daughter of friends of mine, and Andy and I have dug hungrily into our Boat Landing Specials, he picks up the conversation again: "...Suspicious. Yeah, the fact that they haven't nailed anyone for this yet. Even though the city says, after months of digging test holes, they still haven't found the source of the plume, they do have chemical samples to analyze. From my knowledge in the environmental field, I don't think there's a single site in the country, unless it's an open dumping site, where you can't identify whose waste you're dealing with. *We'd* have identified whose it is by now.

"PCE is extremely carcinogenic. It's very volatile, it moves very quickly, it's a very dangerous material -- one of the worst solvents you could possibly have in groundwater.

If Capital Drilling still can't identify the plume, why hasn't the city looked to someone else for some answers by now?"

"Have you asked city council that question?"

"Sure we have. And all we got was a complete glaze-over: 'Capital's taking care of the problem and the plume is unidentifiable.' I'll tell you this. The liability for dumping that stuff could very well be in the millions to clean up. Whoever did it could afford to pay a small fortune to keep from being identified with it."

I digest this for a moment along with my soup and sandwich, or try to -- and find that it doesn't go down as well as lunch. "Could afford to maybe, but do you think one of the companies around here would really do something like that?"

Andy gives me a look as if I'm really the one who's the innocent here, the way I was hoping he'd take the question. "The problem I have with industry -- well, a perfect example of what I see all the time is a hazardous waste project of mine when I was with Environmental Solutions, a remediation company in Huntington. This particular plant, which I'm not at liberty to name, because I had to sign a statement saying I wouldn't -- but it's around here -- grandfathered themselves in with agreements through EPA to get some lesser cleanup criteria, claiming they were going to be proactive in this case. Otherwise EPA would have stretched out the compliance period and made it more stringent for them.

"They had agreed to do this and everything was on paper to go ahead, when the plant began to lose money last year and has been very marginal so far this year. So they decided to extend the study period -- 'Let's see, let's delineate the problem, see how big the plume is,' and so on -- and didn't clean it up. And that's a political situation that is industry-wide. If the money is there, many companies really want to clean up and do something with the problems in the ground -- and this is a 20-year-old problem I'm talking about. But if the plant's losing money or is marginal, or if somebody's a little too greedy, it'll never be done. So, do I think a local plant might say to the city, 'Be quiet and we'll pay you to clean this up our way.'? Look to their bottom line, that's what's going to dictate their decision."

17

About 1970 I began playing around with the idea that it might be possible to *heal* using the same principles involved in dowsing. By this time I had developed all three types of rods I use now: the forked one I use for finding water; the crossrods, for marking the boundaries of an underground stream; and the counter or wand-type rod for determining depth and angle of flow. Held in one hand, this is also the one I use for all other types of dowsing besides locating water.

My daughter Linda had just gotten out of college in Tennessee and come to visit me. The marriage between her mother and me had fallen apart shortly after I got sober, 18 years before. I think she needed me as the burden she'd had for so many years, and when I took over the checkbook and started running my life again, we finally got to where we just couldn't stand each other any more. We got a divorce and Linda went to live with her. Jean married a friend of mine down in Florida, and they put Linda through college.

I was called by the Chandler family, owners of the *Los Angeles Times*, to come do a water survey. Linda went with me to their estate in Arcadia, a suburb east of Los Angeles. I'd been doing a lot of research on energies and various metals relative to body chemistry and health and so forth, and I was demonstrating some things for Mrs. Chandler. I picked up a little figurine of a snail about four inches high, which was surprisingly heavy. I set it down on the driveway and tuned in on it with the counter rod in my right hand.

Now up to this time I had found virtually all objects and materials I examined to be bi-polar in energy. If I held the rod in my right hand so that it was nearly touching an object, the tip of the rod would make a small clockwise rotation over the right side of the object, oscillate vertically over its center, and make a counterclockwise rotation over the left side. But over the figurine, the tip of the rod went to the right and stopped, then to the left and stopped, then back to the right, and so on.

I set this thing back on the lawn and asked Mrs. Chandler what it was made of. She said it was cast from lead. This was my first discovery of the existence of a form of polarity other than the bi-polar energy I had observed so many times before. I went back to the office that night, locked the gates and the door and spent all night and the next day experimenting with lead.

I theorized that lead is poisonous *because* it oscillates its polarity. With its frequencies oscillating back and forth it acts as a sort of degausser. It picks up both positive and negative flows of energy and brings them back into a sort of figure-8 skating pattern: an orbital pattern in the electron structure, complete within itself.

I started looking for other minerals and substances that might do the same thing, by picking out those reputed to be poisonous. Sure enough, mercury, cadmium, selenium, bismuth, formaldehyde, arsenic...one right after the other, as well as rattlesnake venom, bee sting, poison oak and ivy, and many other plants that we're exposed to, such as oleander and dieffenbachia -- anything that has a deleterious effect on the body has a polarity that oscillates. This led me to believe that practically all of our illness may involve the "degaussing", deadening or neutralizing of the polarities in the body so the vital essence of life is unable to flow unhampered through it.

The three aspects of the energy output associated with the body seem to me to be electrochemical energy, which is the mineral output; biomagnetic energy, the energy expressed *around* the body as the aura; and psychoenergetic energy, the computer circuit which *controls* the energy.

My studies indicate that there are three main circuits of the body for this type of energy. In the leg circuit, energy enters through the sole of the left foot, goes up the leg, across the groin, and down the right leg, then out through the sole of the right foot. In another similar circuit, energy enters the body through the palm of the left hand, flows through the upper body, then out through the palm of the right hand. In the last circuit, which I call the "computer" circuit, energy enters through the left eye and exits through the right.

I believe these circuits are over and above, but part of, the 12 "meridians" in the body which the Chinese have been working with as a health and control factor for the past 6,000 years. This has recently shown up in the introduction of acupuncture onto the medical scene in the United States. In working with body energies, trying to pin down various aspects of the flow of energy relative to health in human beings, I find that if you are in the radiation field of anything as simple as a cigarette, you are picking up degaussing energy that will cause illness in your body.

Anyone carrying a pack of cigarettes in a shirt pocket over his heart is actually playing Russian roulette with the frequency that makes the heart beat. I'm quite sure there have been many heart attacks -- in young people 20, 25, 30 years old -- not just from smoking itself but also from having this adverse energy force right over their hearts.

The healing aspect of my dowsing got a significant boost from my exposure to the Esalen Institute, the world-famous "human potential" center founded back in the '60s in Big Sur, California. I had kept in close touch with the Pittineys ever since finding water for them and, under my tutelage, Bill began his own healing experiments with a rod like mine.

The beneficiary of his first major success was Joan Halifax-Grof, a resident psychologist at the institute who happened to be touring his property with her husband. Using the rod and a discharge sink, he dissolved painful lumps in her breasts in about 45 minutes. Dr. Halifax-Grof, the published author of a number of scholarly books and papers, returned to her doctor several days later and was given a clean bill of health. Because of this Bill was asked to come give a demonstration at Esalen. He suggested that I go in his place, and ever since then I have been giving lectures, seminars and healing workshops there.

Dick Price, a gestalt therapist and one of Esalen's founders, and I have worked together on many occasions. He would get on one side of a patient, with me and my rod and a "discharge sink" on the other, and we would "clear his channels" -- remove all the conflict from the patient's body and transmute the toxic things he'd been exposed to.

The discharge sink is a little plastic case containing about 25 different elements which oscillate their polarity; in other words, harmful to the human body. Although it contains items as common as a cigarette and two aspirin tablets, along with about 95 other toxic substances, it took quite a while to put together. Every time I find a new poison I check its compatibility with the others, and if it's compatible I add it to the sink.

If possible, Dick and I try to talk patients out of smoking. Many have quit; I've had reports of dozens of people who have quit cigarettes after seeing our demonstration of what the poisons in their bodies will do to their energy.

Here again, in working with Dick, I made a major discovery quite by accident. I discovered that the thymus gland, located just a couple of inches below the larynx, seems to be the emotional "pop-off valve" and, therefore, the site of the physical manifestation of one's emotional problems. With Dick's probing gestalt therapy stirring up a patient's emotional energy, I found that it was the thymus gland from which debilitating emotional energy -- what I think of as "conflict" energy -- could most easily be discharged from the body.

Then I found that the pancreas also picks up this conflict energy. It seems that it's a sort of physiological dumping ground, because if your emotions are in conflict there is a certain toxicity locked up in your system; and when the conflict is dissolved, this toxicity is dumped into the pancreas. It appears to me that in healing work with the pancreas, the thymus and the pineal gland near the top of the head, energy manifested physiologically from emotional conflict can be discharged repeatedly.

As I work on a particular psychological conflict with a patient, I rotate among these three points on the body a number of times, with my left hand touching the body and the right discharging toxic energy with the aid of my rod into a discharge sink.

Usually after 30 minutes to an hour of working this way with a patient, the conflict and its physiological manifestation, whether pain or some other symptom, begin to fade and, eventually, disappear. I have had an opportunity to check on many of the people I've worked with as they returned to Esalen for further therapy, and their particular problems were no longer evident.

Because of this success Esalen issued me an open invitation to return whenever I had time to spare. They put a notice on the bulletin board of when I'd be there, and I would give a general lecture and private healing sessions or work with Dick Price and his gestalt therapy group.

One night after my lecture on a method of transmuting the poisonous energy of lead, a young man came over at dinner and sat down at my table and said, "I have fifteen Number-Two buckshot in my left arm. You say this is the receiving arm where energy comes in, so this would probably kill off my energy flow. Do you think you can help me?"

I said, "Buddy, I have been praying for you to come onto my screen for quite a few years now because I haven't had a way to test this with a real live person. I've transmuted

114

many inanimate, material objects, but I've never been able to work on anyone with lead in his body."

After dinner we went back over to my workshop, and I worked on him for just 15 minutes. I relieved this boy's congestion and restored his flow of energy and changed his whole life. I've heard from him since and seen his mother, and she says his grades have picked up and his whole personality has changed.

18

One of my Esalen patients, whom I'll call "Cheryl", was a young female massage therapist at the institute with a nine-year-old daughter. The father had started abusing Cheryl in her eighth month of pregnancy, then left her to bear and rear the child alone. As a consequence Cheryl had some hatred and a lot of emotional conflict concerning men and was resisting and repelling them in her life.

To my surprise, when I was checking her out and clearing her circuits, I discovered that the polarity of her gonads and female organs was reversed to a positive factor, just like a man's. I'd never seen anything like this. I checked her hand circuit and it was out, then checked her eye circuit and it was out. I didn't know what to do.

Several years ago I had discovered that I could reverse the polarity of my body so that all my energy was flowing into the right side of all three circuits (leg, hand and eye) and out the left -- then reverse it back again. So I started trying to figure out a way to reverse Cheryl's polarity to see if I could release this conflict from her. I wasn't sure where I was going to get the answer. I told her I'd be back and went outside and stood there for awhile looking at the ocean and the waves coming in. All of a sudden the information I needed was just fed right into me.

I went back in and knelt beside her and asked, "Would you like to try something that has never been tried before?"

"Yes," she said, "if you think it will do any good."

"Well, we're going to do a moon walk," I said, "because I don't think anyone has walked in this space before."

I cupped my left hand over her vagina (she was fully clothed), lining my middle finger up with her conception vessel meridian. I put my thumb and forefinger over one ovary and the fourth and little finger over the other one, then with my right hand I held the tip of the rod just an inch or so from the right side of a jar of minerals from my mine. The tip rotated clockwise in a small circle at first, which is normal, but I tuned in on the minerals until I had completely absorbed Cheryl's reversed polarity. The tip of the rod suddenly went negative, reversing direction. I had reversed my polarity -- which meant that I had reversed hers as well.

I took my hand off of her -- cut loose from her -- then took the rod in my left hand this time and went to the left or negative side of the bottle. Very quickly, in about a third of the time it took to reverse it, my polarity switched back to normal. This is kind of similar to parting your hair on the opposite side versus the side you usually part it on: refusing to lie down in the new direction, your hair falls into place with the first stroke of the comb when allowed to return to normal.

Cheryl had assumed a very soft look. I checked her again and found that her gonads, her conception vessel meridian and her governing vessel meridian had all reverted to the female factor. Of the body's 12 meridians these two, called the "river of life", are the only ones which are different in man and woman.

Her attraction for men was immediate. I had never seen a man touch Cheryl before, but when I came back a few weeks later I watched three different men stop to hug and caress her as she walked across the dining room. She told me that since we had reversed her sexual polarity this was the kind of attraction that was taking place. She hadn't had a menstrual period in five years, and I believe it was two months after our session together that she started menstruating again. I've checked her several times since the session and she remains negative instead of positive.

117

It seems entirely possible to me that within the realm of this reversal of body polarity lies an explanation for homosexuality. I know this is the reason for a lot of divorces because if one of the spouses reverses and the other doesn't they are in total conflict in terms of their polarity. They can't even caress and be pulled together; they would have to force this. Recently I have been fortunate enough to check quite a few youngsters coming into puberty. I find many of them who are reversed at this stage of their life and in emotional conflict, so I feel we have a wide open field for research here.

Another early healing experience was with a clinical psychologist and professor at an Eastern university who had come to Esalen in an attempt to find the cause of an emotional conflict. When he came up to me after one of my lectures and asked if I'd work on him, I began right then as we stood there, by starting to program his head circuit down to his thymus. All of a sudden he dropped as if he'd been shot. I caught him underneath the arms and laid him on the floor.

By this time I'd gotten used to some of the quick changes in people when I'm working on them and didn't let this worry me too much. I gave him an energy boost with my own energy and he came right out of it. When I asked him if he'd ever experienced a similar situation, he answered, "Yes -- two years ago. I had an argument with my wife and went down to my office, locked myself in and went on a marijuana trip. On the second joint the same thing happened: I just dropped flat on the floor."

Apparently, we unlocked whatever happened the first time and let it go back in the opposite direction, allowing him to return to normal. The next morning I was working with Dick Price in his gestalt workshop, and this man was the first patient we got down on the floor and started working on. We went back through this whole marijuana thing with him, found the emotional conflict and discharged it from his body.

I have seen him many times since then, and he's never had any recurrences of the conflict he was in at that time.

This leads me to believe that somewhere in his electrical system there was a short circuit which had been caused by the marijuana. I cleared the circuit and through the reverse action of what had happened to him before, he returned to normal.

These things are happening with such intensity now, with many different people -- especially in the field of reversing polarity in the gonads -- that I believe we're into a whole new method of psychological adjustment. We may have the key to immediate therapy, in which we can handle cases quickly and efficiently, picking up only the conflict areas and discharging them. A person may be able to leave with a lot of his problems gone after just an hour or an hour and a half of treatment.

I don't want to give the impression, however, that the kind of healing I do is only psychological in nature. One day last summer the Pittineys asked me to meet them at Ventana to work on a woman employed there who had a painfully injured knee. While I was working with her, a young man pulled into the service station next to the restaurant in an overheated car. When he took off the radiator cap, boiling water erupted into his face.

He came running around the side of the building with this ice pack on his face, in intense pain. His eyes were wild and he was crying, moaning and carrying on, and you just knew he was ruined. Around a rim of white where his glasses had at least protected his eyes, his face had already begun to swell and discolor. His lips were absolutely tight, he couldn't talk; he made little noises but he couldn't get his mouth to move.

They'd called an ambulance but fortunately it couldn't come right away. If they'd put him in a hospital and put tannic acid on that face, he'd have been scarred for life. He came right to us -- this happens all the time. Many, many times I'll show up just at the right minute to do a healing of some kind, and I don't even try to think about it any more, I just let it flow.

This was the first time I'd ever worked on a burn, and I never actually touched the boy. I just held my left hand in front of his face and moved it around, with the rod in my right hand directed at my discharge sink. All of a sudden a rainbow of about eight different colors came in diagonally across his face, all the way down to his shoulder. I blinked my eyes and looked over at the Pittineys, and it disappeared. When I looked back, there it was again.

It was the color in his aura that was coming out -- just absolutely beautiful. I was the only one who saw it. I see all sorts of auras now in people I'm healing, especially green. A green will get to flashing all over their face and moving back and forth as I'm moving my eyes. It's part of the energy I've been talking about.

Anyway, in half an hour every sign of the burn was gone from that young man's face. And the minute the healing took place and was finished, the rainbow disappeared. He threw his arms around me in utter relief and joy, and do you know what he said? He said the pain was worth the experience! It was really a moving experience for all of us.

Heather Pittiney has seen this young man on two occasions since then, and she says there's no sign of any scars. His skin is perfectly clear. And by the way -- the girl I was working on when he was injured had hardly been able to walk for weeks when I saw her. The Pittineys told me she was out square dancing the next night.

19

Carlotta's in tights, working out to music, when I ring the doorbell. She is polite but cool as she lets me in, her manner -- perhaps mine as well -- implying that she has the role of the injured party here.

"Guess I caught you in the middle of your workout," I offer lamely."

"That's all right, I can't breathe in this goddamn Ohio Valley smog anyway."

"It *is* bad today isn't it. L.A. weather: about as close as we get around here to the atmosphere of a big city."

Carlotta laughs bitterly. "You can say that again. And yet here they are, promoting tourism, when it's not even fit for the people who live here. Tourism and economic development -- as if we didn't have enough chemical plants around here at it is! Let's bring in some more -- forget about cleaning up the air. Give the tourists gas masks."

I'm used to this particular tirade and not about to be drawn into it today.

"...I think your stuff's all in the bedroom at the end of the hall," she says when I don't respond.

But I didn't come over here just to pick up my things. Unlikely though it may be, I'm still hoping some kind of reconciliation can be patched together somehow: not simply by starting in again where we left off a week ago, but with the willingness to try some changes that might make us happier together. Stalling for time, I say, "I wasn't looking forward to this."

"Well, it didn't have to happen, Cork."

"Didn't *have* to maybe..."

"Not if you were willing to be satisfied with one woman in a relationship, instead of living out some adolescent fantasy of being a ladies' man or whatever it is you want out of life. God knows what that might be since you won't share it with me."

"Oh come on, Carlotta, that's not fair to either one of us and you know it. You're not that stupid or wrongheaded, and I haven't been that remote from you. You're always saying I have, but when you do you're just ignoring all that we *have* had together. You're too busy too much of the time feeling sorry for yourself to focus on the positive in our relationship -- which far outweighs the negative, in my opinion."

"Yeh, let's hear it for the buzzwords, Cork. Who's keeping score? How much are the positives ahead by today?"

I make some sort of futile gesture to the effect that Carlotta's just proved my point, and she jumps right on it.

"That's right, score another point for the negatives. You know, Cork, if you were half as good at *showing* your affection as you are in *telling* me about it in that superior attitude of yours whenever we have an argument, there might not *be* so many arguments."

"I can never give you enough, Carlotta. I *am* affectionate -- I'm as affectionate with you as I know how. Not every minute we're together, but you certainly got far more affection from me than anyone else."

"The fact there were others who did at all is the problem, Cork. I won't compete with anyone. I shouldn't have to."

"You're in competition with other women only in your own mind, Carlotta," I say, sighing at this old argument of hers. "The fact is you *do* compete, when there's no reason to. It's a one-woman competition."

In sync for once, we both recognize that this is old territory.

"...If you're just going to get your stuff and leave, I

wish you'd do it so I can get back to my workout," Carlotta finally says in as dispirited a tone of voice as I'm feeling now myself.

"Is that what you want me to do?"

"Don't ask me that question, Cork. You know what I want, I've made that clear enough. And if you're unable to give it to me -- to *us* -- then there's no sense in prolonging things, that's all."

"Do you admit that *you're* unwilling to change or compromise too? That you're as unwilling to try to see things from my perspective as you say I am from yours?"

"I've made a lot of changes in my life for you already, Cork."

"And I have for you too. But now here we are, both feeling we're right and that the other person isn't willing to bend or change. Are you willing to accept half the responsibility for that?"

"Would you just please *spare* me your goddamn pop psychology, Cork! Just get your things and get out -- *please!*"

She *is* pleading with me -- to leave her in peace. Her long lovely face is haggard with weariness and, yes, grief. Better that than admit she's wrong, that she shares some of the blame for our failed relationship? No; she's hurt and confused, worn down by trying to figure out what went wrong and how, what she might have done differently, etc. -- the same as I am. She just doesn't share my hyper-"rational" approach of accepting and ascribing responsibility: "pop psychology". I'm not sure I do either but it seems as good a place to start as any in attempting to diagnose a sick relationship.

In Carlotta's eyes, I'm sure, I just plain don't *care* enough -- to reach out and stop the world with her, our part of it at least. To stop this inexorable process of disintegration, the decline of an almost living entity, a being or beingness

123

that was *us*: relationship entropy. The hell with who's *responsible*.

I guess I don't, do I -- care enough to bend, once again? But bending's not the answer! Carlotta doesn't *listen*, I remind, or reassure, myself. I've told her over and over again that I just can't tolerate her stifling possessiveness, her jealous interrogations. I've apologized and admitted I was wrong in seeing Leslie the way I did. But not once has she acknowledged that any of her behavior has had the least bit of influence on where we are today.

I feel the return of a sort of paralysis I've experienced the past few weeks: an inability to alter the course of events in any way. Like a lab rat that has been exposed to too many electrical shocks and too many blind alleys and now just sits numbly in its cage.

Maybe Carlotta's and my time will come around again, in a different guise, a new form; it may be that this one's run its course, that there's just no use in fighting its demise any longer.

I reach out for her hand and she gives it to me. We stand there a moment looking into each other's eyes, empty now of any blame or resentment, expressing pain without either wallowing in it or displaying it for the other's sympathy or guilt. I give her hand a squeeze and feel hers respond, then turn and walk to the bedroom at the end of the hall for my clothes. When I come back she has already returned to her workout.

20

Living again with my parents is complicated by the increasing constraints my mother's emphysema is introducing into her life. Ever since my return to Lafayette she's been growing steadily weaker and more susceptible to one illness after another; but either sharing a house with her and Dad has made me more aware of her infirmity, or its progress is accelerating -- probably both.

Dad, while depressing in his own implacable state of depression to be around, is actually in the best physical shape he's been in for a long time, after nearly two years now of sobriety. Only his 14 months in a nursing home could have accomplished that feat. Although his stay there was relatively pleasant, thanks both to the excellent nursing home insurance my parents had been wise enough to purchase and to the quality of the facility itself, I'm sure Dad's concern about having to go back is one thing that has helped him stay off booze. His lean body now looks as though it may have several more years in it, though God knows how he'll fill them, with his almost total lack of interest in life.

Mom, on the other hand, still has her great sense of humor and a hunger for human contact, and mourns the gradual erosion of her connections to the world. We've long since mended the hurt feelings from our argument right after I moved in, but Mom's continual and vocal grieving over the deterioration of her health has begun to get to me. Jimmy's right: compassion has never been my strong suit.

One evening after dinner she and I are sitting in the backyard on decrepit metal and plastic lawn chairs whose condition and appearance sadden me because of the way they mirror the lives of my parents themselves. Rustling gently overhead are the leaves of the walnut tree Dad planted years ago from a rotten black walnut the next-door neighbor dug up in his garden and tossed across the fence with the remark, "Here, Miles, plant yourself a tree." Just to play along, unaware the decaying matter even contained a seed capable of germinating, Dad planted it right where he was kneeling in the yard -- a little too close to the house as it turned out. But despite its messy litter of broken walnuts each fall and the generations of raucous squirrels that come for the nuts, then hang around for the birdseed in a long line of feeders supposedly designed to keep them out, the tree has nonetheless been a welcome source of shade for many summers now.

With an hour or more of daylight left, Dad's already gone to bed. Mom as usual is having some trouble breathing in the Ohio Valley's smoggy mid-summer humidity.

"Thanks for joining me out here, honey," she says, smiling warmly; "I was afraid I was losing a friend."

"Don't be ridiculous," I grumble, "I'm your son for Christ's sake."

"You said if I didn't start doing things the way you wanted me to I was going to be on my own from now on."

"I said no such thing. What I said was, if you're not willing to consider any of my advice, or the position of the rest of the family, then you'll just have to start dealing with your medical problems on your own. I certainly never meant I was going to walk out of your life."

"Well, I'm glad we're sitting here together anyway. Before I have to go in for my puffs."

"I could bring your inhalers out here for you."

"No, then I'm going to get under my oxygen."

"At least your emphysema finally got you to quit smoking." Once again I grow weary hearing the same worn phrases being repeated between us -- a sudden mental image of Mom furtively sneaking the occasional cigarette: "You're not are you?"

"After what everyone told me about the danger of blowing myself up? No, I'm not."

"I didn't think you'd be foolish enough to smoke around your oxygen, but you're not in your room *all* the time."

"It sure seems like it," she says with a sigh deep enough for the balcony seats. "It seems like that's where I spend all my time anymore."

"It was your choice, Mom. If you'd stopped smoking --"

"Don't start! If I'd known it was going to be this hard I wouldn't have quit in the first place."

"That's just what I mean."

She ignores the remark. "This is the hardest thing I've had to do in my life. And for what? So I can lie around breathing oxygen all day."

"I think it's great that you quit -- we all do," I assure her. "I just wish you'd done it a long time ago."

"May we *please* change the subject. We don't have a chance to talk much anymore; I don't want to waste the opportunity talking about my smoking."

My eyes are beginning to glaze over when a puff of breeze rescues me momentarily from the umpteenth take of the conversation we've been having not just since I moved in but for the last couple of years at least. It must be two or three minutes later, when the leaves have lapsed back into silence, that I take up the gauntlet again. "So how *are* you feeling these days?"

"Same as ever: terrible -- like what's the point in even getting up in the morning."

"Don't start sounding like Dad."

"No, dear God, don't ever let me start talking like your father. Shut off my oxygen first."

"Glad to see you're still hanging onto your sense of

humor," I tell her, feeling a smile pull some life into my face. "Life would be a lot less enjoyable without that."

"Honey," Mom replies, "I'm afraid life quit being enjoyable for me some time ago. I'm not sure just when."

"Oh, that isn't true and you know it. You still know how to laugh when you're not feeling depressed."

"When is that?"

I don't even respond to this, and a moment later Mom adds, "How to laugh maybe, for whatever that's worth."

"That's where it starts isn't it?"

"Yes and that's probably how it all ends too."

"Life's just a big laugh huh? You *are* down today -- try focusing on something positive for a while."

"I'm trying to...any suggestions?"

My voice rising in exasperation, I tell her, "Just look around you!"

She does, not for the first time since we came out here certainly but now with some exaggeration. Finally she asks, "Did it ever occur to you that it may look different to me?"

"...What you're going through is hardly unique, Mom," I reply, trying to sound matter-of-fact rather than sarcastic. "You're getting old, you're going through what every human being from the beginning of time has had to go through. I'm getting older too."

"Thanks for the insight."

"Well, what do you expect me to say?"

"Nothing, if you can't improve on that."

I feel a sudden tenderness toward her. "This is your *life*, Mom, just as it is. You have to make the most of it."

"I'm trying," she says, a slight quaver in her voice.

"I sympathize with the situation you're in. But *you* have to take some responsibility for how you got here. And for whatever changes you want."

Neither of us speaks again for awhile. Mom goes

through her repertoire of displacement mannerisms while I end up glaring into space.

"...I'm not asking for your sympathy, but a little understanding would be nice," she says at last.

"I'm sorry if that sounded too harsh; but I feel at a loss for anything helpful to say."

"No, if you haven't been there, I guess you can't be expected to know what it's like."

"I just wish...with all the reading you've always done, that you'd spent a little more time getting ready for all this. What you're going through now." This is a subject I've been wanting to broach with her for some time but haven't known how to bring up.

"You think reading would help?"

"It might. It might help you come to terms with..."

"Growing old?"

"With growing old, and everything that comes with it. I feel -- especially after your pointing it out to me -- inadequate to offer anything very helpful since I've never experienced what you're going through. But in a sense I've sort of been preparing for it for a long time. Not so much growing old as dying."

"Well, death is a definite improvement over old age as a conversational topic."

"I know, no one wants to talk about death, unless it's in some morbid way."

"Death *is* morbid."

"It doesn't have to be! Refusing to think about it and talk about it is what makes it that way. Don't you think?"

"Or the other way around. Why are we talking about it now?"

"...I sometimes wonder if part of your depression now has more to do with your thoughts, and fears, about dying than with your various ailments. Is that possible?"

Mom's just as cautious in her answer. "...I suppose it's

possible, yes. I've just never seen anything to be gained by dwelling on it, that's all."

"I understand," I assure her. "See, I *can* be understanding."

We both smile, relieved perhaps to have danced around mortality with such finesse, to have emerged unscathed.

"...So how is it you've been preparing to die all these years? Why haven't I been aware of this?"

"Who wants to talk about death? I think it's something we have to come to *terms* with -- the earlier in our lives the better. But it's not something you sit around and talk about."

"*We* are."

"Yes -- hooray for that!"

"Why on earth is death something that concerns *you* so much? It seems to me you've been extremely well insulated from it."

It's true my life has been remarkably free of tragedy. I think my intellectual curiosity was kindled by a documentary on death which was part of the same TV series Walter Barry appeared in. And by two books on an Indian holy man that I edited for Paul Goldblum, a San Francisco psychiatrist.

When I tell Mom this she laughs and says, "So I'm the lucky recipient of Hindu spiritual teachings filtered through the writings of a Jewish psychiatrist in California, edited by my gentile Midwestern son."

"You should be so lucky." We sit there chuckling. It occurs to me that not so long ago her laughter would probably have brought on a horrible coughing fit; but her lungs, as ruined and weak as they are now, are at least clear of the smoker's phlegm that plagued Mom for so many years: a consolation there's probably no point in mentioning.

"You know, you can always make a mid-life career change and become an undertaker if death interests you so much."

"If you exaggerate like that, naturally it's going to

seem morbid," I reply with mild annoyance. "There are plenty of books on the subject; the best I've ever read is *Denial of Death*, by a guy named Ernest Becker, who won a Pulitzer for it. I'm sure the college library has it if the public library doesn't."

"What's it about, besides death -- my God, the word's worse than my paperwork, I can't get away from it."

"What we've been talking about, basically: how we short-change our *lives* by trying to hide from death. It's the monster under the bed."

"I'm not sure I'm ready for that."

"But you're certainly ready to complain about being depressed and lonely."

"...Am I really that bad?"

"Wellll...yes, you are, Mom -- or else you go into a litany of all your ailments and medications. It gets a little old sometimes."

She sighs and looks off into space for some time before speaking. "...I was thinking, when I'm feeling better, of going to the Unitarian Church on Sundays with Helen. I've tried most of the others over the years, and I can't abide any of them. The Unitarian seems a little less hypocritical than the rest -- or it did anyway the time or two I've gone with Helen."

"That's...great," I say, trying to squeeze some enthusiasm into my voice. "That's something anyway."

"You're not very encouraging."

"Well, when are you going to start feeling better? You've been using that as an excuse for not doing things, taking some action in your life, for months now."

"But I really do feel rotten most of the time, Cork. And when I *try* to do something -- go out to lunch or get your father out of the house for an hour or so -- I feel even worse the next day."

She chokes up and I feel a wave of genuine pity for my mother well up in my heart. If only I could help bring her *real* comfort, not the false sense of sympathy I feel she wants from me!

"...I know it's hard," I say, putting a hand on hers. "That's one of the reasons I get so impatient sometimes with your excuses: I think you're going to have to try something new to get any better. All your medicines and your 'puffs' apparently aren't doing enough. Going to church with Helen might be good for you. At least it should get you thinking about something besides your problems for a while."

"I thought it might too. That's why I'm disappointed that you don't seem any more enthusiastic."

"You know how I feel about church. But if you think it might do you some good, go for it."

"I don't know whether it would or not, I feel I'm grasping at straws."

"We spend our whole *lives* grasping at straws, Mom -- that's the point I've been trying to make! If you've never taken the time to try to develop some kind of spiritual understanding about life, then death and old age are bound to be terrifying and hopeless. But what better time than now -- when you still *have* time? ...It seems so, I don't know, pretentious or outa line for me to be saying this when I don't have any answers you don't have. You're a lot wiser than I am -- you still have a better sense of humor for one thing. For all *my* 'spiritual enlightenment' I'm depressed a lot of the time myself. But I'd be a lot worse if I couldn't step back at times and count my blessings."

"Well, yes," she says, "you still have blessings to count."

"And you don't?" I ask incredulously.

"...Not lately."

"What a crock *that* is! Dad might have an excuse for making such a remark, since he never even watches TV anymore, let alone reads. But you're not uninformed -- how can *you* say something like that?"

"Don't get on your high horse with me!" Mom comes

right back. "Not till you've had to give up smoking after more than 50 years and you're as good as alone in a big empty house, with your friends either all dead or living the kind of life you always looked forward to and almost embarrassed, it seems, to even call you on the phone when they're in town. I know I'm not starving and have a roof over my head, but you don't know how I feel most of the time, Cork. You don't seem to want to know. You may be living here for a while, but we don't spend much time together; and when we do I don't think you really hear what I'm saying."

"I hear you, Mom. Maybe it takes a while for some things to sink in, but I think about what you say. That doesn't mean I know what it's like being inside your skin, of course, but I think I'm being fair and objective --"

"Fair and objective! I'd just as soon have judgmental and self-righteous if you're going to preach."

I can feel the blood rising as I struggle to hold my tongue. "If you're going to be like that," I say hotly, "I don't see any point in continuing our conversation, do you?"

"That's right, walk away!" she snaps -- "since you can!"

21

Lucia, California: a small coastal town midway between Monterey and San Luis Obispo. A man paces methodically over the parched land, another dogs his steps anxiously. In each hand of the man in front, palms up, with handles made of copper sleeves, is a three-foot length of steel welding rod joined at the other end. The man in front is Walter Barry, holding one of three types of dowsing rods he uses to find water. The anxious man trying to keep up with him is a small-time rancher who's just about run out of it -- water he can afford anyway. He's heard of Walter and men like him for years from other ranchers. Like many of his neighbors, he used to ridicule them when they bragged about the water wells dowsers had located for them.

A month ago he found himself phoning a rancher over in King City, about thirty miles east of here, a man he'd made fun of at a cattlemen's association meeting a little less than a year ago. The damn fool had claimed this Walter Barry had found him a 200-gallon-a-minute well on land no better than his, land that's damn near desert.

The rancher from King City is a proud man and when the caller identified himself, what the rancher remembered most about him was the humiliation he'd been subjected to by this same sonofabitch. All the rancher from King City had been trying to do was pass along what he considered valuable information to his fellow ranchers, but from their reaction you'd have thought he was claiming to have found the fountain of youth. Well, he's not too proud to do some good when he gets the opportunity. He invited his caller over to see the well Walter found for him, which is still pumping close to 200 gallons a minute.

"Over the years," says Walter now, holding the dowsing rod out in front of him, talking over his right shoulder to the skeptical rancher from Lucia, "I've developed three different types of dowsing rods for locating water. Each one performs a particular function better than the others. With all of them, I believe it's a correlation of the minerals in my body with the same minerals in underground water that makes the connection; rainwater doesn't affect the rods at all. The one I'm using now I call my 'scanning' rod. It's the best I've been able to come up with for finding the general vicinity of an underground stream. Watch what happens again when we get close to where we marked the near side of the stream."

As Walter crosses the invisible boundary the rod dips abruptly.

"See there? It's realll *sensitive* -- but not quite *precise* enough. So..."

He goes over to a long leather case and exchanges the scanning rod for a pair of L-shaped metal rods. The short leg of each "L" is the handle, encased in a copper sleeve. Holding a rod in each hand so they're sticking straight out in front of him, the long leg on top, he walks toward the spot where the first rod responded.

"...When I want to start layin' out the exact boundaries of a stream, I use my 'cross rods'. Watch what happens when I cross the edge of the stream."

The rods swing toward each other and cross.

"Now I'll keep walking, until I pass over the other side, and..."

The rods uncross and swing back so they're pointing straight ahead again. The dowser returns to his case and replaces these rods with a third one.

"...Now, how *deep* is it? That's the next question, right? I find that out with my 'counter' rod. It's calibrated to

give us the depth of the water in feet -- and the *angle* will
give us the direction of flow. I won't take time now to tell
you how long it took me to learn the rod's 'language', but I'll
tell you this: I found the first clue in the Bible -- right there in
Exodus. Moses did this with the rod, Moses did that with the
rod. Moses struck the rock at Horeb and water flowed....God
said to Moses, 'Take this rod in thine hand, wherewith thou
shalt do signs.'"

Walter stands over the subterranean stream with the
rod in his right hand, and it begins to swing up and down at a
slight angle to the ground. He counts with it: a foot for each
up-and-down movement of the rod. It makes thirty-eight
complete cycles.

"Thirty-eight feet to water. Why that's not gonna take
much drilling at all. You see how this flows now? Probably
originates in a volcanic cone up there in the mountains along
the coast. Thermal energy has pushed it up from deep inside
the earth as steam, until it has cooled and condensed, turned
back into water, which is probably flowing out through a
crack in the volcanic rock up there.

"Then it comes down and flows past here within
what? 150 maybe 200 yards of your house...and continues on
as a little subterranean tributary of some big underground
river flowing down into the valley -- and, eventually, back
into the ocean. A natural cycle that will keep repeating itself
over and over again forever, with water in enough
underground streams like this for everyone on the planet.
While we sit here with our hands tied and our throats
parched, locked into current scientific theory that says the
only way to tap underground water is by drilling into the
water table, period. That, my friend, is a bunch a bull."

Walter is suddenly interrupted by the ringing of his
detachable cellular phone, which he takes from a pocket of
his dowsing-rod case and answers. I'm the caller on the other
end.

"Walter Barry here -- *on location*, atop a vein of the

sweetest flowing water Mother Nature ever put here on God's green earth!

"Hi, Walter, this is a voice from your past: Cork Rockner. I was involved in "The Fourth Dimension", a TV series you appeared in about ten years ago. You're out dowsing for water right *now*?"

"That's right, you've got me on my car phone. Just brought in well number 357 I believe it is -- in arid country you wouldn't think had water within 20 miles of here. What can I do for you?"

I tell him briefly about our contaminated well.

"Well now, that sounds interesting. A little different from my normal line of work -- but not out of my range you understand, I'm not sayin' that. I've dowsed for everything from water to wedding rings. And finding *poison's* really what *healing's* all about. How'd you say you got my name again?"

"Don't you remember? I directed you in that TV special a few years ago. 'Underground Doctors', was the segment you were in."

"Oh yes, I remember," he says. "I brought quite a few wells in as a result of that show. Lotta calls. Not all of them serious but you're never gonna get away from that. Where did you say you were calling from?"

"Lafayette, Ohio. A little town in the southeastern part of the state."

"Hoo -- that's a long way away. Ohio's not exactly my territory. Here in the Southwest's where the serious water needs are. Notice I didn't say 'shortage', because it's hardly ever a *lack* of water that's the problem -- just its hidden nature. It's there, you just have to know how to look for it. What all this 'scientific' talk of aquifers and water tables keeps people from realizing is that the earth has a circulatory system just like the human body. And it sounds like what you all have is some kind of local infection."

"That's a good way to put it," I say. Good old Walter -- hasn't changed a bit.

"Tell you what, here's what I'd suggest. You have any maps of the area where your wells are?"

"Sure."

"Good. Send me whatever maps you have and as much information as you can -- articles in the paper, that sorta thing. I expect you've heard of map dowsing. Most people haven't but I probably bent your ear about map dowsing when we did that show. Before we get too far into this let's see what we can find that way. I'll do that much for you for nothing. If I find something, we can go from there. How's that sound to you?"

"Fine," I tell him, beginning to feel a little excited now that I can detect his interest.

"Good. Send it to me at Box 315, Perdido Canyon Road, Big Sur, California, 93920. Got that?"

I repeat the address for him.

"Good -- I've gotta get back to work now. I have a rancher here payin' a fortune to haul in water once a week, and he's sittin' over a pretty little river forty feet from the surface that should give him close to a hundred gallons a minute when he gets a good well drilled. And free as mother's milk. Good talkin' to you now -- send me those maps."

He hangs up and goes back over to where he was dowsing. The moment he holds out the counter rod, it starts to swing rhythmically up and down, gradually at first, then faster and faster. While I'm sitting at my desk at work, wondering, "What're you getting yourself into here, Rockner?"

22

How to figure a guy like Walter Barry? It's easy to see how he turns some people off, many of them the very people he needs to impress most to have any chance of getting his theories tested on the most elementary scale. He always has to have the last word.

I know that from personal experience. When we filmed him for our TV series, even though I was the one who had cultivated and researched Walter as our representative dowser -- having met and interviewed the Pittineys and others for whom he's found water or who have witnessed or claim to have benefited from his healing -- we had a falling out at the last minute, and the producer himself had to step in and direct the sequence I had so carefully planned. Walter's big ego clashed with my unyielding conception of how to capture it, along with his obvious and apparent achievements, on film.

But I know -- as much as I "know" what I've been taught from textbooks or have heard first-hand from knowledgeable, trustworthy people -- that Walter has found water where no one else believed it could be found. And, as I've already mentioned, I personally witnessed his apparent healing of my seriously ill wife. Besides, a lot of time has passed since he and I nearly came to blows in front of my camera crew.

Before calling him yesterday I reread the transcript of a weekend interview I conducted with him, then documented as fully as possible before our shooting session several years ago. (This, in fact, is the source of the autobiographical chapters on Walter: a fictitious name.) How exciting if even a fraction of his theories are valid -- if there's even just a kernel of scientific truth in his fascinating work. But it's strictly his dowsing skills I'm interested in for now. Can they be used to find toxic contamination as well as water? And can I possibly sell Walter to the city service director of a conservative little town in the Midwest?

Jimmy Majors is sitting in a booth reading the paper, having already finished eating, when I arrive at Brighter Earth for lunch the day after talking to Walter.

"You're late today, Ace. What's wrong, the banks foreclose on you?"

"Not yet," I sigh, sitting down, "but they're beginning to circle." I look up at the ceiling as if watching not entirely imaginary vultures wheeling hungrily against a stark blue sky.

"That sound ominous to you?"

"Not unless you have something against bein' dead meat."

"I'm not prejudiced. Not about that anyway."

Jimmy offers a compassionate smile and puts his paper away. "How are things?"

"The same. I figure we have about six months at the rate we're going."

"Six months till one of the banks calls their note?"

"Well, six months until I have to meet with all of them with some kind of song and dance about how we're about to turn things around. But they're not gonna buy it this time. Not without some major improvement in lumber sales."

"Maybe housing will start to turn up."

"Even if it does, it'll take another six months, at least, to have much impact on hardwoods."

"...Hang in there, Bud." He starts to get up.

"Don't go yet, I wanta tell you about something."

Amy, today's waitress, comes over for my order. There's been some tension between us since the confrontation between Carlotta and me, even though I know it's neither fair nor very intelligent of me to hold Amy responsible. I don't even know how much, if anything, Carlotta's told her about it; she may only be reflecting my own coolness. Jimmy doesn't seem to notice anything, in any case.

"Hi, Amy, what kinda soup today?"

"Old-fashioned bean and spinach-lentil," she replies, briskly professional.

"I'll take the bean, carrot juice, and a corn muffin, heated."

"Comin' up."

I watch her hurry back to the kitchen -- Amy's always hurrying -- although what I'm actually seeing are scenes from my last meeting with Carlotta.

"Okay, so what's the word, big boy?"

"...I met with Andy Byers," I finally reply. "He thinks there may be some kind of cover-up in connection with this contaminated well."

"No shit -- why do you think I had you talk to him?"

"Do you think he knows what he's talking about?"

"It's his business, what he's trained for. Andy *is* a little idealistic at times though. Tends to get a mite testy when the plants around here keep callin' him in not to help them clean up their act but to find out the least they can do to stay legal."

"So you think he may be over-reacting?"

"I don't know, Rockner -- what am I his shrink? I just thought you oughta know what you might be getting into, before goin' off half-cocked with this crazy idea of yours about a dowser."

"That's the other thing I wanted to talk to you about. I just sent Walter -- that's the dowser -- some maps of the well field. If he can locate the source of contamination by map dowsing, I'm thinking of bringing him back here. All I have to do now is come up with the money."

Jimmy's expression of disbelief is fleeting before turning into one more of disgust as he shakes his head. "Didn't anything Andy said register with you?"

"Sure it did. If what he thinks is true, that's all the more reason to find this 'plume' is what he calls it, as soon as possible. I talked to Walter about this yesterday and he seems to think he can do it. But if I decide to go through with it, I'll probably have to find the money somewhere for a test well. I thought maybe you could help me come up with a list of 'environmental angels'. You know people in town with some bucks that I don't know."

"I don't know anybody dumb enough to invest in something like that, Rockner. And I'm not dumb enough to ask them." He chuckles rather scornfully, shaking his head.

"What's so dumb about it? You just wanta sit back and let the city keep pouring money into dry holes?"

"It's none of my business -- and I can't see how you think it's any of yours either. But that's up to you."

"That's right, it is. I could tell myself it's none of my business, but I feel it is. I get tired of reading about how people are so afraid to get involved in things anymore, for fear of getting harassed or sued or inconvenienced. Don't you? I could pretend this doesn't concern me, but it does. The city's losing a lot of money on this. And if the contamination spreads, we could end up losing *all* our goddamn wells!"

"Jesus, don't get your bowels in an uproar, Rockner -- calm down."

Jimmy's right, I *am* getting a little carried away here. After all, he doesn't know a damn thing about dowsing or Walter Barry except what I've told him.

"...I don't think I ever told you, did I, about the time I took Alex in to be healed by this guy?"

"No," he says with a tolerant chuckle. "With what I know about Alex and the rest of your California crowd, though, I'm sure it's not going to surprise me."

"It was quite an experience. She came down with something that started out as a bronchial condition of some kind and couldn't shake it. Couldn't eat or hold anything down, kept losing weight. Finally goes to a doctor, and he tells her he can't do anything for her because it's a virus. This was after we'd separated but I was still aware of all this because I used to take the twins most weekends.

"Like everyone else, I figured she was just dramatizing the whole thing the way she used to everything else. But she just kept getting worse and worse, weaker and skinnier, and finally I realized: here we were, filming all these unorthodox healers for "The Fourth Dimension", and here was Alex, desperately in need of *some* kind of healing. By now it was obvious she really was in bad shape -- she kept saying she was going to die. So I took her to see Walter, who I'd gotten to know when we filmed him for the series -- dowsing for water, though, not healing. We'd already filmed several other healers.

"I just about had to carry her into the motel room where he was staying, and he sits her down and starts going over her lightly with one hand -- his left I think -- while in the other he's holding one of his dowsing rods. First he locates the areas in her body where he says negative energy is concentrated: the thymus gland...the spleen, I think it was...and maybe her gall bladder, I don't remember -- her pancreas maybe. When he touched these parts of her body, the rod would make these big circles in the air. And for him to just barely touch her put Alex in agony -- which made quite an impression on me because for all her melodramatic tendencies, she's always been pretty stoic about physical pain.

"Anyway, once he'd determined where these 'blockages' or 'conflict points' -- I forget what he called them -- were supposedly located, he starts 'draining' each one: with one hand very lightly massaging her and the dowsing rod now pointed at this little plastic case he calls a 'discharge sink', filled with all kinds of poisons, he says: a cigarette butt, aspirin tablet..." (At this point Jimmy can no longer avoid one of his sarcastic guffaws.) "...some mercury, I think. He said

143

this sink of his was supposed to be like a sort of magnet which helps pull out the negative energy.

"When he first touched each of these three conflict points on her body, the rod would go crazy, making these big sweeping circles. But as he worked on her they'd gradually diminish until the rod was still -- then he'd move on to the next point and repeat the whole thing. He must have made about three or four complete cycles; and each time he came back to one of the three points, the rod would react again -- but less than it had before. Finally, after about half an hour or so, the rod was completely still when he touched any part of her body.

"When I took her home, Alex felt so much better she asked me to take her to dinner. She was more lively and energetic than she'd been in months. The next day she had a complete relapse -- felt just as bad as she had before. But the day after that she felt fine again, and was completely recovered."

I lean back now to see how Jimmy's going to react to all of this, surprised at how moved I am myself by the story in recalling it. I haven't told it to anyone in any depth for a long time.

Jimmy just shrugs. "...Great story, Ace -- what am I supposed to do now, applaud?"

"I just thought you'd find it interesting," I reply, equally blasé. "I certainly did -- it's one of the reasons I trust this guy. I was there once when he delivered the goods. He was working with a professor at Stanford last I knew. They published some kind of scientific paper together."

"...To return to life-as-we-know-it here in the Midwest, Rockner, what do you think it would cost to drill a test well anyway?"

"I don't really have any idea. I haven't looked into that yet."

"In round figures I'd guess somewhere in the neighborhood of $10,000 -- maybe more, maybe less."

"You think so? That *is* a hell of a lot, isn't it." I don't automatically assume Jimmy knows what he's talking about, but he's generally more knowledgeable about such things than I am. I figure there's a good chance he's in the ballpark anyway.

"You're damn right it is. Where the hell do you expect to find that kind of money on a moment's notice -- all because some new-age witch doctor with a magic wand says, 'Dig here.'?"

"That's what the hell I'm asking *you*. Who with that kind of money might even consider such a thing? *I'll* do the asking. All I'm asking you for is some names."

Jimmy gets up from the table. "Well, I can't talk about this any longer today, I've got a job interview in Columbus at four. But I'll *think* about it, okay? I'll tell you one thing: if you're so goddamn serious about this, your timing couldn't be worse, moving out of Carlotta's now."

"Carlotta? What the hell's she have to do with it?"

"Well you *know* her brother's as much of an environmental fanatic as she is. He could come up with that kind of money in a minute, if he wanted to. And since he's always looking for some kind of PR gimmick to promote his computer business, he just might go for it -- if Carlotta was behind it."

This had never occurred to me, but Jimmy's right. Damned if I'm going to say anything to her about it though.

"See ya, Ace."

"...Uh, yeah, Jimmy. Good luck with your interview!"

"Thanks!" he yells back over his shoulder -- while I sit there for a minute or two looking into space, until Amy arrives with my lunch. I'm just unfolding today's *Wall Street Journal* when I see Brook come in. Looks like she's here for lunch too, must be some kind of school holiday. For a moment I'm torn between reading in silence and thinking about the conversation Jimmy and I have just had, or asking

Brook to join me. Then she smiles and I motion for her to come over and have lunch with me.

"Hi, Brook, off today?"

She caricatures a look of profound relief and sits down across from me. "No, just extracting the maximum mileage from a dental appointment. How *are* you, Cork? It's good to see you so soon again."

Brook is effusive to the point of what would be obvious insincerity if it weren't for the warmth she radiates. Her smile *seems* genuine anyway, despite its superficial resemblance to the sort of effortless Hollywood smile I saw often enough in L.A. The difference must be in her eyes, which are intent neither on drawing me in nor on dazzling me. In fact her soft but otherwise unremarkable brown eyes must be where this quiet warmth is coming from.

"...I'm surprised we've never run into each other in a small town like this," I say, feeling how easily my own smile responds.

"Me too. I've heard about you though. You grew up here, right?"

"Sure did -- I used to tell people Lafayette was a great place to grow up in, but I sure wouldn't want to live there."

"And now, here you are," says Brook, laughing at my ironic anecdote as if it were actually funny. "So what brought you back here?"

"The family business. My father needed help."

"Well, that was certainly good of you."

"It was the right thing for me too. I was in Southern California for about 19 years, went out there right after I got out of school. But I was just a step away from the street when I came back here -- one of L.A.'s several-hundred-thousand 'writer-producers'. That's a title you don't have to go to school for; it sorta comes with the territory out there."

She seems really interested in what I'm saying so I continue. "I don't know how much good I've actually done here though. The company was in such a hole when I got back it's been next to impossible to pull us out of it."

"You've been a big help, I'm sure."

Somehow Brook makes me believe she means this. But she can't possibly know whether or not it's true since she knows next to nothing about me. "...Some," I say, smiling noncommittally.

"In fact the few things I've heard about you have all been very nice."

"Sounds like my disinformation campaign's working."

We go on in this vein and I learn that Brook is five years younger than I, divorced for a little less than a year after a long marriage. Lives with her two daughters, a dog and a cat. She's a teacher now but has also been a nurse. I can see her in both roles. She's the sort of small intense woman people used to call "perky". Now the description is "high-energy" and you no longer have to be petite to qualify. The term's not even gender-specific.

I can also see in Brook the compassion nursing must demand. Perhaps that's another way to describe the warmth I feel in her presence. She doesn't date, or hasn't yet anyway; still too soon after the divorce. I feel the same way about my breakup with Carlotta. But if anyone were to change my mind soon, it could be this pretty, unassuming dark-haired woman who makes me feel good just talking to her.

Or Leslie. It was my visit to her, after all, that brought this all about. It would be nice to turn it to some good end if possible. But I haven't called her either. There's still an outside chance Carlotta and I may find the magic to start things up again somehow.

23

Once before, a year and a half ago, Carlotta and I separated for a week or two. This was before I moved in with her, when I was still renting a house in the country and we were together only on weekends. Trying to reconcile what had happened with what I was feeling, I wrote the following fable as a way of trying to capture for myself, and secondarily for Carlotta, what I hoped I'd learned from the experience:

"ICARUS GROUNDED"

One day in a land not far away, a land you know of though you may not know you know, a man -- it could as easily have been a woman -- resolved to climb a mountain he had been trying to avoid for some time. As this was a very tall and prominent mountain, like the Grand Tetons or a volcanic peak erupting out of the landscape unaccompanied by foothills or any range it is part of, avoidance had become increasingly problematic. There were few places he could go without seeing it in the distance as part of the landscape, nothing he could work at for very long before his mind returned to the mountain's image even when it wasn't actually in sight.

Somewhere along the way he had become aware that his predicament was a condition of his time, if not of the whole human race. Everyone had his and her mountain they were avoiding or actually climbing. Yes, a few were climbers. Some you could see; the progress of others you were able to infer.

And now again (for he had climbed other such mountains in the past and would no doubt climb more in the future)...now it was time to make this particular ascent. He put everything else aside and began laboring up the mountain's steep treacherous slopes. Progress was very difficult and after awhile it occurred to him that something was holding him back, making the climb even harder than it would be naturally.

It was his wings. (I know, we're throwing a curve at you here. But you see, our hero, our protagonist if you prefer, wasn't aware that he had them either. That is, although he knew he had them, he didn't know *that he knew -- as in a dream where you can suddenly fly or perform some other supposedly miraculous feat and are amazed by this while immediately taking it for granted nonetheless. You must have known at some level about the latent ability, right?)*

Anyway, the wings were dragging him down, holding him back. He stopped to examine them and discovered that they were detachable. This, like the wings themselves, he found both odd and logical at the same time; but it sure solved his problem. He snapped open their quick-release mechanism and sent them tumbling into the abyss -- chuckling at the sight and thought of falling wings.

Now, his burden considerably lightened, he was able to return to the arduous ascent with new energy and enthusiasm. In no time at all he reached the top.

The view was spectacular. He could see into three states, and at least that many states of mind, from here. And more than that: after surveying the scene for quite a while, in that state of intoxication John Denver has memorialized as a Rocky Mountain high, he espied another distant high place which called out to him so eloquently that he knew he must go there (and knew that he knew, this time).

In fact, it occurred to him that this was the very reason for his climb. This distant peak, which he'd never have seen otherwise, was the profound source of his obsession for climbing the one he was on.

Only now, then, did he realize the evolutionary purpose of the wings he had so blithely discarded. What a cruel dilemma! Climbing back down wasn't the answer. Even if he successfully reached the ground again -- a far more dangerous feat than climbing up had been -- he was sure he would never find his way to the peak he could see so clearly -- yet at such great distance -- from here.

In fatigue and anguish he fell asleep. And in a dream his guardian angel (yes, there's one of these too) reprimanded him with the kind of self-righteous moralizing he had always attributed to these creatures, for this reason preferring to think of them, like most people, as strictly imaginary.

"Do you understand now?" she asked rhetorically. "The reason for resolving an issue is not to stake out your 'position' and stick to it, come what may, but to enable yourself to put the issue behind you so as to gain a new perspective, and then to move on -- hopefully, to grow."

Somehow her didactic but gentle reprimand, though a virtual cliché of all such encounters in books and movies, was as ineffably moving as only dreams can be. Probably due in no small part to her parting words: "Don't worry, you must be patient but you'll eventually grow new ones."

Then she vanished, or he woke up, as darkness was falling -- leaving him utterly alone in this high cold place, but with around him the campfires of others like him (or her) on many of the neighboring and distant peaks, extending to the horizon in all directions as far as the eye could see.

*   *   *

Now, a year later, as it begins to seem less and less likely that Carlotta and I are going to get back together any time soon, I spend much of my spare time looking for another place to live and walking the mostly unpaved back roads for exercise and the combination of peace of mind and mental stimulation I find in the fall countryside. Through a local realtor I locate a little octogonally-shaped one-bedroom house surrounded by nearly 30 acres of forest. By the time the sale has closed I've purchased some used furniture, a new double mattress and, from the local classifieds, china, stoneware, glasses and flatware. My parents give me a corkscrew and a set of wineglasses gathering dust in their old Victorian home along with a few other less essential kitchen items.

The family business stumbles along like the Quasimodo of hardwood companies that it is. It's fascinating -- in the same macabre manner that seeing an animal being torn to pieces, say, or its remains being devoured by nature's clean-up crew -- how long an unprofitable debt-crippled company can hang on through sheer inertia. But unless the economy and export sales turn around precipitously this quarter, which absolutely no one is predicting, dead weight will finally overcome our languishing momentum and we'll have to start computing even inertia in red ink.

Red is also running riot in the woods now in a range of shades from orange to violet. But in contrast to our books and bank account, in the surrounding hardwood forests there's lots of gold too. The warm fall colors contrast with the crisp tang of air that seems almost crystalline after summer's haze (the word they still use for smog around here) and humidity. The endless scenic variety -- abandoned and prosperous farms with livestock, mostly cattle, dotting the landscape; the rich umber of newly turned topsoil and sere fields of harvested corn, their acres of dried stalks rustling and rattling in the slightest breeze; country homes, wooded

151

hillsides and streams weaving their melodies pianissimo into the forest silence...such abundance invigorates, astonishes the senses while it soothes my heart and mind.

Most soothing of all is the quiet drifting rain of leaves around me. I've always found the sound of the wind in trees one of the most seductive occurrences in nature. This interplay of one element with another is more than sensuous; there's something of worship, something of revelation in it. Trees are wind harps, on which a force of nature that is scientifically measurable and explicable, though ultimately ineffable, proclaims the essential mystery of life for those who will listen. In this season the whispers of the desiccated leaves are all about transition, renewal, dying to be reborn. I get the message. I take it in.

On weekends and in the afternoon when my schedule allows, I walk five or six miles at a time, hiking half the distance in one direction, then returning to where I've parked the car. The next time out I park where I turned around the last time so each walk is different, a new adventure. I'm getting a feeling for the lay of the land and the way people live on it that I didn't have when I was growing up here.

I'm far more sensitive to the environment than I was then -- or perhaps I should say more *aware* of my sensitivity. Now I perceive my surroundings not just more consciously but with an almost acquisitive sense of enjoyment, even wonder, that I don't remember having before. When I was a boy in town or a teenager hiking through the woods with the family dog, I'm sure that much of the time I felt everything even more vividly than I do now, though of course I lacked the wisdom then to appreciate the miraculous gift of experience and all that lies behind it: life, the senses, the physical world. I took it all for granted.

I certainly didn't ruminate on experience the way I do now. Now, on a good day -- on even a rather ordinary fall day on one of my walks -- I feel as if I'm on the verge of intuiting the very essence of the secret to life: my own, inseparable as it appears to be from the whole of nature.

At such times my separation from Carlotta is not only more easily bearable but endowed with a sense of inevitability; and I'm able to carry the small epiphany back with me into the everyday world, even if it does lose something in transition. Gradually I come to see how I have rationalized events between and concerning the two of us to make them more acceptable to myself: how of course Carlotta's behavior, however much influenced by her prior experience, was *always* a reflection of my own in one way or another. And therefore how futile it is and always was to isolate certain aspects of it and blame them for our problems. Doesn't the exclusive nature of a monogamous relationship inexorably bind one person's behavior to the other's, the way the circle in which they're enclosed wraps the components of the symbol for yin and yang around each other?

But I knew this all along, I just didn't give it enough significance before. After all, how are you going to solve the problems in a relationship without identifying those things the other does that drive you up the wall, bringing them to his or her attention, and asking for some kind of change? I guess it comes down to being willing, or not willing, to listen, I tell myself for the hundredth time. If Carlotta had listened more carefully, would we have been able to focus better on the symbiotic relationship between her jealousy and my inadequate expression of love for her?

Words. All this mental masturbation about a relationship that might have been just makes more poignant the loss of the one we had. One day, standing on a ridgeline at dusk and looking out over several square miles of farmland and rolling hills, I see Carlotta as though she were right before me. The childlike expression on her face alternates between joy and grief but both tear my heart. Oh, Carlotta, why couldn't I have come to you free of the disappointments in my past? Why couldn't the boldness with which I won your heart have *lasted* for once? Why didn't I have the balls and the backbone, the wisdom and the willpower to *live* the overwhelming love I feel for you at this moment? It's real, I know it is!

I just don't know how to keep it alive day after day when the rest of my life keeps intruding and sapping my energy. You could never understand what I meant by having to *work* at our relationship; it bothered you that I would use that word in describing how I felt about us. But it *is* work to change yourself, Carlotta!

It's the hardest work I know.

24

Are you wondering by now whatever came of the telephone conversation between Walter Barry and me? I've sort of dropped the ball on that. He got back to me all right, right away in fact. Said he had a strong hunch about the location of the contamination source from the map dowsing he'd done. So, mixing my sports metaphors here a little, the ball's back in my court now. All I have to do now is go down and convince City Service Director Dean Channel that his people may have been drilling in the wrong place all this time, and that he should allocate funds for a new test well. All this on the word of a man he's never met, from map dowsing the mystery man has performed -- don't ask me how -- on some diagrams I sent him from the local paper.

Or, I can come up with the financing myself somehow. I can realize one of my career ambitions of being a producer, right here in River City. Not of a mere movie in this case but of reality programming of the realest kind, where a community's water supply is at stake. That is, if I'm really (pick one) dumb, foolish, naive or ballsy enough to get involved in this after all.

Was I subconsciously hoping Walter would turn me down, or what? Since contacting him I've continued to scan the paper for more information about progress or the lack of it at the well site, but there hasn't been anything significant. Capital Drilling continues to pour money into test wells that Andy Byers would have me believe are really taxpayer-sponsored ratholes. And speaking of business as usual, Rockner Hardwoods could use a lot more of my attention these days. I'd be ready to tell Walter to forget the whole thing if it weren't for Andy's suspicions of a cover-up. However remote that possibility, it seems to make our contamination problem more urgent than ever.

Resurrecting the short-lived journalism career which began my California sojourn, I've actually been doing some investigative reporting on my own. Almost everyone I've asked about the well has been willing to talk to me: executives at Chemlab and Capital Drilling, Geologic Survey's owner, reporters at the *Lafayette News* and a couple of other leads that have turned up. When asked about my interest I say I'm writing a book; no one's even objected to my taping our interviews with a small cassette recorder.

The only person who still hasn't returned my calls is a city councilman I feel I know well enough to get some honest answers from. In addition, Ohio EPA is due in town any day now to inspect the well-testing project, and I'm going to try to talk to someone on their staff while they're here. In my new role as a small businessman I've learned to be leery of the EPA; we've all heard horror stories of their driving companies out of business. You pay even more attention when you're responsible for meeting a whole raft of EPA regulations yourself. So far, I've found them to be understanding, reasonable people to deal with.

So while I can certainly sympathize with well-meaning companies tangled up in the kind of bureaucratic regulatory nightmares that make good newspaper copy, perhaps I'm a little less likely now to be misled by mismanaged corporate scofflaws who attempt to blame all their financial problems on government regulation. The possibility of a cover-up on the scale Andy suggests is worth sticking my neck out for.

There have been other suggestions that all is not as it should be with the well-testing, now entering its second year, but nothing on the order of Andy's allegations. I thought I was definitely onto something when one of the Chemlab execs gave me the name of a man who'd supposedly witnessed drums being buried at night over a long period of time years ago near the site of the present-day well field.

Why hasn't the paper reported this, I wondered, excitedly dialing a number listed in the phone book. Maybe because the *News* found it to be the same false lead I did. The elderly gentleman claimed he'd been misquoted, that in fact he'd *denied* rumors of any drums having been buried near his home. "I've lived here pretty near all my life," he told me. "If there'd been anything buried here besides a few dog bones, I'd have known about it, believe me."

Possible perpetrators of the contamination have been named: the hospital for one. Riverside Memorial sits on a hill overlooking the river and well site, and in the past has reportedly dumped all kinds of toxic stuff down the drain. Could this have included PCE, and could some of it have ended up in the ground instead of the Thothwillow River? Another plausible miscreant is a company which for many years has fabricated and welded pipe directly across the river from the well field. Could this firm have used PCE at one time as a pipe-cleaning solvent?

But although questions such as these have occupied my mind, they really haven't commanded much of my time since I last talked with Walter. In the press of business obligations and the rest of my life going by, I just can't seem to get motivated to go any further with the project. Maybe after the EPA has had its say about the well-testing, I'll know where to turn next.

I finally had a date with Leslie; it was everything, in terms of feeling anyway, for *me*, that our abbreviated evening together when I was still with Carlotta couldn't possibly have been. But things have gone no further between us since then. It turns out that Leslie is seeing someone else, and I'm the one who failed to make the cut. I was a little hurt by this of course, disappointed; and I suppose Leslie's rejection is making the separation from Carlotta even harder to take. But compared to the loss I feel for Carlotta, this particular setback is a minor one. Besides, I can't help feeling that karma's involved here. How can I possibly feel sorry for myself when, from occasional phone calls I've made to her, I know how much Carlotta is still hurting? The truth is, I don't feel the least self pity.

But as the weeks go by and the silences between our few phone calls -- all initiated by me -- lengthen, I begin to feel a need for the kind of nurturing Jimmy talked about. Or if not nurturing exactly, at least the warmth of a woman's arms around me, the warmth of a woman within my own. I keep remembering the lunch I had with Brook some time ago. *There's* a woman who appears to be warmth incarnate. But I haven't seen her for quite a while, maybe I'm exaggerating; maybe memory has embellished her sweet smile, raised its emotional temperature a few unwarranted degrees.

This sort of conjecture just makes me more interested in her, out of curiosity if nothing else. But there is more, some part of my nature keeps telling me. Finally I call her, we have a pleasant conversation, I find her even more amusing than I'd remembered and just as warm-*sounding* anyway. I ask her to come to dinner -- one of my first invitations to my new house -- and she accepts.

New Age Books & Crystals

Fri Jun 7-96 12:29pm #0012 H

Title/ISBN	Qty	Price	Disc	Total	Tax
DOWSING FOR LOVE					
0964925216	1	17.50		17.50	1

	Subtotal	17.50
	GST (Tx1)	1.23

Items	1 Total	18.73
	Cash	20.00
	Change Due	1.27

Final Sale
Exchange or Credit Only

25

Jimmy calls the office the next day to invite me out on his boat after work. He's going to be taking it out of the water over the weekend and reminds me that I haven't been on the river with him since early in the summer when Carlotta and I went skinny-dipping with him and his wife Sarah. This is partly due to the breakup between Carlotta and me and partly because for the first time since my return to Lafayette, my daughters weren't able to vacation with me this year. In summers past I've spent many afternoons and evenings skiing with Jimmy and his girls, Carlotta and my own, or cruising with Jimmy and a cooler of beer up and down the Ohio or its tributary the Thothwillow.

Jimmy's boat is a beautiful old solid-wood Sportsman Chris-Craft, mahogany trimmed with teak, that spends most of each summer in the shop or his garage being worked on. Even when shipshape its 115-horsepower inboard isn't powerful enough to make "Woody" much of a ski-boat. But its classic looks and status, the nostalgia-inducing throaty rumble of its unreliable but undeniably ancient ('58) engine -- the aquatic equivalent of Hollywood mufflers on a '55 Ford -- give Jimmy all the pride of ownership one could ask for in recreational riverine transportation. For Jimmy, pulling-power alone is no match for the sentimental pull of the past.

His is one of a flotilla of mismatched pleasure craft bobbing gently alongside the Lafayette Boat Club's floating dock upstream from the mouth of the Thothwillow: everything from outboard bass boats to phallic-looking cigarette boats, pontoon-supported houseboats, and cabin cruisers large and seaworthy enough for coastal ocean travel, though none of these is likely to get much closer to the Gulf of Mexico than Cincinnati.

We remove Woody's waterproof cover, stow our towels and beer, and Jimmy maneuvers out into midstream, holding the engine to little more than a deep guttural idle because of the no-wake zone prevailing for three-hundred yards on either end of the dock. I hand a beer to the skipper, open one for myself and lean back against the padded seat, inhaling the cool evening breeze flowing like another, lighter river along the surface of the Thothwillow. The way my tired, tense body is relaxing as we head upstream, it feels as if it too may reach a state of liquefaction before we return to the dock.

Jimmy and I don't say much at first, then languorously bring each other up to date on my family business and his job-hunting, which has resulted so far in two offers he's turned down and a West Coast interview he'll be flying out to next week. I can tell his apparent nonchalance is more an attempt to keep his hopes in check than lack of interest in a position that sounds perfect for him career-wise. It would also take him back to Phoenix, a move he's ambivalent about because his daughters would probably stay here.

As usual, he asks about my parents, to whom he's been close since we were in high school together, as I have to his. I start to reply with the same old "Oh they're OK, considering," but decide instead to share with him the concern I'm feeling for both of them these days. Maybe it's the river, maybe it's because he may be leaving soon.

"Dad's about the same," I begin -- "I don't think he'll ever get over going into Chapter 11, even though he's the one most responsible for getting us back out again."

When we were growing up together in the forced perspective of adolescence which made this small town the greater part of our world, Jimmy and his twin brother idolized my father, a dashing, stylish man who worked and played hard. Johnny in particular saw him as the swashbuckling

160

owner of his own company: successfully dealing with the rough kind of men who've always been associated with the lumber business; continually investing in new and better equipment; buying timber holdings and financing small sawmills in the area to augment his own hardwood production; taking half a dozen phone calls every night after dinner -- yet still able to call his time his own.

Dad often attended football practice on fall afternoons and drove us to our junior high games, where he was always the loudest, most involved spectator on the sidelines. President of the Tiger Boosters Club our junior year when we were undefeated and ranked sixth in the state, he was instrumental in obtaining new lights for the high school stadium. One of his tractor-trailers hauled them here from somewhere in the South

From the age of 12, I worked for my father every summer, first as a one-boy cleanup crew with rake, shovel and wheelbarrow, then as a lumber-handler. We spoke the same taciturn, often wordless language; the first half of a sentence between us was usually enough. Like any teenager, I felt he was often and unfairly on my case, but we got along. I respected him.

After his dreams for me no longer coincided with my developing sense of self-awareness, we experienced an extended period of estrangement. I skulked around the house for months, struggling to find the better part of myself, while Dad tried to hold his tongue. Wearying of this at last, he gave me $500 and the Chevy Impala I'd been driving and said, "Get the hell out to California if that's really what you want -- make something of yourself."

After that I was always glad to come home again. Those were my parents' good years, and they were there for me whenever I needed them. Now the time of famine's upon them, or so they perceive their lives. None of Dad's horses came through for him: the fullback with bad knees, the standardbreds he invested in when flush with success and money; last and most painfully of all, the business that had become so much a part of him he was mortally wounded when it finally gave way beneath him.

My mother, on the other hand, though she's stuck with what's left of Dad and the ruins of her failed if enduring marriage, refuses to give up. My thoughts turn to her as we head upriver.

"Mom and I aren't getting along very well at all," I tell Jimmy, finding my voice again. "Just your typical elderly parent quandary, I guess. She's miserable and the only advice I can offer she's not interested in hearing."

"Which is?"

"I'll probably feel as weird talking to you about it as I do with her -- but I think what might help Mom most right now is more of a spiritual perspective than she seems to have. Her health, her social life, most of the few dreams she still had are all falling apart. What's she have left? But where the hell do I get off trying to tell my mother how to become more spiritually inclined?...You know what I'm saying?"

"Sure, I guess so," Jimmy replies.

"You sound a little uncertain -- do you disagree? You know Mom almost as well as I do."

"That that's what she needs, or that you're the person to tell her?"

"Well, both."

"I'm not sure *anyone's* going to be much help to someone who's not ready to hear that kind of message."

"Yeah, I think you're right. On top of all my usual reasons for getting impatient with her, I end up feeling like such a self-righteous asshole."

Jimmy laughs. "*I* can understand that but that doesn't mean your mom feels the same way."

I give him the finger with one hand, take another swig of my beer in the other. "Yesterday, she asked me to help get some of her medical records straightened out for her. I said, sure, I'll be glad to help. Then she hands me this bulging folder full of doctors' bills, pharmacy receipts, AARP and Medicare forms and I don't know what else, and I see the mess things are in...I get real short with her and stalk out of the house with this overflowing folder, half-snarling. So much for good intentions when the real world intrudes, right?

"I told Mom, hey, I can only spend so much time with you and Dad, and if I'm going to spend it doing errands and paperwork, I can't spend it *visiting* with you. As if she has much choice. Dad always had one of his secretaries take care of that sort of thing. You can imagine how intimidating all this must be to her now."

"Hell, we all hate paperwork."

"Don't we. I eventually got hers done -- took damn near a whole morning. But the gracious way I went about it, she'd have been better off doing it herself."

"I'm sure she appreciates it, Rockner -- probably all the more so, knowing how much *you* hate it."

"She sure knows it now."

I'm well into my second beer. We're cruisin' along with no other boats in sight, moist heavy air riffling my hair and T-shirt, the cottonwoods and sycamores along both banks of the Thothwillow accentuating the river's broad channel. Though the sun's already dropped behind low rolling hills to the west, a mackerel sky of scattered cumulus and altocumulus commemorates its departure in gaudy reds and purples mirrored in turn by the river's shimmering surface. Squinting against the wind and bright water dazzles my work- and routine-dulled mind; before long I find myself waxing philosophical.

"The world sure is polarized where spirituality is concerned isn't it? I mean, on one hand you have the fundamentalist contingent, flogging the dogmas they use to judge the rest of us: the main focus of their various belief systems, it seems to me -- right?" Jimmy doesn't answer but seems receptive enough. "And at the other extreme of course are the 'secularist' non-believers. For them, spirituality is an escapist fantasy for the weak and mentally deficient. The fundamentalists have *co-opted* spirituality, and the secularists are too crippled by academic educations dictating what's real and what's not -- all those years of running on mental training wheels -- even to *consider* the possible existence of a spiritual dimension. It's a tainted concept."

"...What the hell are you talking about, Rockner?" Jimmy finally asks with that sarcastic smile of his. But in the mood I'm in now I'm undeterred.

"*Mom* -- she has nowhere to turn, no role models to follow. People who actually *experience* a spiritual dimension in their lives -- that sustains them and enriches their lives, without putting others down -- aren't much heard from in our society. And Mom isn't willing to look very hard for answers on her own."

"What kind of answers?"

"To what's troubling her so! She sure doesn't want to think about death, or the consequences of aging. So where does that leave her? 'Just tell me which tranquilizer to take. What antidepressant do you recommend?' All she can think of is how alone she is in the world now. Why is the whole goddamn intent of organized religion to create *distinctions* -- and then defend them to the death -- when the essence of spiritual longing is to put them behind us? To break *out* of our mentally conceived shells that isolate us and cut us off from experiencing life?"

I pop the tab on the last beer in the six-pack and, since Jimmy seems to have nothing to say at the moment, rave on. "It's not enough we have to argue about whether or not there's some kind of higher power and a *meaning* in life. Those who can agree on that have to kill one another over rules and regulations. Distinctions." With a sweeping gesture meant to include both the evening and the magnificent natural setting surrounding us, I ask rhetorically, "Why can't we just look around us, acknowledge the miracle of our being a part of all this and, regardless of its source, agree simply that nothing less than *reverence* is the proper response?"

"Reverence? You think reverence is going to make your mother feel better?"

"I think it's impossible to feel thankful for being alive and depressed at the same time. You can't feel both at once."

"Have you told her that?"

"I've tried to. But it's so hard to say that without sounding preachy or judgmental. She's said so herself. So I chicken out -- even though I believe in my heart that's what's best for her. I can't even tell Mom I love her and really mean it. I know it's true, but I usually can't *feel* it when I say it, so I'd rather not say it. You know what I mean? Reverence I have no trouble with, but love...that's a tough one."

"I know, that's always been a problem for you, Ace," Jimmy chuckles. "I don't know why."

"...Someone once asked the mother of a friend of mine in L.A., a Catholic, which of her eight children she loved the most. She thought about it for a moment, then said, 'Well, I guess the one who *needs* it the most.' *That* I can understand, you know? If Mom were sick or dying -- some kind of crisis, maybe when it was already too late -- then I'd be able to feel plenty of love, right? As it is...it makes me wonder, when Mom gives me this loving smile -- because of something I've done for her maybe or for no reason at all -- and all *I'm* experiencing is a sense of duty."

26

The week before my Saturday night dinner with Brook is a busy one. Several buyers from the wholesalers we do business with stop by, as well as a contingent from Japan, another one from Taiwan accompanied by people from the Ohio Department of Development, and a guy from Germany looking for a good source of white oak. I also have a meeting to discuss back payments due on one of our forklifts which the dealer is threatening to repossess; an inventory audit by the bank with whom we have a revolving working capital loan secured by lumber; the weekly management meeting with our production staff; a visit from a company wanting to see our new federally-funded wood-waste system, which is saving us a bundle by greatly reducing the consumption of natural gas by our boilers; scheduled appointments with a handful of people who want to sell me something or provide some kind of service I can't afford to be without...in addition to the normal multitude of less significant demands on my time. The one I'm looking forward to least is the management meeting. "What's going on," everybody wants to know, "are we going to make it or not?"

Saturday finally rolls around and it's a gorgeous late fall day -- football weather. I get up early enough to get most of the cleaning done so I'll have time for a walk. Lately I've been hiking on a gravel township road along a ridge that takes me twenty minutes or more to drive to. But it's worth it: the views are spectacular, and a car comes by only about every fifteen minutes or so, if that. I'm feeling great when I get back. I shower, put on some music, pour myself a glass of wine and go out on the deck to wait for Brook.

The Chardonnay sharpens my anticipation to just the right edge. It feels very pleasant to be sitting here in the late-afternoon sun waiting for someone new to enter my life. I notice the cat react before I hear Brook's car myself.

Hidden from County Road 36 by trees, my house sits in a clearing at the end of a long winding gravel drive; approaching vehicles are halfway from the road before they can be seen or heard. I'm surprised to see Brook drive up in a classy little Fiat convertible with the top down. My nameless cat does her usual disappearing act at the arrival of strangers, and I get up and walk through the house to meet my guest, wondering whether this is the beginning of a new chapter in my life or just a stimulating interlude.

Brook is wearing a pretty summer dress in a soft clingy knit fabric which shows off her shapely figure. She seems a little startled when I hug her, but conversation flows easily enough from the moment she walks through the door. She oohs and ahs over how my little glassed-in bachelor treehouse looks out over the forest, and I can tell that she really sees the charm and beauty in the place. I think some people see it as small and poorly furnished, period.

She looks at all the photographs of my daughters, in the beautiful hardwood picture-frame moulding the company has been unsuccessfully trying to market for the past year or so, makes friends with my cat, then sits with me on the deck sipping demurely from her glass of wine.

"Do you know that I've seen you out walking before?" she suddenly asks me.

"You have? Where?"

"Oh, several places. I run, and I used to see you from a distance, always from behind. I recognized you from your walk."

"No kidding. Why didn't I ever see you -- were you avoiding me?"

"Of course not," she says a little indignantly. "I'm not out there to meet people when I run."

"I'm not either -- when I walk I mean -- but I'm surprised we never passed each other."

"The only person I can remember talking to is an old man who gave me his favorite walking stick when he found out he had cancer. Mr. Rinard. He was a neighbor of mine, a widower. He used to walk for four or five hours at a time."

"How'd you happen to talk to him?"

"The first time I saw him I was coming back to my house. I was ready to stop and walk for a while to cool off anyway. After that I always stopped and walked with him."

She gets a distant look in her eye for a moment but then brushes it aside. "He knew something about every house we'd pass -- not just the people who were living there, but the different people who'd lived there for generations. He was a clerk in a hardware store in town for forty-some years. I don't know whether you'd know this, but when you're a clerk in a small town you're almost like a counselor to people. He told me stories about each house and farm we'd pass, the dogs he'd defended himself from with his walking stick...do you know, when he gave that to me the end of it was worn so smooth by his thumb after all those years, it was indented a little and just as smooth as glass."

Brook's story establishes a deeper level of intimacy between us. When I ask her about teaching, she tells one funny story after another about the kids in her reading-disability classes. The more mischievous they are the more she loves them. It's not hard to guess how they must feel about her, with her quick infectious laugh and her sense of humor.

"This one little boy, third grader named Timmy Potter's, my favorite," she tells me. "Hates school, mean as a snake sometimes, ornery..." She lets the word trail out as if the bounds to Timmy Potter's orneryness have yet to be surveyed and duly recorded in his already bulging office file.

"Can't read of course or he wouldn't be in my class, but he's years ahead of anyone else I have in street smarts.

He's either going to be very successful or in jail most of his life, I don't know which."

"These days maybe both."

"That's true," she agrees, chuckling. "The other day he came in and told Larry -- that's the principal -- that so-and-so had used the 'J-word'. Larry's sitting there at his desk trying to figure out what the heck the J-word could be. But his mind's a blank, and Timmy can't sit still for more than 30 seconds, tops. Finally Larry says, 'The J-word? What's the J-word, Timmy?'

"Timmy says, 'You know...the J-word,' with this cocky little smile on his face as if Larry's just puttin' him on, trying to get him to say it.

"'I don't know what the J-word is, Timmy,' he says, 'you're going to have to tell me. Come over here and whisper it to me if you can't say it out loud.'

"So Timmy comes around the side of his desk," -- here Brook's face begins to get a little red and she starts to giggle at the same time -- "and whispers the word in his ear." By now she's laughing so hard she can't go on -- or is reluctant to.

"So what was the word?" I ask, laughing now too, simply because she is.

"I can't repeat it," she says, "but it's more commonly referred to as the 'F-word'."

This sets Brook off again in another peal of her musical laughter. "Larry came in and told me right after class, and we couldn't stop laughing for five minutes."

"The J-word!" I'm laughing too, as much from Brook's losing it right now as from anything else, though I can see the two of them -- Brook and the principal -- throwing up their hands at the task the community expects of them, giving in to helpless if not hopeless hilarity at such a priceless example of the position our schools are in these days.

"It's what we face every day," Brook gasps, wiping

her eyes. "The J-word," she mutters, shaking her head.

When I get up to fix dinner, she goes out on the deck to enjoy the sunset for a few minutes, then comes back in to examine my landscape photos in the living-area part of the house and to check out some of the titles of the books on my shelves before coming over to keep me company. My galley kitchen is no more than a lineup of sink, appliances and counter space along one wall of the living area. She stands there watching -- close enough for me to hug her a couple of times -- asking interested questions about my cooking and talking to me while I throw together a tossed salad, then sauté some bay scallops and shrimp. Brown rice with raisins and pecans has been simmering on a back burner for half an hour.

Looking down into Brook's smiling eyes, I try to read what's going through her mind but without much success. A couple of times I start to kiss her but each time she gently turns her face away, then looks back at me with an expression asking for understanding -- and, I hope, patience.

After dinner we end up sitting on the floor in front of the fireplace, though it's too warm for a fire, and at her request I read some of my poetry. I have to haul over my laptop to do this and read rather awkwardly off the screen since I don't keep any of my writing here at the house. She seems at least moderately impressed and pleased that I'd want to share the poems with her, but it isn't until I've read one called "Asymptotic Journey" that she chooses to comment beyond a simple, "That's nice," or "I like *that* one."

"ASYMPTOTIC JOURNEY"

From the Greek: *asymptotos*
  not meeting
Remember parabolas & hyperbolas
the sets of curves we constructed
in high school algebra?
One was in a class by itself

170

Asymptote: the mind bender
The curve that approaches
always approaches
some limit like the X or Y axis
   without ever getting there

No matter what value you plug in
no matter how long or how often
that stubborn curve
the apotheosis of intransigence
and approach/avoidance behavior
just keeps gearing down
into ever more micro dimensions
of mathematical being

A glide path whose absolutely smooth
   trajectory
unblemished by the slightest deviation
the greatest pilot can only envy
the glide path that never gets there

Contemplate for a moment
the incredible saga of the curved line
spending all eternity
getting closer and closer
to its destination
and never
ever
arriving

Actually
it has a vaguely familiar ring
doesn't it?
Come to me
my asymp-totic BA-a-by!
   or
Gon-na take an as-symp-tot-ic jour-ney...

I sigh and get out of bed
to wander out onto the front porch
in the dead of night

On this warm October evening
in a sibilant whisper
the oak tree's dry leaves
seem to murmur
the answers to life's oldest mysteries

I listen intently
to the melodious revelation
that surrenders not even a syllable
  to meaning
though it transmits it whole
Or transcends it

I listen and am soothed

The moonless sky is so clear
I can see constellations
normally invisible here
Cassiopeia
vain queen of Ethiopia
to the left of the red oak
Her unfortunate husband Cepheus
glimpsed through its shimmering boughs
What matter that she and I are
  estranged
when the leaves assure me
that all we know is suspect
We yearn for what we have

What matter my fickle heart
my silverplated tongue
tarnished by silence
Her deflated hopes and pride
her self-pity
Our unconsummated reach

Later
I walk the gleaming ribbon
  of asphalt
that follows this ridge
out to where both descend again
into planted fields and bottomland

So clear and dark is the night sky
that for the first time in years
for the first time since
returning to my hometown
I can see the Milky Way!

I am awestruck as always

Looking with such longing
at the glorious center
  of our galaxy
I am reminded of a kid on some prairie
  highway
gazing at the distant bright lights
  of the Big City

Then I remember the definition
  of "asymptote"
I came across years ago
and catch my breath

Is it true?
Like lovers desperate to merge
with the beloved
like seekers longing to know God's plan
are we destined forever only to reach out
to *approach* the heart's desire?

In our lives on this tiny planet
far out on the galactic rim
will we always remain just
"tangent at infinity"?

When I finish there's rather a long silence, then Brook asks me to read it again and I do. This time she says, "I like it a lot, but I'm surprised it sounds so fatalistic. Did you mean it that way: that we're sort of stuck somewhere -- humanity I mean -- 'tangent at infinity', and we're never going to be able to progress beyond this point?"

The fact that she finds the poem worth discussing

takes me pleasantly by surprise. "Well, remember, it's posed as a question: *are* we destined only to reach out and never actually achieve some of the things we desire the most? I think it's a legitimate question, don't you?"

"Oh, sure I do -- I was just surprised to hear you ask it, I guess. I don't know why I should be, I don't know you that well after all."

This opens a discussion of our personal interests. I decide to tell Brook about my currently-in-limbo dowsing project, including my resistance, now that I've come this far, to taking the next step. Her enthusiastic curiosity soon has me telling her everything I know about the subject -- not much, although as you've observed, more than most people care to hear.

"...Whether you're talking about a magic wand, a witching stick, or a dowsing rod," I say, "you're talking about some kind of 'psychoenergetic' instrument -- is one thing it's been called -- that, if it works at all, apparently does so by means of some kind of non-physical energy that science doesn't recognize. And since I've *seen* dowsing rods work, I think it's just a matter of time until science comes to understand this kind of energy and incorporates it into a better, fuller understanding of the world we live in. Then, from understanding, should come all kinds of practical applications.

"So in other words, I guess where I'm going with all this is, sure, I *do* think we're bound by certain limitations, whether you're talking about individuals or mankind in general. But I think many of them are only temporary. Maybe they all are. Dowsers, with their 'magic' sticks, may be pointing the way to a future few people can imagine. You see what I mean?"

Brook nods her head rapidly, arching her eyebrows to show her interest.

"Or another way to look at it is that the dowsing rod may represent -- not only symbolically but in a very concrete example -- a bridge to a whole new dimension of reality, that has always been there but that's been beyond the knowledge of most people. Beyond the *consensual* knowledge that basically determines what society considers 'real' and what's not real....Am I making any sense, Brook, or am I just spouting gobbledygook at you?"

"No, no, I understand what you're saying, I *think*," she replies. I sense that she understands more than she realizes, and the best thing for me to do now is shut the hell up. "You'd think, though, that in this day and age if dowsers are really able to find water, scientists would have been trying to find out how they do it long ago."

"You'd think so, wouldn't you. But, you know, scientists aren't the only people who'd rather look the other way than change their minds about what's real. Even our film crew, when we were shooting the TV series, got so they just didn't give a damn one way or the other about whether what we were seeing was true or not. It wasn't just skepticism, or cynicism -- it went beyond that; I felt it a little bit myself. I guess something strange enough, and significant enough, that it could conceivably change your notion of reality, you'd just rather not think about if you don't have to. Maybe that's a defense mechanism built into the human mind. Maybe it's just as well that we *don't* change our minds too easily about something that fundamental. But if it is then I think, like any defense mechanism, it gets in the way a lot of times when it shouldn't. It stands in the way of changes that *should* be made -- that would be to mankind's advantage if they were.

"Another problem is the type of individual who tends to get involved in any kind of scientific exploration outside the establishment, like dowsing. You get a guy like Walter Barry, cut off from the scientific community -- *frozen* out of it is more like it -- and he begins to feel a little defensive after a while. Downright self-righteous in Walter's case. It's hard to blame them, but it sure doesn't do their cause any good."

Brook, who has been listening intently the whole time, suddenly hits me with a real zinger. "Why on earth if you believe all this are you so reluctant to go in and talk to Dean Channel about a dowser? How else are people going to learn? The worst thing he can do is say no."

Damn! the woman is something else. "Good question," is my lame answer.

She makes a few more encouraging remarks, gives me a snappy little pep talk, but I think we're both tired of talking by now. What I really want to do is touch her, hold her in my arms, nuzzle my face against hers, against her body. She's so petite, the soft curves of her body are so inviting. Her slim brown legs are as shapely as a showgirl's, in miniature. But either I sense that she's not ready for this, or I'm not quite myself. So instead I go in and get some body lotion from my nightstand and offer her a foot massage: the *piece de resistance* of any dinner for two at my place. I used to give them to my daughters all the time; they'd chirp like baby birds for foot massages.

Brook doesn't sing for me, but she closes her eyes sensuously while I'm working on her small feet. I spend a good twenty minutes on them, she's almost asleep when I finish. And then?...well, it's about time to call it a night. Nothing more's going to happen. I'm certainly not going to try to force it to; by now Brook's sense of time seems as natural, as suited to her, as the playfulness in her eyes or her quick smile, and I feel in tune with it as well.

I walk her to her car, where we exchange one last long warm hug. I'm not sure she'd like me to kiss her goodbye. But I do anyway, gently. And when she feels no pressure in the kiss, I feel her relax and kiss me back, lightly. Then we pull away just far enough to look into each other's eyes. It's been a good night, hers say, with an expression of faint surprise as if only now is she realizing just *how* good. I couldn't agree with her more.

27

Bright and early Monday morning after my Saturday night dinner with Brook I'm in Dean Channel's office with a map of the well field in a file folder on my lap, telling him more about my years in L.A. than he ever expected to hear. I can see him wondering why, even as he appears to be taking a genuine interest in the concise career summary I've related a number of times since returning to my hometown.

"'Psychic phenomena' huh? Well I knew you'd been involved in some kind of TV series in California. I never knew what it was."

"Some of it was pretty hokey stuff," I admit right up front as I'm usually careful to do, "but other things I was really impressed by. Some of the unorthodox healers, in particular. But what I came in here to tell you about, Dean, is what I learned about *dowsing* while we were doing the series."

"Uh huh, dowsing -- for water you mean," he replies guardedly. "I always heard it called 'water witching' around here. Used to use a hazel rod, I believe it was."

"Right," I agree, feeling myself nodding my head a little too affirmatively, pleased with how the conversation is progressing. I decide to back off a little. "But apparently, what you use isn't really that important. My father told us when we were kids about a man who found a gas line over at the lumberyard with nothing but a pair of coathangers."

"No kidding?" He's smiling now, interested, putting himself in the story. "I can see our sewer line inspectors wanderin' around town with a coathanger in each hand, can't you? Keepin' the budget down, we'd tell people."

We both chuckle at this. Then I can sense him feeling the subtle but peremptory reverberations of time's winged chariot rumbling through the bowels of the city building and decide it's time to cut to the chase.

"...Anyway, dowsing's fairly common in Southern California. There are a lot of homes and ranches out there that get their water from wells located by dowsers. We filmed one of the most successful of any of them, a guy named Walter Barry, in our TV series. Had all kinds of testimonial letters from people he'd found water for. I met some of them: one couple lived in this huge house made out of bridge timbers, overlooking the ocean in Big Sur. Beautiful home on top of one a those cliffs you've probably seen photographs of along Highway One. God knows how many acres -- several hundred anyway. She was the daughter of one of the founders of Lockheed, when it was restructured back in the '30s. Walter Barry found three wells for them. They couldn't say enough for him."

"I know where you mean. The wife and I were out there three or four years ago. We have a son in the oil business in Bakersfield."

Wondering whether Dean's still stuck there along scenic Highway One or, God help him, in Bakersfield, I decide to keep the narrative momentum rolling. "Really? Well you know what I'm talking about then. Anyway, Dean, I contacted this guy the other day and told him about our contamination problem here with Well Six. Then I sent him some articles from the paper, including a couple of diagrams of the area."

"...I'm with you so far," he replies a little doubtfully.

"The reason I sent him the diagrams -- there's a kind of dowsing you may not be familiar with, Dean, that appears to be as authentic as any other kind. I say 'appears' because I don't claim to be any more of an expert on this than you are, just more exposed to it than you maybe. Anyway, it's called map dowsing. You dowse using maps, rather than being at the actual location."

I give him the same brief explanation that so impressed my mother weeks ago -- about this being just a preliminary step, not a substitute for on-site exploration -- then pause, having caught myself leaning forward there at the end, crowding Dean a little. He's getting restless; how's he taking this so far? He gets up, comes around to the front of his desk and perches on the front corner in front of me.

"Go ahead," he says, "I'm still following you. It's getting a little far out there for me, though."

"I know -- bear with me just a little longer."

"Fire away."

"I'm not *too* naive. I know the city can't get publicly involved with a dowser, not here in the Midwest. But what about some kind of behind-the-scenes arrangement, where there's no city money involved, not up-front anyway? The reason I ask, Dean, is that this Barry thinks he's found the source of the contamination -- by map dowsing."

I open the file folder and take out the map of the area I've brought with me but keep it to myself for the moment. Dean, growing increasingly fidgety, starts to get up and interrupt, but I manage to hold him off a little longer.

"Let me just add one more thing if I may, Dean," I plead, raising my hand. "I'm pretty sure I can make a deal with Barry to come back here and verify the location -- by dowsing here at the actual site -- so it won't cost the city a dime. And it doesn't have to be public knowledge; I'll take care of that part myself. Then, if it turns out that he can't confirm the location -- or if, for *any* reason, you decide not to go any further, we just let it go at that. Nothing's been lost, and no one needs to know anything about it. But if he *does* come up with some convincing evidence of where the source of the contamination may be located, we could drill a test well there and maybe end up saving the city thousands, maybe *tens* of thousands of dollars. What do you think?"

Dean can no longer restrain himself from getting up and pacing.

"...Well, I appreciate your interest, Cork, I really do. It takes guts and a real sense of civic responsibility to come forward with something...different like this. But I have a responsibility too. When you say 'convincing evidence', convincing to who? What might be convincing to you and this Water, I mean Walter, Barry wouldn't necessarily be convincing to the city. Do you see what I'm saying? And it would be awful hard to keep something like this secret, off the record as you say.

"I'm not saying anything against dowsing, you understand. I don't know enough about it to say for or against. Maybe out West, where you say dowsers are used a good bit, something like this would be a little more feasible. The public would be easier to educate. But here...I just don't see how it would work. It could very well end up being a disaster in fact."

"...I understand your position, Dean. I figured it'd be a hard sell."

"The other problem is, there probably wouldn't be enough time to *drill* a test well based on anything he found. At the next council meeting -- that's, what? ten days from now -- we're going to ask council approval to drill another round of wells, and we've already determined their location. I don't think there'd be time to bring this guy in here and drill another well before we got started. And I sure wouldn't want *two* drilling companies working there in the same area....Where does your man think the contamination's coming from?"

Is this an opening? I lean forward eagerly to show him the map of the area. "Here in this vacant lot northwest of the well field. I went down there this morning and looked at it. It's real wet there -- marshy almost."

"I know where you mean. We almost drilled there ourselves, but the results we've gotten so far indicate the contamination's in the other direction, near the softball field. That's where we're going to drill next: right along the first-base line and into right field. We're going to upset a lot of people, I'm afraid."

Something else I can use! "Yeah, I can imagine, especially if you don't find anything. Let me ask you this then, Dean. What if I *can* get a test well drilled in time -- and *I* come up with the money somehow? Would you permit that? If I took all the financial risk, and didn't hold up the drilling you want to do?"

"...Do you have any idea what that would cost, Cork? We're talking about a well maybe 200 feet deep through rocks and heavy gravel. Then we'd have to leave the pipe in the ground and put in a well screen so we can continue to monitor water quality. All that's not cheap: could be as much as $10,000."

Damn, Jimmy was right on the money. Just when I'd begun to think of snatching victory from defeat's pitiless Spielbergian jaws. "...I'm still willing to try. If it's all right with you."

"Wellll...as long as it's not city money, and you use a reputable drilling company -- I'd prefer you use the same people we are if they're available, they know the conditions here...I guess it's all right with me. I'll have to tell Bill Spriggs, the city attorney, about this. He'll probably raise hell but I can deal with him. There'll be a number of conditions you'll have to adhere to of course."

Anxious to bring the meeting to a close now, Dean thrusts out his hand and adds briskly, "Let me know what happens! Good luck."

"Thanks, Dean!" I exclaim, standing and gripping his big rough hand gratefully. But my brain is already whirling from the meeting's sudden reversal. Turning to leave his office, I feel a little dizzy. Is this what they mean by being careful about what you ask for, because you might get it?

28

"Walter? Cork Rockner. They agreed to let you do
it!...Right -- now all I have to do is come up with the money
somehow for a test well....I know, that's *my* problem. But
here's a problem we both have. We've gotta get you here, and
the well drilled, in the next ten days. How soon can you get
here?...Well, they're gonna start drilling a whole new series of
wells then -- unless we convince them to do
otherwise....Yeah....Really? Great! You want me to make the
reservations?...I'll call you back just as soon as I have 'em.
All right, next question: I'll front the plane tickets of course,
and all your expenses while you're here, but I'm wondering if
you'd be willing to make a deal with me on your dowsing
fee?...First of all, how much is it?...Wow....No, no, that's fair
enough. It's just more than I can handle, that's all.

"...Well, here's what I was thinking: From what you've
told me this sounds like the first time you've gotten involved
in an environmental issue quite like this, right? so I thought
maybe --...Well, *sure* it's environmental -- *I'd* say it's
environmental....Exactly. I was thinking it might represent a
whole new line of work for you: a whole new marketing area,
if you want to call it that....Right. With that in mind, would
you be willing to take only part of your fee up front -- say
half at the most -- in exchange for, let's say, twice the
remaining half, if you're successful?...Well, yeah, I could
probably get 'em to come up with three times. I think we
could live with that.

"Here's another thing: you've worked with a lot of
drillers, maybe you can help me come up with some ideas on
how to finance a test well....No, I don't mean it's your

responsibility, but any help you could give me along those lines would be greatly appreciated....Okay, Walter, I'll call you back as soon as I have the reservations....Yeah, this is gonna be a real adventure. See ya."

Ten days. Not much time to come up with $10,000 or whatever a new test well would end up costing. That's my assessment *before* actually beginning any prospecting. When I start putting together a list of potential donor/investors (they'll be investing in the safety of the city's drinking water after all) and making some initial phone calls, the limited time available for my fund raising seems to contract to the length of a long weekend.

There are all kinds of excuses for eliminating most of the names on my list when it comes to picking up the phone and actually calling them. I haven't put the bite on anyone yet; my calls at first are all to friends and acquaintances just to find out in a roundabout way who might have money to put into something like this. Although Jimmy finally suggested a couple of names neither of them has panned out.

I've raised money before but that just makes doing so now all the more difficult. A few years ago, long before I ever dreamed I'd be living in Lafayette again, I came back and raised $25,000 in local development financing for a movie I hoped -- and still intend -- to shoot here. Investors in that limited partnership have been extraordinarily patient and understanding; the last thing I want to do now is arouse their ire with a new project most would probably view as bizarre at best.

I've also solicited several thousand dollars in contributions the last three years for the community's nationally recognized arts and crafts festival. And, again, I'm not too thrilled with the idea of approaching these same loyal supporters for more money, no matter what the cause. Last but far from least, my hesitation stems from the death struggles of the family business and its many past-due accounts strewn around town.

This still leaves a number of legitimate prospects, but by the end of the week I've cautiously sounded out many of them to no avail. The rest are out of town, fail to return my calls or in other ways, subtle and otherwise, let it be known they're not interested in talking to me on this subject.

In the meantime, Brook and I have made a tentative date for a walk together the first nice weekday afternoon, which turns out to be Thursday. Even though thunderstorms are predicted there are only a few large scattered clouds in the sky when we start out together from my house after work.

I'm no arm-pumper and for my 6' height I'm short-legged. Like most small women Brook's a naturally fast walker. So we get a nice easy compatible pace going, talking at first but then gradually saying less, seeing more, feeling what it's like to be walking down this nearly deserted road together, holding hands with our arms swinging rhythmically between us.

Brook tells me more about life at home with her kids, I tell her about my own daughters, my great respect for single parents who do the actual child rearing, as opposed to absentee fathers like myself. She swipes a late tomato from a garden near the road and manages to eat it without dribbling juice down her chin or leaving her hands sticky. Examining the dried remnants of a toad squashed down into the gravel, she confesses to me her fascination for road kill.

She knows the names of some of the wildflowers we pass, I identify a few of the trees, although for a "lumberman" I'm tree-illiterate. "I'm ignorant about computers too," I tell her, "but I believe my bark is worse than my byte." Knowing even less about computers than I do, however, she doesn't get this, although she's tickled when I sheepishly explain it to her and confide that punning's not something I'm normally guilty of.

"I hope not!" she says.

Meanwhile, towering cumulus -- cumuli? -- have

begun to stack up and darken in the west. The lighting gets dramatic as the low sun finds ways to angle great shafts of light through them like heavenly golden staircases *a la* Cecil B. DeMille, his production designer obviously influenced by Maxfield Parrish. Country roads often follow a ridgeline, and with all this weather gathering over us this one seems to be thrusting us up against the sky. The wind picks up and distant thunder rumbles beyond the horizon. "If you ever get too old to find this exciting, you're in trouble!" I say to Brook, my voice raised.

"You think maybe we'd better turn around?" she asks, more delighted than concerned about the prospect of getting drenched.

"We'd better," I agree, "but you know we're going to get soaked anyway."

There's no place to run for cover and we're two or three miles from my house by now. You can see where it's raining in the distance. We try to cover as much ground as possible as the landscape to the west becomes steadily obscured by a translucent scrim sweeping toward us, but when the rain finally catches us in its icy embrace we give ourselves up to it.

It just pours down; the drops get fatter and heavier until all at once it's hailing. Hailstones the size of pebbles, of marbles, though nowhere near as hard, pepper the road and our soaked bodies while we spin slowly around with our arms extended, palms up, like trance dancers, big grins on our faces, soaked to the bone. I don't remember ever being so drenched before. Several cars stop for us, but we just laugh and thank them and wave them away, our clothes and streaming hair plastered against us. By the time we get to my house the rain is little more than a mist, but we're both cold.

"We can shower together or you can go first by yourself," I tell her, turning on the hot water and welcoming the steam that rolls off of it.

"N-no, you g-go first," she chatters.

185

"No way, get in here, you're freezing!"

"I'll b-be all right -- hurry up!" she insists.

No sense delaying this any longer. I peel off my wet clothes, hop into the tub-shower and pull the sliding glass door shut. The hot water is heaven but I'll have to make this quick. I'm just starting to suds up when the shower door opens and Brook steps in, white with cold and shivering miserably.

"I c-couldn't w-wait," she manages to get out.

Of course I wrap her in my arms at once -- she *is* cold -- absorbing the chill from her firm electric flesh, feeling the goosebumps all over her exquisite little body. My hands and arms come alive around her while she continues to shiver uncontrollably against me. But then gradually her movements soften and liquefy as the hot water streams down upon us, cementing our bodies which are soon moving in unison. When I kiss her our lips, too, are sealed by the warm water flowing over our faces.

Later we sit in front of the fire, Brook in a T-shirt and bulky sweater of mine and my sweatpants. My back's against the loveseat which faces the fireplace at an angle, with Brook leaning back against me enclosed in my arms. She's already called home to tell her kids why she's late.

"...I'm not really in the habit of asking men out," she says rather tentatively -- "in fact I'm still not much in the habit of *going* out. But some friends of mine are having a little get-together Saturday night and I wondered if maybe you'd like to go with me."

"Sounds like a great idea, Brook. Sure -- I'd love to."

"Good! One thing I have to warn you about first though. Remember Jimmy kidding me about our 'sweat baths'?"

"Yeah, I remember," I say, grinning.

"Well, we call them 'sweats', like the Indians have. They're part social gathering and part...well, like a cleansing ritual -- do you know what I'm talking about? Is that too far out, or does it sound like something that might appeal to you?"

"Hey, I'll try anything once," I reply with mock bravado in a macho tone of voice. "Actually, I've been wondering about it ever since Jimmy mentioned it. It sounds like some of the things we used to do in L.A."

"I thought that might be the case. I'd never have had the nerve to ask you otherwise."

"Why not?"

"Well, for one thing, most people do them -- the sweats I mean -- in the nude."

"I figured that."

"I was trying to work up the nerve to ask you to go with me, but I guess seeing each other naked isn't much of an issue anymore."

"Maybe it's not for you," I say, pouring it on really thick here, "but I don't think I'll ever get over seeing that body of yours in the raw."

"Oh, I like that," she says, playing along and snuggling up against me. "I like your body too, Mr. Rockner. The name suits you, buster."

I can tell she means this although she's flattering me, unfortunately. I grunt non-committally.

"Hey, nobody sees more bodies than a nurse," she persists. "You should be proud of yours."

I'm not, but I sure feel good in it right now.

29

By Saturday night I still haven't raised a dime for dowsing. I've already told Brook how her pep talk on our first date galvanized me into going in and selling my idea to Dean Channel. As we drive out to the sweat, she asks me where things stand and I confess that it doesn't look as if there's any way this project is going to happen. "I put enough down on my house when I bought it," I tell her, "that I could probably take out a second mortgage and finance the drilling myself. But I'm already personally liable on several of the company's notes and back taxes. I'd be a damn fool to extend myself any more right now when we could be in Chapter 11 in a month or two."

This threatens to lead to a discussion of the business -- the last thing I want to talk about -- and I thrash around looking for somewhere else to steer the conversation. It seems I've only gone from bad to worse when I suddenly find myself babbling about how it has become more and more apparent that Jimmy was right: the best prospect by far for a project like this would normally be Bud Knowland, Carlotta's brother. I've even discovered from one of my phone calls that right now he is in fact looking for some kind of "green" promotion, as my informant described it -- a way to sell Bud Knowland along with all of his computers, peripherals and software.

And of course, in explaining why this is now out of the question, we end up talking about my relationship with Carlotta and how it ended. Although Brook is interested in the subject, even fascinated by it, it's a fascination that makes us both uncomfortable -- as does the fact that I brought

Carlotta up in the first place. Silence has settled over the car by the time we arrive at the Savages' house in the country, where the sweat is to take place.

Not coincidentally, tonight is the harvest moon -- that's the full moon nearest the autumn equinox, for all you city folks. Brook has already told me her friends try to schedule their sweats as close as possible to the full moon in a month when they're going to have one, and it so happens that September's falls on a Saturday. I guess the fact that tonight is the harvest moon makes this sweat extra special.

At the end of the Savages' long recently slagged driveway we find half a dozen vehicles parked at random behind their renovated farmhouse. People are seated on logs around a large crackling bonfire blazing up midway between the house and a dilapidated-looking old barn. Reflecting the flames is a dome-shaped enclosure which Brook tells me consists of old sleeping bags and comforters covered with plastic to help hold in heat, laid over a framework of saplings which have been cut, bent into shape and tied down.

"I know most of these people from the arts and crafts festival," I tell her, "I just don't know any of them very well."

"Well they know you well enough for me to be bringing you. They're pretty careful about who comes, and Sonia said it was all right."

"I guess it isn't the sort of thing you'd want to broadcast," I agree.

"No, this isn't California; people could get the wrong idea. A friend of mine who doesn't know I'm one of the people she was talking about told me she'd heard that after the sweats the men go off naked into the woods and howl, and the women, also naked of course, come beat them with sticks."

We get a good chuckle out of this, then Brook adds, "Besides, it's an intimate experience. You want the people sharing it with you to be there for the same reasons you are."

"Simpatico huh?" I say, giving her a hug as we walk toward the fire.

"Simpatico," she says, smiling. She swings her hip playfully against me. "Hey, you sure you don't mind doing this in the nude?"

"Not if you think I'll measure up," I reply. She laughs, and Sonia Savage's husband Tom, standing by the fire with a pitchfork in his hands, spots us and calls out.

"Brook! You're just in time. Come on over."

"Hi, Tom. You know Cork, right?"

"Sure do -- glad you could come, Cork."

Tom is a hearty, boisterous fellow about 30 or so. He thrusts his hand out to me and proceeds to introduce the rest of the group, all somewhere in their 30's or early 40's. "This is Steve and Paula"...(She's a cutie with boyishly short hair; he has a full ponytail, not your fashionable little yuppie foal's tuft.)..."Reba and Nathan"...(He has straight shoulder-length hair framing a bald head, she's in loose-fitting clothing of her own design, which I know she sells successfully at arts and crafts shows all over the East and Midwest.)..."Karen and David"...(I'm surprised to see Karen, whom I know from a small print shop where we do business; her small body has been twisted by some crippling disease, and I wonder whether she intends to get naked with the rest of us. David gives us a thumb's-up welcome.) "Over there is Susanne"...(an earth mother who greets us with a warm smile..."and that's her husband Tony over by the sweat hut," (slender with long dark hair and an impish grin which he's sharing with Sonia, our hostess, at the moment).

"Have a seat, you two. We're just taking in the bricks," she says. "I'm Sonia, Cork. Good to see you, Brook." Sonia has an interesting slightly husky voice with a lilt in it, which somehow gives me the impression of someone floating with life more than fighting or struggling with it.

After greeting everyone Brook and I sit down on a

log in front of the fire. Tom thrusts his pitchfork into the coals and comes out with a red-hot firebrick.

"Fire in the hole!" he hollers.

Tony lifts a corner of the sweat hut's opening flap and Tom disappears inside with the brick balanced rather precariously on the tines of the pitchfork, then backs out with it empty. I notice that the couples are beginning to drift off into the shadows to undress.

Brook hands me a bath towel. "You can undress and leave your clothes inside the barn if you like," she says. "There should be a light on in there."

"Okay," I say, not particularly surprised that she still feels too shy to undress in front of me.

I walk over to the barn and she disappears into the dark. The night air is chilly against my bare skin, but I linger just outside the barn for a minute or two until I see others beginning to emerge from the shadows, their nude bodies either subtly reflecting or silhouetted by the fire. Either way it would be difficult to see specific features if you were looking for them, and I'm doing just the opposite: avoiding looking at anyone too closely, probably in this way trying to protect my own privacy somewhat.

I don't notice Brook until she's right beside me. I can tell she feels at least as awkward as I do, although she takes my hand and gives me a small forced smile. We have to stoop to enter the sweat hut, then crawl through a small opening into a pitch-black interior -- warm but not really hot yet and musty from the smell of the mildewed sleeping bags and comforters that make up the roof. There's no way to do this without exposing your ass royally, but I figure I can be as game as anyone else, and I make a point of looking the other way as Reba precedes me.

I can't see a thing inside. "Which way do I go?" I ask, feeling a little foolish.

"There's room over here," someone says -- "to the left." Hunkered over, the dirt floor of the hut cold against my feet, I feel my way in that direction -- carefully avoiding the firepit in the center -- until all at once I'm up against bare flesh, then ease my butt down onto a section of log with my back brushing against the side of the hut. Brook settles beside me a moment later, and then we all just sit there in the dark while the firebricks gradually begin to heat up the interior.

Finally Sonia asks, "Everyone have enough room?" There are murmurs of assent and she adds, with humor in her tone of voice: "Welcome, Cork, to our humble sweat hut." Brook gives my hand a squeeze. Already I can feel a sweat breaking out on my forehead, and my eyes and nostrils have begun to smart from the dry heat.

"Mmmmm..." says Sonia, "this feels so good. *Ahhhh.* I don't know about the rest of you but I've really been looking forward to this."

"*I* certainly have," says the person beside me, who only now do I realize to be Karen, apparently no more self-conscious about her body than any of the rest of us. "This past week's been murder. I think we got more orders out last week than the whole rest of the month put together."

"I'll bet Sid was a lot of fun to be around then, wasn't he." I recognize this as Tom's voice.

Karen snorts in what seems to me a sort of affectionate contempt. "He was frantic. Too much business makes him more uptight than no business at all."

Once again there is an extended pause, much longer this time, punctuated only by inarticulate animal sounds of pleasure and relief as everyone settles in. Then, although it's too dark for me to see clearly what he's doing, Tom appears to dip a cup into a bucket behind him and sprinkle water onto the red-hot bricks in the firepit. This produces a hissing cloud of steam and more exclamations -- including some not of pain exactly, but imbued with a sense of stoic endurance.

I'm starting to wonder just how long I can hold out; I'd hate to be the first to give up. At least one other couple came in behind Brook and me and are between us and the flap

I'd have to negotiate somehow in the dark to get out. I can see myself slipping on the slippery dirt floor and falling into the firepit.

Finally a new voice, a woman's, breaks the claustrophobic silence.

"Tony and I are going away this weekend. We've rented a cabin at Old Man's Cave. It's our tenth anniversary." This must be the earth mother, if I remember the introductions correctly.

"That's right! Congratulations, you two," someone else replies, followed by sincere-sounding comments from the others.

Susanne (it must be) says, "Thanks," and her husband -- in a tone pitched expertly between sincerity and irony -- adds the obligatory, "Seems like ten months at most."

"...It's beautiful there in the spring," Sonia says after a chorus of "Ahhhs" both sarcastic and genuine has died down. "Be sure to go to Ash Cave too if you have time."

"We're just gonna go...with the flowww," replies Tony.

Another long pause. Then all of a sudden someone -- Nathan I believe it is, although I'm starting to get all these voices in the dark confused -- lets out a big warwhoop followed by a Native American-sounding chant, and some of the others join in, all of them making their own sounds at different pitches. The chanting eventually trails off into another extended silence.

By now I'm extremely uncomfortable and remembering why I've never been much into saunas. The heat is more than oppressive, it's suffocating. My throat is so dry it feels as if it's about to close up. But no one else seems to be unduly suffering; if they can make it I ought to be able to. I'll hold out for another ten minutes or so anyway.

Bless her heart, Brook could have been reading my mind when she asks, "...Who has the drinking water?"

"It's over here, Brook, are you ready for some?"

"Please." *Please* is right.

"I'll pass the cup around." Someone starts a large tin cup clockwise around the circle. It's a popular move, and by the time the cup gets to me there's just a medium-size swallow left. What there is of it tastes heavenly.

The drink of water seems to have revived everyone a little, even me; there are murmurs in the hut again, people are stirring. I can feel Brook looking at me in the dark before she addresses the whole group. "Cork, I hope you don't mind my mentioning this, but I know it's something everyone here would be interested in...Cork's asked a dowser to come in to try to find the contamination in the city's wells."

This takes me completely by surprise, but before I have time to react one way or the other, Tom says, "Really? That's great, Cork." Several others chime in too.

Then the guy with Karen says, "I didn't even know they were contaminated."

"I didn't either, I stopped reading the 'Snooze' years ago," says Reba, the clothing designer. "But I'm not surprised. We have our own cistern."

"I heard about it somewhere," replies Sonia, "but nothing about a dowser. How on earth did you get the city to approve that?"

"...Well, its actually supposed to be kind of confidential," I say, rather at a loss for words.

This makes Brook feel real good of course. "Oh, I'm sorry!" she blurts out, and I reach out for her arm to reassure her, feeling like an ass for putting her on the spot.

"That's all right, I didn't mean you can't say anything about it. The city just wouldn't want it to get in the paper or anything, that's all. As long as it's kept quiet, they don't have anything to lose. They're not putting up any money. They're sure not having any success the way they're going."

Susanne's husband Tony asks in a tone of disbelief: "You mean the city's really going to let a dowser come in here and tell them where to dig?"

"Well, the city service director is anyway," I say. "The problem will be finding the money to dig where the dowser says the contamination is. That's expensive."

"How much?" asks Tony.

"About $10,000."

"If the city's not going to come up with the money, who is?" Tom wants to know.

I'm growing increasingly uncomfortable with this conversation. "That's the other problem. I guess we'll have to cross that bridge when we come to it."

"Some bridge!" says Tony, laughing.

"I know. That gives you an idea how much this is costing us -- the city, I mean. They can't afford to keep screwing around with this much longer. And I have less than a week now to come up with the money for a test well before they start drilling somewhere else."

"*You've* gotta come up with it?" asks Tony incredulously.

"Where do you think you'll get it?" Sonia asks, interceding in an entirely different tone of voice.

"Who knows?" I admit, chuckling ironically at the impossibility of my position.

But Brook won't let me leave it at this. "Tell them what Jimmy said," she urges.

I can't imagine where Brook's going with this. I trust her too much to think for a moment that she's just trying to make me look foolish, but what's her point? Once again she squeezes my hand and I decide to go along with her, not knowing how else to get out of this gracefully anyway.

"...Jimmy Majors -- do you all know Jimmy? -- says I have lousy timing. He thinks the best prospect is Bud Knowland."

"Carlotta's brother?" asks Sonia.

"Oh yeah, he bought that Computech franchise a few months ago didn't he." This is a completely new voice -- must be Steve, Paula's pony-tailed husband, an artist who encases colored glass in beautiful egg-sized clear glass spheres he calls orbs.

"What makes *him* such a good prospect?" demands Paula.

"PR," says Steve. "What a way to tell the community, 'Hey! Here I am, folks -- I'm in the computer biz now.'"

"That's what Jimmy said. He's got a point; you know how vocal the Knowlands are about the environment."

"So what's stopping you," Nathan asks me, "have you approached him yet?"

There's an awkward moment of silence before Nathan apparently remembers what everyone in this small town seems to know.

"Oh, yeah...." he says and lets it go at that.

Sonia steps in to fill the void. "I don't think you should let that stop you. If he's really the best person to ask."

"From what I know about Carlotta, I don't think she'd stand in the way," Paula concurs. "Would she?"

"No, I don't think she would either," I agree. "But I wasn't that close to her brother to begin with; now I'm sure he'd have no interest in talking to me. If I was going to ask him, I'd pretty much have to go through Carlotta."

"Oh -- I see," says Paula.

"I'd say you've got yourself in a real Catch 22 situation, Cork," adds Tom.

"...I'd go ahead and ask her," insists his wife.

"I would too." This is Brook in her first comment on the subject.

"Sure, what have you got to lose?" adds Paula. "I don't know how you two left things, but I never thought of Carlotta as a vindictive sort of person. It's awkward, sure, but that's the way life is sometimes. What do the rest of you think?"

"I don't know Carlotta at all," Susanne answers, "but if you can really bring a dowser in here who can clean up that well, I say ask her. I think it sounds exciting."

"That's what I say," declares Tom. "Go for it!"

Ever the hostess, Sonia asks, "What do you think, Tony?"

"Well, if you really want my opinion...$10,000 is a lot of money to ask someone to gamble on finding a contaminated water well. You've got more balls than I do, man."

"Yeah but think of the publicity he gets if the guy's successful," Steve persists.

"That's a big 'if'. Think of the money lost if the dowser's wrong."

"But that's for Bud to decide, David," says Paula. If he doesn't want to take the risk, fine -- who can blame him? But you won't know if you don't ask him."

"The same thing goes for Carlotta. You'll never know how she'd take it either, unless you give her the chance."

I'm sure I'm not the only one who's relieved when it turns out that Sonia's remarks are the last on the subject. A moment later Nathan begins to chant again, and then others take it up until everyone has joined in, even me. I feel a sense of exhilaration when I let my own barbarous voice out amongst these relative strangers. Can you sweat out inhibitions, I wonder, or in letting go have I ceased to be a stranger here?

30

"Of all the goddamned nerve, Cork, you must take the cake! It's not enough that you've made my life miserable, now you come and ask me for money on top of everything else? I don't believe you!"

Trying to keep my voice under control, I reply, "I'm not asking *you* for the money, Carlotta. I just asked if you'd be willing to help set up a meeting between Bud and me. Don't you realize how difficult it was for *me*, to come up here? But I don't know where else to go, there isn't time. I've already asked everyone else I can think of. I thought this might be the sort of thing that would concern you too."

"That's right -- try to make me feel guilty about it! This is an *environmental* issue, so I should forget all about what's happened between *us* and help you come to the rescue of the city's water supply."

"I'm not trying to make you feel guilty, Carlotta. It *is* an environmental problem -- a serious one -- that's why I came to you; I'd never have come otherwise. I know the environment's even more of a concern to you than it is to me. And what the hell could be more critical than the contamination of a whole community's drinking water?"

Only slightly more subdued, Carlotta says, "This is all on your say-so though, Cork, and I don't know how much I trust you anymore. I don't trust your *judgment*, that's for sure. So why should I get mixed up in some off-the-wall stunt like this with you? A *dowser*! It's not even my money to lose."

"Well if you don't trust *me*, would you be willing to meet with Walter Barry when he gets here? Everything depends on what he finds out anyway. I wouldn't even recommend going ahead unless he convinces us he's located the source."

"He's not going to convince *me*, Cork -- I don't know anything about dowsing. I'd be taking the word of someone I don't know and someone else I no longer trust. With a lot of my brother's money riding on my decision. Why should I put myself in a spot like that -- for you especially? I don't how you can even ask me to."

"*Bud* would be the one who'd make the final decision, Carlotta, not you; it wouldn't be your responsibility. All I'm saying is that if you were willing to meet this guy, Walter Barry I mean, I think you might be favorably enough impressed to be willing to introduce him to Bud. It would be up to him to decide."

"Right, then I'd have put *him* on the spot. And I'm sure Bud doesn't know any more about dowsing than I do. You're asking way too much, Cork, for someone who just walked out of my life the way you did. And you're adding insult to injury by suggesting I should get involved in this for environmental reasons. That's the city's responsibility, not mine or Bud's. Why isn't the city willing to pay this dowser if he's so reliable?"

"Well you're being naive if you think --"

"No, *you're* the one who's being naive, Cork -- to think you can just walk in here and ask something like this of me and expect me to give it to you. It's insulting that you thought you could. What *did* you think? That I'd do it because I want you back? Or that I'm such an environmental fanatic I could be talked into anything -- by someone who treats me like shit and then walks out of my life? *That's* 'naive' for you, Cork."

"...I guess you're right -- about being naive, I mean. You're wrong about the rest though, Carlotta: about my trying to take advantage of you. I understand your saying no; under the circumstances, that's really what I expected. But I hope you won't hold it against me for asking. I thought it was something important we might do together, in spite of all the problems we've had. That's where I was being naive."

I turn to go and Carlotta accompanies me to the door.

"With Bud's money, right." She laughs bitterly. "Well, thanks for the investment opportunity, Cork. Maybe next time."

"Don't call us, we'll call you, huh?"

"Something like that," she says, opening the door for me.

"Someday you're going to realize I care a lot more for you than you give either one of us credit for."

"Ha! Do you really think I look down on *myself* because of your lack of caring?"

"I don't know *what* all your self-pity and insecurity stem from, Carlotta."

Shaking her head with that same bitter chuckle, she says, "Good-bye, Mr. Wonderful."

Walking to my car, I hear her massive baronial front door close heavily behind me.

31

My fruitless visit to Carlotta was on Sunday. Monday morning, over coffee at Elby's with Jimmy, I read in the paper that the Ohio EPA is scheduled to begin inspecting the well field today. An hour or so later I'm talking to Clara Teague, from OEPA's Division of Remedial Response, in front of Well Six.

"According to someone who should be in a position to know," I tell her, "it should've been possible by now to identify the company that dumped this PCE. Is that true?"

"That they'd have left a corporate fingerprint you mean?"

"That's a good way to put it!"

"I wish it were that easy. Chemical analysis can often tell us the particular process that created the toxic waste we're left with -- but not who did it. Unfortunately, PCE was a very common industrial solvent at one time. Many companies used it, for a lot of different purposes."

"So then it wouldn't be possible to pinpoint the company that used this?"

"Not scientifically and definitely not legally. Even when we know damn well who a polluter is, proving it in court is another matter. There are companies who choose to spend millions in legal fees rather than using the same money or less to clean up after themselves."

We chat for a few more minutes, but I've already learned as much as I'm going to from Clara Teague. I don't automatically assume that she's right about this and Andy's wrong. Another person I've spoken to earlier is Henry Marsh, Geologic Survey's crusty owner. Along with the EPA's bureaucratic procrastination and labyrinthine regulations, he made a point of criticizing the agency's professional expertise -- due largely, he said, to their exorbitant employee turnover. "When their people have been there long enough to learn something," he told me, "industry hires them away at a lot higher salary and puts them to work plotting strategy against, guess who? the EPA themselves."

On the other hand, Ms. Teague's remarks are in line with what I've been hearing from most people. With the possibility of a cover-up appearing more remote now than ever, I'm supposed to pick Walter Barry up at the airport this afternoon.

An hour or so after lunch I'm finally plowing through the morning and weekend mail when my secretary Irene enters.

"The bank just called about their payment for this month."

"Which one?"

"First National. Century Trust called yesterday and Citizens' isn't due till the middle of the month."

"What'd you tell them?"

"What we've *been* telling 'em. That we'll be late again but we won't get a whole month farther behind."

"Did they buy it?" I ask, sighing.

"They weren't too pleased...but I think we'll be okay for a while."

"Did you call Hardwood Design about their bounced check?"

"They're sending another check over this afternoon."

"Is it --"

"But it won't be a cashier's check."

"Je-sus Christ! Ten to one this one will bounce too."

"Probably."

"Well, I guess if First National will accept it *we* may as well."

"Doesn't look like we have much choice."

"Did you fax Portland Pacific's invoice to them yet?"

She nods. "They said they'll send a wire out first thing tomorrow. We should have it in our account the next day at the latest."

"Why the hell can't they send it out today? We might start bouncing checks tomorrow."

"I think we'll be all right. Dee -- that's who I usually talk to and she's pretty reliable -- said there was some sort of mix-up with the container number or something."

"Great! Was it our fault or CPI's?" (That's our freight forwarding company in Columbus.)

"As near as I can tell it must have been theirs. We had the right number on the invoice and the shipping papers."

"Then call 'em and give 'em hell. They know better than that. Here Portland is wiring our money in advance and we can't even give 'em the right container number."

"Is that all?" Irene asks.

"Yeah, I guess -- oh *shit*, no! I almost forgot. Citizens is coming in for an inventory audit late this afternoon."

The news takes Irene most unpleasantly by surprise. "...They are?"

"Yeah, that's what Tom's call was about a few minutes ago. Are we going to be all right?"

"Not unless I can move some payables around. Hardwood Design had better get here with their check before the bank closes. But even that's not going to be enough."

"I'll call and make sure they do. You find out what you can do with your payables and get back to me. You always manage somehow."

"But it's getting harder all the time."

"I know. Do what you can."

She starts to go, then turns. "Oh, I just remembered: there's a woman waiting to see you."

"Who is it?" I ask, annoyed.

"I think she said her name was Brook or something like that."

"*Brook*? Great -- send her in!" I feel the afternoon brightening all of a sudden.

Beginning a futile attempt to tidy up my desk, I give it up as hopeless as Brook enters, looking anything but all-business even though she's dressed as professionally as one could ask of a teacher, in skirt, sweater and heels.

"What a pleasant surprise!" I say, standing and motioning for her to sit down in one of the uninviting vinyl chairs facing my desk.

"Hi Cork, sorry to just barge in on you like this, I hope I'm not interrupting anything important," she says in one breath without a pause.

"Not at all, Brook," I assure her, "you've just rescued me from Monday's mail. Sit down. Can I get you some coffee or anything?"

"No thanks, I'll just be a minute."

"I hope longer than that. Welcome to the Executive Suite. What is it they say about a busy executive's desk being messy?"

"I don't know," she says, laughing, "but if there's a positive correlation I'd say you must be putting in sixteen-hour days."

"Even that wouldn't be enough. So I'm lucky to get in eight. What's up?"

"Well, I ran into Jimmy a little while ago and he told me you hadn't had any luck with Carlotta...and I just wanted to stop by and give you a word of encouragement I guess. I was driving by anyway."

"That was sure nice of you, Brook. Yes, I guess you could say Carlotta was less than enthusiastic."

"You're not going to give up are you?"

"You mean with the dowsing? It looks like I'll have to -- even though Walter's flying in this afternoon, it was too late to stop him."

"I wish I had the money -- I'd give it to you in a minute."

"Well I wouldn't take it. Not unless you could afford to lose it. But I certainly appreciate your support, Brook."

"I know it's easy to say I'd give you the money -- when I don't have it -- but I believe in you, Cork; and I believe in what you're trying to do."

"Well, thank you, Brook," I say, surprised and moved. "That's the nicest thing anyone's said to me in quite a while."

"And I mean it. Don't give up -- surely there must be some way to make this happen."

"Oh, I'm sure there is but, you know, I've got so many problems here with the business...and everyone thinks I'm either crazy or on some kind of ego trip with the dowsing. I even wonder myself whether I'm just trying to create some kind of grandiose Hollywood production number out here in the boonies or something -- you know what I mean?"

"I don't believe that for a minute, Cork. I think you've seen an opportunity here that no one else can, and your 'producer' instincts have taken over -- something like that. I've read up on this now myself. I went down --"

"You have?"

"Yes. I went down to the *News* and asked to see all the back articles they had on the well problem. And I agree with you that this is a lot more serious than people realize. I mean, I read about it myself at the time and didn't give it that much thought either."

"Well, I've convinced *someone* anyway."

"You're daggone right you have. What are you going to do? Are you going to have your dowser check the well field anyway?"

"Oh sure -- might as well, since he's going to be here."

"Well if what he finds confirms his prediction of where the contamination is, I think you've just *got* to find a way to dig a test well there."

"You're really serious about this aren't you?"

"I told you I believe in you, Cork."

Brook gets up to go and I get up with her.

"You keep giving me new energy, Brook. I'm gonna call Dean Channel right now and see if I can cut some kind of deal with him."

I give her a big hug, so swept up in her enthusiasm -- already thinking of what I'll say to Dean -- that I've not yet begun to marvel at how this has become almost as much Brook's project by now as my own.

"Good luck, Cork."

"I'll be sure to let you know what happens," I promise her.

"I'll look forward to it."

Awkwardly, I feel I should kiss Brook but I don't. Is it because of the office setting? That's part of it; it would feel about like making love in a service station or something. There's an imaginary sign over my office door that reads, "Thanatos: abandon Eros, all ye who enter here." But that's not the whole story, something else is holding me back. Whatever, Brook leaves and I return to my desk and call Dean Channel.

"...Dean Channel's office please....Dean? Cork Rockner. I've been thinking. You know the dowser's coming in this afternoon, right?...Well, I've had no luck at all so far in raising any money for a test well. But I wonder if it really has to be as expensive as I've been telling everyone. The real expense will come if we find the contamination and have to leave the casing in the ground so the well can be monitored, right?...That's what I thought....Uh huh. Oh, I know it's gonna cost some bucks, believe me. Let me ask you this though, we really didn't get this clear between us. If it turns out we do find the contamination with our own test well, the city will reimburse us won't they?...That's what I thought. And if we don't find it, we're not going to have any of the expense associated with monitoring, right?...Good, that's all I wanted to know. It's going to be expensive but maybe not as much as I thought. Thanks, Dean."

I punch out another number on a different line.

"Jim Meekle's office please....Cork Rockner....Jim? Cork....Good, how are you?...I want to talk to you about taking out a second mortgage on my house....Well, ten-thousand I guess, but I hope to be able to repay part of that immediately....You're probably not going to believe me when I tell you -- do you have time to see me this afternoon?...Great! I'll see you then."

32

When I meet Walter that afternoon at the small commuter airport serving the area, I'm not prepared for how much he's aged in appearance. On the phone it was apparent that his self-confidence and enthusiasm for life haven't diminished in the least. His hearty greeting and jaunty walk to the baggage claim area and immediate nonstop monologue confirm that he hasn't changed in spirit. I drop him off at the Holiday Inn next to the interstate where I've made a reservation for him, with plans for dinner at the Boat Landing. The dowsing is to take place under cover of darkness.

At 8:30 that evening the well field is deserted. The above-ground superstructures of well casing and pump-motor platform loom in the dark like so many identical drilling platforms in a placid sea. Scattered over ten acres or so, the seven water wells are only dimly illuminated by a mercury vapor lamp standing guard over a small parking lot at one end of the field. I get my flashlight out of the glove compartment while Walter removes the tool chest he carries his dowsing rods in from the back seat of my car. For this task I assume he'll be using his scanning rod, the forked metal analogue of a witchstick.

Shining the light on the newspaper diagram he used for his map dowsing, I indicate our location so he can orient himself. "Over there's the vacant lot where you think the contamination is," I say, pointing toward the northwest corner of the well field. "Must be about an eighth of a mile or so from where we're standing."

"All right," he says, studying the map. "I'm going to

try something different this time. The scanning rod alone will show us where there's water underground, but what we need to find is contaminated water. So I'm going to try holding the discharge sink in my left hand along with the handle of the rod, like this. It's a little awkward...but I think it'll work out all right. Whether it'll actually help us find the contamination or not, we'll just have to wait and see."

I feel the dinner we enjoyed earlier begin to congeal. You mean he's going to be winging this? It never really occurred to me when I emphasized on the phone how dowsing for pollution could become a valuable and lucrative new field, that Walter would have had so little experience with this he'd be learning on the job, so to speak. But before I can voice my concern, he's heading off in the dark with the rod out in front of him like some kind of new-age fertility symbol.

I catch up with him, then tag along just behind and off to one side, aiming the flashlight out in front of us. For the next thirty minutes, at least, we go on like this, with Walter methodically crisscrossing the northwest corner of the well field and adjacent lot in some kind of random pattern that makes absolutely no sense to me. It reminds me, in fact, of the seemingly aimless meandering of ants. But since he seems just as fixed as they in following his own hidden path, I keep my mouth shut and merely light the way.

"...You sure this is the same area as the map you sent me?" he asks finally.

"Sure I'm sure," I answer, feeling queasy again. "Why?"

"I just don't seem to be gettin' the kind of vibrations I'm used to. I grant you this is a little different from your normal dowsing -- this is dowsing for *bad* water. Still, I should be gettin' *some* kind of signal, unless the sink's interfering in some way. I hope not because this is my tuner for the contamination frequency. I put a drop a that tetrachloro-whatchamacallit in it before I did the map dowsing. Worked then, oughta work here too."

I'm beginning to wonder if we really are in the right place. I came down here right after Walter mailed back the diagram, in daylight, so I'm reasonably certain that we are, but it wouldn't hurt to check again.

"Stop for a minute, Walter, and let me check the map."

We study it and agree that we've covered the whole area on the map fairly thoroughly.

"Well, the next question," he says, not discouraged in the least that I can see, "is how accurate this diagram is. I've worked from maps before, lots of times, and I can tell you they're worse than useless half the time. Why don't we extend out toward the river as far as those willow trees and up as far as the road?"

"The ground's really soft out that way," I warn him, "but I'm game if you are."

We haven't gone more than a hundred yards into this mucky area when all of a sudden the rod begins to vibrate.

"Do you see it?" Walter asks.

"I see it," I reply, holding my breath.

He slows down but continues walking...and the rod dips dramatically.

Turning to me with a typical Walter Barry smile -- cocky but somehow reverent as well -- he says, "There she is -- right below us."

Walter spends another hour or so mapping out the contaminated area: first with his crossrods to determine its boundaries -- roughly a circle with a diameter of some thirty or forty yards --; then the counter rod, held in his right hand and braced against his thigh, to gauge its depth. The contamination plume appears to "crown", in Walter's terminology, about 120 feet below ground and then to taper off to a greater depth around the circumference of the circle.

Comparing the location and dimensions of the contamination with those he determined earlier by map dowsing, Walter is convinced they're virtually the same. It's the diagram in the newspaper that's inaccurate, he says, and I find this assessment plausible enough. The two sites are fairly close together in any case -- and far removed from the softball diamond where the city intends to drill next.

We're both pretty pumped by now; neither of us wants to end the evening yet. But knowing that Walter is -- or was, at least, when I last saw him -- a recovered alcoholic, I'm at a momentary loss about where we should go to celebrate. He takes me off the spot, however.

"What's your classiest bar in town?" he asks. "I'm buyin'. I don't drink but I'll bet you do, and I'll be satisfied just to sit and eyeball the ladies."

All the way to the cocktail lounge at the historic Shawnee Hotel, I'm wondering whether Walter hopes to find someone to share his bed with him out at the Holiday Inn. And the more I think about it, the less unlikely it seems to me that Walter Barry could persuade some attractive woman to discover what it's like to make love to a man who's twice or three times her age yet just as alive and vital as she is.

The Shawnee's cocktail lounge is a real showplace for fine hardwoods -- many of which came from our retail store when the lounge was remodeled a few years ago -- and Late Victorian architecture. Situated at the confluence of the Ohio and Thothwillow Rivers, the hotel has survived several major floods, the most significant of which are commemorated by plaques marking the high-water marks. Visitors find it hard to believe that the town could ever have been so deeply submerged, but before the U.S. Army Corps of Engineers tamed the Ohio with massive roller dams between Pittsburgh and the Mississippi, flooding was just a fact of life in river towns like Lafayette.

These towns still have their unofficial flood-watchers who monitor the rise of the Ohio and its tributaries on gauges along the banks and predict the time and depth at which the swollen torrents will crest. Then merchants and home-owners rush to move stock and furniture from their basements -- in years past, to the second floor. In 1913 and '37 even the second story wasn't high enough in much of the downtown area. To kids like myself growing up in the higher parts of town, floods were always an exciting time when our residential streets would be lined with every kind of refugee vehicle imaginable which had been moved up out of the way of high water.

Walter and I sit down at a table overlooking the Ohio and its intermittent traffic of towboats pushing long lines of barges up- and downstream. He's favorably impressed with all the woodwork, like the solid cherry bar, and the turn-of-the-century ambiance. I order a draft and Walter joins me with the first of several Chargers (made with bitters, club soda and lime) which he nurses over the course of the evening. The conversation's as one-sided, and fascinating, as I remember from the days in California when I was first learning about the art -- Walter would no doubt say "science" -- of dowsing.

When we get back to discussing our current project, however, I find myself answering one question after another until pretty soon I'm doing much of the talking. It occurs to me that Walter's probably tired from his flight even though we're three hours ahead of Pacific time. I narrate the difficulties I've had in getting the drilling financed and then, prompted by his obvious interest, tell him a little about the Knowlands and Carlotta and me. This gets him started on his own love life; he seems to get a second wind.

"My first wife stayed with me through all of my alcoholism," he begins after our waitress has brought us our third round of Chargers and draft beer. "She was never a heavy drinker; she'd take one or two if we were at a party and that's all. While I went along all this time, for over 20 years, drinking an average of a quart of whiskey a day and, on weekends, a half a case of beer to go with it plus anything else I could get my hands on. This little woman stuck right with me through the whole thing. I had become her burden, I guess, and she got so she really needed that burden.

"But a very peculiar thing happened. After I got myself sobered up and back on my own two feet again, took over the checkbook and started running my life a little better, our marriage began to fall apart, until it finally ended in divorce. I can truthfully say that ninety percent of our problem was Walter, it wasn't her at all.

"After we divorced, she married a friend of ours from Florida who had lost his wife from cancer. Shortly after she remarried, Jean's health began to deteriorate. She went to the University of Florida Clinic and had some tests and found that she had cancer too. Her liver was three times the normal size, with this huge tumor. Her new husband had quite a bit of money and he sent her all over the world trying to get something done for her, but in 1971 she finally died."

Walter relates this matter-of-factly with little emotion, outwardly anyway, but he locks onto my eyes for what he's about to say next.

"Since I've been into energy transference, I now believe that Jean picked up all the conflict that should have gone into *my* liver, with all the drinking I did for so many years. She followed pretty good health habits herself, yet she's the one who died of cancer, and my liver's never given me any problems at all. I think this may be a key that should be investigated by the medical profession: one member of a family making another member sick and coming out of the whole thing smelling like a rose."

"I thought this was already somewhat accepted in medicine," I reply.

"Not to this extent, not where one person actually dies of the symptoms from another person's abuse of his body. And the alcohol- or drug-abuser or what have you escapes any symptoms whatsoever -- as if the other has accepted them along with the psychological burden as well. I really think this sort of thing deserves looking into."

"You're probably right," I reply. "What happened after your divorce -- did you meet someone else soon?"

"Before the divorce, actually. After Jean and I were separated, I was closing out my garage business in Santa Monica so I could put all my efforts into my mining operation. I walked into the State Board of Equalization one day and there was a beautiful redhead sitting there, making arrangements to get her tax number for a new business she was forming in Westwood. I was quite smitten and made a date with her.

"We started going together pretty steady. I was spending a lot of time up at the mine, and she and I got to going up there on weekends. She was a beautiful woman. She could drive a truck or skiploader or bulldozer -- anything you wanted her to -- but she was still very feminine. She'd opened a dress shop on Westwood Boulevard and was quite successful with it.

"After my divorce we decided to get married. I should have picked up on the fact that her mother, her son and two grandchildren came before anything else; but we got married and bought a big five-bedroom house, with a guest house in back and a six-car garage on a huge lot covering nearly an acre out in the Van Nuys district. We all moved in. Her family moved into the good house, and we moved into the guest house."

I'm just taking a drink of my beer when he makes this last remark, and it's so unexpected I almost choke on it. Walter grins at my reaction.

"Doesn't sound like me does it? Well, we were sharing the expenses of the whole thing, and it got to where I was doing all the work in the yard while her son was in the studio making pottery and her grandchildren were lolling around doing nothing. I finally laid it on the line for her. I said we're going to move and let your family have this place -- since it's

214

theirs anyway -- and we got into a big rhubarb over that and I moved out. I moved into my office and warehouse on Sepulveda Boulevard and built a little apartment in back of my office.

"We got a divorce, a real rough one. She wanted to nail me for half of the mine, $5,000 cash, and $500-a-month alimony on an 18-month marriage! I went blazing in with both fists and both feet and whipped it down to where she didn't get anything but the equity we had in the house and some furniture and so forth. And I was really fond of this woman. It seems that this old psychological trauma from my mother abandoning us when I was a child has shown up in my relationship with every woman I was ever with. As soon as I'd get settled nicely with one and have everything going right, I'd pick up two more somewhere who I could go to and do this whole hurt business again that I was quite famous for. I guess I still am, although I've gotten rid of a lot of it."

This really hits home. What excuse do I have for the way I've handled my own relationships with women? Nothing comparable to what Walter has related. I'm just another wounded soldier in the battle of the sexes, whose war wounds keep me from being able to commit myself to a long-term relationship when I'm convinced that this is what I really want.

Walter's excuse I can buy, but what hope is there for the rest of us, made gun-shy by broken hearts, failed romances or shattered dreams? Then I catch myself in this moment of self-pity and -blame and push my half-full beer mug away in disgust. How the hell did I get on this kick anyway?

33

Walter's on a roll. At eleven o'clock he's still going strong.

"I went along single for several years after the second divorce. My water discovery business was picking up and I was doing quite a lot of traveling. I had a bid to go up to Eugene, Oregon, to do a survey on a ranch up there sometime in 1971 or early '72. I walked into the airport to get my ticket and felt a vibration, something warm and nice, directed my way. I turned around and looking at me was the most beautiful red-headed woman you ever laid eyes on. She had a shape like a thoroughbred race horse, and she was standing there smiling at me." I smile, picturing Walter the centaur mounting his beautiful roan mare, but he doesn't take note of this.

"I was in a T-shirt and a pair of boots with ranch jeans shoved down into them, and I had my dowsing rod strapped onto my suitcase. I looked like a real farm boy going somewhere. But the whole time I was making out my ticket, this woman was putting a beautiful smile my way. By the time I finished she'd left and was standing in line at the gate. They put me on standby, I got there too late for a reservation. So I walked up and handed her my card and said, 'If I don't get on the plane, give me a call.'

"She says, 'I live here and I'm going up to San Francisco.' We stood there and talked for a few minutes and then everyone got on the plane including her, and they started calling the standbys. They got down to one other person and myself and then finally called for one more -- they had one last seat and it was mine. I got on the plane and it was right in back of this gorgeous redhead. I sat there with my heart pounding and my blood running warm and watched her all the way to San Francisco. She made friends with everyone around her, even very sweetly got a man to put out his cigar. They came with the cocktails and she didn't drink one; she didn't smoke a cigarette...and by the time we got to San Francisco I was in love just looking at the back of her head.

"We got off the plane and I went directly up to her and walked down to the baggage claim area with her. I asked her where I could see her and she said she would be at the San Francisco Hilton and for me to stop by there when I got back from Eugene. I did and we went along together for about a year and then decided we'd better get married -- which was a mistake."

Walter pauses for a beat in his narration, just long enough to give me a knowing look, then continues. "We had gotten along famously up until the marriage ceremony because we were separate beings that kinda went our own ways and didn't interfere with one another too much. We had a beautiful relationship -- good sexual relationship, everything -- and the minute we got that knot tied came the corral and the halter, the 'where have you been and who were you with?'

"Again, I had the extra woman and she knew it. It's always been a necessity for me. I guess if I'm going to travel the freeway of love, I'm going to have a spare tire in case I get a flat -- that seems to be the pattern, it's been going on for years. We're still married, I see her occasionally when our paths cross. She's a beauty director for Anita of Denmark Cosmetics, and they send her all over the world to do advertising for them -- and she *is* a walking advertisement. So as of now I don't know exactly what our status is, but we'll probably never get back together."

Whether it's because I'm a good listener or because he hasn't had a chance to talk like this to anyone for a while, Walter has that distant look of the past in his eyes. I really am interested in this part of his life, a part he didn't divulge to me when I interviewed him several years ago, so when he asks, "Shall I go on, you wanta hear more?" I nod my head eagerly.

"I was giving a lecture at Esalen one Sunday afternoon before I moved up north. In the group was a lovely woman about 29 or 30 years old, and she came up to me and said, 'Your work absolutely enthralls me. I've been through a week of training, and they taught us about these same energies, went right back through the history of man, and this really intrigues me. What you're showing us here is everything they taught us except they didn't know what the answers were.' She asked if I'd like to do some psychological work with her and I said yes, I'd love to.

"I was staying over at the Chappellet Ranch with the Pittineys, and the following morning I got a call from her. 'I live at a ranch on top of a mountain,' she said, 'and if you'd like to do some work with me, I'd love to come pick you up and bring you back up here. Your van won't make it because it's too long. I'm on a real winding road and it takes a Jeep or something to get up here.'

"So I left the Pittineys' and met her down at a little grammar school she'd mentioned; parked my van and went up to her place. I did about eight hours of intensive psychological work with her, trying to find some of the things that were bugging her. We found a situation with her mother that went back to the age of three when her mother grabbed her and rubbed her nose in her own excrement and held her down in that position, trying to toilet-train her. That trauma was still with her.

"It took about two and a half hours to find this and have it manifest and get it out. The physical manifestation showed up in the descending colon as a heavy oscillation of the rod. I got quite an energy discharge from it, quite a bit of warmth. We went through this thing several times, and every time it discharged energy until it finally went away.

"Then we went to her relationship with her father, and in working on this we couldn't get any magnetic tie with him at all, absolutely nothing: no manifestation of hatred or anything, even when she was relating how brutal he'd been to her mother, how she'd had to beat him off of her mother with an umbrella. We kept going through this and going through it, and the rod wasn't indicating any conflict in the thymus or the third chakra, until all of a sudden it dawned on me that this man couldn't possibly be her biological father because there was no magnetic link with him. Then she said, 'Oh my God, I know who my father is!'

"After putting the picture together she realized that her father was a priest who is now in the Vatican in Rome. Her mother had given her a letter of introduction to him when she and her husband went to Europe -- he won a trip to Europe on his outstanding work as an architect. When she walked into this man's study, he looked at her and started crying, and then *she* started crying, for no apparent reason at all. He made a special appointment for her and her husband to go through the Pope's gardens, and they were given a place of honor at a meeting with the Pope and the president of Italy. So we relieved the conflict connected with her father, her *real* father.

"Then we went through the conflict with her husband, and as we started putting this picture together, it became quite evident that he was bisexual and doing a lot of playing around with his boyfriends, showing up on two occasions wearing someone else's underwear when he was supposed to have been out working somewhere. She bought all his clothes and knew every stitch of clothing he had, so our work merely confirmed what she'd suspected. When we got into this area she had a physical manifestation on the left side of her body: from her clavicle all the way down even with her navel there was a rash like scarlet fever about four inches wide. You could feel the heat coming out of it as I discharged it.

"Here's the interesting part though," Walter says, straightening up in his chair to stretch and then leaning back onto the table. "Her family had always been very mean to her and never had too much to do with her. They'd very seldom written her a letter or called her on the phone. About three days after this therapy, she started getting phone calls and loving letters from her parents -- for virtually the first time in her life, she told me! So this leads us right back into the magnetic lock I believe links people together. She changed and so her whole family changed.

"Well, she confronted them on the phone with the whole thing about her being illegitimate, and everybody clammed up. Since then they've been lavishing a lot of love on her and have invited her to come home, which they hadn't done for years. I got very fond of this girl, and since I wanted to move to northern California or the Bay area -- I had my eye on Palo Alto -- I asked her if she'd like to go along and she said yes. She had a seven-year-old daughter who was absolutely fabulous, one of the most beautiful, intelligent children I have ever seen; I really got hooked on that little girl.

"So Sue and I decided to move in together and started looking for a place in the Bay area, but we couldn't find anything -- everything kept steering us right back down to the Carmel Valley. We finally ended up renting us a nice house on the side of a hill which is ideal for the Institute of Bio-Energetic Healing, the legal structure which gives me the right to practice spiritual healing. We moved in together with the daughter and put her in school.

"Sue was a good typist, with shorthand skills, who was very valuable in my work. I had a lot of traveling to do. I took her up to Stanford with me on two or three occasions, and I had to do water surveys in Arizona, Nevada, Oregon and all over. Since I was away quite a lot, I decided to put some money in the bank for her -- opened up an account with $1,000 in it -- and we were getting along, I thought, famously.

"There was a little dissension, a little trouble at times; on several occasions she referred to men as male chauvinist pigs, which should have given me some clue as to how she felt. But I went away on a little trip over to Winnemucca, Nevada, and was gone for several days. When I came back the house was a shambles. All of her stuff was moved out and she'd even left the doors open and a lot of lights on. I couldn't understand why she'd just up and moved like that.

"Then I checked the bank account and it was gone -- I thought, well, that's quite a loss. The phone bill came in, there was $157 worth of long distance calls on that. I started paying this stuff off, and then my Bank Americard came through and there was about $800 worth of stuff charged to that account. I'd put a check guarantee on my bank account for her. By this time I was getting a little angry. Then I happened to look in a drawer where I had a box of jewelry, including my father's watch, which I was very fond of. This was one of those big Walthams with a snap case on it. It was given to my dad in 1911, the year after I was born, for designing and building the first 3,000-board-foot sawmill in the state of Florida. It was quite a ceremony. Three days before he died he handed it to me and said, 'I won't be needing this anymore.' I was planning on passing this watch down to my grandson.

"Well, when I discovered that this was gone, along with a Tiffany watch and a bunch of jewelry of all kinds, I *really* got angry. I was going out looking for her, and then I thought about this beautiful daughter -- what effect any kind of arrest or anything would have on her -- and I just dropped the whole thing. I paid off all this stuff and got myself back to normal. I don't know where she is now, but that was a pretty good lesson for an old man. I hope."

Walter grins broadly and I smile back, but what I'm thinking about after his marathon tale of woo and woe is how men and women hurt one another so. Despite his gift of dowsing and healing which he has devoted half his life to understanding and developing for the sake of humanity (it certainly hasn't made him wealthy), Walter seems to have been no more successful than I have in affairs of the heart. His heart chakra where humanity and his work are concerned may be huge -- and I believe it is -- but man-to-man, and especially man-to-woman, it's as errant and fallible as anyone else's. It's not clay feet we human beings as lovers have but clay hearts.

Neither of us says anything for a while, both of us lost in our own thoughts, and as I sit mulling mine it suddenly occurs to me why I was so reluctant to kiss Brook in my office this morning. I think it's because I find the intensity of her interest and belief in me, as expressed in my dowsing project anyway, unnerving. I find it hard to believe, even distrust it perhaps. Either it's all something of an act, or it's actually sincere, which is the most disconcerting -- *say* the word: most frightening -- possibility of all. How is one to be worthy of such trusting, or should I say credulous, and unsolicited support?

"You know, what we need, Walter, is a dowsing rod for love," I tell him, only half jokingly. "If you can dowse for water and use a dowsing rod to heal, why can't we dowse for love?"

"...Well that's a good question," he replies, surprised. "I never thought of that. I expect you can if that's what you set out to do. Tap hidden reservoirs of love to bring into human consciousness, something like that." He says this in a tone of ironic exaggeration but I can tell that he, too, is only half joking.

"Something like that. You think it's possible?"

"Anything is possible, my friend. If I've learned anything in my seventy-plus years on the planet, I've learned that. We're as far removed from the kinds of beings we have the potential to evolve *into* as we are from the furry folks we've descended from. You can't stress too strongly the word 'potential' however."

On that note we decide to call it a night.

34

Tuesday, the day after our discovery, Walter and I meet with Dean and manage to persuade him to come out to the well field for another top-secret dowsing session. He shows up that night as promised and is impressed with Walter's self-confident spiel and the consistent performance of his dowsing rods. If nothing else (and of course I believe there *is* more), Walter is a consummate showman; if he can get a prospective client out to where his rods, doing everything but speaking in tongues, say there's water, he's usually got himself another commission.

I'm sure my willingness to front the cost of drilling plays a major role in Dean's decision to go along with the new location as well. Initially, the only person other than the city attorney that he'll have to let in on the reason for the change will be water director Russ Fawcett, and Dean says he's sure he can secure his confidence.

After work the next day I stop in to see my parents. City council is meeting tonight and since one of the items on their agenda is approval of the next round of drilling, I want to be there. I decide to have dinner in town before the council session, giving me an hour to spend with Mom and Dad -- although, as usual, Dad has no interest in joining Mom and me in the back yard. She fixes herself a Perfect Manhattan (half sweet and half dry vermouth) and I carry it and my own drink, the same blend of vermouth without the bourbon, out under the walnut tree for her.

"Good of you to stop, honey," she says when we've settled into the deteriorating lawn chairs that I've been putting off taking down to the basement for the winter. "What's going on in your life?"

"About the same, nothing new." (I'm sure as hell not going to tell her anything about my secret project until it's either a *fait accompli* or the major fiasco she fears.) "Been a beautiful day hasn't it?"

"It certainly has. This is the latest I can remember Indian Summer's lasting."

"I was afraid you'd missed most of it."

"Well, I didn't get a chance to enjoy it as much as I'd like, but that doesn't mean I wasn't aware of how nice it's been."

"...You feeling any better?"

"I'm not going to talk about me, you said you were tired of hearing about my problems. But Dorothy's in the hospital. She fell in the bathroom and broke her back again."

Dorothy, my parents' next-door neighbor for the past forty years, is an enormously attractive, good-natured widow in her late-eighties who has probably broken more bones in her lifetime than the entire NFL suffers in a season; yet she still retains an indomitable determination to enjoy life. "What a shame," I mutter, shaking my head. I can feel her latest injury in my groin, where a sort of queasiness often accompanies the report of someone else's pain.

"Do you think you could possibly take me up to see her when she can have visitors?"

"Of course, be glad to."

We nurse our drinks, thinking about Dorothy's brittle bones and gritty courage. It was her husband Carl who bequeathed the walnut tree to us.

"I've been thinking of what you've said about trying to develop...a more spiritual outlook on life," Mom says tentatively. "But, other than going to church, I don't really know where to begin."

"Gonna put me on the spot huh?"

"That wasn't my intention."

"I'm glad you asked," I tell her. "I've been thinking about it too, ever since you complained of my preaching."

"When was that?"

"Never mind, if you don't remember I'm not going to bring it up now."

"Can you give me some pointers without being too dogmatic about it?"

"Is that how I sound?"

"Maybe that's just how I'm hearing it."

"God, I hope so." I do feel on the spot all at once -- Mom's actually considering my suggestion. The conversation the other night on Jimmy's boat pops into my head: where the hell do I get off advising my mother on "spiritual" issues? *Oh, quit questioning your motives or qualifications and follow your intuition!* "...Well, I think the first thing is to get your attention off of yourself, off your problems. Don't you?"

"That's the *first* thing? It seems to me that's the whole point."

"If that's *all* you did, how would you sustain it? How would you keep yourself from coming back to your problems again?"

"That's what I'm asking *you*."

"I'm not saying pretend you don't *have* problems, that you're not lonely and unhappy, but you don't have to dwell on them either."

"That's a relief."

"Yeah, see how easy this is?"

I smile at her but she makes a face, one of the facial tics from the stress of growing old that have become part of her conversation over the years. "And just how do you suggest I avoid dwelling on them?"

"You won't think I'm being dogmatic if I tell you, will you?"

"Oh, probably," she says, "but let's hear it anyway."

"Well, according to Paul Goldblum, the psychiatrist whose books I edited, from both a psychological and spiritual approach the secret is detachment. Instead of trying to *repress* the loneliness you say you feel most of the time, maybe the trick is to learn how to just...*detach* from negative emotions. Let go of them. See the difference?"

Mom's not impressed. "I understand the difference in *meaning* -- but isn't this just a semantic exercise?"

"Maybe at first," I admit, "but why don't you try it for a while and see what happens? Let your loneliness come, don't try to fight it -- really *feel* it...then just let go of it."

"That's all?" She takes a long sip from her drink and rattles the ice in her cocktail glass. "I'm glad you're not charging me for this session."

"It's always easier to talk about solutions than actually going through with them," I reply, feeling defensive in spite of myself. "But that doesn't mean they can't be worthwhile does it?"

"If this is just the first thing I need to do, what's next? How do I keep from coming back to loneliness after I've learned how to 'detach' from it?"

Her question surprises me; I thought she was already bored with the subject. "You have to focus on something positive."

"Like what for instance?"

"I can tell you what works for me. Gratitude."

"*Gratitude?*"

"It's really hard to feel depressed and grateful at the same time."

I know she's getting impatient now, but I reluctantly continue, as if our discussion's developed a life of its own. "Can you think of anything to be grateful for, at the moment?"

"Nothing comes to mind. This beautiful weather maybe."

"Well, that's about you isn't it? It's your weather -- your experience of it anyway."

"That's the dumbest thing I ever heard of."

"Why's it so dumb? That's a fundamental spiritual contention: there's no 'other', no distinction between you and what you perceive."

"No difference between me and the weather?"

"Between you and the weather, between you and me, between you and anything."

"Oh, Cork, I'm afraid this is all beyond me. It has about as much practical value in my life as all the rest of this... spiritual talk of yours."

"Well, we agree on that at least. Now all I have to do is convince you there *is* some value."

"In these 'bedtime stories' of yours? Why can't you just give me a little more of your time?"

"Why can't you be content with what I give you?"

"...If this were chess," she says, "I'd say we just traded pawns, wouldn't you?"

"I guess so," I agree, chuckling.

"Okay, so that we don't end up checkmated again --"

"Stalemated."

"Whatever. So we don't end up stalemated again, you're saying I should focus more on being *grateful* for a day like this -- is that correct?"

"Voila! She walks, she talks..."

"She hears, she parrots...and gets a cracker for her effort."

"Stale probably."

"Oh that goes without saying: stale and about as nutritious."

A surge of emotion makes me speak out all at once: "You *are* this day, Mom! Everything in it, everything about it. The more you can *feel* what your mind and senses make you aware of, the less you'll be able to feel sorry for yourself. Imagine doing this all the time -- getting inside everything you come in contact with."

"Wait a minute, I thought you just said I already *am* everything around me."

"*Touché* -- you *are*. So *feel* it, otherwise, what good does it do?"

"I see -- at least I think I do, through a glass darkly perhaps."

"That's good enough for now. 'Bedtime stories' huh? That's good, I guess that is what they are in a way. Well, you used to read me bedtime stories; maybe now it's time to return the favor -- only these stories aren't make-believe."

"Says you -- as if either of us had any way of knowing....You were never afraid to go to sleep; why are you so sure I'm afraid of dying?"

"I'm *not* -- I hope I'm wrong."

"If I were, how would being grateful for life keep me from fearing *death*? I'd think that would have just the opposite effect."

"I think they go hand in hand," I reply, really warming to the subject now. "Being grateful -- as a way of life I mean -- can change the way you *feel* about life, in my experience. It can give you a whole new attitude. An *acceptance* of the way things are -- and aren't -- that includes the knowledge that, like every other person in the history of the world, you're going to leave it some day. I don't know which comes first: reverence for life, or the sense that we so-called individuals are inseparable from it -- but I'm coming to believe they go together."

I look up into the swaying branches of the walnut. "What makes me love the way the leaves are rustling in the breeze right now is the way observing this pulls me in until it feels almost as if *I'm* up there blowin' in the wind." I extend my arms, close my eyes, and do a little leaf improv. "Without a care, without a worry -- see what I'm saying? Can you believe your tight-assed first-born can actually let go like that?"

"No," she cackles, "as a matter of fact -- I *don't* believe it."

I can feel a big grin on my face. "It's pretty subtle."

Mom's thoroughly loosened up now, like the live audience at a sitcom taping. "Change your attitude with gratitude -- sounds like an advertising slogan. But I thought 'attitude' had become synonymous with having a chip on your shoulder."

"In this society it certainly has; we can't imagine attitude being anything but negative. That comes with the spiritual vacuum we're living in."

"Being grateful," says Mom, turning serious herself, "is what my morning prayer is all about."

"I didn't know you *had* a prayer."

"Ever since my Al-Anon days, when your father's drinking got out of hand. I started saying Al-Anon's Serenity Prayer, then just gradually made up my own."

"What's the serenity prayer?"

"Oh, you've heard me say that, surely: 'God grant me the serenity to accept the things I cannot change, the courage to change the things I can, and the wisdom to know the difference.'"

"That's nice -- you're right, I have. And *your* prayer's different now?"

"Yes, I thank God for the people who make my life worthwhile -- you for one. But to me, gratitude isn't reverence, it's not religious. Religion's something you *live*."

"That's what I've been talking about!"

Mom begins to stir and I know she's ready to go in. "I don't think being a leaf for a while is really the answer I'm looking for, Cork."

"Of course it sounds weird when you put it into words. Don't you see though? Somehow reverence brings about an identification with the things we're grateful *for* -- we *become* them. We need to understand now, while it can still do us some good, that when we die, when we're 'gone', a part of us will still be here, in all the things we really loved."

"I wondered where all this was leading."

"I know -- I can see you're getting antsy to go in."

229

"It's time for my puffs."

I get up to help her out of her chair.

"I'm afraid all this is a little over my head, honey," she says when she's firmly on her feet, cane in hand. "But I appreciate your taking time to explain it to me."

"I wish it could've done you some good though, Mom. I'm afraid you didn't get much out of it."

She takes my arm as we walk toward the house. "I did get something out of it. Something that means a lot more to me than understanding all your spiritual concepts."

"What's that?"

"You know very well what it is," she says, stopping to smile up at me. "Even if you do have yourself half-convinced otherwise. All this talk of yours tells me, whether you show it or not, that you really do care about the old hag after all."

"Of course I do, Mom," I reply at once without thinking, my voice cracking a little. "I *love* you."

35

The drilling rig and its two-man crew have been on the site since Thursday, the day they were scheduled to begin drilling near the softball field. The ten days Dean Channel gave me to convince him to drill here turned out to be even less than that. Council met on Wednesday as it always does, nine days after my initial meeting with Dean, and approved the next round of drilling, as Dean had assumed they would; he'd already arranged for the drillers to begin the following day. But they're drilling in the area where Walter believes the contamination is.

Now, a little after 9:30 p.m. Sunday, we're an hour or so away from 120 feet, the depth at which Walter's counter rod has told us repeatedly the contamination is located. The two drillers are tired but willing to go to 120 feet and a little beyond, if necessary. I've been getting more nervous by the hour as the drilling has dragged on. Originally the crew had predicted they'd be at 120 feet by noon Sunday, leaving them sufficient time to strike the set and arrive at their next location somewhere in northern Ohio on Monday, as scheduled. Needless to say, we're really pushing that schedule now. They had to radio in for permission to stay as long as they have.

Walter had confidently predicted that we should begin to see some signs of contamination at around 100 feet or so, but we haven't seen a thing so far. He and I are standing near the rig when Dean returns from dinner.

"If it's really down there we should be hearing about it pretty soon, shouldn't we?" Dean asks as he joins us.

"Whaddaya mean, "*if* it's down there"? Walter replies good-naturedly.

"They've averaged almost 30 feet a day," I add apropos of nothing except my own anxiety.

"I've seen drillers do 35 easy, but you've got some fairly coarse gravel here," Walter reminds Dean.

"Yeah, we've been lucky to *get* 30 feet a day on our other test wells. I think we've averaged more like 25, 26," he agrees.

"Dean, do you think we'd have seen some sign of contamination by now if the main source really is at 120 feet?" I ask, anxious for an assessment other than Walter's of where we stand right now.

"Well, not necessarily -- not with the photo ionization detector anyway. That doesn't mean some of the samples we've been taking won't show trace amounts when they've been analyzed. Normally, you *might* expect to have detected some signs by now, a faint odor maybe. Has the crew reported anything since I left?"

"No, they haven't. That's why I asked."

"Now don't you get yourself all worked up there, Mr. Rockner," Walter intercedes. "If the rods say it's down there, it's there. Maybe not *exactly* where I think it is, because I'm not as used to dowsing for chemicals as I am for water. There may be some peculiarities I'm not familiar with. But it's down there, you can rest assured on that."

"I'd like to, Walter, believe me. It's just that four days of this have begun to get a little wearing, you know what I mean?"

Walter glances at Dean, then says to me, "Why don't you go get something to eat. It'll be an hour yet before they hit 120 feet."

"Too nervous to hold anything down," I confess. "I *am* going to go pick someone up though. I want her to be here when we hit 'paydirt'."

"I *hope* to hell it's paydirt," says Dean. "And I wish

there were someone we could hang this on. But more'n likely it's been down there for years."

"You'd still think whoever dumped it here should've known it was eventually going to pollute the groundwater," I reply, watching Dean carefully for the slightest sign that he knows more about this than he's ever let on.

"Sure they knew, they just didn't stop to think about the consequences. They didn't *want* to think about them," Walter grumbles.

"Dean, one thing I've been meaning to ask you: why hasn't city council ever put the test drilling up for bid? I understand we have a couple of local companies who want to bid on it."

"We do," he says. "Chemlab and Geologic Survey have been lobbying for a joint engineering study for a year now. We're going to give 'em a crack at it if this next round of test holes doesn't give us the answer."

"You *are*?" I ask, surprised that I haven't heard this from Andy.

"They should have been allowed to bid in the first place. It was just politics that they weren't. Capital Drilling's been around longer and done more work for the city than they have, and I guess the severity of this problem's had council kinda spooked from the start. But all that's gonna change if Capital -- or Mr. Barry here -- can't deliver this time around."

"...So much for the latest conspiracy theory," I reply, feeling foolish along with everything else now. "See you in a while -- keep your fingers crossed." I'm glad to get out of here for a few minutes. I just hope I won't be bringing Brook back to witness a complete fiasco.

When I pick her up and she finds out I haven't eaten since early this afternoon, she gets a bowl of her delicious potato soup and an English muffin into me while I tell her about today's progress, or the lack of it. I'm trying not to be pessimistic after coming this far, but in my mind's ear I can

233

hear the meter running, with *still* nothing to show for it. In her inimitable fashion Brook manages to be sympathetic and encouraging at the same time. She's excited about being in on what must be the community's best-kept secret right now. I hope to God it stays that way if we don't find anything, but that's not very likely.

When we drive up to the drilling site, I see it through Brook's eyes this time and capture some of her mood. The rig's 35-foot mast, lit eerily from below by a generator-operated portable light tower, could be a slender monument, from Greek stele to totem pole, as interpreted by some kind of machine-worshipping cargo cult. Surrounded by various lengths of pipe, heavy incomprehensible tools, and a mound of mud and sand already removed from the hole, the truck-mounted cable rig has been jacked up onto 4x4s to keep it level and away from the hole.

At this depth, the crew is testing every two feet now, which means that the entire drill stem -- five or six 20-foot lengths of hollow rod and several shorter "change rods" -- has to be winched up by cable from the three-inch hole every fifteen minutes or so and replaced by the sample-taker, at the end of a second cable.

The sample-taker is a five-foot pipe with a sliding rod inside and a hinged cover called a "flapper" at the bottom end. When the rig's 200-pound hammer slams down on the sliding rod, the sample-taker is driven down into virgin soil at the bottom of the hole, compressing it and forcing it into the sample-taker through the hinged flapper. Removed from the hole, a three-to-four-foot core sample is tapped out on the ground, and the driller's assistant sticks a photo ionization detector into it to reveal any possible trace of contamination.

Then the drill stem is lowered back into the hole and the rhythmic pounding, which assaults our ears now, is resumed, in a laborious, repetitive process which has been going on for four long days.

36

Two hours later, the mood is far from positive at the drilling site. Even Brook's perennial optimism seems to have become infected by my queasy doubts about finding anything before the crew is forced to quit. In place of Walter, whom I haven't seen since my return, the city water director is now at the site. Sworn to secrecy last Thursday by Dean, Russ is beginning to look more and more concerned -- resentful even -- that he let himself become party to drilling at this location in the first place.

"Where are they now, are they past 130 feet yet?" he asks no one in particular.

"One-thirty-one," says Dean. "Still no perceptible odor or P.I.D. reading."

"What's a P.I.D. reading?" Brook asks me.

"P.I.D.'s short for 'photo-ionization detector'," Dean replies, overhearing her. "It's a little hand-held gizmo with a probe and a small built-in pump, so you can hold it over the hole and suck in an air sample. If there's any measurable gas in the air, it'll light up a lamp on the P.I.D."

"And when you uncover the contamination, some of it'll get dispersed into the air?" Brook asks.

"Exactly," says Dean with a big bleary smile. "Ain't science grand?" He and Brook chuckle punchily, which should give you some idea of how we're all feeling by now.

"I sure hope *Walter's* science comes through. Right now I wouldn't be willing to bet on it."

"Cork, whatever it is Walter has I sure as hell wouldn't call it science," says Dean -- "despite that scrapbook of success stories he carries with him."

"Oh, I've *seen* the results," I reply wearily, no longer trying very hard to counter Walter's growing opposition here on the sidelines. "I just don't know what his hits-and-misses ratio is."

"His batting average," says the water director.

"Yeah, his batting average. He probably doesn't keep any negative clippings or letters. You don't know where he went do you?"

"No, I don't," Dean replies, "but whether he's back here or not, I'm gonna have to release the crew pretty soon. They're exhausted -- I'm tired just lookin' at 'em."

"I talked to them a little while ago, Dean. They said since this is their last day on the site they're willing to keep going if you give 'em the OK."

"Well, I know you're anxious to find something, Cork, and I sure don't blame you, I'd like to too. But I can't allow these guys to keep drilling until they drop, or have some kind of accident. You understand."

"Sure, I understand, Dean. I wouldn't want you to. I wish to hell Walter would get back so we can find out what he thinks the odds are that we'll still find something." Brook puts her arm around me and gives me a hug; I smile back weakly, grateful for her insisting earlier on Walter's trading his room at the Holiday Inn for the guest bedroom at her house. The rental car he's been driving all over the place since his arrival is costing me plenty.

"I don't mean to sound disrespectful," Dean replies, "but my guess is he'll say they're the same sure-fire odds they've been all along. I admire self-confidence, and I guess in his business you're dead before you start if you don't have it. But you've gotta be willing to face facts too, and the fact is we've gone well beyond where he said the contamination would be."

"I know, you're right," I admit. "I can't afford to spend any more money anyway."

A gloomy silence descends over the four of us. Why

the hell was I so sure of success in something as arcane as dowsing so long as I found a way to pay for it, as if money were the only issue here? As if success were just another commodity? Was I going to buy my way into the ranks of Aquarian explorers like Walter Barry? Yes, that's exactly what I was trying to do. I'm a dowser wannabe.

It's almost at the exact moment that I'm expecting Dean to tell me he's going to have to call the drilling off when I spot Walter and, of all people, Carlotta walking toward us.

"Look who said she wanted to come watch us find that contamination!" he announces for all to hear.

I'm sure if I could see my face in a mirror right now, my mouth would be hanging open. As tired and discouraged as I am, as nonplused at seeing these two together, I feel a *frisson* pass through me, an electrification of my spine alerting me that I'm either losing my mind or have become aware suddenly that I'm caught up in something beyond my comprehension.

Carlotta, guarded-looking and all-business, takes a quick appraising look at Brook, then turns to me and says evenly, "Hello, Cork."

I guess hearing her familiar voice snaps me out of my stupor. "...Well, hi, Carlotta...what, what're you doing here?" I manage to stammer.

At the same time I hear Walter saying to Dean, "I told the crew to take a break while we figure out what to do next. They're beat."

Dean is somewhat taken aback by this assumption of authority. "...Uh, well, okay, Mr. Barry. What do you recommend?" he asks in a manner clearly suggesting that a lot rides on his answer.

"Walter's been filling me in on your project here," Carlotta says to me. "I just came to see how you're getting along."

I can see that despite, perhaps because of, the awkwardness of the situation, Carlotta's enjoying my

237

confusion over her appearance here with Walter. "Not so hot I'm afraid. This is our last day and the crew's already into double overtime."

"We're right there," Walter declares emphatically, "I can feel it: another hour or two at the most. You don't have any choice now but to go on."

"I don't see how I can permit another two hours," Dean contradicts him. "I think you need to consult with Cork here. He's financing this, you know."

"...Reality sets in," I reply, shrugging.

"Reality's one thing," says Walter, on the defensive now -- "I'm all for reality. But before *giving up* sets in I think you oughta ask Ms. Knowland here what we've been talking about for the last hour or so."

Everyone looks questioningly at Carlotta and she nods for me to move off to the side with her where we can talk in private. I think to glance at Brook, who nods vigorously.

"...What's going on?" I ask lamely when Carlotta and I have moved far enough away to talk quietly without being overheard.

"Your friend Walter's really something. He came over to see me a few days ago and tried to talk me into bankrolling this. I thought you must have put him up to it and told him off on the phone, but he swore up and down that all he got from you was my name and that you didn't even know he was calling."

"That's right, I didn't. He never said a word to me about it. I couldn't believe it when I saw you two together just now."

"He's pretty sure of himself, isn't he. I finally agreed to see him for just a few minutes, but he ended up staying a couple of hours. What a character!"

"Well...what did you decide?"

"I told him I wasn't going to do it -- and I wasn't

going to ask Bud to either. I told him it was all very interesting -- but not my problem."

At this point I'm more confused than ever. "...So why are you here then?"

"I had a few days to think about it; I guess my curiosity was starting to get the best of me. Then Walter called this evening and said he'd do a water survey for me for free if I got involved in your dowsing project."

"*He did?*" I'm flabbergasted by this piece of information.

"Sure did. You know, I have a pretty steep water bill in the summer with all the watering we have to do to keep the lawn from dying, and my horses and garden and all. He said I'd never have to pay a dime for water ever again. But why isn't the city willing to pay for this? I see you've got the city service director here."

"Dean's been skeptical from the beginning. Now he's about ready to call it off -- can't say that I blame him."

"But Walter says you're almost there."

"*Walter* says. He may be right for all I know, but Dean's far from convinced. He put his ass on the line for us and he's just not willing to leave it there any longer. And I'm running out of money. I don't know how much we've spent yet, I'm afraid to find out -- but it's way up there."

"That's what I want to talk to you about. I can't ask Bud to risk *his* money --"

"Jesus Christ, Carlotta! No one's asking you to -- you already made that abundantly clear."

"You interrupted me. I've thought it over and, under the circumstances, I'm willing to help out myself."

"...You are?"

"You've gone so far already; it seems a shame to stop now. I have a hunch Walter knows what he's talking about. I talked to two of the people he found water for in California, he gave me their phone numbers. Now I want a well of my own," she says, grinning.

"The trouble is, this is the drilling crew's last day, tomorrow they have to be somewhere else. And when drilling's resumed here it'll be at a different location."

"Which Walter says will be a waste of time and money."

"He already told you that huh?"

"He put it a lot more colorfully than that," Carlotta replies with a laugh.

"I'll bet. Anyway, as late as it is now, I'm not sure Dean will even let them start up again."

"Well if he does, I'll split the cost of drilling with you."

"...That's great of you, Carlotta. But I've already spent too much as it is. I don't think --"

"I mean I'll split the whole cost with you. Whatever you think it's cost you so far, I'll pay half. The city will reimburse us if they find the contamination, right? That's what Walter told me."

Dumbfounded, I confirm this for her. "...What brought about your change of heart? Never mind, forget I asked; whatever it was, *thank* you, Carlotta. Let's go speak to Dean about it."

"No, you speak to him. I'm leaving."

"Leaving? You mean you're just gonna leave everything up to me to spend your -- *our* -- money?"

She shrugs. "Most of it's already spent. Besides, there ought to be *something* I can still trust you with, Cork." Catching sight of Brook looking quickly away, she says, "The drilling wasn't the only thing I learned about this week. I hope the two of you are happy together. I hope she knows what she's getting herself into."

Carlotta's bitter smile is full of hurt, but beneath it is the strength that brought her here tonight. Maybe even, I dare to hope, an implicit promise of the resumption of our friendship, on a different level. I have the sudden impression that her look of pain is merely the fading after-image of the old relationship, built on wants and needs and assumptions which in some sense we've outgrown -- this despite the fact that there is much we still don't understand and much we were wrong about. Beneath this remnant of the old, then, may lie the real core of our friendship. Or do I presume too much? My questioning gaze elicits no answers. Carlotta gives Brook -- who smiles gutsily, though a little uncertainly, at her -- a sidelong glance in passing.

"...She said she'd split the cost of drilling with me," I inform Brook in a tone of incredulity.

"I knew it was something like that," she replies, beaming.

"How did you know?"

"I could tell from the way she was looking at you."

This is all happening too fast for me. "...I don't know whether to ask Dean to let them continue drilling or not."

"*Why not?!*"

"Well, I've asked a helluva lot of him already, maybe too much -- I'm amazed he's gone along with it this far. Maybe we'd just be throwing good money after bad. Eventually you have to be willing to admit you made a mistake and give up, right? 'Know when to hold and when to fold.' And now I'm responsible for Carlotta's money as well as my own."

"Cork, if that's what's really worrying you, then don't stop now."

"That's easy for *you* to say."

"Just...trust me on this, okay?"

I don't know what to think, except that Brook's decisiveness seems to ring true somehow, as if it expresses something I'm feeling but not quite conscious of. All right, she said to trust her -- I will. Somehow I feel a little like a relay baton passed from Carlotta to Brook. It's time I took a stand here.

"...I'll go see what Dean says."

Walking over to where Walter, Dean and Russ are

standing, I feel more decisive myself with each step. At least it seems that way.

"Dean, let's drill just a little longer. I think we're close. I *know* we are, I feel it."

"You sure?" It may just be my wishful thinking but Dean, too, appears ready to be swept up in our infectious sense of conviction, although at the moment he's still hanging onto his professional skepticism.

"Sure he's sure, can't you tell?" Walter blurts out.

Dean looks at his watch. "...It's damn near one o'clock, Cork. How much longer do you wanta go?"

"I don't know, till dawn if they'll work that long," I reply immediately without stopping to consider my answer. "If we haven't found it by then, we'll quit, period -- no if's, and's or but's."

As if he himself can't believe how far out on this limb he's willing to crawl, Dean shakes his head. "Go see if they'll work that long," he says finally.

"Oh they'll work all right," Walter says. "Let's get 'em started again in the right spirit."

I'm about to walk away with him when I suddenly remember Brook. "Come with us!"

Her face brightens. I give her a big one-armed hug. It has suddenly occurred to me that there's nothing unmanly or irresolute in my being passed baton-like from Carlotta to Brook, if that's the way my mind wants to picture the transition. I don't even try to formulate this in a thought at the moment, but I know it's something I'll think a lot about later: Somehow the transition is as important in my life as either of the relationships in themselves. It extends them, in fact, as it extends me. Each of these women has given me so much, and now Carlotta, in effect, is passing me on to Brook, for the working out of a new phase in my ongoing relationship with the world.

Thinking of it like this brings tears to my eyes. Is this

a true insight, I wonder -- an epiphany -- or the fuzzy thinking of fatigue? Right now I don't care.

"Whatta you think of our dowser here, Walter?"

"*Me*?" Brook exclaims.

"No one else has done any more than you to make this happen," I assure her.

She still isn't buying this. "Well, you have. And Walter, for heaven's sake....And Carlotta's helping to *pay* for it."

"That's true but I'd have given up if you hadn't kept encouraging me."

"All I can do is *find* water, I don't make it wet," contributes Walter, bless his heart. "Thanks for the inside information, by the way."

...So it was *Brook* who helped put Walter in touch with Carlotta! She's actually blushing. "See?" I say, hugging her again, "we all had to become dowsers in our own way to make this happen."

Walter's analogy is only one of two statements tonight that I'll remember, word for word, for the rest of my life. The other is uttered a moment later by Dean Channel.

As the three of us start off toward the drilling rig, I hear Fawcett, finding this all very hard to believe, ask incredulously, "You're really gonna let 'em keep diggin'?"

I turn in time to see old straight arrow Dean, a big smile on his face, reply with a grand theatrical gesture that I'd have thought entirely uncharacteristic of him: "Yessir...keep diggin' -- till the sun's first rays reflect off the Thothwillow River. Till they turn it into the Shawnees' 'Bright Horn' again."

The water director gives him a strange look and says doubtfully, "...You don't really think they're gonna find anything do you?"

Dean laughs heartily and throws a big arm around him. "Stranger things have happened, Russ," he says. "Stranger things have happened."

243

EPILOGUE

Yes, *but*. At best, real life is a process of two steps forward, one step back, right? And sometimes it's more like the reverse. Getting ahead in life isn't so much a matter of eliminating the backward steps as learning how to cope with them, how to keep them from undermining our optimism and self-confidence.

So, *yes*, Walter's dowsing located the source of contamination in our water well. *But*, this wasn't the unalloyed triumph I had envisioned. It turns out that tetrachloroethylene is a type of solvent known as a "dense non-aqueous phase liquid" (DNAPL). These can't be contained underground; they tend to spread out, forming subterranean pools or plumes which pollute groundwater in an aquifer the way smog spreads through the atmosphere. Ohio EPA warned the city, If you unearth that stuff, you're going to have to haul it away -- all of it. Taking "x" number of truckloads of contaminated soil -- assuming we could even manage to get all of it -- to wherever the nearest toxic-waste disposal facility is located could have ended up costing Lafayette's taxpayers millions of dollars.

OEPA's suggestion was to drill what's called an "interceptor" well which, as the name implies, would -- if we were very fortunate -- capture the contaminated groundwater before it could pollute any of the other wells. And what were we to do with this polluted groundwater? "Aerate" it by pumping water from both the contaminated and interceptor wells through aerators on top of the wells -- and then into the Thothwillow River. That's right, after as much of the contamination as possible has been dispersed into the atmosphere, the PCE concentration will supposedly have become diluted enough to be harmless.

Was Walter's service to the community futile then? Not really; *finding* the contamination was an important step in dealing with it after all. And so far we have kept the other six wells from becoming polluted. I was, in fact, completely reimbursed for Walter's fee and expenses, and the city paid for the cost of drilling. Walter, Dean and I all gained a certain amount of local notoriety for the parts we played in the affair. Since our success was considerably muted so was the praise I suppose I'd looked forward to. (Perhaps my mother was right about this to some extent after all.) Some people never have accepted the city's picking up the tab for a dowser, especially when the only concrete result they can see is city water gushing night and day into the Thothwillow River. This became even more of an issue when a water shortage the following summer compelled the drilling of a new well.

While the controversy over who was to pay whom and how much was still raging, I called William Tiller, professor of materials science and engineering at Stanford University. He had collaborated with Walter on the first in a projected series of scientific papers on dowsing. I figured he could lend valuable credibility to our cause if we needed it. It turns out that the first paper in the series was also the last. It wasn't just Walter's ego and intransigence that were problematic. Prof. Tiller said he had become increasingly suspicious that, whether intentionally or otherwise, Walter was subtly influencing the response of the wand-type dowsing rod they were using in their experiments.

Of course, where dowsing for water is concerned it would do Walter no good whatsoever to manipulate his rods; the only thing that matters is whether or not he finds water, period. In the experiments conducted at Stanford, however, it wasn't water that was being sought but confirmation of Walter's elaborate theories of how and why his rods work: what it is they're actually responding to. So his scientific colleague secretly devised a way of detecting whether Walter was "pre-determining the motions of the wand" in any way. To put it bluntly, Walter flunked.

"I don't think he was doing this in any way intentionally or fraudulently," Prof. Tiller told me. But the test did persuade him that at least subconsciously Walter was physically manipulating the wand to make it behave in accordance with his theories. "I think of him as a sort of 'Rainmaker', like Burt Lancaster in the movie of that title," he said. "Walter's a terrific con man who also makes *something* happen. He's charismatic, with lots of energy which he doesn't understand."

Needless to say, I made no mention of this conversation to anyone in Lafayette but Brook. Lest you assume from this that Walter was more a charlatan than a genuine dowser (whatever the hell that is), however, let me add this interesting piece of information: In working with Walter, Prof. Tiller learned how to use the dowsing rods himself. He said that after amicably severing his professional association with him, he still uses "polarity-based materials" to give himself and others strength and still practices self-healing, although not with the wand.

For Walter, then, two steps forward, one step back. If he has been frustrated in his attempts to have his theories validated by an established scientist, perhaps the influence of his work in the private life of a public figure in academe will eventually further his cause -- even if it is long after he's dead. (Let's hope not too long after we've depleted the water table in various parts of the world.)

Walter did find Carlotta's well for her, by the way. They brought it in less than a month after his successful dowsing for the city. As he promised, she hasn't paid a cent for water since, and she's using it as extravagantly as she does the free gas on her property. How do I know? Well, I guess time is a healer too.

Brook and I are married now. Her own dowsing skills and whatever it is I've learned from all this seem to be working for us. We have a good time with each other; I don't waste as much energy as I used to worrying about my past repeating itself.

The family business finally went bust. There have been few hard feelings that I'm aware of among our creditors, though I suspect there may be some disgruntled people out there. Most, however, realize that we did the best we could under the circumstances. "Business is business," they say. "What's the use of holding a grudge?"

There really are a lot of nice people here. I've been back in Lafayette for almost ten years now, and even though Jimmy Majors -- divorced and living in his beloved Phoenix again -- keeps telling me the West is still where all the action is, I'm no longer in any hurry to leave. It's funny: for all my regrets about returning, if I hadn't come back, not only would I never have met Brook or Carlotta, but I'd never have encountered this story either. I'm thinking of making good on the white lie I told people I interviewed, and writing it all down someday.

THE END

APPENDIX A

The following scientific paper, published in 1974 by Prof. William Tiller (former head of the Materials Science & Engineering Dept. at Stanford University), in collaboration with California dowser Wayne Cook, was to have been the first of a series in an unprecedented university-affiliated scientific investigation of the dowsing phenomenon. As was noted in the Epilogue, the series never progressed beyond this initial paper. Prof. Emeritus Tiller is the author of 64 scientific papers.

Psychoenergetic Field Studies Using a Bio-Mechanical Transducer

Part I: Basics

by
William A. Tiller and Wayne Cook

Introduction

Over the course of the past century a variety of psychoenergetic devices for monitoring "non-physical" energies have been investigated. These devices include the Eamans' relaxation circuit[1], the Cayce appliances[2], the Lakhovski oscillator[3], radionics instruments[4], and a host of others[5]. However, the development of these devices has been severely limited by our inability to clearly define all the functioning elements involved in the device operation, and to delineate the essential protocol to be followed for widespread reproduction of the results by others.

In general, there are three categories of psychoenergetic devices to be understood and developed: **(A)** A human being who has already reliably constructed these extrasensory systems within his own organism. He observes a phenomenon and then gives one a verbal description of what is "seen". **(B)** A living system, plant, animal or human, to which is attached an electrical or mechanical readout device. Here, the living system transduces the "non-physical" energies into either electrical or mechanical correlates which then stimulate a meter or chart response on the readout device. In this category we have **(i)** the polygraph machine hooked up to a plant a la Backster[6], **(ii)** acupuncture-point monitoring devices attached to humans or plants[7], **(iii)** Kirlian photography devices attached to humans or plants[8,9], **(iv)** biofeedback devices attached to humans[10], **(v)** a dowsing wand in the hand of a dowser, etc.

   (C) The third category of devices are direct reading devices built from non-living materials according to the logic of these "non-physical" dimensions rather than to the logic of the physical dimension with which we are all familiar. Here, the device might sit on a table and we would mentally concentrate or emotionally express ourselves from perhaps 5 to 10 feet away, for example, and we would produce a direct response on a meter or chart in the device. At the moment, the only devices in this category appear to be the Soviet psychotronic generators and the Sergeyev detector[11].

   The present paper is concerned with the second category of devices and specifically with a biomechanical type of device which is similar to that used by dowsers. The main human subject in the study was the second author [Wayne Cook], who will be referred to throughout as WC. Although the first author [to be referred to throughout as WAT] was not initially able to function as the human transducer in the device, he was eventually able to do so, and some joint studies will be reported on. In this first paper, we will limit ourselves to the description of results that shed light on **(a)** the suspected mechanism of operation of the device, **(b)** human body polarities and main body energy circuits, **(c)** responses from different materials, and **(d)** the global interaction principle operating between different elements of the study system.

We offer these results not with the conviction that identical results will be produced by others, but with the realization that we are dealing with an exceedingly complex experimental system, a portion of which is some adaptive circuitry within the human part of the instrument; and that, even if only partially reproducible by others, these results may help someone else to give a more proper and complete description of that universal reality we are seeking to understand.

Device Description

WC, in his water dowsing, generally utilizes three types of instruments which are illustrated in **Fig. 1**. The most familiar type of divining rod **(Fig. 1a)** may be made from 3/32-inch steel welding rod, parallel or intertwined over about a 9 1/2-inch length at one end and spot-welded with silver solder. Copper sleeves (~1/4-inch diameter) about 6 1/2-inches long are located 2 inches from the opposite free ends of the welding rod. The joining is made using either epoxy or silver solder (normal solder gives strange effects). The full length of the instrument is about 36 inches, and the copper handles are mainly for comfort. To hold the instrument, the hands are held palms up with forearms bent at roughly right angles straight out in front of the body (arms relaxed). The fingers are wrapped around the copper sleeves with the thumb on the side of the rod (pointing back towards the body). This is generally used first in the sequence to locate the general vicinity of an underground stream.

The second step in the sequence is to utilize the angle rods illustrated in **Fig. 1b**. These are made from 1/8-inch welding rod about 3 feet long. The 6-inch open sleeve may be made from copper, brass, steel, etc., which rests on a half-nut stopper joined to the welding rod by epoxy or silver solder. An angle rod is held in each hand by gripping the copper sleeves and holding them vertically in front of the body at the same distance from the body with the tips slightly depressed below the horizontal. Thus, the rods extend horizontally in front of the body and are free to swing in a horizontal plane. This is used to locate the edge positions of the stream and to map out its detailed path.

The third step in the sequence is to utilize the counter rod illustrated in **Fig. 1c**. It consists of a 1/16-inch-diameter spring steel rod about 26 inches long with a half-nut epoxied on one end and a 1/2-inch diameter, 5-inch-long, thick-walled steel tube expoxied to the other end. This device is held in the right hand and is used for indicating the depth of the stream, its linear rate of low, its volume flow rate and the direction of flow.

In the present study we were not involved in the location of water and thus will not discuss how one proceeds to accomplish that end. For our studies we utilized only the counter rod or wand type of device and thus will restrict further comments to it alone. Most of the investigations were made utilizing the wand as depicted in **Fig. 1c**; however, for a special experiment, a handle such as illustrated in **Fig. 1d** was attached.

The experimental procedure was generally to grasp the wand with the right hand, which is firmly braced against the right side of the body with the left hand held either free of the body or touching the left side of the body above the beltline. The tip is located in the immediate vicinity of the object or body location under test and the motion of the tip of the rod observed. The general mode of tip motion is elliptical with either clockwise or counterclockwise steady rotation or oscillatory rotation. In the extremes, this leads to five distinctive periodic modes -- clockwise circular rotation, counterclockwise circular rotation, oscillatory circular rotation, vertical linear oscillation and horizontal linear oscillation -- as illustrated in **Fig. 2**. On a finer scale of tuning, information distinction is present in the angle of linear oscillation relative to the horizontal and in the degree of ellipticity of the motion (aspect ratio of the ellipse). In our studies, we discriminated only the five simple modes of wand motion shown in **Fig. 2**.

Some Polarity Results on Different Materials

We have found four different categories of materials which we have listed as bi-polar, unipolar (positive), unipolar (negative), and oscillating polarity.

Bi-polar: This is the most common material or object response and, with the wand held in the right hand and placed close to the object as in **Fig. 3**, produces a right-hand (clockwise) rotation **(Fig. 2a)** on the right side of the material; a left-hand (counterclockwise) rotation on the left side of the material **(Fig. 2b)**; and vertical oscillations directly over the top of the material **(Fig. 2d)**.

With the wand held in the left hand, the directions of rotation are reversed. If the wand is held on the same side of the material or object for too long a period of time, then after rotating to the right (positive) for a period, the motion becomes erratic and the operator begins to feel tension in his arm and his body begins to feel strange. Next, the wand begins rotating to the left (negative), and he finds that his body polarity has been reversed (see next section). Most household objects and materials fall into this category. These designations of positive and negative were chosen to correspond with the motion observed with the north pole (positive) and the south pole (negative) of a magnet.

Unipolar: For this kind of material, the wand exhibits only right-hand rotation or only left-hand rotation no matter what the location of the wand relative to the object. Most unipolar materials are of the positive variety and generally fall in the category of beneficial herb; e.g., ginseng, gotukola, fo-ti-ting, etc. The male gonads and the male sperm are also of this polarity. To date, the only unipolar material of the negative variety that we have located is the female gonads and the corresponding secretion. The two secretions combined on a glass slide yield the familiar bi-polar response.

Oscillating Polarity: With this class of material, it does not matter where the wand is spatially located with respect to the object (so long as it is close). One observes that the tip rotates to the right and then stops and rotates to the left and then stops and reverses again, etc. In this category we find a variety of metals such as mercury, lead, cadmium, arsenic and a variety of poisons like rattlesnake venom, etc. In the food category, we find that pork, shellfish, rabbit and insecticide [-tainted produce] fit into this pattern.

In all of these studies, if the wand is in the right hand, the left hand needs to be held within 6 to 16 inches of the object in order to have any motion generated in the wand tip. The exception to this is when the operator either holds some of the same material in his left hand or it is in contact with certain parts of his body, or if he contains the substance within his own body.

Another point that should be made at this juncture is that, although WC and WAT obtain identical responses in most materials tested, there are some materials that produce different responses for us. One example is the mineral azurite (hydrated copper carbonate), which always yields a positive polarity for WAT but always yields an oscillating polarity for WC. A second example is ordinary black coffee which is bi-polar for WC but is an oscillating polarity for WAT (decaffeinated coffee is found to be bi-polar for WAT). A third example relates to WAT and his wife (who has a slight hypoglycemic condition) and their individual response to a can of soda pop. For WAT, it is bi-polar but for his wife Jean it is an oscillating polarity -- presumably because of the high sugar content.

Finally, the results obtained with combinations of different materials are worthy of comment. It is found that two-member combinations, produced by placing jars of each side by side, can lead to a wand response that may be the same as one of the members or different from either of them. For three-member combinations, the same options hold. In Table I, the results for WC and WAT with a variety of material combinations are given.

Some Polarity Results on the Human Body

The polarities of all people studied to date fall into two categories: **(a)** macroscopically bi-polar and **(b)** macroscopically unipolar (positive) with wand motions as illustrated in **Fig. 4.** For these results, the experimenter was facing the subject and holding the wand in his right hand. For most people, one finds that the left sole, left palm and left eye exhibit a positive polarity. Likewise, the right sole, right hand and right eye exhibit a negative polarity. In 1% to 2% of the cases, the polarities were reversed.

Along the centerline (front and back) of a bi-polar person, a vertical oscillation **(Fig. 2d)** is observed. No such centerline effect is observed for a unipolar person. On a positively unipolar female, one finds (front and back) a negative polarity region centered on the gonads and having a radius of about 6 inches. Unipolar adults are a fairly rare event; bi-polar nature is the more common.

The fingertips of both the bi-polar and unipolar person are the same. On the left hand, the thumb (negative) is opposite to the palm; the index finger is the same as the thumb (negative); the forefinger gives a vertical oscillation; the fourth finger shows the same polarity as the palm (positive); and the baby finger also shows a positive polarity. It should be noted that the index-finger side of the forefinger shows negative while the opposite side shows positive, yielding a combination result like **Fig. 2d.**

On the right hand, the results are exactly the opposite the left. On both hands, these results are obtained by holding the wand tip close to the fingerpads with the fingers outstretched and well separated from one another. The back of the hand is opposite in polarity to the palm except for the left hand of a positively unipolar person.

One is tempted to try to correlate these polarity results with the acupuncture meridians that end at the fingertips. But while there are some correspondences and relationships between the presently discussed energy polarities and the yin and yang polarities of acupuncture meridians, there is no absolute correlation. This can be seen, for example, by noting that the meridians ending at the fingertips alternate yin and yang and are symmetrical on the left and right hands. Here, these polarities are opposite on the two hands and do not alternate with adjacent fingers.

Moving to the feet, the wand response is simple for a unipolar person -- it is the same adjacent to any part of the foot (except the sole) as the macroscopic polarity. For the bi-polar person, the story is different. At the sides of the foot, as one makes a complete circuit around the foot one finds alternate polarities in each of the four quadrants, with vertical oscillations along the midline as shown in **Fig. 4a**. There is also a split along the midline between the feet, and the polarities of the feet are mirror images of each other. On the top of the feet, at the base of the toes, the polarity is the same as the macropolarity for that side of the body.

At other joints of the body, there are no dramatic changes for a unipolar person. However, for a bi-polar person, the polarity reverses in the middle of a bone and reverses again at a joint with another bone. Further, around the circumference of the bone, the polarity reverses in adjacent quadrants of the four quadrants just as was seen with the feet.

It was possible to determine in which direction the energy that gave rise to these polarities was flowing by the following simple experiment. If we pick up an object, say a jar of oscillating polarity material, in the left hand and hold it for a minute before setting it down, then with the wand in the right hand, hold the tip close to the jar, we obtain the proper tip motion even with our left hand far removed from the jar.

After a few minutes, the amplitude of oscillation dies down to zero. If we repeat the experiment but this time pick up the jar in the right hand, then after having set it down, try to check for wand motion, we find none unless the left hand is placed in the vicinity of the jar. This same experiment was carried out with the foot circuit, wherein the oscillating polarity jar was contacted via either the left or right sole (with socks on), and similar results were obtained: i.e., contact with the left sole led to wand motion, whereas with the right sole, no motion occurred.

From this experiment we have concluded that energy streams enter the body via the left hand, left sole and left eye, and exit the body via the right hand, right sole and right eye. Waves of right-hand circular polarizatioin flowing in the direction of this energy stream would be consistent with these polarity results. From this experiment and the one outlined below, it seems that we are dealing with three main circuits of the body for this type of energy. These circuits have an easy and a difficult direction of flow and are somewhat interconnected, rather than being totally isolated from each other.

The circuit pathways have been somewhat delineated by following the experimental setup shown in **Fig. 5** when WC was still bi-polar. A molecule foreign to the body is placed on a table and monitored by the wand while another sample of this molecule is placed at various locations on the body. If it is placed at location 1 in the left hand, wand response (bi-polar) occurs, suggesting that a linking circuit via the air has been made. With the sample fastened to the leg at location 2, no wand response occurs, providing that both feet are on the ground. If only the left foot is raised 18 inches off the ground, there is still no wand response; however, if only the right foot is raised 18 inches off the ground, wand response occurs.

This series suggests two important factors: **(1)** The

leg circuit consists of energy entering the sole of the left foot from the ground, traveling up the leg across the groin, down the right leg and back to the ground via the sole of the right foot. (2) If the sample is not linked in a critical energy loop with the sample "s", then no wand motion can occur. When both feet are on the ground, the sample at location 2 is linked only with circuit (a) (see Fig. 5), which is isolated from the source "s". When the left foot is raised, energy can flow in circuit (c), but this does not link 2 with s. When the right foot is raised, energy can flow in circuit (d) which links with s. If the location of the sample is shifted to point 3, wand response occurs no matter what is done with the feet, which suggests that the hand-trunk circuit and the leg circuit interconnect at point 3.

If the location of the sample is shifted to either ear (point 4), then no wand response occurs, which suggests that there is a local head circuit that is not linked with s. Finally, if the sample is placed at point 5 at the back of the neck, wand motion occurs, suggesting that the hand circuit and the eye circuit can couple at this location.

Our conclusions based upon this and other studies is that only the circuits (a), (b) and (e) of Fig. 5 are detectable in the human body; i.e., we found no ear circuit, navel circuit, etc. Now that WC is unipolar, a slightly different character of wand response has been found. This will be discussed in later papers of this series. [There were no further papers.]

As a final comment in this section, it has been noted by one of us (WC) that all young babies tested to date have exhibited a positive unipolar wand response. At some later point in life, the body becomes bi-polar. However, it does seem to be possible to return oneself to the unipolar state since both WC and WAT were bi-polar when these experiments were begun almost two years ago, but switched to unipolar about eight months ago. Some of the protocol factors involved in this body polarity change will be discussed in Part II of this series.

Interconnections

It has already been noted that the wand response is not just a function of the material under study but is also a function of the inner circuitry of the wand holder. When conducting studies with certain unknown materials, new shape configurations or extended sequences of operations, one or several of the operator's three main circuits may temporarily cease to function; i.e., give no wand response. We have learned a number of techniques for reinitiating the circuits, and we can soon repeat the experiment. However, on many occasions, WC can be experimenting on one side of the room while WAT is sitting 12 feet away making notes. Then, one of WC's circuits will suddenly go out and WAT can feel a sensation in his own body. On checking his circuits, he finds it to be out also. Thus, not only are WC and the material being studied part of the measuring energy circuit, but WAT is also part of that same circuit even though he is 12 feet away.

It has been found that members of the same family generally exhibit a similar connectedness; i.e., an energy circuit effect on one member gives rise to a similar effect on the same energy circuit of a closely linked member. Whatever kind of energy is being dealt with here, it seems to connect all members mentally or emotionally involved in the experiment as part of the human component of the measuring circuit.

Postulated Mechanism of Device Operation

There are five key observations that allow one to speculate on the essential elements of a mechanism. These are: **(1)** If the wand is gripped by its handle **(Fig. 1d)** in a vise, with fingers wrapped around the steel sleeve and with objects brought into the vicinity of the tip, no motion of the tip is observed; however, if taken out of the vise and held normally, tip motion of an organized character occurs. **(2)** If the wand, without the handle **(Fig. 1c)**, is held by the steel sleeve (fingers wrapped around it) and the tip is pointed directly at the center of the object (along a radial line), then negligible motion of the rod is observed. However, if a finite perpendicular exists between the wand axis and the object being studied, then motion is observed.

(3) The mode of motion exhibited by the wand tip is independent of the spatial direction of approach to the object by the subject; i.e., N,S,E or W, etc. (4) If a specific element is brought up to the wand and this same element is contained in the body to a measurable degree, motion ensues even though the left hand is held removed from the element sample. If the specific element is not contained in the body to a sufficient degree, no wand motion is detected. If one holds another sample of the same specific element in the left hand, wand motion ensues and increases in amplitude above that for the former condition. (5) The tip motion results determined by different operators studying the same object are sometimes different even though the results are consistently repeatable for the same operator.

Observation (5) suggests that at least one necessary element for wand response is energy passage through the operator; i.e., he is an integral part of the information response system, and the specific type of response depends upon his internal energy structure. Observation (2) suggests that more than energy passage through the operator is needed for wand-tip motion; i.e., energy must also react directly on the wand tip. Observation (3) suggests that the type of energy being sensed by this device is being emitted radially by the object.

Observation (4) suggests that our internal circuitry functions somewhat like a double-detection or superheterodyne receiver of the type used in AM, FM and microwave radio. Simplistically, the energy stream, acting as a carrier wave, is rippled with information relative to the specific element (either external to the body or internal in the body) and enters the left side of the body via the left hand, etc. In addition, the element information enters the right side of the body via the wand. Via processes of frequency mixing, amplification and detection at an unconscious level, the left side information is matched against the right side information. If they match, then a new signal is generated at the unconscious level which is then brought to conscious registration via some specific involuntary mechanism of the body.

This registration signal could be on one of several different frequency bands, each designated to yield a different specific type of registration response at the conscious level. The magnitude of the registration signal is determined, in part, by the magnitude of the signal on the carrier wave passing through the body and, in part, by the amplification capacity of the individual's internal circuit (which can be increased by practice).

Observation **(1)** suggests one possible involuntary registration mechanism for transferring the unconscious result signal to the conscious level; i.e., that physical movement of the muscles of the hand and thus of the wand handle is triggering information display by the wand tip. In all, we seem to be dealing with a kind of biofeedback loop involving very small signal strengths. The body seems to have weak sensors for these signals which are effectively amplified by the motion of the wand. As we all know, one may excite a very heavy swing to large amplitude excursions by a sequence of properly phased but very small amplitude pulses. We seem to have the same principle operating here.

This possibility is emphasized by taking the modified wand **(Fig. 1d)** and holding it firmly in a vise. In this case, the wand yields no motion when an object is brought up to it even though the operator has his fingers wrapped around the steel sleeve. However, if the vise is detached from the edge of the bench and placed on a resilient substance which, in turn, rests on the bench top, then one does begin to see a slow buildup to large amplitude and motion. *One also sees very* *small undulations of the vise on its flexible cushion.* Of course, conservation of momentum would require this.

Before moving on, it should also be noted that when the modified wand **(Fig. 1d)** is held by the U-shaped guard rather than by its normal handle (the steel sleeve), tip motion still occurs and, for some people, the motion seems to be better regulated than that found using the unmodified wand of **Fig. 1c.** It should also be noted that other readout mechanisms besides involuntary hand muscle movement may be possible.

Some Other Relationships

(a) To the Eemans' Relaxation Circuit: Eemans[1,2] developed a circuit that could be used as either a relaxation or a tension circuit. This is illustrated in **Fig. 6** and consists of an individual plus copper mats and copper wires. The back of the head and the right hand were found to be of one polarity. The base of the spine and the left hand were found to be of the opposite polarity. The individual (clothed) is aligned along the magnetic flux line with head to the north and feet to the south (ankles crossed). If he is right-handed and connected in this way, he will just relax in this particular circuit, and this brings about a balancing of the energies in his body. If the hand connections are reversed, a tension circuit is built which right-handed people find almost unbearable after a little while. If the individual is left-handed (energy-wise), the situation is reversed. These were the findings of Eemans[1,2], and they have been substantiated by this author [WAT] using a variation of the basic technique[11].

From the point of view of our results discussed earlier, we would attribute the utility of the Eemans' circuit to an equalization of some "biological potential" within the three main body circuits. The left hand draws energy from the head circuit, feeds it through the trunk of the body and into the leg circuit. In this way, one might expect that the three circuits would be essentially "shorted out" and equalize their potentials. This would be so providing that departures from the relaxed state led to higher potentials existing in the head circuit than in the leg circuit. Of course, for truly left-handed people, the situation would be reversed.

If our theorizing is correct, then the copper serves only as a conductor and one can obtain similar effects by just using the bare hands. This has been tried by WAT and it definitely works! A simple protocol is as follows: If the body is stressed or one has a headache, lie on a bed or the floor, somewhat on your left side, with the left hand at the back of the head (base of skull) and the right hand at the base of the spine. Cross the left ankle over the right and try to relax. In about 15 minutes, the body will begin to comply and, with continued time, one progresses into a deeper and deeper relaxation state. The body orientation with respect to north does not seem to be of major importance. This can also be carried out with the body in a sitting position.

It is worthy of mention that male and female lying in an embrace, each with left hand on partner's base of brain and right hand on partner's base of spine, should tend to produce a deep harmonizing attunement with each other as well as a relaxation state. We would speculate that this is caused by our partner's "vibes" flowing through our body, and vice versa. This special sense of attunement seems to last for several days to a week for WAT and wife. There exist other beneficial circuit connections that will be discussed in later papers of this series.

As an extension to these observations, we have noticed that the conventional method of handshake, right hand to right hand, does not allow energy to flow from body to body and, in fact, depletes the energy current through both bodies. If one wishes to truly greet another via energy exchange, then right hand should hold left and left hand should hold right of the partner. In this way an energy circuit is formed and "current" flows through both from one to the other. A similar situation exists with respect to eye to eye contact.

(b) To the Cayce Appliances: Both the "wet cell" and the "radioactive appliance" described by Cayce[2] utilized a solution jar in the circuit with the human body. This jar contained particular solutions depending upon the condition needed; i.e., **(1)** gold chloride to supply nerve energies for rebuilding nerves, **(2)** spirits of camphor to supply general healing forces, **(3)** atomidine to supply cleansing of the body[2].

It seems that, for healing, it is not necessary to have the physical substance present -- rather, it is important to have the vibratory quality of the substance. When the current flows through the solution, the energy stream picks up the vibratory quality of whatever is in the solution jar and moves this quality into the body on the current acting as a carrier wave. If there are centers within the body, or molecules, which absorb and radiate in the frequency band of these vibrating qualities, then they will just absorb the resonant wave patterns. These elements, molecules or glands will gain, in fact, the value that they would have gained from the minerals themselves. Thus, the function of the solution jar is to serve as a current-modulating device.

With respect to the body connections for the electrodes from these devices, Cayce advised the following: "Attachments are made as follows: Mark the terminals and always attach the same terminal first to the body. First day, right wrist and left ankle. Second day, left wrist and right ankle. Third day, left ankle and right wrist. Fourth day, right ankle and left wrist. Then you repeat this about three or four times."[2] We can note that, in all cases, the current would flow through a portion of the leg circuit and the trunk-hand circuit. By changing the electrode locations from day to day, all portions of these circuits would have been irrigated by the current flow.

(c) To the pendulum and to Vivaxis: It has long been known that using a pendulum held from the hand by a string, one is able to obtain a set of pendulum motions which confer information. These motions correspond almost exactly to those illustrated in **Fig. 2**. We can thus conclude that the pendulum is also able to respond to the same energies that stimulate the wand. However, fewer people exhibit sufficient body conductivity for this energy to produce wand motion than those who can produce motion of pendula. The number should really be the same but, since the pendulum can be moved by a smaller force, mental interference (conscious or otherwise) is greater for the pendulum. Correlations between these two techniques will be discussed in later pages of this series.

The techniques of the subject Vivaxis[4] utilize angle wires of the general type presented in Fig. 1b. It is felt that the wand technique, discussed in this paper, responds to the same energies as the Vivaxis' angle wires. In future papers this correspondence will be explored.

Utility for Healing

By placing one's left hand on his own body or on someone else's body, energy of the type discussed in this paper can be removed from that location. By placing one's right hand on his own or on someone else's body, this energy can be introduced at that location. If an individual has a pain at a particular location in his body, then he or someone else can diminish the pain by placing the left hand on the location with the right hand held out from the body to release the energy stream into the atmosphere. The left palm acts somewhat like a fan or suction pump to pull the energy stream from the subject's body at that location and passing it out through the right palm. It is presumed that this energy stream carries with it some measure of the energy causing the pain.

Several important factors modify the efficiency of this process: **(1)** If the individual removing the pain is a poor conductor of this energy, then the impedance to current flow will be high and only a small current will flow, and the process will take a very long time; i.e., it will be inefficient.

(2) If one makes contact with the acupuncture meridian and acupuncture points for that pain area, the impedance will be lower and the current flow higher. **(3)** If one presses on the acupuncture points with the fingertips, the impedance seems to be further decreased, yielding higher current flow. **(4)** Although one can discharge this energy into a variety of media, a type of polarization or saturation quickly occurs so that the potential difference driving the discharge current decreases and the magnitude of the current decreases. The best type of sink for this energy discharge found to date is an oscillating polarity material. A combination of oscillating polarity materials, presumably providing a much broader frequency band than any single member, seems to be the most efficient.

The most effective procedure seems to be to place the wand in the right hand and hold the tip four to six inches from a jar of oscillating polarity material. Then, with the left hand, locate those acupuncture points that seem tender to the touch (even through clothes). An oscillating motion will appear at the wand tip, the radius of the circle being directly related to the severity of the condition. The left finger is maintained on the point until the amplitude of motion dies down to zero (which may take several minutes).

Often the finger touching the point may feel almost painfully hot and often the hand holding the wand will respond likewise. A sharp sound report, "crack", is often obtained by WC when he releases the wand. It is beneficial to break the circuit every few minutes to eliminate any internal polarization that may have been set up. This procedure continues periodically until no further wand motion is noted. From the small amount of experience we have had to date, almost any subject can relieve many of his aches and pains by using the wand technique. Even though he may not be a good conductor, holding the wand in the right hand and letting the tip touch the oscillating polarity jar is sufficient to produce a small leakage of discharge current. One may do this while watching television or reading, talking, etc. The discharge sink should always be placed on the right side of the body and at least 18 inches from the body (and handled with the right hand only).

Reservations

The authors have two main reservations about this work: **(a)** the motion of the wand can be influenced by the operator's mind through voluntary muscle action and **(b)** we seem to be an adaptive organism whose essential circuits for this measurement are still in the process of change so that results obtained a year or two from today may be slightly different from those obtained today. When WAT first began to obtain wand motion, it was extremely easy for him to make the wand move in either direction by only slight mental concentration.

It is not at all surprising that this should be so and that mentally generated voluntary muscle signals could swamp out the sensor-signal-generated involuntary muscle signals. Fortunately, with practice, the magnitude of the sensor signal seemed to increase and the ease of mentally "cheating" decreased. It is extremely important to try to remove any mental bias during a measurement because it is relatively easy to let voluntary muscle control slip in if we are looking for a preconceived result. Conversely, if we approach a measurement with a detached mental state, we may obtain clear and unambiguous readings.

We have also found that these energy circuits become fatigued after several energy reversals so that, if insufficient time is allowed between repetitions of an experiment, the results are found not to be reproducible. It seems that a type of internal polarization can be developed in the energy circuits with repeated use, and time must be given for the system to relax to the same initial state before repetition should be tried. Certain foods taken into the body can also influence the measurement reproducibility shortly after eating.

Summing Up

Our attempt here has been merely to outline some of the basic principles involved in this bio-mechanical transducer measuring system. We think that a new type of energy is involved and, although there appear to be some interesting considerations here, we recognize that nothing definitive has been proven yet. In the human body we seem to be working with the following general type of reaction equations:

Structural ---> Chemistry ---> Energy ---> Mind
states   <--- states   <--- states   <--- states

Medicine has, in the past, largely focused on the link between chemical states and structural states. Now it seems that we are about ready to take the next step of working directly with the energy-state level. We feel that the bio-mechanical transducer is a useful tool for learning something specific about these energy states and how they interact with both the chemical and the mental states of man.

Perhaps the most significant point to be emphasized is that, concerning the energy studied here, we are an integral part of the flow pattern and spectral distribution. In the measurement of the process, we cannot be separated from the process. Thus, our mental, emotional and physiological states have a subtle influence on the details of the process. This must be understood and accepted if we are to make progress in this type of research area.

References

1. L. E. Eemans, "Co-operative Healing" (Frederick Muller, Ltd., London, 1947).

2. W. A. Tiller, "Energy Fields and the Human Body, Part II," in Symposium Proceedings, "Mind-Body Relationships in the Disease Process," p. 70 (A.R.E. Clinic, Ltd., Phoenix, Arizona, 1972).

3. G. Lakhovski, "The Secret of Life" (Health Research, P.O. Box 70, Mokelumne Hill, California, 1970).

4. W. A. Tiller, "Radionics, Radiesthesia and Physics," in Symposium Proceedings, "The Varieties of Healing Experience" (Academy of Parapsychology and Medicine, Los Altos, California, 1971).

5. M. L. Gallert, "New Light on Therapeutic Energies" (James Clarke Co., Ltd., London, 1966).

6. C. Backster, "Evidence of Primary Perception in Plant Life," International Journal of Parapsychology 10, 1968.

7. W. A. Tiller, "Some Physical Network Characteristics of Acupuncture Points and Meridians," in Symposium Proceedings on "Acupuncture" (Academy of Parapsychology and Medicine," Los Altos, California, 1972).

8. S. Ostrander and L. Schroeder, "Psychic Discoveries Behind the Iron Curtain" (Prentice Hall, New York, 1970).

9. W. A. Tiller, "The Light Source in High Voltage Photography," in Symposium Proceedings, "Second Western Hemisphere Conference on Kirlian Photography, Acupuncture and the Human Aura" (Gordon and Breach, New York, 1974).

10. E. Green, "Biofeedback for Mind-Body Self-
     Regulation: Healing and creativity," in <u>Symposium
     Proceedings</u>, "The Varieties of Healing Experience"
     (Academy of Parapsychology and Medicine, Los
     Altos, California, 1971).

11. W. A. Tiller, to be published.

Figure Captions

No.

1   The different types of sensing devices used by a
    dowser.

2   The five most distinctive types of wand tip motion.

3   Illustration of wand tip motion about a bi-polar
    material.

4   Polarities around the human body for **(a)** a typical

    bi-polar human and **(b)** a unipolar human being.

5   Sample locations used to discover the pathways of the
    three main body circuits.

6   Illustration of the Eemans' relaxation circuit.

Table 1

Material	WC Observation	WAT Observation
Peg Leg mineral	Bi-polar, body circuits OK	Bi-polar, body circuits OK
Isotone	Positive polarity, body circuits OK	Positive polarity, body circuits OK
Discharge material	Oscillating polarity, body circuits OK	Oscillating polarity, body circuits OK
Peg Leg + discharge material	Oscillating polarity, body circuits OK	Oscillating polarity, body circuits OK
Peg Leg + discharge material + isotone	Positive polarity, body circuits OK	Positive polarity, body circuits OK
Azurite	Oscillating polarity, body circuits OK	Positive polarity, body circuits OK
Li	Positive polarity, body circuits OK	Positive polarity, body circuits OK
Mo	Positive polarity, body circuits OK	Positive polarity body circuits OK
Azurite + Li	Positive polarity, body circuits OK	Positive, but less than azurite above
Azurite + Mo	Zero polarity, body circuits knocked out	Positive, and stronger than azurite + Li
Azurite + Mo + Li	Zero polarity, body circuits OK	Zero, and body circuits knocked out
Isotone + azurite +Mo + Li	Zero polarity, body circuits OK	Positive polarity
Diethylstilbesterol	Oscillating polarity, all body circuits oscillate and one feels shaky	Oscillating polarity, all body circuits oscillate and one feels shaky

Figure 1

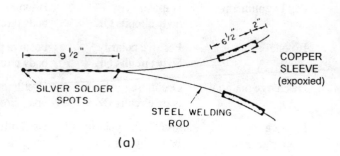

(a)

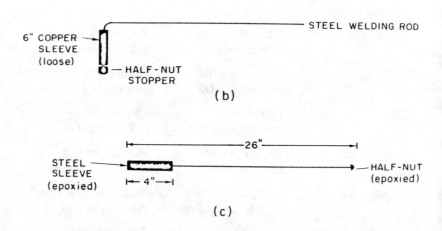

(b)

(c)

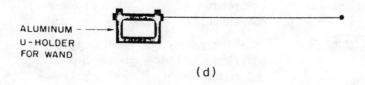

(d)

Figure 2

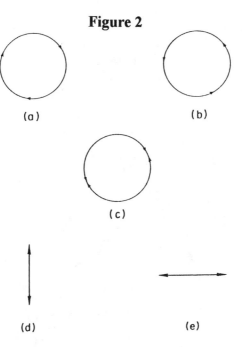

(a)

(b)

(c)

(d)

(e)

Figure 3

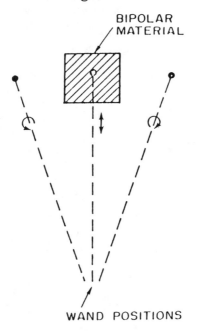

BIPOLAR
MATERIAL

WAND POSITIONS

273

Figure 4

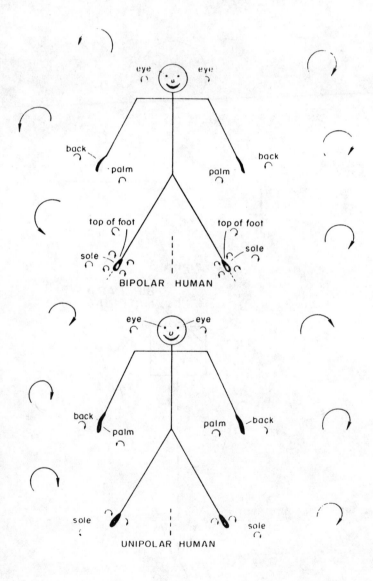

BIPOLAR HUMAN

UNIPOLAR HUMAN

Figure 5

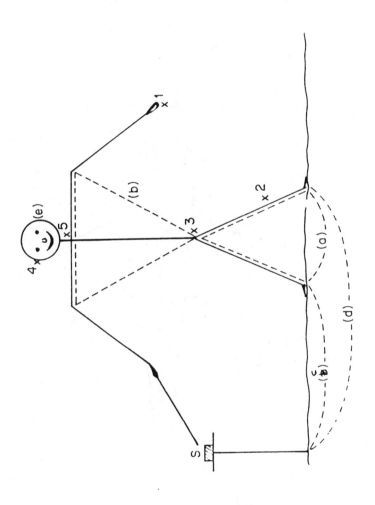

Figure 6

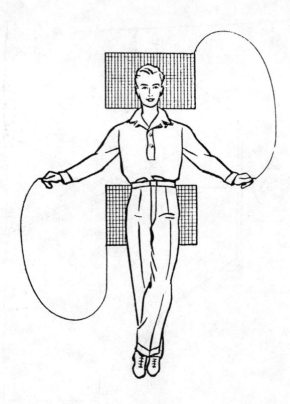

APPENDIX B

"Walter Barry" is a combination of two real-life dowsers, both now deceased. All the biographical material in the story was related to me by Wayne Cook in a weekend interview prior to our filming him for "The Fourth Dimension". Map dowsing of the contaminated well field, however, was performed by the late Don Wood and his partner Elaine Ralston, who is still operating Dowsing Unlimited, the business in which she was partnered with Don in upstate New York. They didn't actually dowse on site because in real life there was no Cork Rockner to initiate the metaphorical communal dowsing which helped bring the fictional Walter to "Lafayette".

When informed of my having written *Dowsing for Love*, which included her father, Nancy Wood graciously sent me the following testimonial letters from Don and Elaine's many satisfied customers. The ones I chose to use are only about half of those she mailed, which in turn, according to Nancy, are only a fraction of the letters of thanks her father and Elaine have received over the years.

To me they are remarkable not so much for what they attest, since I've become more than merely open-minded in regard to dowsing's efficacy. Don and Elaine's success in *eliciting* such an outpouring of testimonial gratitude is what impresses me most, knowing of Wayne Cook's difficulty in getting people to thank him in writing for the many wells he located.

I'm pleased to be able to share these letters with you -- from communities and developers, businesses, private individuals and well drillers (often dowsers' biggest skeptics, until they've worked together) -- and hope you'll take time to read them. Selected for their broad range of detail, most of the letters have one element in common: the initial skepticism of their writers toward hiring a dowser.

But, other than love, what's more precious than water? The need for it will continue to override society's prevailing fear and loathing toward anything that seriously questions our notion of reality. The increasing scarcity of pure drinking water on our planet, in rich and poor countries alike, may finally compel the scientific establishment to follow the courageous lead of people like Prof. Tiller and intellectually curious dowsers like Wayne Cook in explicating and embracing the ancient phenomenon of dowsing.

WILLIAM M. COHEN   ARCHITECT
210 FIFTH AVENUE
NYC, NEW YORK 10010
212 686 7281 FAX 212 213 1424

APRIL 16, 1992

DON WOOD
ELAINE RALSTON
BOX 273
ROSE AVE.
TILLSON, N.Y.

DEAR MR. WOOD AND MS. RASTON:

I WOULD LIKE TO THANK YOU FOR THE JOB YOU DID AT THE GEBAUER PROPERTY. THE WELL DRILLERS FOUND WATER WITHIN TEN FEET OF THE DEPTH YOU HAD SAID AND THE YIELD FROM THE WELL WAS DOUBLE THE AMOUNT YOU HAD PREDICTED WE WOULD FIND.

I MUST ADMIT THAT I AND MEMBERS OF MY OFFICE EXPRESSED OUR DOUBTS THAT A DOWSER, NOT USING A SCIENTIFIC APPROACH WOULD BE ABLE TO FIND WATER. I AM HAPPY TO REPORT THAT AFTER THIS POSITIVE EXPERIENCE I HAVE BECOME A PROPONENT OF DOWSING. YOUR STORIES ABOUT PAST JOBS AND THE DIFFERENT KINDS OF PROBLEMS THAT A DOWSER CAN SOLVE WERE FASCINATING TO ME.

YOURS TRULY,

William M. Cohen

WILLIAM M. COHEN

DOWSING FOR LOVE

DANCING ROCK, INC.

P.O. Box 435
Bearsville, New York 12409
(914) 688-7600
(914) 679-9055

APRIL 25, 1991

TO DON WOOD AND ELAINE RALSTON :

I WOULD LIKE TO THANK BOTH OF YOU FOR COMING UP TO DANCING
ROCK. MY PROPOSED THIRTY-SEVEN LOT SUB-DIVISION. DUE TO THE
CONTROVERSY OF MY PROJECT THE ULSTER COUNTY HEALTH DEPARTMENT
REQUIRED THAT WE DRILL TWO TO THREE TEST WELLS AT THE HIGHEST
BUILDING ELEVATIONS ON THE MOUNTAIN (APPROX 1300 M.S.L.).

DON AND ELAINE CAREFULLY SELECTED THE TWO EXACT DRILLING SITES
BY DOWSING THEM AND CONSULTING EACH OTHER FOR THE "CROSSING OF
VEINS". THEY PREDICTED WATER AT THE HIGHEST WELL TO BE AT 170'.
THEY ESTIMATED A YIELD BETWEEN 11 TO 21 GALLONS PER MINUTE.
THE HEALTH DEPARTMENT REQUIRED AT LEAST FIVE GPM AND STATED
SEVERAL TIMES THAT THEY EXPECTED TO SEE DEEP WELLS. THIS WELL
HIT WATER AT 171' AS THE CHAIRMAN OF THE PLANNING BOARD AND RICHARD
RISELEY, MY ATTORNEY WATCHED AS JUST MINUTES PRIOR I TOLD THEM THAT
THE DOWSERS PREDICTED WATER AT 170 '. WE DRILLED TO 198' AND HAD A SUSTAINED
PUMP TEST PERFORMED FOR FOUR HOURS AFTER STABALIZATION. THE TEST
DEMONSTRATED 10 GPM.
DEAN PALEN, CHAIRMAN OF THE ULSTER COUNTY HEALTH DEPARTMENT WAS VERY
SURPRISED AND SAID HE NEVER EXPECTED A YIELD LIKE THAT ESPECIALLY AT
THAT DEPTH.
OUR SECOND WELL GAVE US EVEN A BETTER YIELD. 15 G.P.M. AT 298'

279

DANCING ROCK, INC.
P.O. Box 435
Bearsville, New York 12409
(914) 688-7600
(914) 679-9055

WE HIT MOST OF THE WATER AT IN THE LOW 280'S. DON AND ELAINE DOWSED
SEE NOTE
IT AS LOW AS 203' TO ABOUT 262' ʌ THEY PRTEDICTED A GOOD YIELD AND THEY
WERE CORRECT (11 TO 21 G.P.M.) THE THIRD WELL WAS UNNECESSARY AFTER
THE TWO RESULTS.

IN SUMMARY DON WOOD HAD DOWSED SEVERAL WELLS FOR ME PRIOR TO THIS IN 1985
AND 1986 AND WITH HIS ADDITIONAL PARTNER, ELAINE , I SINCERLY RECOMMEND THEM

TO ANYONE WHO WHO NEEDS TO DRILL A WELL. THEY ARE GOOD AT WHAT THEY DO,
VERY RELIABLE, AND VERY NICE PEOPLE TO SPEND TIME WITH IN SEARCH FOR
THE OPTIMUM WELLSITE.
YOURS TRULY

LARRY HEIMEL

Note by Don and Elaine;

Our actual predictions were this; One vein at 203' to 212', 11 to 12 G.PM.
The second vein (crossing vein), at 253' to 262', 9 to 10 G.P.M.

A THIRD WELL: On his partner's property (and adjoining his property), was
drilled to 300', somewhat beyond our predictions and getting very little
water. Elaine and I went to the site and with a crowbar & sledge hammer we
freed up the veins, which the rotary drill rig had sealed. They ended up
with 14 G.P.M.!!!

 **OROWEAT**

To: Elaine Ralston & Don Wood   Sep. 91

Dear Elaine & Don

Thanks for coming to Livingston N.Y. Entenmann's
apple processing plant to dowse a new well
for us. Good producing wells and good water
are hard to come by in this area.
The new well, #4, when it was drilled produced
approx. 25 GPM. at first, at your recommendation
we had Jim Eckerson dry ice it, now we
measured 35 GPM at 303 feet as you
predicted.
I asked you to try to improve the flow in
wells #2 and #3 and you did that by
diverting nearby water veins into them.
#2 increased from 4 to 7 GPM, #3 from
2 to 5 GPM. Our #1 well has allways
given us 18 GPM, so with your help we
more than doubled our capacity, we
should be in fine shape for years to
come.
      Once again thank you for this fine
dowsing job, Elaine and Don.

                              Walter Becker
GENERAL FOODS BAKERY COMPANIES, INC.   Facilities Manag.
55 PARADISE LANE, BAY SHORE, NY 11706

281

J. T. ECKERSON, INC.

Water Well Drilling - Pump Sales and Service

ROUTE 9W

MILTON, N. Y. 12547

PHONE (914) 795 - 2250

February 15, 1988

To Whom It May Concern:

I run a well drilling business in Milton, New York. It was established in 1946 by my father and I've been involved full time since 1973. Ever since I was a small boy, I remember my father using brass rods to find the best spot to drill a well. I also dowse for my customers if they ask me to. However, if I'm going to drill in an area that I know has a poor water supply or the customer needs a large quantity of water I give Don Wood a call. Don is the only professional dowser I have ever used. I've never had a reason to look for another.

When I go to a job site with Don he is always good about explaining what he is doing to the customer. If they are willing, he gives them a try at dowsing with his help and then they try themselves.

I have used Don for approximately the last seven years and both my customers and I have been happy that we did.

I'm not out to just make as much money as I can. I try to give my customers the best goods and service as possible and quite often that involves dowsing.

Very truly yours,

James T. Eckerson, Jr.
President

JTE,Jr./pef

282

Andrews Welldrilling, Inc.
Andrews Pump Service, Inc.
Clapp Hill Road
LaGrangeville, New York 12540
(914) 223-3375
Fax # (914) 227-6988

March 20, 1991

To Whom It May Concern:

I have been in the water well business for the past 10 years. When I'm going to drill in a area where the water is known to be inadequate or if our customer is looking for a large quantity, I call on Don Wood and Elaine Ralston in Tillson, New York. They are a professional dowsing team.

When I go to a job site with Don and Elaine, they always are good about explaining what they are going to do to the customer. They even ask the customer if he or she would like to give dowsing a try. It's quite amazing that the customer will sometimes pick the same spot as Don or Elaine. I have used Don and Elaine for several jobs and both my customers and myself are pleased with the results.

Here are some of the results:

(1) This customer was looking for a well to supply his house and horse barn without iron in the water, (he had an allergy to iron mineral), the well was 240 ft. with 60 GPM and **NO IRON**.

(2) There was a restaurant that had two wells and they were always running out of water, the third well was dowsed and the results were a well depth of 525 ft. with 20 GPM. Needless to say, they now have plenty of water.

I try to give all my customers the best possible service and when it involves dowsing, I recommend Don Wood.

Very truly yours,
ANDREWS WELLDRILLING, INC.

Thomas J. Andrews
President

283

DICK CROY

EASTONE ASSOCIATES
1392 RIDGE ROAD • SYOSSET, N.Y. 11791   516 - 692-8760

February 29, 1988

Mr. Don Wood
Box 873
Rose Avenue
Tillson, NY 12486

Dear Mr. Wood:

We would like to take this opportunity to advise you of the outcome of
the well you located for us on the Vellano Beacon Land Development
Corporation property in the Town of Fishkill, New York.

As you know, last year we had retained ground water geologists to locate
water sources for our proposed residential housing project. Their
efforts were carried out at considerable cost and with limited success.

The new well was drilled to a maximum depth of 240 feet with the first
water bearing fracture being encountered at approximately 160 feet. A
72-hour pumping test was carried out at a flow rate of 200 gallons per
minute. At the end of the test the total static drawdown was approximately 50 feet. The estimated yield of the well is in the order of
350 gallons per minute. Final results of chemical tests for water
quality have yet to be obtained. However, preliminary results indicate
elevated quantities of sodium and chlorides but well within health
department allowances.

Needless to say, we are very pleased with the results of your efforts and
will not hesitate to request your help for possible future needs.

Yours sincerely,

Bache Bleecker

284

TEFFENS & ARCHARD

REAL ESTATE INVESTMENTS

5 N. FRONT STREET
NEW PALTZ, NY 12561
(914) 255-9171

5/24/88

To Whom It May Concern,

Don Wood. Dowser. has been of service to our company. STEFFENS & ARCHARD is a land development and home construction business. Don Wood first began dowsing for us in 1986.

The art of dowsing had both my partner and I very curious and skeptical at first introduction. Don Wood had come reccomended to us by several of his former clients. Since his fee was most reasonable we decided to give dowsing a try.

Don located our first six wells at the TALL OAKS project in Rosendale. These wells astounded us. The results were uncanny, depth and flow were as Don Wood had dowsed. He was far to accurate for chance. We drilled wells #7 & 8 without dowsing. Wells #7 & 8 were the deepest and most costly. We quickly returned to dowsing and the services of Don Wood.

Don Wood has saved my firm thousands of dollars. His skill and sensitivity make our product better. Clients of ours are pleased with their wells and know that as developers we took every possible step to produce a home that includes a good well.

We are proud to reccomend Don Wood as a dowser of skill. He has demonstrated that his dowsing abilties are the best insurance to a good well. Although he has never made any guarantees or warrantees STEFFENS & ARCHARD will never do another well without first consulting with our dowser.

Please feel free to contact me if your are questioning using his services. I would be most happy to answer your questions and will strongly advise that before you spend thousands of dollars on a well that you take out a little well insurance and contact a dowser and if you want the best contact Don Wood.

Respectfully.

Richard Steffens
President

285

Rosendale Plains Homeowners Association,Inc.
P.O. Box 121
Tillson,NY 12486

December 3rd,1992

Dear Don Wood and Elaine Ralston:

On Sept. 24th,1992, you and Elaine were able to locate a new potential source of water for our community water company. Our local water company consists of 43 existing homes, housing approximately 154 residents.

We were advised by DEC and our state Department of Health that we needed a second source of water to complement our existing deep well. After obtaining the necessary permits, we needed to accurately locate the most advantageous source, for both quantity and quality, since our existing well was a sulfur well in need of continual treatment. Our existing well also delivers 12.5 gallons per minute.

You and Elaine determined, after dowsing, that we would find water at approximately 268 feet and that our end result would be from 16-20 gallons per minute.

We hired the Eckerson Well Drilling Company and they drilled, cased and grouted 140 ft and found water at 260 ft down. We decided that since we hit 10 gallons per minute at that time, we would go another 120ft. The end result was approximately 17 gallons per minute. After the 24 hour pump test, discharging 21,000 gallons of water, our well was still delivering 16.3 gallons per minute and the original static level had almost been recovered.(The beginning of the pump test showed an initial delivery of 20 gallons per minute.) The water was sulfur free and the New York State mandated test results showed the water to be free of any contamination.

The two wells (our other well was dowsed by Don Wood) will deliver a total of 28 gallons per minute, running alternately. The water will be chlorinated and then pumped into a 14,000 gallon concrete holding tank on our community property. The holding tank uses two jet pumps to actively deliver the water through a series of 2 and 4" water mains to each home. This service meets all DEC and Department of Health regulations for purity and quantity.

We wish to thank Don and Elaine for the fine service. We saved countless hours and thousands of dollars by getting the necessary water the first time.

Sincerely yours,

Maryann E Sheeley
President

E & E Construction Corp.
BUILDER CONTRACTOR, GENERAL CONTRACTING
BULL MILL RD · RD # 1 · BOX 361A
CHESTER, NEW YORK 10918
(914) 783-6473

July 19, 1988

Dear Mr. Wood:

On June 10, 1988 you and your protege located three wells on my property. All wells came in good; deeper on two then anticipated, but all with plenty of water. As I told you, this particular area is known to not have substantial water.

I have a few more wells to locate in the future, and will be calling on you and your assistant.

I can also assure you that I will not drill without consulting you or another reputable dowser.

Sincerely,

Oddvar Egenes

S & A CHAISSAN & SONS, INC.

FRUIT GROWER, PACKER, STORAGE
481 CRESCENT AVE.   HIGHLAND, NY 12528
(914) 883-7069
FAX: 883-6505

May 20, 1993

To whom it may concern:

Elaine Ralston and Don Wood were hired by S&A Chaissan & Sons, Inc. to help us determine where to drill a well. They determined the site and also told us how many gallons of water per minute to expect and to what depth we would have to drill. When the well was completed, we actually were getting more water than they had expected at the same depth.

We were very pleased and would highly recommend their services.

Sincerely,

Dennis Chaissan
President

P.S.

Don and Elaine predicted that a maximum of 338 feet we would have a flow of 38 to 41 G.P.M. The final results were that at 350 feet we had 45 G.P.M.

DOWSING FOR LOVE

FENIMORE ROAD • MAMARONECK, N. Y. 10543
P. O. Box Z
Telephone (914) 698-8400

August 26, 1986

Mr. Don Wood
Box 873, Rose Avenue
Tillson, N.Y. 12486

Dear Don:

On behalf of the Board of Governors, members,
Bob Alonzi and myself, I wish to extend our thanks
and appreciation to you for your outstanding
performance in dowsing at Winged Foot Golf Club.

Through your great ability, we have already installed
pumps in 2 wells that we dug in the area you had
recommended. We are now getting a good amount of
water from those wells. I know there are many out
there who are in need of your services, and if you
wish at anytime to have anyone call me to verify
your great ability - please do.

Thanks again from all of us.

Sincerely,

WINGED FOOT GOLF CLUB

Jim. Nolletti

James L. Nolletti, CCM
General Manager

TOTAL OF 256 C.P.M.
FROM THESE 2 WELLS.

Thunderoc Farms Nursery
Box 319, Rt. 9, Rd. 2, Germantown, NY 12526
(518) 537-4686

June 4, 1988

Don Wood
Box 873, Rose Ave.
Tillson, N.Y. 12486

Dear Mr. Wood,

We would like to take this opportunity to express our
gratitude for your recent help in locating a shallow well
at our nursery. We must admit we were a bit skeptical
about calling in a dowser, but were amazed with your
results. We placed a well point at your site, set the point
12' to 15' and we're getting approximately 19 gallons per
minute.

We water every night using a ½ horsepower pump and
have not been without water.

Yours very truly,

Thomas H. Kirby

Thomas H. Kirby
President

290

CLEARWATER EXCAVATING CORP

(914) 669-5150   Hardscrabble Road   North Salem, N. Y. 10560

January 23, 1990

To Whom It May Concern:

    As incredible as this may sound, we hired <u>Don</u>
<u>Wood</u> and <u>his partner Elaine Ralston</u> to <u>dowse</u> the best
site to develop for a well. After we drilled <u>the well</u>
which <u>produced 22 gallons per minute,</u> we requested Don
and Elaine to <u>come back</u> and try <u>to move veins</u> of water
<u>to increase</u> the <u>flow of water</u> in the well. In a subse-
quent <u>12 hour test</u> after moving veins the <u>well</u> tested at
<u>45 gallons per minute!</u>

Gilbert S. Shott
President

GSS/cmk

P.O Box 162
Cottekill, NY 12419

July 7, 1986

Mr. Don Wood
Box 873, Rose Ave.
Tillson, NY 12488

Dear Mr. Wood:

I must apologize most profusely for not having written you
in a more rapid manner to thank you for dowsing our well.
You dowsed on November 17, 1984 and indicated that I should
get at least 10 to 12 gallons per minute of water between
212 to 220 feet. They hit water at a little over 200 feet
and completed their drilling at 248 feet. They put the
pump down to 230 feet and I am happy to say that we get
20 gallons per minute.

Enclosed is a copy of the well log showing the make-up of
the earth as they drilled through it.

Once again, thank you very much for your help.

Sincerely yours,

George P. Vogel

MARCH 12,1985

0-30 FEET	HARDPAN
30-70 FEET	GRAVEL
70-150 FEET	CLAY AND BOULDERS
150-160 FEET	MILLSTONE
160 FEET	CASING AND DRIVE SHOE
160-180 FEET	MILLSTONE
180-205 FEET	GRAYSHALE
205-215 FEET	MILLSTONE
215-230 FEET	GRAYSHALE
230-248 FEET	REDSHALE

230 FEET HIT 20 GPM

September 28, 1987

Don Wood
Dowser
Box 873, Rose Ave.
Tilson, N.Y. 12486

Dear Don,

You have not only done it again -- but you have outdone yourself too!!
I know your predictions are generally accurate so when you said 180-190ft.
at 9 to 11 gallons per minute, that's what I was prepared for...........
And then I thought: this might be an opportune moment to experiment just
to see how great the power of thought can really be. There is no doubt
that we create our realities -- but when I asked you to join me in visualizing
the well digger hitting a vein with about half your predicted footage
(and to have more gallons per minute, at that) I was not prepared for
quite such an astonishing success. For the well digger only had to go
down ninety-six feet, hitting an artesian well that flows at over fifty
gallons a minute!!

Thanks again for so accurately picking the one right spot on all that
land, then successfully helping to direct more water to it, closer to
the surface. Dowsing is not only an effective way to substantially cut
back on overall construction costs, but a graphic reminder to all of
us of our interconnectedness with the elements of nature.

With gratitude,

NONIE CAROLL
6313 RIVKA ROAD
SAUGERTIES, N.Y. 12477

Andrew Sauer
1 Baccara Drive
New Fairfield, CT. 06812
June 3, 1986

Dear Don Wood,

I would like to thank you for using your dowsing expertise
in locating a well for our new home. the well is located at a
depth of 240 feet producing 30 gallons of water a minute.

The story that goes along with our well is truly remarkable,
and will never be forgotten. Thought you may be interested in
hearing it. Our builderknew he had to drill in the area you
located for us, so we all were sure the rig was located properly.
That morning they started drilling, that evening we received a
phone call from our builder that they drilled over 200 feet and
there was no water, but they would continue in the morning.
So of course we called you for your opinion on how far we should
drill. To our surprise you told us that we had already hit water,
and there should be water in the well already. The next morning
we went to our property and there it was, water, , already coming
* out of the well! You were right again!!
Thanks again, for locating a great well, and making the construction of our new home a truly memorable experience. You really
are incredible.

Sincerely,

Andrew Sauer

Andrew Sauer

* AN ARTESIAN.

7-1-86

Dear Mr. Wood

This is just a note to let you know how I made out on my water well.

As you know I am a trooper with the State Police and was somewhat skeptic to say the least. But after drilling 650 ft. for a quart per min. I had nothing to loose.

We drilled where you said which was only seventy five feet from my first hole. You mentioned there were two vains crossing the first being 130 ft and the next about 370 ft. You were right! — we hit water about 1 gallon per min. at 127 ft which you figured and we hit 40 gallons per min. at 390. Which is the biggest flow of water in the entire area. Average being 2 or 3 gall./min.

I only wish I had come to you first.

Thanks so much

JOHN J. SCHETZEL
P.O. Box 545
ELLENVILLE, NY 12428

DON BEESMER CONSTRUCTION INC.
Commercial & Residential

RD 1 Box 392 A-1. Stone Rd.
West Hurley, N.Y. 12491

PH 914-331-0685

Sept. 6, 1988

Don Wood
Box 873 Rose Ave.
Tillson, N. Y. 12486

Dear Mr. Wood,
    I am writing to thank-you for knowledge and help concerning our water problem.
    As you know, we recently purchased a home in the West Hurley area and after about two weeks discovered we had very little water except for what was seeping in the well.
    Upon recommendation from several people I decided to call you. I thought this would be worth a try and better than to have to dig a new well. You came and diverted two veins into our well. After about ten days with still not much water we called in a well driller to bring in a pounder to clean the well out and we were surprised that when he started bailing he was getting well over 14 gal. a min. with a static level of 115 ft. and a 231 ft. deep well.
    The well driller said" there is no needto go deeper, the dowser did the job."
    Needless to say we are delighted to have all the water we need and without the expense of drilling a new well.
    Thanks again for your help and the help of your assistant.

                          Sincerely,

                          Donald Beesmer

296

January 5, 1984

Mr. Don Wood
Box 873, Rose Avenue
Tillson, N.Y. 12486

Dear Don,

Regarding the water problem in my trailer park in Highland, I had tried the following methods as possible solutions without success:

1) Installed service to stand-by well on property; thereby having two wells in simultaneous operation.
2) Removed flow restrictor from stand-by system to increase output of system.
3) Redrilled main well by an additional 200 ft.
4) Installed 1000 gallon concrete reservoir with its own pump to act as a reserve supply of water for high demand times.
5) Redrilled main well again to a depth of 630 ft.
6) Drilled a new well to a depth of 200 ft.
7) Pressure tested entire system for underground leaks.

You were my last resort and you seem to have worked a miracle! From every indication, the water problem appears to have been solved. My only hope now is that the solution will be permanent.

Needless to say, I am impressed with your success and would recommend your services to anyone. I only wish I had started with you. I could have saved a lot of money, time and aggravation.

Thank you and it was a pleasure getting to know you.

Sincerely,

John H. Dugue'
Broker/Owner

JHD:jp

ERA® - ADVANCED REALTY SERVICES
895 South Road
Wappingers Falls, New York 12590   914-298-9000

Each office independently owned and operated.

G. LECOURS DRILLING
R.D. 1 Box 71
Red Hook, NY 12571
914-756-2003

February 29,1988

To Whom it may concern;
  I have faith in Don Wood's dowsing ability.
  He has dowsed a lot of the wells that I
have drilled. He has had a high sucess rate as far as
depth and gallons per minute.
  I would recommend his services to anyone.

       Sincerely,

       Gervais A. Lecours
       Owner
       G. Lecours Drilling

APPENDIX C

I'd like to close by giving Wayne Cook the last word. He usually had it when he was still alive, and I see no reason to change now.

Around 1971 I got to wondering about the Feather River Canal and all the money that has been spent to transport rainwater hundreds of miles from north of Sacramento to Southern California in concrete aqueducts. This is minerally depleted water that falls through a polluted atmosphere to the ground, where there are cigarette butts and all kinds of crud, before washing into rivers and lakes -- from which it is finally pumped at enormous cost and waste to irrigate the near-desert landscape of Los Angeles and Southern California. Minerals are God's battery put into every living thing to make it function electrically. Because plants, animals and human beings need minerals, we need minerals in our water supply, but we won't get them that way.

I also got to thinking about the possibility of someone bombing the canal or one of its many dams, letting all the water out and throwing the whole farm community dependent on this water into utter chaos by having the crops fail. This could be done by any of the underground terrorist organizations because there is no way to protect hundreds of miles of aqueduct and all the dams, reservoirs and other facilities connected with the project.

So I started to formulate a plan to present to the Department of Water Resources, the government body responsible for the state of California's water resources. I decided the best way to do this was to go up through the chain of command in Sacramento so I wouldn't step on anyone's toes. I got past the information desk at the statehouse to two men with the same name though they were unrelated. One was between 25 and 30, the other was about 55.

Because I was a taxpayer and a citizen and a voter, they took me into a conference room and listened to me for about two and a half hours. What I wanted was for them to give me a Jeep with a spring-loaded chair on the front of it with a safety belt, and a good safe driver behind the wheel. He would take me along the access road to the Feather River Canal, and at every underground river we crossed that was over an "x" number of feet wide I would stop and check it out and find the direction of flow: every river that flowed under that canal for an "x" number of miles, to be decided on by the government and myself.

I didn't mention getting paid for any of this; I was willing to donate my time for a test. I told them, "We'll find these rivers and go in there and core-drill them -- check the underground water potential."

I know where there are two rivers flowing under the canal in Lancaster, in the Antelope Valley just north of Los Angeles, alone. There's one north of Avenue K which is over 125 feet wide, and another north of Avenue L which is about 90 feet wide, both flowing west to east under the canal -- with many others that could be found along that access road.

In those rivers with good potential, I wanted the state to put in 24-inch casing and diesel pumps independent of the electrical system, so we would have a standby system for pumping good clean underground water into the canal. This would be mineral-rich water instead of that minerally depleted alkali rainwater with all the pollution in it that they're catching up north and bringing south. If there was a disruption in power in a dam, from a bombing for example, or a dam break or something, all they would have to do is put up a temporary dam across the canal, and start pumping -- which I thought was a damn good idea.

The younger man was very interested; the other guy acted like he had just stepped in something and was wanting to get somewhere to clean off his shoes. I did a little work with his junior colleague on polarities, and he said he felt some energy flowing through his body that gave him a tingling sensation in his hands. I handed him the crossrods and he held them over the bottle of minerals I had, and they crossed for him. The older man wouldn't even touch them. He wanted me out of there just as quick as I could get out.

I asked them if they would present this to someone further up the line and see if they could set up an appointment for me to make a presentation to some of the department's engineers and geologists. The younger one said, "We'll talk to the head of the department, and see what happens. When you come back through the next time, give us a call."

Two or three weeks later I happened to be going north again on a water job and called the younger man from downstairs in the lobby. When he answered the phone and found out who it was, that phone suddenly felt like I had just opened a deepfreeze. He hemmed and hawed and finally said they weren't interested, they didn't want any part of this.

I went back home after finishing my work up there and laid everything out in a letter to the department head. I sent him documentation of some of the wells I had found and letters of recommendation, and offered to give him a field trip absolutely free of charge. This was the letter I got from him:

> This is in reply to your letter of December 13, 1972, in which you requested another meeting with the Department of Water Resources personnel for the purpose of explaining your theories on water dowsing, which would include a field demonstration.
>
> I carefully read the literature that you enclosed and, using this information in conjunction with your prior visit to our office, see little need for an additional visit. It appears to me that your techniques have been thoroughly described to us.

The Dept. of Water Resources uses geological methods to determine the extent of ground water resources. The methods produce excellent results and will be used by us in the future.

Thank you for your interest in the water resources of California.

I was quite disappointed with this letter; I thought he should at least have taken a look. I got angry and said to hell with this, I'll go find a good two-fisted newspaper reporter and we'll attack them through the press. So I went over to the *Sacramento Bee* and got an audience with the metropolitan editor. He listened attentively and said, "Well, I'm very much interested in the story, but the man I'd like to write it isn't here now, he's on vacation. The next time you're in Sacramento come by."

I was so enthused I went back in a couple of weeks. I made the trip up there especially to do the story; I had called and the man the editor had mentioned was back. This reporter came out and looked at me like he had been on about a two-week drunk, and the minute I talked to him I knew I should back out, I felt bad vibes on the whole thing. But being so anxious to get this before the public, I went ahead with the story anyway.

We went out on a little field trip, and I showed him how I could pick up underground water. His cameraman, who was very much interested, took some photographs, and I thought maybe I'd gotten through to him after all. But this guy came out with an article on my best water discovery and my picture splashed all over the front page, calling me a silver-haired, silver-tongued con man who was trying to get the state to appropriate a huge sum of money so I could make a profit out of some of my witchcraft -- and this went all over central California.

So I backed off and I thought, well, you were crazy to tackle this thing in that direction because you know what the press is like anyway: they won't get your name and address or anything else right. About a year later I did an underground water survey for the Transcendental Meditation organization in the mountains above Santa Barbara. In going up to this place we passed then-Governor Reagan's ranch, which was dry as a bone. I asked the man I was with if there was any water on the ranch. "No," he said, "I don't think so. There's no development there at all.".

So I sat down and wrote Gov. Reagan, offering to give him a field demonstration on his own ranch to show him the potential of dowsing for underground water. I told him I knew in my heart that there is enough circulatory water coming from geothermal activity underground to give every plant, animal and human being all the water they need for all eternity. Water that goes through a purification system when it is turned to steam and that picks up adequate minerals to sustain life when it is sent back through the arteries in the earth.

I got an immediate answer from the state secretary of resources:

> The development, preservation, improvement and utilization of water from all available sources is a matter of great concern. Certainly geothermal resources show promise of being one of our resources of water and power. A number of agencies...are at present engaged in studies and exploration of geothermal resources, particularly in the Imperial Valley.
>
> Because of the large number of private agencies involved in geothermal resources development, the State is concentrating its effort at present on appraisal of geothermal resources and its [sic] impact on the environment. I thank you for your recognition of and concern for the water problems of the State.

Thanks but no thanks. The geologists go out and study the sand structure and the rock structure and say there should be water here, so they get an expensive well-drilling rig and start core drilling all over, and once in a while they'll hit one of these underground streams. When they do they say the water table is such and such in this area. If there's a water table, why don't they hit water every time they drill? I don't think there's any such thing as a water table. If there were a water table, Death Valley would be a lake about 260 feet deep because it's that far below sea level.

As an offshoot of a lecture I gave at the Naval Postgraduate School, someone wrote to Bill Tiller, former head of the of Materials Science and Engineering Department at Stanford University. Bill called me and asked me to come by the college next time I was up north, which was about three weeks later. I got into Palo Alto about 4:15 or 4:30 in the afternoon and called Bill and he said, "It's pretty close to my quitting time and I have a 5:15 appointment, but why don't you run by and we'll shake hands, look each other over, and the next time you're through we'll get together and I'll take a look at some of your stuff. I'm very much interested in what you've discovered on polarities and body energies."

So I went by the university and arrived at Bill's office about a quarter of five. After we'd introduced ourselves I said, "I'll give you a quick demonstration so you can make your 5:15 appointment." Two and a half hours later, after he had called and canceled his appointment, we finally broke it up and decided to work together.

When we began I gave Bill the rod and showed him how to use it, and for months the thing never moved in his hands at all. But he also knew full well that there was some foundation and fact in what I was doing. I caught him studying me and watching me but he kept me coming back. Every month I would come back for our two days of research, and we started really pinning these energies down. We went into all sorts of tests on various materials and combinations of materials and elements. About eight months after he first picked up the rod, all of a sudden this thing started working for him. I attribute this to the fact that he had finally unlocked his energy from his skepticism.

Bill and I had a sort of ritual of checking each other's polarities before we started work. One morning he came in, and his energies were down to zero. I checked his feet and hands and nothing was moving so I asked him what he had that was new. He pulled out a keyring and it had a tiny piece of plastic with his initial on it. I laid it down on the table and checked it, and the rod showed that its energy was oscillating. It had been processed with mercury or formaldehyde. Having this in his pocket had knocked his energy down.

I had discovered some years before that the plastics industry uses mercury and formaldehyde to harden plastics and to keep them from changing color or bleaching in the sun. They put mercury into glasses frames, and the minute you put mercury that close to your brain, at your temples and across your nose, everything starts slowing down.

Up to this time, whenever I found a pair of glasses that were degaussing somebody's energy we would go to an optometrist and I would spend a couple of hours going through glasses frames, trying to find some that weren't contaminated and having the individual's lenses transferred to them.

I was sitting there on Bill's desk with this keyring in my hand, and for some reason or other I closed my left hand around it and held the end of my dowsing rod a few inches from one of my discharge sinks. I held onto the keyring, turning it over in my hand, for about three minutes; all of a sudden the oscillation quit. I laid the keyring down and checked it again with the rod, and its energy had become bi-polar now instead of oscillating. I kept checking it every 15 minutes or so, and it stayed that way, until I finally decided I had actually changed the orbital pattern of the electrons, transmuting a poison into a harmless energy.

From then on every time we found something whose energy was oscillating we would attempt to transmute it. I

305

discovered that I could hold a .38 cartridge in my left hand and transmute the lead's energy into a harmless bi-polar factor so you couldn't get any lead poison from it. (It wasn't too long after this, by the way, that I transmuted the buckshot in the arm of the young man at Esalen.)

In 1974 Bill and I published a scientific paper, planned as the first in a series, entitled, "Psychoenergetic Field Studies Using a Bio-Mechanical Transducer". That's the scientific name for the single wand-type dowsing rod used in our experiments with energy. The paper was presented to an A.R.E. [Association of Research and Enlightenment] medical symposium, "New Horizons in Healing" in Phoenix, Arizona, in January of that year.

But after doing research with Bill at Stanford for three and a half years, he told me he'd run out of money. I think it's a shame that in America you can't get one dime for this type of research. You can get a half-million-dollar grant for checking the love life of the snail or some damn fool thing like that that's of no value to anyone and take years spending the money, but when it comes to the nitty-gritty of finding some money for research into the type of thing we're into, the only place you can get it is from private investors or some foreign country.

All of the chaos and all the blocks that have been put in my path to keep me from becoming a wealthy, established-type businessman lead me to believe that I have a destiny I am supposed to fulfill, probably in the field of healing and scientific research. Because, other than dowsing, everything of a business nature that I've attempted, including several inventions I haven't even mentioned, would get up to within a quarter-inch of success and then fall apart and set me right back to where I had to pull my belt in and start changing things, in particular my own life -- until I've finally channeled it into where I am now.

In dealing with the public, I have gone strictly to the spiritual for an explanation of the application of the energy involved in dowsing and healing. I have adopted as a sort of first principle the fact that the Bible says God is love. You apply the energy factor to this and you find that love is energy -- positive to negative energy -- and I call this the Logistics Of Vibratory Energy: LOVE. Energy flowing from the power of God through the power of Christ into every living thing, going back into the generator to be regenerated and cleansed and put back on line for the use of plant, animal and humanity throughout all eternity...so that we can live as healthy, intelligent people for the rest of our lives -- with all the underground water we need, full of all the necessary minerals to support us.

Somewhere along the line we're going to have to look at how we live on this planet from a completely different standpoint. Get rid of the dollar greed and go after success on the basis of humanitarian love. Let's see if we can't straighten this whole thing out.

ORDER FORM

Telephone Orders:
Toll-Free: (800) 484-1624 + (MSI Code Number) 7036

Postal Orders:
Watershed Books
1300 Glendale Road
Marietta, OH 45750

Please send the following books: _____

_____

I understand that I may return any books for a full refund, for any reason, no questions asked.

Name:_____

Address:_____

City:_____**State:**_____**Zip:**_____

Telephone:_____

Sales Tax:
Please add 6.5% for books shipped to Ohio addresses.

Shipping:
Book Rate: $2.00 for the first book and $.75 for each additional book (surface shipping may take three to four weeks).

Air Mail: $3:50 per book.

Payment:
Check: ____

VISA: ____ Master Card ____

Name on Card: _____

Card Number: _____ Exp. Date ____/____

Call *toll-free* and order now!